Praise for

"Hunter's brand of supernatural ... and entertaining . . . Filled with high-stakes tension, Hunter's storytelling is vivid and descriptive with edgy, sharp dialogue laced with humor."

—RT Book Reviews

"Once again, Hunter proves she's a master of the genre."

—Romance Junkies

"A lot of series seek to emulate Hunter's work, but few come close to capturing the essence of urban fantasy: the perfect blend of intriguing heroine, suspense, [and] fantasy with just enough romance."   —SF Site

"Readers eager for the next book in Patricia Briggs's Mercy Thompson series may want to give Faith Hunter a try."   —*Library Journal*

"Hunter's very professionally executed, tasty blend of dark fantasy, mystery, and romance should please fans of all three genres."   —*Booklist*

"Hunter deftly manages risk and reward, and Jane's ever-growing tribe manages to bond amidst pressure from all sides."

—All Things Urban Fantasy

"Hunter is a master of the game-changer and cliffhanger."

—Kings River Life Magazine

Books by Faith Hunter

The Jane Yellowrock Novels

Skinwalker

Blood Cross

Mercy Blade

Raven Cursed

Death's Rival

The Jane Yellowrock World Companion

Blood Trade

Black Arts

Broken Soul

Dark Heir

Shadow Rites

Cold Reign

Dark Queen

Shattered Bonds

True Dead

The Soulwood Novels

Blood of the Earth

Curse on the Land

Flame in the Dark

Circle of the Moon

Spells for the Dead

The Rogue Mage Novels

Bloodring

Seraphs

Host

Anthologies

Cat Tales

Have Stakes Will Travel

Black Water

Blood in Her Veins

Trials

Tribulations

Triumphant

Of Claws and Fangs

OF CLAWS AND FANGS

FAITH HUNTER

ACE
New York

ACE

Published by Berkley

An imprint of Penguin Random House LLC

penguinrandomhouse.com

Library of Congress Cataloging-in-Publication Data

Names: Hunter, Faith, author.

Title: Of claws and fangs / Faith Hunter.

Description: First edition. | New York: Ace, 2022. | Series: Jane Yellowrock

Identifiers: LCCN 2021051762 (print) | LCCN 2021051763 (ebook) |

ISBN 9780593334348 (trade paperback) | ISBN 9780593334355 (ebook)

Subjects: LCGFT: Short stories.

Classification: LCC PS3608.U59278 O37 2022 (print) | LCC PS3608.U59278

(ebook) | DDC 813/.6—dc23/eng/20211021

LC record available at https://lccn.loc.gov/2021051762

LC ebook record available at https://lccn.loc.gov/2021051763

First Edition: May 2022

Printed in the United States of America

1st Printing

This collection of short stories is in memory of Teri Lee Akar.
My life and my writing are darker without you.

SHORT STORIES FROM FAITH HUNTER

Dear readers, fans, and friends,

When I released the comprehensive short story collection Blood in Her Veins, *I thought I was done with short stories and novellas and novelettes. Ummm. Nope. Apparently not. There were a number of my stories that came back available from anthologies that had been out a while, and some that had been used for PR or as freebies over the years and were then taken off the Internet.*

This compilation is because you clamored to have all the remaining short stories and novelettes in one place, and my publisher and I listened.

*Of Claws and Fangs is a fun hodgepodge of stories from many characters within nonlinear timelines of the Yellowrock world and the Soulwood world. There are a few stories that most of you have not seen because they were published in hard-to-find anthologies, or released in serial format for the newsletter (you do know I have a newsletter, right?) or serialized in blog tours. All those for PR purposes were removed quickly from the Internet. Some have now been lightly edited to fit this compilation. This means that they have been published in this format before. There isn't much new here except the short vignette about Miz A. I hope you enjoy having everything in two places—*Blood in Her Veins *and* Of Claws and Fangs! *Ummm. Not that I will stop writing shorts and novellas. I can't see that happening anytime soon!*

For now, grab a cuppa of whatever you like to sip on, curl under a blanket, and enjoy your old friends.

Faith Hunter

CONTENTS

Candy from a Vampire   1

Make It Snappy   6

It's Just a Date   24

Life's a Bitch and Then You Die   36

Black Friday Shopping   52

How Occam Got His Name   57

Shiloh and the Brick   69

Beast Hunts Vampire with Jane   77

Of Cats and Cars   80

Beast Hunts Pie-bald Deer   114

Jane Tracks Down Miz A   117

FROM ANTHOLOGIES:

Anzu, Duba, Beast   122

Eighteen Sixty   143

Wolves Howling in the Night   149

Death and the Fashionista   172

My Dark Knight   191

Bound into Darkness   213

The Ties That Bind   305

OF CLAWS AND FANGS

Candy from a Vampire

A vignette first published online, on my blog, as a serial blog tour short for Halloween in 2017. It is from the point of view of Leo Pellissier, a view of his thoughts, for which my fans have often clamored.

Leo Pellissier stood outside the Royal Mojo Blues Company, a bucket—a cauldron, really—filled with individual servings of candy in front of him. Each piece was wrapped in paper, or foil, or foiled paper, with the ingredients in tiny print on the back, showing calorie content and fat content, which was significant, and nutritional value, which was negligible. He had always thought that was the point of candy, that it was to be nothing but sugar and fat and delicious. A treat, back in his day, a sweet that was earned when he had done something good, like staying on his pony through a trot, over small fences, or translated a particularly difficult Latin tale into the French or Castilian or Greek, as his tutor demanded. His hand beaten with a thin strip of wood when he failed, and his presence at dinner denied. Treats when he succeeded. It was the way of his father's house. Carrot and stick. Or candy and stick. It had been effective then. Now children could have sweets at every meal. And on All Hallows Eve, even more.

It was scarcely past sunset and the streets were filled with adults in various stages of inebriation, accompanied by various stages of nudity, the closer to Bourbon Street one drew. Costumes that did far more than hint were everywhere, even here at the Mithran Council Chambers. But here, as tradition dictated, there were children. Many, many children.

Halloween in the French Quarter of New Orleans had been changed forever when Marilyn Monroe had attempted to turn John Kennedy in the Oval Office and been staked for her trouble. That next year, 1963, Leo had appeared for the first time, in full tuxedo and a black cloak, with scarlet silk lining, to hand out candy. Personally. The children had been bused in from all over the city at Mithran expense. And back then, a parent thought nothing of putting children on a bus and sending them off for a party, which was what he had put on for them, all along the street in front of the chambers.

There had been humans dressed as storybook witches in every doorway, some with hot cauldrons full of liquid pralines that they ladled onto waxed paper, allowed to cool and solidify, and gave away, others offering popcorn balls or caramels. Jugglers, clowns, artists of every stripe were encouraged to display their wares. Musicians stood on every street corner, with baskets or open instrument cases before them for tips. There were pony rides. The press wandered among the crowds, taking photographs for the *Times-Picayune* and to show on CBS or NBC or ABC, all across the nation. The party had been a ploy to improve public opinion of the newly revealed Creatures of Darkness, as described by a young, up-and-coming newsman whose name he had long forgotten.

The street party had been successful at the time. Now, fewer parents allowed their children onto the chartered buses, instead throwing parties for them in the safety of their schools or in private homes. And when they did allow the children aboard, the parents came too, holding their child's hand. These days monsters on the streets might be human, intent on much worse than stealing a little blood.

There were fewer and fewer newsmen and newswomen on the streets to photograph the decades-old tradition. Perhaps in a few years, he would discontinue the party, or perhaps make it bigger. He could add wine tasting and beer tasting, and persuade restaurants to bring their foods to taste, in order to attract an older, more sophisticated crowd.

But there were still a few here tonight. Children and reporters both. Enough each year to brave the Quarter for the joy of taking candy from a vampire. And this year, one of the candy makers was a *real* witch, one he recognized from her dossier. He nodded regally to Suzanne Richardson-White, an earth witch with a gift for making pralines that rivaled Aunt Sally's. It was a sign of improvement between the races that she was here, in public, sharing a street with a Mithran. On All Hallows Eve. She nodded back, an amused expression on her face.

A little girl with bright red hair raced up to him, her brown paper sack held out in two tiny fists. "Twick or Tweat, Mr. Pewisir."

"Oh, please. No tricks tonight," Leo said, reaching down and lifting up enough candy to turn the little girl into an instant diabetic. He let them all fall in a cascade of *shushing* sounds into her bag. He felt the moment the cameras focused on him and the little girl, and he smiled his public smile, toothy but totally human, the smile that the whole world knew.

"Thank you, Mr. Pewisir," the little girl said, before racing away to the next candy station.

"You're welcome, my dear," Leo replied, though she was no longer there to hear, and a tiny tot in a cowboy suit took her place, his father standing behind, smiling, as if remembering the time he took the bus to this section of the French Quarter to receive candy from a vampire.

The hours wore on, and the crowds thinned. The moon rose in a hazy night sky.

Suzanne dipped up the last of the candies and closed her booth. She packed her mini-cauldron and the brazier that had kept the melted sugar hot. He watched from beneath the streetlight as she moved, her body encased in a corset, the laces holding and reshaping her curves, her breasts thrust up high and rounded. Her flowing witch's dress was made of silk and netting, the fabric catching the night breeze as if a spell caused it to float. She wore ankle boots with tiny spike heels and the kind of old-fashioned buttons that had to be closed with a hook. He had always loved taking such shoes off a woman. And corsets.

Leo smiled. The girl was all of thirty, a graduate of Tulane. He had learned that acting on such thoughts was considered improper for anyone, especially for an old man such as he. Jane Yellowrock had made him re-think many things that he had once taken as his due.

"Shall I pack everything away?" Del asked, interrupting his reverie.

Leo turned to her and smiled his nonpublic smile, the one he kept for retainers and blood-servants, especially those he depended upon for security and a pleasant life. "Thank you, Del. Yes, it's late."

Del spoke into a headpiece, calling in the menials who would clean up and take down the candy stand. She was efficient and beautiful and far too bright and accomplished to be acting as a caterer, though as primo, that was part of her job from time to time. Perhaps too often.

"Del? . . ." She looked up at him, instantly alert for any need he might have. He studied her in the wan yellowed light that tried unsuccessfully to replicate gas streetlights of his early years in New Orleans. "You look lovely tonight. Are you happy in my employ?"

Del's blond brows went up in surprise, wrinkling her forehead. "Thank—Sir?"

She sounded . . . nonplussed. As if he never asked such things of her, of any of his dependents. And perhaps he had not done so, not in a long while. Had ruling made him hard and insensitive? Jane had insisted this was true, the last time he called her for some small service. Her exact words had been, "Do it yourself, your Royal Fangyness. This is my day off. And maybe it's time to stop being such a royal ass." She had hung up on him. And while he had raged, he had also enjoyed the exchange, her indifference, her rebellion, her refusal to bow before him.

To Del, Leo said, "I have been remiss in asking. I want you to be happy in my service, Del. I want you to find joy here, in New Orleans, fulfillment and satisfaction. What can I do to make certain that happens?"

Security closed in around him, urging their small crowd to move down the street. A limo pulled around the corner. Behind him, the kitchen servants began to tear down the candy stand. He and Del walked toward the approaching limo, their legs illuminated in the headlights.

"I don't know what to say," Del admitted as the limo slid to a stop beside them. The door opened and Derek Lee, head of security, stepped out, scanning the darkness for threats. Del slid in, her blond, upswept hair and pale skin catching the light. But her eyes were brighter than he had seen in some time.

Yes. Jane was right. He had been more than remiss. "Well, think about it. You are not a menial, but skilled and capable. Your legal degree and aptitude make you too valuable to waste on tedious and humble tasks. You have proven both ability and loyalty." He smiled again as Derek took his place across from them and closed the limo door. The armored vehicle pulled into traffic. "I am prepared to entrust my personal legal affairs to you. Perhaps I shall also ask you to oversee the financial affairs of the city and the clans. Such jobs as these"—he indicated the darkness and the stand that fell behind them—"could be better administered by a secretary or personal assistant."

Del's eyes lit up. "I know just the woman. She's bright and sharp and detail-oriented."

"I trust your decision." He waved languid fingers in the air. "See to it. And for her first task, have her schedule a meeting with you and my law firm."

"Yes, sir." Her voice sounded breathy. Excited. "Thank you, sir."

"Think nothing of it. Happy All Hallows Eve."

Make It Snappy

"Make It Snappy" was first published in *Urban Enemies*, an anthology from Gallery Books (2017), edited by Joseph Nassise. The story is from Leo's point of view and is set in the modern-day world of Jane Yellowrock, but a few years before Jane and Leo Pellissier meet.

Leo eased the girl's blond head off his shoulder. She was asleep, dreaming blissfully about their encounter, his mesmerism and the power of his blood ensuring her happiness. He ran a hand over her hip. Her body was rounded and plump, the perfect vision of beauty until modern times. Now when he visited those sworn to his service, he was often offered scrawny, bony creatures with no curves, no soft and pleasing warmth. She murmured in her sleep, pleasure in her voice and on her face.

Many of his kind preferred the scent of fear, the unwilling, the blood-bound. He preferred his meals willing, even if only by bargain. This one came to him at dusk, when he woke, offering herself in return for a simple favor. He tried to remember her name as he dressed. Cynthia? Sharon? Simone? She had been an easy read, offering all of her past but for one small corner of her thoughts that was closed off and darkened, perhaps some trauma, some childhood fear. He'd left it there, in the depths of her mind, silent and untouched.

He strapped a small blade to each wrist, positioning the hilts in their spring-loaded scabbards. Shrugged into his crisp dove-gray shirt and black suit. Tied the contrasting charcoal tie. No denim or T-shirts for him. He had worked too hard for too many centuries to dress down in casual clothing, using comfort as an excuse for a crass lack of style. His uncle had taught him the social advantages of education, intelligence, and elegance, and while he was delighted the old Master of the City was dead, he

wouldn't toss out the lessons learned at the knee of a dominant, successful Mithran, particularly his sire.

He smoothed back his hair as he walked toward the door. The sheets
on the bed shifted when he reached the entrance, and he paused to look
back. The young woman was sitting up, watching him, a hand at her throat
where his fangs had pierced her as he fed. Her face was wan and uncertain.
"You won't forget?"

Forget? His brow quirked up in amusement. The woman was his, with
or without his compliance in her little family matter, her useless bargain.
Women were such an easy indulgence. But still, he was concerned with
her "favor" for business reasons, and it would not take him long to resolve
it. "I shall do more than remember. I shall accomplish your request before
the sun, *ma chérie*. Marcoise will no longer have the power to cause pain."
A small smile lifted his lips. "Perhaps we may meet for dinner, just before
dawn, *d'accord*?"

"C'est possible," she said in a schoolgirl French accent. She ducked her
head, her long hair sliding forward to curl around her breast. "You know
where to find me."

"I do." She had recently come to work in the Royal Mojo Blues Company, a music, dance, and cocktail bar catering to Mithrans, the vampire
citizens of New Orleans. As the Master of the City, he had right of first
taste of all the new blood. Mixed with wine, he had found hers to be pi-
quant, saucy, with undertones of currants and laughter. When she had
begged a favor in return for a night in his arms, he had readily agreed.

Leo tapped down the stairs of the town house she shared with another
girl from Royal Mojo Blues and out the door, into the street. His guards
gathered close, summoned on the cellular telephone used by George, his
primo blood-servant. Security was much easier since the invention of the
devices, though at some point his vampire enemies would discover their
use, he was certain.

The limousine approached quietly from down the street, riding low,
the weight of its armor holding it close to the asphalt. Once inside, Leo
said, "One more stop tonight. Back to the club." The club where Marcoise
worked as head bartender. Where his bargain with the girl would be satisfied.

"Why, boss?" George asked, his upper-class London accent deliberately coarsened to fit his new persona, his new identity. Like most blood-servants, George had outlived his natural life, his papers and his past reinvented again and again.

"The sister of *ma petite fleur* received an inappropriate and unwanted advance from Marcoise."

George's brows drew down.

"According to *la fille*, several of the other girls were similarly approached, with the implication that they would lose their employment if they refused his attention, a clear violation of his service to me."

George shifted his eyes from the street to meet Leo's. "Inappropriate and unwanted advances? And that becomes problematic to you, my master?"

Leo lifted an eyebrow at what might have been censure in the tone. "They are mine. When would I not protect what belongs to me?"

George bowed his head, the gesture formal, the gaze between them broken. "My apologies, my master. It's of no matter."

Leo thought otherwise. George was conflicted and wished to speak but was holding his tongue, his scent burning with an internal struggle. He was known to have a tender heart for females, having seen his sister abused and his mother killed by those who used them. They would speak of this later, after the situation with Marcoise was addressed. "Her sister acquiesced and has not been seen since their date. I shall attend to the issue."

George scanned the street and the sidewalks to either side as they drove, searching for enemies, problems, threats. Such loyalty as existed between them was rare, but their relationship began in death and violence and had joined them closer than most. Leo knew his primo's mind and heart; they were bound, blood and soul.

They pulled up in front of the club, the lights bright inside as the cleanup crew attended to postclosing duties. Leo lifted his cuff and checked the time on his Versace Reve Chrono, though he knew, almost to the second, when the sun would rise. His kind always did. "I'll be only a moment. Security will wait outside."

George opened his mouth to protest. George was always protesting something. Leo lifted his finger, silencing his primo. "I will speak to Marcoise alone. You may cover the outer exits. You may not enter. The cleaning crew will be working and, as former military, they will be armed. I will calm them. I will not have a bloodbath in my club."

George hesitated, clearly thinking about the numbers of potential victims and hostages. "Derek Lee's company is new," George said. "I'm not certain of the extent of his knowledge, or of his biases."

He did not need to add *Many have refused to work for the vampire Master of the City of New Orleans.*

He raked through his hair with his long fingers, worried.

"Alone," Leo insisted, and tapped on the window. The chauffeur opened his door. "Thank you, Alfonse," Leo said. He was always polite to the help.

Into the night, he exited with all the grace of his kind, part ballerina, part snake, part spider, all predator. The night smelled of humans and blood. Saliva filled his mouth, hunger riding him. The girl earlier had been a tasty diversion, her body a delight as she used it to seal his promise, but this . . . this was the hunt. There was nothing like it, and even civilized Mithrans such as himself knew the desire, the overriding craving for shadowing and stalking prey.

Leo leaped to the door, his speed creating a pop of sound as the air around him was displaced. He keyed open the lock and entered. His men, left behind, rushed to guard the entrance and provide the protection his kind seldom needed. He slipped inside, into the shadows. Standing behind a brick pillar, he watched the cleaning crew, scenting them. The men were all dressed alike, in one-piece gray uniforms; they were healthy, their blood touched with alcohol and marijuana. He had known it for centuries as hemp, MJ, ganja, and by a hundred other names and grades and varieties.

He took in a slow breath and parsed the chemicals in their blood. The marijuana smelled . . . odd. Impure. He watched as a small man, no more than five feet, five inches tall, lifted a bucket and then, oddly, dropped it. The pail landed with a clatter and splash of water on the concrete floor, and the man stood, hunched over, staring at the mess as if mesmerized. Certainly confused.

Leo sniffed again. There was something mixed with the marijuana, some chemical he did not recognize. The small man took a breath, a faint gasp of sound. He fell.

Leo held still, as only undeath allowed. The other men rushed to help. Another fell, his head bouncing on the floor. A third dropped. And another. Only Derek was still standing, the boss of the crew. Leo had hired Derek Lee's fledgling company because of his service in the military, though the man was destined for far more. Derek pulled a weapon and backed to the bar, the brass rail at his spine, analyzing the room, the short hallways.

Leo said, "You did not partake of the smoke offered to the others."

Derek swung his weapon toward the column hiding Leo. "Who's there?"

"Leo Pellissier, Master of the City. The smoke? The *weed*?"

"Owner of the Royal Mojo. Fanghead. And no, to the weed," Derek said, his weapon steady on the brick pillar. "One of the guys brought it. Said his brother had gotten a deal on the streets."

"Mmmm. And a gift is always a good thing?"

"No."

"And what shall you do to the man who injured your cohorts?"

"Better you don't know." Derek's voice was harsh, unyielding.

Leo chuckled. "There is more here than meets the eyes."

"No shit, dude. I got free weed, four downed boys, and the Master of the City hiding behind a brick column. How 'bout you come out. Make nice-nice wid me."

"How about we take down whoever is waiting for us in the office? I smell six. One is a Mithran, one is female and bleeding, one is a dead human."

"My men?"

"They are breathing. I will offer them healing blood if they are not awake before dawn."

Derek considered. "You take the fanghead. I'll take the others."

Leo stepped from behind the column, hands where they could be seen.

"You seem certain that you can contain the humans," he said. "Three against one?"

"This trap wasn't for me. Makes sense it was for you. I'm supposed to be down and out so they won't be expecting me."

"Better things, indeed," Leo murmured to himself, reevaluating the young man. "You are correct that this is a trap for me. I was sent here by a woman, to chastise an employee named Marcoise. You don't perhaps know if he is with the others?"

"Beats the hell outta me."

Leo chuckled. "I shall enter at speed and engage the Mithran. If there are humans held against their will . . ."

"Understood. No collateral damage. After this, I suggest you get a better security system. Cameras woulda gone a long way to keeping this place safe."

"Undeniably so." Behind him, he heard the door open and George's scent blew in. George seldom followed orders he felt were unwise. "Do not shoot my primo. He follows," Leo instructed Derek. Silently, he led the way to the back, Derek following, and George behind.

At the door to the office, Leo paused, pressed his ear to the crack and listened. There was silence on the other side, the scent of blood and pain and gun oil wafting from beneath the door, but no scent of a fired weapon. He gently attempted to turn the knob. It was locked.

He nodded to Derek and to George, both armed, weapons at the ready.

He stood back, positioned his body, lightly balanced on both feet, and kicked out with all the strength of a well-trained Mithran. His foot impacted the door where the lock's bolt entered the strike plate. The frame splintered, the door banging open. Moving with faster-than-human speed, Leo leaped inside. Still in the air, he took in the room's layout in an instant.

Three humans bracketed the doorway. Two with cudgels, one with a long rifle, the battlefield kind, fully automatic, created to bring down multiple enemies. If it hadn't been pointed at him, he might have approved of the choice. And the girl, in the center of the room. Fastened to a chair with duct tape. Unconscious. Bleeding. Near death. No Marcoise in sight.

The true enemy stood in the back of the room, holding two silvered blades, his fangs down, eyes scarlet and black in fighting form. Shock sped through him in recognition. *El Mago.* Leo had left the mage on the fighting floor, his body in pieces, over three hundred years ago on a visit to Madrid. The fiend was dead. Or should be.

Leo snarled, bending his legs to touch down. Heard three shots from the door. Derek, behind cover, taking down the shooter. George screamed, a battlefield roar, intended to shock the other two humans. Leo landed, let his body fall forward, over the chair, taking it and the girl bound to it with him, into a roll, and shoving her and the chair across the room, out of the line of fire. He drew two small steel blades and rose upright, into El Mago's face. Inside his reach. Thrust both blades into his abdomen, twice each. Stab-stab, high, low. He withdrew the blades for another double thrust.

Pain ratcheted up and through his body. He looked down. El Mago had dropped the longswords and performed the same maneuver on him—two shorter blades were buried inside him. Agony shredded his belly. The blades were silvered.

And then El Mago yanked upward, the blades slicing into his core, then out to the sides.

Leo fell to the floor, the blades still buried in his body.

Standing above him, El Mago extended an arm and turned over his hand. White crystals poured from a black bag. *Salt?* Sea salt? Crystalline flakes of a brilliant white fell over him. El Mago removed his blades, wiped them on a cloth. Darkness descended upon Leo, his vision telescoping down into nothingness. The sound of gunshots was a muffled hollow drumming as the darkness stole even that.

When Leo woke, El Mago was gone and his own scions had filled the office of Royal Mojo. He was fighting exhaustion, thirst, and a rage that he could scarcely control. Not since he went through the devoveo, the decade of madness experienced by all his kind when they were turned, had his need for blood been so strong that he could not force his fangs to retract. The broken thing, the girl who had been tied in the chair, had been bled almost to the point of death. She was being attended to by Katherine, life coaxed into the girl, so that she need not be turned. Another drop of blood lost, and she would die a true death. Still, he could think only of sinking his fangs into her throat and draining her dry. Even Marcoise's dead body, bloodless and cold, on the floor across the room, smelled appealing. Marcoise, the bait to this trap, which had been sprung on him with such exquisite perfection, had been dead for hours.

"Master?"

George stood behind him, his heart strong and pounding. He had been honed into a weapon so perfect his body was little more than a sheath for the blade he was. Hot, perfect blood, pumping through his primo. *Son sang est rempli d'énergie, puissant, merveilleux sang.*

Leo spun up from the floor like a snake striking, too fast for George to dodge. He sank his fangs into George's throat.

He heard gunshots. Felt the impacts. Whirled to confront his enemies and took a stake to the belly. Leo fell to his knees at the feet of his assailant. His own love. Katherine.

He slid to the floor, where he lay in a spreading pool of his own blood, paralyzed by the ash wood that pierced him. Above him, around him, other Mithrans, his scions, rushed to heal George, whose blood was spurting across the room.

Heal George.

He had attacked his own primo, the human blood-servant who most trusted him. The human he most trusted. Shock flowed through him, filling the empty veins that had been drained out on the cement. Katie bent over him, her silvery-blond hair upswept, her long teal gown split up the side, a bastard-sword at her hip.

She toed him, cocked her head far to the side, her eyes luminous and thoughtful. Very, very quietly, she murmured, "I know you can hear me. Understand this, *my master.* If I wished your lands and hunting grounds, I could take them this night. If I wished to be forsworn and yet powerful enough that such treachery was no matter, I could take your head.

"You attacked your primo without provocation and mortally wounded him. Had I not been informed that things had gone wrong and seemed off-kilter this night, your George would now be turned and in *my* scion lair, not yours. Had I not arrived in time here, you might have died at the hands of these humans.

"Now you are at my mercy. However, I am loyal still, and do not wish to rule. This bargain we shall strike. Someday I may require all your power and influence to save me, to protect me, keep me in my undeath and not true dead. At such time, you will remember this moment and provide such assistance as I might need. Until then you are in my debt." She stood straight, her body positioned so that he might see up her split skirt. "Think on this as you bleed, my lord and master."

If he had been able to draw breath, Leo might have laughed, knowing that Katie meant both her threat and what she displayed. Had he been able to move at all, he would have run a questing hand up her leg. His love ran a bordello in the French Quarter, and half the state's elected and law enforcement officials had visited her at one time or another. Her peek show was a reminder of her strengths—human friends in high places and a sexual libido and prowess unmatched in his centuries of experience.

She drifted from view, her grace and balance impeccable in her five-inch stilettos. Katie had been a small woman in human life, and, after so many centuries, with each generation of humans growing taller than the last, she was apt to be taken as defenseless and vulnerable. But his lover was never that. He was truly in her debt. After this night, he would be in the debt of many.

His blood ceased to flow. His hunger was growing prodigious. His eyes were drying out—perhaps the most uncomfortable of his small miseries. The cleanup was well under way, his people moving around him, working silently. No one had attempted to remove the stake embedded in his belly, not with Katherine wearing her *Duel Sang* bastard-sword. It had been forty-two years since Katherine Fonteneau had dueled for position in his clan, but no one who had seen it would ever doubt her wicked expertise with the blade nor her cunning strategy.

Leo Pellissier, Master of the City, owed his Katherine much this night. Though he would make her pay for the paralysis, humiliation, and discomfiture, it was the kind of punishment that would take place in his bed.

One good thing came of the enforced immobility: the time to remember, to reflect. El Mago had been on the far side of the room when he entered. There had been a sword in each hand. The sorcerer had been wearing long sleeves that hid his arms, likely places to conceal weapons, such as the short blades he had used. Hidden blades were Leo's own strategy. Clearly El Mago remembered from the last time the tactic had been used against him, when Leo had killed him. *Almost* killed him.

Leo had been predictable. The mage had *expected* him to step inside his reach. He had dropped the swords, incapacitating him with the blades in his own sleeves. He had carved his way deeply into Leo's entrails.

It was time to rethink his dueling methods. But . . .

Silver should have rendered him incapable of healing without massive amounts of blood. Yet when he awoke, his belly was uninjured. There had been a scent like silver and marzipan. The scent of bitter almonds. Cyanide was not lethal to Mithrans, but when coating a silvered blade, unable to purge from his body after entry, and allowed to fester with an unknown spell that both healed and fettered him . . . Leo did not know what effect that might have. His ancient enemy had intended to disable him, not kill him. Or, at least, not right away.

It was clever: the bag of white powder upended over him had healed his flesh over the wounds, so that he and others might not know what had happened. Buried within his body was poison, silver, and a spell—the spell that was perhaps the reason he had attacked his primo. Either one he might have defeated, but all together were deadly, had he not been stopped with a stake to the same damaged area.

The bag El Mago had upended over him had seemed to contain a white powder, crystalline flakes like salt. It had made a quiet *shushing* as it left the cloth sack and fell upon him. When Leo stood after he awoke, nothing had fallen from his clothing or his person. He remembered the sound of Katie's shoes on the floor as she walked through the room. There had been nothing between her soles and the concrete, no grinding or crushing or near soundless compression of some softer material.

He was poisoned. Likely dying. What seemed a minor inconvenience only moments past loomed large. If someone didn't remove the stake, and soon, so that he might ask for aid, it might be too late.

Another hour passed. Pain had begun to grow in his belly, cold and harsh and remorseless, spreading through his empty veins and arteries. By the time Katie meandered back, he knew with certainty that he was dying.

She knelt beside him, aligning their faces. Her eyes, hazel gray, met his. She had applied fresh scarlet lipstick, and when she smiled it was the smile of a court courtesan, practiced and perfect and only slightly sadistic. "My master, you look miserable," she said. "But perhaps it will cheer your unbeating heart to know that our George is once again fully alive and will neither perish nor be forced to take our curse. No? No comment?" She shook her head, making a small *tsking* sound.

Katie bent and kissed him, her lips as cold as his own. She held the kiss before pulling away, and as she did, she took a breath, then froze. Her remarkable eyes widened. "Bitter almonds."

She ripped his shirt open, revealing his abdomen and torso. "*Mon dieu.*" Katie yanked the wood from his belly and ripped the flesh of her left fingers with her fangs, her blood spurting. She dug her fingers into his flesh, inserting her blood at the point of the original damage. She ripped her right wrist and placed it at his mouth. "Drink, sire. *Drink!*" When he did not swallow, Katie shouted, "Get the priestess!" Then, to herself, "Oh no."

Astonishment flashing across her face, Katie staggered back and fell to the floor beside him. She held up her left hand. The fingers she'd tried to heal him with were blackened and smoking. "Poison. I am poisoned. How is this possi—" She swooned.

Leo felt his body lifted and carried to the front of the club. He was placed on the bar, where he could see only the bottles and the brass-backed mirrored wall behind them. Not a silver-backed mirror, but one in which his kind might be seen as more than a blur. Katie's body was placed on two tables shoved together.

The outclan priestess, Bethany, floated into the room and stood over him, her dark skin catching the lights, her skirts swirling in brilliant shades of blues. She sniffed his small wound, then Katie's hand, which appeared in the mirror as blackened and smoking. Bethany pointed at three humans and said, "Feed her copious amounts of blood. Bring in more servants. Tonight, Katherine is a Naturaleza." Which meant she would drink humans down if they were not careful.

Returning to the bar, Bethany tore her own throat and climbed over Leo, her limbs moving like a praying mantis on the hunt, elbows and hips high. She placed her ripped flesh at his mouth and began to chant softly in her native tongue.

Magic swirled over him like a dense fog from the Mississippi River, a coiling mist of opaque light, whirling and twisting, enveloping him. Sliding down his throat. Convulsively, he swallowed. Again. And again. Magic and blood twined and flowed down his throat. Magic pressed into his abdominal wound and snaked through him and curled tight with the blood of the priestess.

The magic of the assault spell that had woven itself into him parted before the onslaught of the priestess's own power. He felt strands of El Mago's spell snap. Agony speared through him. He gasped. Lifted one hand and gripped Bethany close, drank, sucking down her healing blood. He lost track of time before she peeled herself away and a human took her place. And then another. Trying to heal the damage of the poison, the silver, and the magic with blood.

After the third human was wrenched away, he gasped out to the near-est blood-servant: "George?"

"He is well, my master."

"Katie?"

"Healing, my master."

"The two human girls? Bring them to me. Now."

"Yes, my master," the voice replied. "You and you. Go get the girl from the apartment. You and you, bring the one from the office."

"What's happening?" someone asked.

"Better you don't know, dude," Derek said, moving for the door.

Leo closed his fangs gently, slowly, on a blood-servant's throat. And drank.

The pain was bearable but the rage was still hot within him. He had drunk from Bethany and from ten humans, taking a little over a pint from each. He had ingested over a gallon of blood, and he could have taken more, but he had an enemy to find before dawn. El Mago. The mage would not be allowed to reside in his city if he had to cut a swath through the populace to find him.

In the private restroom of the office, Leo washed his face and brushed his teeth, his fangs, and the hinge structure that operated them. He combed his black hair and tied it into a queue, then took a moment to inspect his abdomen and torso. They should have displayed dreadful wounds, but they were unmarked. He dressed in the clean clothes that had been brought from his clan home on the west side of the river, but this time he strapped a small weapon to his right leg. The Smith & Wesson .380 semiautomatic pistol was loaded with silver/lead rounds. He belted his dueling swords around his waist and checked himself in the brass-backed mirror. Human customers in the bar hated it, but for Mithrans it was the only way to see a reflection. His flesh picked up the golden tones from the brass, looking far more human than his pale skin in the bright lights. Satisfied, Leo rifled through the zippered bag holding his clothes and pocketed a cell phone. Some wise person had placed a folded sheet of paper between the clamshell halves with instructions on how to use it. Fortified, Leo stepped from the restroom and walked across the room through the lines of his humans to the girls.

The one who had been tied to the chair was stretched out on a chaise, her head in the lap of the other one. The victim was named Audrey Salick, and she looked vaguely Asian. Her sister, the blond temptress who had shared Leo's bed earlier in the night, was named Margaret Coin. The same mother. Very different fathers.

"Audrey," Leo said softly, his voice a low purr as he wielded his mesmerism. "You have been healed. The memories of your abuse muted. Are you well?"

Audrey lifted her head off her sister's thigh and blinked blearily around the room. "I'm fine, I think." She focused on the Mithran standing behind Leo, the Mithran who had healed her, and pointed a finger. "I know you. You're Estavan." Her brows came down in a scowl. "Hey! Did you . . . ? Did we—"

Estavan moved to the back of the couch and took her hand. "All is well, *mi hermosa ave.*" *My beautiful bird.* Leo's lips lifted at the endearment. Estavan loved women and he was already half in love with this new one. "All is well," Estavan finished. He lifted her hand and bowed over it to kiss her fingers. The woman sighed. "She is well, my sire. And she knew nothing about tonight's ambush."

Leo set his eyes on Margaret. "But this one. She knew much," he said.

Margaret pressed her body into the couch, her blond hair coiling about her. Her blue eyes filled with tears. "He had my sister. I didn't have a choice."

"We all have choices, my dear. Estavan, take your new blood-servant."

"No!" Margaret screamed, even as Estavan leaned across the couch and lifted Audrey into his arms. He whisked her through the door, into the bar. "No," Margaret sobbed, one arm out as if to drag her sister back. "I was supposed to be saving her."

"In return for . . . ?" Leo asked.

"A week of . . ." She drew in a sobbing breath and her mouth pulled down in shame. "Servitude."

"A week in a Mithran's bed," Leo clarified. "A vampire who called himself El Mago."

Margaret nodded, tears reddening her pale skin.

"Then you shall have five weeks in mine, as payment for the trouble you have caused. For now, we will start in small sips. Give me your wrist. And this time you will withhold nothing, not even the trifling dark place in your soul that hid the knowledge of my enemy from me. The trivial dark spot that I should have forced my way into when you were compliant."

"No. No, no, no, no."

"She's wearing an engagement ring, boss."

Leo turned slowly and looked at his primo. His voice took an edge. "So she is. Had she come to me and told her story, I would have saved her sister and set them both free. I have been magnanimous to all human cattle in my city. I have made it clear that they may come to me at any time. She did not. She chose to fear an enemy, to become one herself. You would have me punish her according to a law older than my own?" According to the Vampira Carta, the written laws that all Mithrans adhered to, he could have taken her life for such an infraction.

"No." George shook his head. "I'm not—"

"This is about your sister and the shame she was dealt. I understand. And for this reason alone, I will not banish you, nor strip you of power. But for now, leave me." Leo smelled Alfonse in the room. "Alfonse, take my primo home. See that he stays there. The rest of you, wait in the main room. Drink. Enjoy yourselves. I'll be an hour."

Leo left the room, licking his new paramour's blood from his lips and taking with him all she knew. Margaret Coin would make a lovely addition to his collection of blood-servants. She was willing, no matter that her earlier interest was reliant upon fear for her sister. Now she had tasted his blood and she was his. He would recompense her betrothed for the loss of his future wife. George would disapprove, but George often disapproved.

Leo stepped silently into the main room of Royal Mojo and said, "My enemy is at the Hotel Monteleone, in the Ernest Hemingway suite. He has magic, spells of confusion and obfuscation and false health. He has silver and poison. I will compel no one to fight at my side, nor will I condemn any who walk away. But I ask for aid and fighters who might join me."

Katie made a soft sound with her lips: *Pfttt.* "I am yours to call. You need no one else."

"You are my love, not my warrior, nor my security team. This is not your fight."

"And if you die true dead? You have chosen no official heir, yet all will turn to me. You know this. You have planned it. You would leave me shackled with the city and its restive Mithrans? Dreadful responsibility for one such as I, who has dedicated her life to pleasure. Such boredom, tied to the boardroom of negotiation and mediation." Katie tilted her head and gave him the same smile she had offered him when he lay on the floor, paralyzed. "It has been long since we fought your old . . . *enemy* together. Since the day he turned on you, breaking his blood bond to his sire and yours. All recall when he used magic on Amaury Pellissier rather than a blade, the day he broke his word, broke his vows. Proving his blood and birthright were the lesser, tainted by dishonor." She drew her sword, the sound like a caress as it left the decorative scabbard. "Let us go to the Monteleone and play with your wily nemesis."

Bethany said, "I carry a trinket that will allow a Mithran to see magic as I do." From a finger, she removed a wooden ring, carved from a tree from her homeland in Africa. She had worn it as long as Leo had known her, which was many centuries. "Capture the mage who forced you to attack my George. And before he dies, tell him that his death would have been infinitely more painful at my hand. Catch. And go." She tossed the ring. Leo's hand swept up and he caught the ring. He slid it onto his finger and instantly he saw a purple haze about the priestess, her magics swarming for a moment with darker purple particles before she inhaled and pulled it all back inside her.

Leo paused outside the elevator, the Hemingway suite at the end of the hallway. It was one of the most elegant in the extravagant hotel, with two bedrooms and a large sitting room for social engagements. He glanced at his cohort and grinned, fangs down, remembering the last time they had entered this suite. It had been a week of revelry at Mardi Gras, a dozen young tourists, far too much alcohol, and ceaseless sexual escapades.

Katie chuckled, a wicked sound, and ran her fingers up his back. "If we are back in your lair before the sun, my love, we might reenact in great detail. For now, you shall inform me what you see in the seating area and engage our enemy if he is there. If he is not, then we shall clear the parlor, the bedroom on the right, then the room to the left. Oh. And Leo, *mon amour*, will you please demolish the door? These are new Jimmy Choos." Katie swept back her split skirt, again displaying the stilettos and a great deal of leg.

"Of course, my darling, though what I had in mind is perhaps more anticlimactic than you might wish." Leo strode to the door, pulling a room card from his pocket. He swiped it and the door clicked open. "I borrowed it from the front desk."

"I do believe that I adore you."

"As I do you," Leo said, easing the door open a crack, clenching his fist around the ring. "No magic."

The door opened silently to reveal the large parlor—the pale green of its walls, long upholstered couch, and heavy draperies producing a sense of serenity. The antiques, tall ceiling, crystal chandelier, and heavy moldings established elegance. The merrily burning fire generated a comfortable ambience for the three humans standing before it on the room-sized Persian rug. They were well-armed toughs, incompatible with the luxury, far more suited to a barroom or pool-hall brawl. They were not expecting Katherine Fonteneau.

His love blew past him at speed, and in three perfect cuts slashed the throats of all three. Before he was dispatched, the last one shouted, giving away their attack, though Leo had never supposed they might enter without such a warning.

"You could have left one for me," Leo said.

"I have never been called generous except in the bedroom."

"True, my love. But in bed you are Hathor, Aphrodite, and Venus all together."

"I am," she agreed.

They raced into the bedroom on the right. It was empty, though it smelled of sex and fear and the bedcovers were rumpled and smeared with blood.

The marble bathroom was empty. Leo followed Katie to the bedroom on the left. At the doorway, he placed a hand on her shoulder, stopping her. Into her ear, he whispered, "Magic."

Where? she mouthed.

Leo pointed into the corner behind the door. There was room for only one of them. The other would have to clear the room and provide protection from rear assault. Katie pouted, her lips pursing around her canines. "Poo," she said. She inserted her sword in its scabbard, out of the way, and slammed back the door. She tucked, dropped, and rolled past it, into the room.

Leo followed her through. Kicked the door closed behind them. Revealing the space behind the door. Empty. Except for a haze of reddish magics with particles of black swarming through it. And the faintest haze of a Mithran hidden within.

With a single thrust, Leo speared through El Mago's heart, whipped his flat-blade left and right. With a backhand cut, he slashed his old adversary's throat. The fog of magics dissipated, revealing El Mago, falling to his knees, his long black hair up in a fighting queue. Blood spouted from his throat. His black eyes flashed in shock.

Leo dropped his swords and grabbed up his ancient rival. Covered the torn throat with his own mouth, and began to drink. He slid his mind into the mind of El Mago, following the pathways of their earlier years, before their conflicts. He drank down the old jealousy, the hatred, and the betrayal they had given birth to. He absorbed the plans and the hopes and the future as El Mago wished it to be. He understood.

The European Mithrans were coming for the Americans, as soon as ten years. They wanted his land, his Mithrans, his cattle. They wanted to rule the world; what better place to do so than from the United States of America? *His land.*

He would not give it up.

Leo dropped El Mago and, with an economical swipe of his sword, removed his head.

Katie bent down, inspecting the body. "You killed him before we left for the Americas. Only someone powerful might have healed him from the mortal wound you administered." She tilted her head to Leo. "You have enemies. Will you grieve again, for his death?"

"I will not." Leo pulled out the cellular phone and followed the instructions. "Pellissier Clan Home," a woman answered.

"This is Leo. Send a cleanup crew to the Hemingway suite of the Hotel Monteleone."

"Leo. The Master of the City?"

"Of course. Who else would make such a call? And send a car to collect Katherine and me. We shall be walking down Royal toward St. Louis Street. We require a male blood-servant and the human Margaret Coin, champagne, and privacy in the limo. And . . ." He considered the odd phrase he had heard his people use. "Make it snappy."

Leo Pellissier, Master of the City of New Orleans, dropped the cellular phone and held out his arm to his beloved. "Come. Let us take in the city before the sun rises."

Together they left the Hemingway suite and the body on the floor of the bedroom. Perhaps this time El Mago—Miguel Pellissier—would stay down. Re-killing his brother was tiring.

It's Just a Date

First published online, as a serial short, as part of a blog tour in 2016. In the timeline, Jane is the Enforcer to Leo.

"It's just dinner."

"It's a date, Jane," Jodi argued. "With a guy who works for Leo Pellissier, the vampire Master of the City of New Orleans. There is a clear conflict of interest between him and NOPD."

"There's no conflict of interest at all," I said. "No. Take it off. The red looks too bright with your blond hair."

"You know zilch about fashion and color," she countered, but drew the shirt off over her head. "You are currently wearing purple socks with brown ankle boots, a black shoulder rig, red holster, a royal blue tee, and beat-up blue jeans. Except for the boots, you look like a shortsighted, color-blind person who shops for high fashion at Goodwill and Cabela's."

"Nothing wrong with any of those things," I said, pulling up my jeans legs to see my socks. The purple was pretty. "Besides. I have time to change before our triple dinner date. Nor is there a conflict of interest," I went on, hoping she didn't notice the word *date* buried in that sentence. "Wrassler doesn't work for the mob, doesn't have a record, and is charming. You're just too chicken to start dating again." Jodi pretended to be too busy yanking on a gorgeous pale yellow shirt that still had the tags on it to reply to me. I narrowed my eyes at her. "Chicken," I said, distinctly. "Chicken. Chicken. Chicken."

Jodi, head of the woo-woo department of the New Orleans Police Department, shoved her head through the neck and scowled at me. "What if he doesn't like me? What if we have nothing in common? What if he's bored. What if—"

"Stop," I yelled, managing not to laugh. "He watches you like a hawk any time you're near. You both like guns and politics and protecting people. I promise he will not be bored. We're going to Stephan's and they have a band starting at ten."

"He does?"

I wasn't sure what part she was referring to, but she sounded hopeful, so I just said, "He does. He's smitten. And the yellow is perfect. Put on the necklace so I can see it all." Jodi averted her head, carefully not looking at me as she hooked the wire-wrapped citrine around her neck, and I had a revelation. "You bought that shirt just for tonight, didn't you?" Jodi didn't look up but she blushed a bright pink. "It's silk." I grabbed the tag. "And it's freaking expensive!" She didn't look up, but her lips pressed together and her color went higher. "You like him too! Holy crap. Jodi's in Looo-ooove. Jodi's in Looo-ooove."

"Jane Yellowrock, I swear by all I hold holy that I will shoot you if you say another word."

I let the teasing fall away. Softer I said, "You've been carrying a torch for each other for a long time. You deserve some happy time. Some down-time. And if you bought that shirt with Wrassler in mind, then you made a perfect choice. You look gorgeous without looking like bait."

Jodi blew out a breath that fluffed her bangs. "Okay. Fine. I'll see you at eight. Now skedaddle. I worked a scene until four and I need some beauty sleep."

I dressed with special care. It had been weeks since my honeybunch—not that I'd ever call Bruiser that to his face—and I had been on a real date. Something other than fast food or grabbing a few hours together had become a rarity, and dinner at a new multi-star restaurant was a treat, even if we did have four others sharing the limo. No fun and games on the limo floor tonight, but getting a blind date in place for Wrassler and Jodi was an invitation we couldn't refuse. The two had been giving long looks when the other was too busy to notice, making excuses to be in the same room or on the same case together. I had even caught Jodi twirling her hair when she was talking to him. And Wrassler had bought a new suit and new shoes that fit his prosthetic leg better than his old ones, and he wore it whenever she was around. They were crazy about each other but neither would make the first move. And I would suck as a matchmaker. So Eli, one of my partners in Yellowrock Securities, and Sylvia, his sweetie-pie (ditto on not saying that aloud) set up the date. It was pretty romantic.

I heard my own sigh as I pulled on a pair of dress slacks with false pockets. The legs were wide enough that I could carry a blade and a small weapon strapped to my thigh. I had a .380 that was the size of my palm, and a six-inch silvered blade. I went nowhere these days without a weapon, even the nearly useless ones I carried tonight. I pulled on a long-sleeved black T-shirt and a necklace with a topaz stone focal, and loosely braided my hair. I stabbed two silver stakes and one wooden stake into it once I had it all twisted up into a messy bun.

In the mirror I looked casual but elegant. And Bruiser liked the way my legs and butt looked in these pants. Just to remind him what awaited him if we ever found the time.

I adjusted the weapons so they didn't show on my legs and decided they weren't enough. I texted Molly—my BFF and earth witch—that I was going into her trinket box, and dragged it from the top shelf of my closet. I unlatched the small olivewood box and studied the charms that Molly kept ready for my use: petrified wood discs hand-carved in bas-relief, a wooden cross with a dead crucified Jesus on it, a wooden ring made of three kinds of wood laminated together, a hair ornament with a wooden leaf dangling on a short chain.

I touched several and decided on the charm that I hadn't had the courage to wear in a long time. The last time I had used this type of working I had killed the only other skinwalker I had met in modern times. It tingled with harnessed power, hot on my fingertips. By touching it, I had locked and loaded the charm. The petrified wood disc was hand-carved to look like a spray of leaves. I slid a stake through the holes in the back and added it to my hair. It looked like a hair ornament where it dangled at the crown of my head.

It looked innocent enough, but it was designed to explode into a magical attacker and dissolve both flesh and spell, leaving the assailant an empty, lifeless husk. Wearing it, I felt better about my lack of steel weapons. While I was at it, I slid on the wooden ring too. It had been hand-carved, created to provide me temporary protection from aggressive spells. It gave me a fifteen-second window to get away if I was magically attacked.

Pretty cool, though it was a onetime-use amulet and, once used, couldn't be reloaded.

I opened the door to see Bruiser on the front stoop, leaning against the post that held up the gallery overhead. His dark hair was hanging over his forehead, a little too long, his Roman nose slightly reddened from a day in the sun. His dress slacks were pressed to a perfect crease, the sleeves of his white shirt were rolled up to show off his well-muscled arms, and his shoes were polished to a high shine. The only odd note was the double shoulder rig that would be hidden beneath his sports jacket when we got to the restaurant. His lips turned up in reaction to my perusal, and he held out a single dark red rose, the exact shade of my favorite lipstick. Scent had nearly been bred out of red roses, and because my skinwalker senses made flowers with scents a bad prezzie, the rose was perfect for me in every way.

I accepted the bloom, and the heat in his eyes made it seem as if I were accepting something far more valuable than a flower from him. His fingers caressed along mine, lingering on the ring I wore.

"Jane," he said. Just that. My name.

And something that was both icy and scorching raced along my nerves, beneath my flesh.

Mate, my Beast purred. *Would rather have cow than plant.*

Mentally I shushed her, and shoved aside the image of Bruiser meeting me at the door with a raw steak in his hand. "Hiya, Bruiser," I said, moving back to invite him in. I stepped into the kitchen for a vase, my low heels clicking. I could feel his eyes on my butt the whole way.

"Get a room," the Kid grouched, proving me right.

I grinned. Bruiser laughed. He was closer than I thought, his mouth suddenly at my ear as he reached around and took the narrow white vase from my hands. He pinned my hips to the counter with his body and held me lightly in place as he filled the vase with water and placed the rose inside. He was Onorio hot. Burning through my clothes to my skin. A human that warm would be in a hospital, packed with ice bags. I took a breath and smelled his faintly citrusy scent.

"Shall we place it by your bed?" he murmured, his lips moving on the side of my arched neck. His heat shot through me like lightning. I dropped my head back to his shoulder. At six feet, I couldn't do that to many men without hurting myself, but Bruiser was a tall man. "So it can be seen when we wake?"

"You'll make us late," Eli said, the words bland but somehow amused.

Without raising his voice Bruiser said, "Your timing is dreadful, as usual."

"His timing is fantastic," Syl said. "But you two can romance after we eat. I'm starving."

"Triple date," Bruiser said, straightening. "I have a feeling it will not go well."

We arrived at Stephan's with a few minutes to spare, the lights in the four-star Cajun-Creole restaurant shining bright through the sparkling windows. The place had been refurbished and enlarged, the kitchen hidden behind a wall, the lighting all copper, the tables all quartz-topped with cast-iron bases, the seats all high-end leather.

Stephan's had originally been a diner, and had closed down after a fire just before I arrived in NOLA. When the place reopened a month past, it was no longer a dive that specialized in fried foods and crawfish but an elite and expensive joint that required either lots of time on the waiting list for a reservation, or someone with moxie and power to get one of the twenty tables sooner. Someone like Bruiser, the MOC's former primo.

We were shown to a large, U-shaped, leather-seated booth in back, big enough for us all with room to spare, but with limited linear length for us all to face the front door. Each of us was hardwired to sit so we could watch the entrance, and while the others were jockeying for position, I slid in, facing one of the back entrances that opened on the alley and the small courtyard. If I was a bad guy and had reconnoitered the restaurant, that's the way I'd come in.

I placed the cloth napkin on my lap and waited until the others realized why I'd sat. The women figured it out first. Syl drew a file and started working on her nails with false patience. Jodi just rolled her eyes and rested a hip against the table, waiting.

The three alpha males looked both ways, considered the layout, and looked at each other, and with that peculiar communication of battle-weary warriors, they each took a seat. Bruiser shoved me over so he could take the aisle. Eli maneuvered around next to me in the center of the U and pulled Syl in after him. Eli was the most limber and slightest of build. He could leap over the table faster than either of the others. Wrassler held out his strong right hand and encouraged Jodi into the seat next to Syl, so he could take on the other aisle seat. Wrassler was the biggest and the slowest, due to the injury he'd received in a battle at vamp HQ. Didn't make him less valuable in a fight. Just meant he took a different job and different position.

We three well-armed women shared a look that said *Aren't they cute?* and let the guys position us where they wanted. Not that we didn't each decide how we would respond to a threat. Finding the best defensive positions was hardwired into us too.

Together, we were that mixture of races and genders common to New Orleans and bigger cities: Black, white, tribal, cop and civilians, VIPs of vamp politics and ordinary folks, all sitting together. Eating together. Ready to defend our fellow diners from an outside threat, or a hidden threat from within. Together we were a small army.

The waiter was a good-looking local kid, skin a reddish brown color that suggested a gorgeous mixture of tribal, Black, and white. He had a local patter and graceful social skills, as he gave a half bow to our table. "How y'all doing tonight. A pleasure to have a such beautiful group of people in Stephan's. Hope you're hungry. Tonight there are three specials on the menu and a wonderful selection of wines to complement the meals . . ."

I tuned him out. Not just because I'd have the beef, and everyone at the table knew it, but because the head of NOPD district eight, Commander Walker, and his wife had just entered Stephan's. At the same time, a thin trail of smoke was wending its way down the aisle from the direction of the restrooms at the back of the restaurant. And the smoke was purple.

The purple smoke trailing along the middle of the aisle didn't act like regular smoke. It didn't spread out and dissipate into the room. It didn't rise as if heated. It moved almost as if with purpose, in a straight line down the aisle, past our booth, toward the entrance of Stephan's. Toward Commander Walker and his wife, who were being seated.

"Problem," I said, interrupting the waiter's patter.

"Black magic witch working?" Bruiser asked. He had already seen the smoke.

I sniffed. "Smells like it."

In an instant everyone moved. Bruiser ducked out and under the purple smoke to the front of Stephan's to warn the commander and start clearing the space. Eli went under the table instead of over it and was in the aisle before I noted he had moved, a small weapon at his thigh in a two-hand grip. In a fast, bent-kneed walk, he moved to the rear of the restaurant. The instant he was past, Wrassler stood and pushed the waiter down and to the side. "Get out!" he whispered in a stage whisper that carried through half the restaurant. Everyone nearby looked up. When they moved too slowly, he grabbed up the couple nearest and started clearing the place physically. Syl followed Eli, weapon drawn. Jodi was calling in the local magical hazmat team.

For once, I stayed seated and took pics, sending them to the Kid and to Molly, my BFF witch friend with the text: Problems. Smoke spell. Suggestions?

Instantly, I got a reply from Molly. GET OUT!!! All in caps with three exclamation marks.

Instead, I darted into the kitchen and grabbed the head chef, a sous chef, a dessert chef, and three scullery types. With the words "Terrorist attack. Get out and get under cover," I shoved them toward the loading exit, an extra door directly from the kitchen into the delivery alley. Terrorists was a lie, but *terrorist* was much more likely to result in compliance than saying *magical attack*.

"The burners!" the head chef said, pulling away.

"I'll get 'em." I yanked his collar and shoved harder to the back, bunching them into a herd and heaving them into the dark. Shutting the door so they'd think twice about coming back in.

I raced over and cut off everything that was hot. *Cow!* Beast thought. The smells were delish and Beast wanted to taste everything in every pan, especially the half-raw steak. I ignored her and spun back to the restaurant.

But my way was blocked. By a purple wall of smoke.

The sound of sirens arriving was crisp on the air. Shouting. Bright lights, purpled by the odd cloud. The restaurant wasn't empty. I could still smell Bruiser and humans at the front, and Eli and Sylvia at the back. It made sense. Someone had to coordinate the response teams, which meant Jodi and Wrassler would be outside with the populace and the first responders. Syl, the chief of police from Natchez, wasn't leaving Eli, and Eli and Bruiser weren't leaving me. Crap.

Two thirds of their concern was stupid. Bruiser and I weren't human. We were more likely to withstand magical attacks than humans. Eli and Syl were human, and were just as likely to die from magic as any other human, well-trained warrior and cop or not. Military and paramilitary measures were no help against magical workings.

Worse, the wall of spelled purple smoke was growing, expanding. It had filled the hallway and the restaurant and was moving into the kitchen. It should have dissolved and dispersed after Commander and Mrs. Walker left the scene. But . . . it was getting bigger. So maybe it had a secondary target.

My cell dinged and I risked a glance at the screen. Molly had sent a text. Does it have eyes? How many? Claws? Fangs?

I texted back, No. Is filling space. O2 replacement? I was asking if it intended to suffocate us. Then, the purple-smoke-cloud-spell shifted, roiling, as if blown back by a slow wind. It changed shape. I texted, Now I see claws. See fangs. One set. No eyes yet.

It's after you? she texted back, guessing the same thing I had. I told you to GET OUT!!!

"Ducky," I muttered, pocketing the cell. I shouted, "Bruiser, Eli, Sylvia, get outta here. NOW!"

From the front of the restaurant I saw a flash of gold, like a sizzling length of horizontal lightning. The kind that goes cloud to cloud, not heavens to ground. Through the air I heard cursing and a shriek of pain. Then the footsteps of half a dozen human holdouts as they finally took Bruiser's word and skedaddled.

I heard Eli and Syl speed away, down the hallway toward the front entrance, their steps odd, as if they crouched low to avoid the fog. I raced to the back of the kitchen and swung open the door again. Outside was more of the purple vapor, the spell rolling outward, from the restaurant into the neighborhood. I took a step back inside, narrowly avoiding the plumes of magic.

On the far side of the smoke, Eli and Syl crouched, backing up the alley. Looked like they had gotten out just in time. My partner stared at me through the purple smoke, face empty of expression. Battle face. The face he had worn so often since I was hit by magical lightning and he and Bruiser had carried my burned body through the city.

"Can you jump through it?" Eli asked, his tone calm, too calm. Glacier cold.

The spell sensed the open door and boiled in. It brushed my skin with a burning, stinging sensation, like steam, not smoke, hot and wet, not hot and dry, a sensation like tiny needles made of scalding mist, slicing and piercing into me. I leaped back, brushing the purple away. Where it had touched me, I was stained lavender in swirls and parallel lines, like some kind of tribal markings. Or like a spell tattooed into my flesh. Marking me. Why? To what end?

My blood was rising to the surface and pooling like bloody blisters. It hurt where I touched my skin, like a burn from hot steel, but it looked nothing like a burn. It looked as if my blood was being pulled from my veins to puddle just under my skin. I hissed. "No. Can't jump through that."

Eli crouched, as if ready to dive back inside. To save me. I slammed the door. Locked it.

This was bad. This was very bad.

"Jane!" Eli yelled from outside.

I eased farther into the kitchen, seeing the mist coming at me from two sides. Backed up until I could feel the heat from the ovens and burners that were still trying to cool.

The gold lightning sizzled again, and this time I flinched. I couldn't help it. I'd been hurt by lightning. I was still trying to get used to the idea of thunderstorms and weather fronts. And now this . . .

"I've got her," Bruiser said, from the front room, presumably to Eli, outside. "Jane," Bruiser said to me. His voice steadied me. I took a breath that tasted like the ashes of violets in the back of my throat.

"It's marked me with something like tattoos," I said. "You?"

"It tried." Bruiser walked through the kitchen doorway from the restaurant proper.

The purple smoke-mist rolled away from him, like a wave spun away from the shore when it was spent. The mist moved almost as if Bruiser was damaging it, and when he put on a burst of speed, it sparked where it touched him. His skin was burned with the purple swirls, and flaked off. Just as fast, his magics repaired the damaged skin. But I smelled his blood. His Onorio magics were offering him protection, but he needed out of here. Fast.

He reached my side and took my hand. "No purple etchings or burns here. What does the spell in the ring do?"

It was the hand wearing the wooden ring amulet. "Ahhh," I said, relief shooting through me. "It gives me fifteen seconds to get away from an *attack* working. And it looks like it gives me some kind of localized protection even without being activated." For a moment I was blank on how to activate the ring, and then it came to me. A lot of Molly's more weaponized spells required a drop or two of my blood to activate them, but this was less a defensive working than the kind of thing witch children learn when they are tutored in magic. It was a game. I made a fist and rapped with the ring on the countertop, *tap-tap-tap*, fast. I felt the purple mist-smoke spell stutter and sputter and I grabbed Bruiser's hand. "Come on!"

Together, we raced through the restaurant and into the night. Lights and sirens were everywhere, first responders still arriving, and Commander Walker and his wife were walking back through the mob of local LEOs, coming back to the entrance and the media gathered there. "Oh crap," I said.

Bruiser must have read my mind because he dropped my hand, raced ahead, picked up the commander—not a small fellow—and his wife, and carried them kicking and screaming away. And the purple mist followed them. It rose into a shape like a huge maw, a shark mouth, full of golden-electric lightning teeth, sharp as razors.

So it wasn't here for me after all. Or not just me.

I reached up and yanked the hair ornament out of my hair. If Molly's gift didn't work, I was out of ideas. "Get down!" I shouted. And threw the disc into the purple smoke-vapor maw. The wooden disc clipped an electric fang and whirled deep inside the mouth, like skipping a stone off another stone.

It exploded inward, into the shark mouth. It blasted the smoke-formed head into purple dust and exploded back through the restaurant, taking apart every molecule of the working. A magic hand grenade. Purple dust blasted out into the street through the open doors. The purple cloud shimmered away.

I spotted Jodi working the scene and Wrassler propped against a marked car, a big, totally-smitten grin on his face. When he saw me looking, he made a megaphone of his hands and shouted, "Best first date ever!"

I laughed and the laughter caused me to start coughing up purple dust.

From the corner of my eye I saw movement. At the entrance of the alley, a small woman raised her arm. *Gun.*

I reached for my weapon. Hidden in my clothes.

Four gunshots sounded. Overlapping. The woman fell back against the wall.

Eli and Syl moved toward her, weapons extended. The woman gasped several times, her chest moving. Then she lay still.

The commander, cell phone in hand, pushed his way through the crowd and stood over her. "Cancel the ambulance. We need the medical examiner and crime scene." He closed his phone. "Natalia Bussey. A witch who cursed her unfaithful lover in 2004. The witches didn't stop her, so I did. I put her away in a human prison. I was notified six weeks ago she had been paroled."

"And you didn't think it necessary to tell me?" Mrs. Walker asked, her tone like liquid steel. "We'll discuss this at home. Tonight."

The commander blew out a breath. "Yes, dear."

The commander's wife looked at me, her eyes flashing with banked fire. "Thank you, Ms. Yellowrock."

"You're welcome, ma'am."

I didn't stay for the mopping up—dusting up—of the spell, nor did I hang around for the press conference. Bruiser dealt with city politics and the press. Jodi and Wrassler hung out with the cops working the crime scene. I hitched a ride home with Eli and Sylvia, took a long hot shower, and put lots of Molly's healing lotion on my burned, bruised skin. Meanwhile Eli and Syl shared a bottle of wine and made plans of a more amorous nature.

I went to bed. Alone. I thought I'd not sleep, but I must have slipped into dreams because I woke when my Onorio climbed into my bed and wrapped me in his arms. Which was a grand way to end a very bad triple date.

Life's a Bitch and Then You Die

First published as a serial short online in 2017 and takes place while Jane was sick. It is from Beast's and Wesa's point of view, and it answers some questions asked by fans about secrets Beast keeps. In the timeline, it takes place before (and perhaps after) "Of Cats and Cars."

I studied the landscape through Beast's eyes.

Good hunt in snow, she thought at me.

Uh-huh.

Would be better to hunt bison with Ed, in Ed car.

We don't have Ed. He's in France. We don't have Ed's car. We don't have bison. Yeah, I know about that hunt bargain so don't give me a hard time.

Bison ranch is there—she turned to look in the direction of one of three bison ranches in the area—*to setting sun.*

If I'd been human-shaped I'd have sighed, but *Puma concolors* didn't sigh. With just a hint of irritation in my mental tone, I thought, *Those bison are not wild animals. They are . . .* I tried to find a word she understood . . . *pets. We don't kill pets.*

Beast chuffed in disgust. *Stupid pets. Stupid human rule. Beast will hunt cows with trees on head. Beast will kill cows with trees on head.*

For the record, that's probably bulls with horns, but whatever.

Beast looked back down. *Beast sees deer tracks in snow. Smells deer on wind. Will hunt deer.*

Yeah, yeah. Whatever. Go for it.

I caught a glimpse of Brute, the white werewolf, in the trees off to our left, his body blending into the drifts, following us, his path at a pincer angle. Beast would never admit that she liked hunting with the werewolf, but she did. She moved more slowly, allowing him to catch up to her. She thought, *Brute is stupid werewolf. Brute is slow werewolf. Beast is best ambush hunter.*

Uh-huh, I thought back again.

Thirty feet up, she stepped on a limb. It gave, cracking, a sharp sound like a gunshot. She froze into stillness, eyes taking in her options. The branch looked like the other winter-bare limbs all around, but it cracked again. It was dead. Pieces fell, spinning for the ground.

Trickster tree! Beast took two quick steps back, gathered herself, and leaped to another tree, and then another. Behind us, the branch where she had stood fell and crashed to the ground.

Her claws gripped and shoved as she raced down a strong branch, closer to the ground. Though her paws were designed to prevent snow accumulation, ice tried to wedge into the paw pads. More than five trees away from the trickster tree, she stopped and shook her paws, one at a time, slinging the snow away.

She leaped again, landing on a lower limb with that cat balance and grace no human could ever master. I hunkered down in her mind and let her hunt, my thoughts wandering. We did a lot of that these days, me hiding in Beast's body, her in control, making the decisions, chasing deer in the mountains of Appalachia, annoying the white werewolf who had come to live with us. With the exception of picking on the wolf, she acted like a housebroken Big-Cat. She was having a ball, loving every minute of it.

I was bored outta my mind.

Spotting Brute, who had moved ahead, taking an animal path between bushes, Beast moved upwind, through tree branches, following the deer tracks below, in the latest snowfall. It was midwinter, in a year that had already recorded more snow than the usual thirteen inches, and we had two more months of winter left. If the weird weather pattern continued, it could be a record-breaking snow-year for the Asheville, North Carolina, area. The human members of our family were currently out snow skiing and snowboarding and having a blast while we hunted. I couldn't bring myself to care about the snowfall. Or much of anything these days.

My human body was dying and my Beast body was the only part of us that was healthy. So while my clan worked on the property and buildings that I had bought with the Dark Queen's cash, and played in the snow, and tried to figure out how to heal me, I got to let Beast hunt, twiddle my virtual thumbs, think about the failure of the Sangre Duello, and delve into memories best left untouched.

It was like picking a scab just to see it bleed. It was stupid. It accomplished nothing. It didn't help me heal. But since me actually healing and not dying from the cancer growing in my human belly was unlikely, staying in Beast's body beat living sick. For now.

Beast caught the scent of deer, ripe and pungent.

She crouched, her tail held tight to her torso, as she paw-paw-pawed ahead. Her back paws landed in the prints of her front paws. She was silent, unseen, moving high in the trees. Below, Brute glanced up and flicked an ear to the far left. Beast flicked her tail in response. Still hunched, she eased along an oak branch that brought her close to a springhead and a runnel of water, the deer tracks leading directly there. Temps were cold enough for the rivulet to be frozen over, but the springhead pumped still-liquid water to the surface where it puddled in a slight depression in the ice before it ran off and froze in a tangle of ice threads leading to the frozen creek below.

Brown color and movement drew my attention.

Beast was tightly focused on the movement between the trees where a hugely pregnant doe, a mature doe, and two almost juveniles were pawing at the ice. One was a male. Small *tocks* of sound echoed as the more mature deer pawed, teaching the younger ones how to get at water in winter, their two-toed feet scratching and beating at the springhead, widening the depression of clear water.

Beast watched, studied the position of the deer, where their eyes were pointed, where their ears twitched. She listened to the steady *tocking* sound, considered the direction of the wind. These were all things she did unconsciously as she waited on the wolf to get in position behind the small male deer. She had taught Brute—by fighting him away from a doe, leaving bleeding scratches in his white fur—which of the herd to hunt and eat. She always saved the females and took down the males, even when she was hungry. Beast was patient. Deeply focused on the deer.

Since I wasn't interested in the kill scene and the feasting that would follow, I seized the opportunity and slid into Beast's memories, the ones she kept from me to keep me safe. Or to hide truths from me. Having lived inside her brain for so many decades, I was curious as a cat. I slid through memories of hunting for catfish in a bayou. Landing on a boar and suffering a dangerous injury. Fighting an alligator, a big honking alligator. *Stupid cat.* I found older memories of other hunts.

Deeper, in a shadowy corner of her mind, I found a memory I should have known about. In it, Beast was racing away from a hunter.

Smell of white-man on wind. Stink of white-man-guns. *Hate white-man. Hate white-man-guns.* Needed kit sleeping in mind, but did not wake her. Raced for river. *Fastfastfast.* Over broken stone and fallen trees. Leaped high to top of rock pile.

Felt sting. Heard sound of white-man-gun. *Boom.*

Rolled in midair, tumbled off. Falling. Hit ground. Smelled blood. Was sick. No. Not sick. Wounded. Was shot by white-man-gun.

Pain clawed through insides. Got to three paws, one front leg hurt. Blood flowed fast over chest pelt and to ground. Crawled toward river. Could hear water. Roar of water, like sound of Big-Cat purring. But Cat was dying, not purring. Fell. Landed in snow. Blood everywhere.

Needed sleeping human kit to wake. Sank claws into sleeping human kit in mind. *Wake up, Wesa. Need you.*

What? Human kit curled long front paws and put to eyes. Cleaning eyes awake.

Am dying. White-man is here. White-man shot Cat. Must take form of human kit.

Don't let white-man find us, she thought. Fear raced through her. *White-men are killers only.*

Will shift to human shape. Will shift back to hunting Cat. Will be hungry. Will not be able to feed.

Okay. Take my form, she thought. *But keep away from white-man.*

Looked back. Did not see white-man, but he was making loud paw noises as he walked. Was too close, but Cat was dying. Cat found image of snake in deeps of human kit. Shifted. Cat screamed. Human kit screamed.

Coldcoldcold. Winter was early. Hunger hit my belly, an ache for meat and for *elisi*'s fried corn-cakes. Hunger in my middle like *tlvdatsi* claws when panther and Wesa fought and merged. Bad hunger. Bad cold. Looked at body. Had human shape. Dried blood made flakes and fell from body. Remembered knife and killing white-man, long ago. Had been good. But Wesa-in-human-shape had no knife. Wesa had lost father's knife long ago. Wesa-in-human-shape crawled under pile of branches and curled up in leaves for warmth.

Heard footsteps. Crouched tiny. Thought. Water is near. Could reach water and swim away.

Footsteps went past. Saw shape of man in white-man-clothes, with white-man-stink, of sweat and poison and stinky things that make the Earth and the children of the Corn Mother sick.

White-man passed on by. Air and ground fell silent. We shivered in Wesa-human-shape, bare skin with no pelt. Would die soon in this shape.

Time moved. Birds flew on air. Squirrels peeked out of nests, staring at Wesa-human-shape. Hunger made belly ache. Noisy silver metal bird with strange beak flew overhead. Owls hunted and claimed territory. Finally decided that white-man was gone. Crawled from pile of sticks and looked around. Tried to smell with human nose, sniffsniffsniff, and did not smell white-man. Stood. Heard river. Place of safety. Wesa was thirsty.

Feet hurt in human-shape as Wesa raced to small river. Wesa climbed down many rocks to edge of water and drank. Was hungry. Wanted corn-cakes fried in fat. Water was not enough. Wesa still hungered. Touched chest, ribs were sharp like knives against flesh. Wesa fingers found a scar, round shape on bare skin of chest. It was a new scar. Had nearly died from white-man-gun.

Sank down on back feet, bony knees to bony chest, arms around knees. Was cold. Skin of fingers was blue. Thought about hunting Cat shape. Thought about *tlvdatsi* shape. Shifted. There was much pain.

Was Cat. Was healed. Stood. Walked toward water.

Heard crack of white-man-gun. Felt sting in rump. Spun and raced toward water. Jumped into water. Raced up far bank. Reached top. Felt tired. Looked at rump. Was white-man-metal-thing sticking out of rump.

Rolled over, pulling white-man-metal-thing out. Was not much blood. Cat ran and ran. Stumbled over own paws. Cat was hungry and tired. Too tired to run. Too tired to fight. Eyes almost closed. Rolled over. Saw white-man boots walking closer. Knew was about to die. Slept.

Woke. Light was bright. Body did not move. But was not dead yet. Slept again.

Woke. Hurt. Hurt bad. Taste in mouth was bad, like eating dead thing, rotting in mud. Bright lights. White-man-lights. Smell of Cat-piss. Smell of metal. Smell of white-man-poisons.

Rolled over. Found had pissed on pelt. Was bad smell. Sick smell. Cat was . . . in cage. Eyes did not work. Tongue did not work. Was . . . in *cage*. Cage not on ground, but up higher. Nose said was on top of other cages.

Eyes began to work. Mouth began to work. Was not dead. Smelled own blood. Tried to stand. Could not stand. Cage was too small. Hair had been removed from legs, above paws. Could see skin and lines where blood ran. Small wound was on each leg on bare skin. Licked. Tasted Cat-blood and white-man poisons. Claws had been cut smooth. Not sharp. But not broken. Could regrow claws. Could make claws sharp again. Touched tongue to teeth. Killing teeth were still long and pointed and sharp. Pulled body in tight. Paws beneath chest and belly. Tail around feet, tight. Watching. Waiting. Eyes saw slight movement. White-man sat with back of head to Cat. Was prey position, but Cat could not make kill from cage. White-man did not know Cat was awake. Did not look at Cat.

Other cages were across space. All cages had animals inside. Cats and dogs and wolves and foxes. All predators. All smelled sick. Smell of piss and excrement was strong. No creatures looked at Cat. All looked away. Even wolf. Afraid. Ashamed to be in cage.

Wesa woke too. Thought into mind, *White-man-gun made sick. Hate white-man.*

Heard noise. White-man moved to cage. Smelled of strong plants and cooked meat. Onion and garlic, Wesa thought. Onion-and-garlic-white-man face came close enough to kill fast, but cage was in way.

"Well, I see you're awake. How's my pretty *Puma concolor*?"

Did not know sounds. Tried to growl. Mouth did not work right yet.

But smelled water. Found white-man-metal that held water. When tongue worked, Cat drank. Metal taste was bad.

White-man opened tiny door in Cat-cage. Put stinky meat into cage. Smelled of water and thin blood. Was part of bird. Cat did not want to eat, but Wesa thought, *Eat. We need strength to escape.*

Cat ate strange chicken. Could not stretch out. Was not room. Muscles hurt. Pissed and shat and slept. Dreamed of hunt and roaring water and white-man in bloody killing teeth.

Woke again. Lights still bright. No night came to white-man-place. Was always day. Place stank of many animals, fear, pain. Had to piss. Growled. No white-man came. Had to piss in cage again. Pissed on own feet again. Would kill white-men who made Cat piss on own feet. Lay down. Looked at place. Was warm and dry like good den. But was too bright. Could not see outside. Could see no opening to den.

Loud noise clanged. Metal-on-metal. Echoed. Hurt ears. Cat curled in ear tabs. Turned head to look and saw shiny metal thing swivel down and then wall bent. Crack appeared in whiteness of bending wall.

Wesa thought, *It's a door. That's the way out.*

White-man entered. Smelled of cooked meat. Was Cooked-meat-white-man.

He touched white box and made it glow green.

He pulled metal from bottom of Cat-cage and stole cat piss. Put metal back. Sat at green-glowing-box and made slow tap sounds.

Cooked-meat-white-man went away. Time passed.

White-man entered through door. Was another white-man. Smelled different.

Wesa thought, *Smells of white-man-soap.*

Soap-white-man went to box in corner. Sat. Box still glowed green. White-man made fast tapping noises, like sleet on stone. Kept back to Cat like prey at water-hole. But was not prey. Had caged Cat. White-men were strong predators.

Was many white-men. Was Onion-and-garlic-white-man, was Cooked-meat-white-man, and was Soap-white-man.

Soap-white-man did not turn around, but made strange noises. "You look just like a *Puma concolor*. But you aren't. Charles saw you shift shape into a human child and then shift shape back." Soap-white-man spun to see Cat. Eyes were blue like kit-eyes, but was not kit. Was predator.

What is Charles? Cat thought.

Charles is white-man-name, Wesa thought.

"We have your blood. Your hair. X-rays. A CT scan. A piece of tissue you'll never miss, I promise. Urine. Stool. I don't know what you are, yet. But we'll know your secrets soon." Soap-white-man went back to green-glowing-box and made more tapping.

Cat thought about metal thing that swiveled in bending wall, called door. *What is metal swivel thing in door?* Cat asked Wesa.

I think it opens the door. It moves and then the door opens. They use their hands to open it. Watch.

Waited. Watched Soap-white-man.

Metal thing turned. Door opened. Onion-and-garlic-white-man entered and door closed. Metal thing turned back up. Onion-and-garlic-white-man began to give water to caged animals. Cat watched carefully as he opened tiny doors to cages. Was metal thing that turned down, like door metal thing but smaller. All doors worked same. Metal thing that turned down.

Wesa thought. *Door latch. I have fingers. I can open door latches.*

Cat heart began to race. Was way out. But. Needed Wesa fingers. Needed Wesa in new way. Had used human kit before, many times, to keep alive when body was injured. But had never needed Wesa fingers. Never needed Wesa mind. Never needed Wesa to escape trap. Wesa was baby bobcat and human form. Wesa had many uses. Now had new use.

White-men talked. White-men gave water in metal thing. White-men talked more.

Green box went black. White men went away. Cat thought. Looked at cages. Looked at thing on cages that turned down. *Door latch. Can turn door-latch-metal-thing down without Wesa, if can get out of cage.*

Wesa thought, *I remember them from time with* elisi *and* edoda. *But you can't get out of cage without my fingers. It takes fingers to work a door latch on the other side of the cage. And when you do get out, fingers can open all other cages faster than Cat. All animals out will make a big problem and make it easier for Cat to get away.*

Cat did not want to need Wesa, who had stolen body and mind. Cat slept. White-man-lights stayed on. Time passed. Latch went down. Onion-and-garlic-white-man made box glow green. Fed animals and Cat stinky meat. Cleaned cages. White-men came in and out. White-men smelled of foods and white-man-stinks each time, but different each time. Time passed. Green-glow-box went black. White-men did not come back. Green-glow-box was dead.

Now, Wesa thought. *Change to Wesa form and use fingers. We will get away.*

Cat did not want to be Wesa. But did not want to be in cage. Thought of Wesa form. And changed shape. Painpainpainpain.

Wesa hurt. Was hungry. Hair was long and in my way. Shoved hair out of eyes, back behind ears. Drank water from metal bowl. Body was cold on white-man-metal-cage. Reached fingers through cold metal and turned door latch down. Door did not open. Carefully, to make no sound, Wesa shook cage. Door opened.

Cat looked out through Wesa eyes. Demanded, *Change back to Cat!*

No. We have to get out of white-man building first. Wesa jumped to floor and went to green box that was not green. Was black and dead. Saw other metal things, different kind of latches. Wesa pulled on latch. Drawer opened. Inside were things of metal and paper and smooth stuff that was not metal or paper. Wesa looked for a knife. No knife. Looked in other drawers. Found a tiny knife in a red case. Opened it.

Cat has best claws, Cat thought.

Yes. But still need fingers to get out of here.

Wesa went to cages and turned all the latches down. Some animals got out. Others stayed in back of cages. These were wounded in soul or body.

Wesa went to door latch and turned it down. With fingers. *Cat needs Wesa*, she thought.

Cat did not answer.

Wesa looked out. Saw tunnel, like long tunnel in cave, but with flat floor and flat walls. Was dark in cave, and tunnel had other doors with latches. Wesa opened door wide and wolf and fox raced into tunnel. Wesa found heavy metal thing to prop door and to make door stay open. Bobcat and lynx raced past into tunnel.

Wesa smiled. Was fierce smile, showing teeth. Wesa raced into tunnel and turned down each door latch, stuck head inside. Looked. Sniffed. Some rooms were light, some dark. Some rooms smelled of poisons. Some of white-man-food. Wesa hungered but did not look for food.

All rooms were empty of white-men. Last door opened to show strange floor that went up and down. Wesa raced up. Wolf and fox and one bobcat, another wesa, but old, came too. Running up strange floor. Running. Ignoring hunger in human belly. Running with predators, all together. Wesa held her knife, ready to kill.

Found door with latch at top of strange floor. Carefully, Wesa turned latch down. Cold air blasted in. Naked skin without pelt made bumps with cold. Outside it was night. Was a flat place, covered with snow. Was dark, with no white-man-lights. Had low walls, but no roof. Wesa found heavy thing to hold door open. Then ran to wall. Looked down. Was long, long way down.

Cat can jump down, Cat thought, *and run away.*

See fence? Can jump over fence? Fence is too tall.

Cat looked out through Wesa eyes. Saw things close to fence. *What are things there, hilly things covered with snow?*

Is other roofs, Wesa thought. *Can run across other roofs to that one close to fence. Go up to top of pointy roof. Then jump over fence.*

Yes. Shift to Cat.

Cat looked at wolf through Wesa eyes, thinking. *Wolf is hungry.*

Wolf stared at Wesa. Licked jaw.

Wesa swiped with knife claw.

Wolf and fox ran to other wall. Cowered like prey.

Bobcat leaped to top of wall and walked around, looking down. Bobcat did not need help. Bobcat would get away. Wolf and fox would die before jumping. Cat could not help wolf and fox. Wolf and fox predators might hunt Wesa while human kit changed to Cat shape. Was danger.

Looked at other tall place. Was not too tall, but wolf would not jump so high. *Can climb up there?* Cat asked.

Can climb up there. Wesa ran across snow and pulled things over to wall at tall place. Climbed up, then pushed other things off so wolf could not follow.

Was good to have fingers, but Cat would not tell Wesa.
Wesa thought of Cat.
Was painpainpainpainpain and darkness.

Woke in Cat form. Smelled wolf and lynx and other animals from cage.
Was hungry. Hungry enough to eat wolf or fox or lynx or bobcat.

No. Will not use fingers again if Cat eats other caged animals.

Cat growled. *Wesa is stupid. Should eat.* Wesa did not answer. Cat
jumped down to flat roof and walked to low wall and to next low wall.
Jumped up to top of low wall and then down to hilly-shape-roof. Was slick
and nearly fell, but caught balance. Moved carefully across hilly-shape-
roof and jumped to next one. Clawed to top of roof and studied distance
to cross to fence. Gathered self. Leaped. Pushing off with back paws.

Air and wind and night and fence went under belly. Cat landed on
ground in trees.

Felt something near. White-man! But was not white-man. Was lynx.
Lynx had jumped too. Looked at Cat. Lynx made hissing sound. Lynx
raced away. Bobcat landed near. Bobcat spat and hissed and raced into
woods. Cat raced into woods.

Heard white-man-noise.

Looked back. Saw white-man with white-man-gun. Charles. Would
kill white-man-Charles. Laid careful trail away from place of cages. Many
cat paw prints in snow. Watched for good ambush place. Was hungry, but
did not hunt and eat. Saw good tree hanging over small water place.
Stopped and drank good cold water, no metal taste. Then walked through
water upstream. And leaped from water into tree. Climbed up to limb and
jumped to next tree. And next tree, moving back to spot where Cat entered
stream. Last tracks. Picked best limb. Crouched. Waited.

Smelled white-man-Charles. Heard white-man-Charles. He moved
through snow, white-man-paws noisy to Cat-ears. Charles followed cat
paw trail in snow. Went to water edge. Cat waited. Patient.

White-man-Charles bent over prints. Cat gathered self. Leaped. Front
claws caught head and neck of white-man-Charles. Body landed. Shoved
white-man-Charles into water. And under. Was shallow. Cat caught white-
man-Charles neck in fangs and started to shake. Was killing move.

But white-man-Charles rolled over and pulled white-man-claw-knife. Said strange noises. "Kill you, you Beast."

Watch out for knife! Wesa shouted in head.

Cat swiveled body.

White-man-Charles hit Cat with claw-knife. But caught only loose coat. "Kill you, Beast! Die!"

Cat ripped out throat of white-man-Charles. Jumped back.

White-man-Charles bled and thrashed and died.

Cat drank blood and ate meat. Was good. Tore through clothes-pelt and ate heart and liver and lungs. Was good. Lay beside kill and licked own wound made by white-man-Charles. Was not bad. Was not deep. Would heal.

Tore off good thigh meat from white-man-Charles. Carried meat into woods and up into tree. Left meat there for food. Went back to carcass and tore off more good thigh meat. Saw lynx and bobcat. Turned away, tail twitching. Little cats could have carcass of white-man-Charles.

Carried thigh meat into hills, far away. Climbed tree far away. Leaped from tree to tall pile of rocks and found place free of snow, like small den. Curled into rock. Watched sun rise. Ate more white-man-Charles meat. Thought. *Cat is best ambush hunter.*

No, Wesa thought. *White-man-Charles called us Beast. Cat and Wesa are Beast. Beast is best ambush hunter and best human-kit-get-out-of-cage. Together are Beast.*

Better than Cat? Cat snarled in threat.

Yes. Better than Cat. Beast got out of cage. Beast killed and ate white-man-Charles. Was good meat. Wesa and Cat are Beast.

Cat who was now Beast thought more. Sun made day warmer. Brighter. Asked Wesa, *What other words did white-men say?*

Do not know white-men-language.

Beast chuffed with disgust. *Beast knows all cat languages. Knows all dog and wolf and fox language. Why does Wesa not know white-man-words?*

Would have to be with white-men long time to learn white-man-language and understand white-man-words.

Beast watched world grow brighter. Thought at Wesa, *Wesa should take human-kit-shape and be human and learn white-man-words and white-man-language. Can kill many white-men if we have words and language.*

Wesa thought at Cat. *Want to—*

Beast lunged and fell. The landing was brutal. It knocked me away from the memory. She took down the small juvenile buck, claws and killing teeth buried in the back of the buck's head. Brute leaped on his thrashing hindquarters. The buck squealed and screamed and thrashed. The does darted away and were gone. The buck died.

I waited. Thought.

We were back at the inn and winery I had purchased when I was looking for property when I ran away to die. I entered through the oversized cat flap by the front door. Brute followed. I was nice and clean, while his white coat was stained with brown dried blood. He'd be getting a bath, which my Beast found amusing. Brute hated baths.

Before she could stop me, I took control of her body and padded us to Alex's office, off to the side of the kitchen. I put our front paws on his desk and rose up until we were standing with our weight on our back paws, our heads level.

"Hey, Beast," he said absently.

I lifted a paw and put it on his hand, holding it down. Alex turned to me, smelling of bacon and pancakes and maple syrup. He smelled delicious and Beast wanted to lick him, but I held her back.

"Not Beast?" he asked.

I shook our head.

"You need to talk?" He pushed the specially modified keyboard at me. I chuffed and shook our head.

"In Jane form?"

I nodded once.

"Go shift. I'll find the boys. We'll be ready."

I dropped down and trotted to the suite I shared with Bruiser. It was upstairs in the left wing of the inn, and it was huge, two times bigger than my bedroom in the house in New Orleans, and the bathroom was lavish. Everything about the inn and winery was luxurious and extravagant. I lay on the floor of the bath and thought about my own shape. The one with cancer that was slowly dying. The pain wasn't bad this time. Surprisingly.

I woke on the icy tile of the shower and pushed myself to my knees. Then to my feet. And held on with all my might. I didn't intend to stay in human shape long. The pain was too horrible. I shoved my hair behind my ears and secured it with an elastic. I dressed and made my way to the elevator, because the stairs were beyond me.

I entered the office and sat gingerly on the sofa. That and the coffee table and the office desk and chair was all the room held for the moment, though more furniture was on the way. Eventually. Eli slid a plate of scrambled eggs onto the coffee table in front of me and placed a mug of hot mint chocolate in my left hand, a handful of ibuprofen tablets in the right. He had dozens of supplements on order, natural stuff to help with the pain, but the ibuprofen was all I had for the moment. I threw them back and drank down the chocolate. It tasted delicious, but my appetite was decreasing and the nausea was increasing. It wouldn't be long before I wouldn't want to eat, or be able to eat.

I heard Bruiser come in. "What's happening?" he asked as I wolfed down the eggs. He smelled of snow-skiing and spice and alcohol from a hot toddy.

"Janie came in from hunting and wanted to see us," Alex said.

I swallowed. Between bites, I told them about the memory I had discovered, giving them as much information as I could and as much detail.

"Government? Military? Private research facility?" Eli asked.

"Didn't feel exactly like either," I said. "Maybe a private lab with ties to the military? Or something like that? Or not?"

"Can you figure out a time for this memory?" Alex asked. "Maybe by the computer screen you saw?"

"The monitor was a small square with a green screen, no graphics, black type. The screen was part of a grayish box like an old—very old—PC. There was a large computer housing and the keyboard was in a large housing too. Lots of wires. No mouse." I finished off the eggs. "The unit's parts were all different colors of gray. Nothing matched exactly."

Alex nodded. "Probably a hand-built system using whatever parts they needed. That was common in the late seventies and early eighties. So were green screens."

"That gives us a starting point. How did you get out?" Eli asked. He pushed my empty plate away and replaced it with a pad and a pencil. "How much of the compound did you see?"

"I can't draw worth crap."

Eli lifted his eyebrows just a hair, a challenge.

"Fine. Okay." I took the pencil. But the pain in my belly was growing and I couldn't stay in this form long. And I wanted some sweet time with Bruiser before I had to shift back or die. I sketched out the cage room, the hallway, the rooms to either side, labeling them according to smell. "I went up two flights of stairs. Maybe three. I found a rooftop entrance covered with snow." I drew the rooftop and the wall. "Then the roofs to the left, the fence, and the woods. The approximate location of the creek where I . . . where Beast killed Charles."

There was a time when I wanted to believe that Beast had never eaten human flesh. That time was long past.

"To be clear. She ate Charles?" Bruiser asked softly.

I felt a little light-headed and a little nauseated. Maybe the sickness. Maybe the recognition that I was a monster. "Yeah."

Eli grunted one word. "Good."

"I hope he didn't give her indigestion," Bruiser said.

They were trying to tell me it was okay, no matter what Beast did. That Beast and I were the same being and not the same being. I had to look at life differently from an ordinary human. *Right.* I managed a laugh, more breath than anything else. "Right," I said aloud. "Okay. I'm thinking this happened a decade or so before I became human, but I had to be human age of around twelve because there was no mass transfer."

"When you walked out of the forest with bullet wound scars on you," Eli said, thoughtfully.

I nodded. I still had the scars. I only kept scars that meant a near-death wound. I had a lot of them these days.

"If so," Eli said, "then the research facility, or whatever it was, could be close to where you were found. I'll do some investigating and get some drones up when the snow clears."

"And if you find it?" Bruiser asked.

Eli grinned and it was a scary sight. "Road trip, my man. Road trip."

"And then?" I asked.

"Life's a bitch and then you die," Eli said.

"This is our job, my love," Bruiser said. "We'll deal with it while you concentrate on getting well."

Like that's gonna happen. However, I nodded. "I'm changing back to Beast soon. But I have a little time?"

"Let's go upstairs," Bruiser said. "I'll take any time with you I can get."

"Ditto," I said.

I stood and took his hand. Our fingers interlaced. With my other hand, I reached up and scrubbed my knuckles over his two-day beard. "I like it," I said.

Bruiser smiled. "Maybe I'll keep it, then."

"Oh please," Alex said. "Will you just go on upstairs and do the big nasty. I'm trying to work here."

Bruiser laughed and pulled me to him.

Black Friday Shopping

A Soulwood story. It first appeared online as a gift to fans in 2017. It takes place around the time Nell joins PsyLED as a probie.

"Mama says Walmart is the devil's storehouse," I said, hiding my badge in my jacket lapel pocket and making sure my weapon was secure and out of sight in its Kydex holster.

"Nell, sugar. You never been in a Walmart?" Occam stopped and pulled me to a stop with him by the simple expedient of catching my jacket sleeve between thumb and forefinger.

"Course I been in a Walmart." I eased away from his touch and he let go. Occam knew my history and was always careful when it came to trapping me. Neither of us liked cages of any kind, him being a were-leopard who'd spent twenty years in a cage, and me being an escapee from a polygamous church. "I just think about Mama anytime I go to a place she would disapprove of. And Mama would highly disapprove of me shopping at a Walmart on early Black Friday, after Thanksgiving dinner—what she would interpret as the devil's holiday."

"Well, let me lead you into sin and destruction"—he shot me a sidewise glance and a cat grin—"at Walmart."

I knew he could smell my blush. Occam wanted to take me to dinner and a movie. A date. Like normal people did. But I wasn't normal and neither was he. And I wasn't sure how to date, what to do, or what to talk about, or how to act. I'd sorta put him off, which had made the occasional mischievous banter more pointed.

Determined not to be teased without a rebuttal, I said, "They got steak and pork and salmon and shrimp and chicken in there. You gonna go all furry and raid the refrigerated meats?"

Occam snorted and led the way. "I'll try to restrain my cat, Nell, sugar."

I made a *hmmming* sound and followed him into the chaos and insanity of a Thanksgiving evening at Walmart.

We had been sent by JoJo at HQ to take a long walk through Walmart while keeping an eye out for someone who might be casting curses at the shoppers or the store itself. The week before Thanksgiving, there had been half a dozen unusual accidents in the store, from a rack of children's Santa-style pajamas collapsing and taking down four other racks, to a shelving unit full of Christmas trees falling on one shopper, to a row of three car batteries exploding in the automotive shop, to all the freezer compressors in the frozen foods section burning up at the same time. Other than a customer wearing tinsel, the fire department arriving to put out a small fire, and the mess of a lot of melted seafood and ice cream, there had been no major danger or human injury. But the customer who had worn tree lights after the Christmas tree shelving fell on her was a sensitive and claimed to smell magic, hence our presence in the store on late Thanksgiving, undercover, as shoppers.

Occam snagged a buggy and we melded into the crazy.

Two women were fighting over a sale item made of camo-material. Another woman yanked an item out of the hands of a disabled woman. Fortunately, someone "accidentally" tripped the shopper-thief and the item was returned. In the bedding section there was insane fighting over the last set of Marvel Comics superhero sheets. In the toy section, several shelves were empty already. In the food section the frozen turkey bin was empty and shoppers were yanking turkeys out of the hands of the poor clerk as he was restocking. And there was a near riot in the electronics section. Occam called it in to the local PD and we kept an eye open until the cops waded into the melee and arrested two women who were wrestling on the floor over an Apple tablet case that glowed in the dark.

We trundled through the store, eventually leaving the buggy in an aisle and just people-watching. An hour in, I felt a wash of magic, like sparklers cascading over my skin. I pointed. "That way. Fast."

Occam took off at a jog while I walked slower, checking out the shoppers for anyone who looked like they might be casting mischievous spells on the customers, the store stock, and the store building. I spotted a little girl, standing off by herself. She was wearing boy's clothing—too big for her, none too clean, and worn in tattered layers. I slowed, taking her in, knowing that something was wrong here.

There were dark circles beneath the child's eyes. She hadn't bathed or washed her hair in a while, her face smeared with that particular orange shade of Cheetos. Most telling, her ankles were bare and dirty above brand-new bunny slippers with the tags still on. And there was an aura of magic about her, like a soft blue haze.

To her left, a glass-topped case cracked and fell to the floor. Inside, an entire rack of jewelry slid to the floor on top of it, fake diamonds glittering. Shoppers raced in and grabbed up whatever was on the floor, one woman scooping glittery jewelry into her pocketbook, her hands like brooms. Security guards and the police from the electronics fight descended into the mess and arrested more people.

I watched the little girl as she watched the action. Occam looked back and caught the direction of my stare. He moseyed over, easy to do because he was wearing cowboy boots and jeans for this undercover op. "A kid? Naw," he murmured.

"She's the source of the magic. And I don't see anyone watching for her. I think . . . I think she's homeless. I think . . . she's living here. In the store. Stealing food. Maybe she was abandoned? Or homeless and got lost? Thrown out by her parents because weird things were happening and they were afraid of her? Doing magic by accident maybe?"

To her right, an entire row of cosmetics hit the floor with a clatter. The little girl didn't even turn that way.

"Who do we call?" Occam asked.

"Social Services for sure, but she'll need a foster who can handle a witchling."

"T. Laine," he said, speaking of the unit's resident witch. It was her day off, but she'd come for this. Occam pulled his cell to text JoJo at HQ. He also managed to wander around behind the wild child to cut off possible escape.

We didn't approach the child, just appeared to shop as we wandered around her. She didn't move.

Half an hour later T. Laine showed up and we formulated a plan to approach the little girl.

Lainie knelt near the child, as if inspecting a scarf on an endcap. She twirled her fingers, creating a flare of light, quickly extinguished. The little girl whipped her head to the side, her eyes on T. Laine. Without looking at her, Laine said, "It's not bad. It's not dangerous. It's just a gift, like being able to see or smell or taste."

"You'un's a witch. You'un's gonna burn in hell. Maybe on a stake first."

My heart fell to my feet. The little girl was speaking church-speak, the accent that set the members of God's Cloud of Glory apart from most other people of Appalachia.

"Nope," Lainie said, quickly adopting the accent I had used all my life until I joined PsyLED, the Psychometric Law Enforcement Department of Homeland Security. "Ain't nobody gonna hurt me. 'Cause I'm a police officer and I got a gun to go with my magic. I can keep myself safe."

The little girl blinked, slowly. "Safe?" The single word was a tone of disbelief, hope, and pain all at once. "I ain't never been safe."

T. Laine's face underwent a series of reactions, too fast to interpret, but leaving tears in her eyes. "I'll keep you safe. My name is Lainie. What's your name?"

"Rebecca the witch."

"Well, Rebecca, how about we go to the McDonald's over there in the corner, get a hamburger and a milkshake." Laine held out her hand. Slowly, Rebecca placed her Cheeto-grubby hand into Lainie's. Together they walked to McDonald's, placed an order, and took seats in the back, heads bent close in conversation.

"Looks like Lainie's got a houseguest for the night." Occam handed me a crisp hundred-dollar bill. "She'll need some stuff. Go shopping. I'll keep watch."

I nodded and found a buggy, taking the aisles through the toys and dolls and stuffed animals and then children's clothes and toiletries, picking out both sensible and frivolous things to wear and play with. Working out all the holy hell I was planning to bring down on the church come morning.

I finished shopping fast and paid with Occam's hundred, adding everything I had in my pocket. Because Christmas shopping mattered.

A social worker appeared through the doors slightly before ten p.m. T. Laine and Rebecca the witch left the store, hand-in-hand. Occam and I took a break in McDonald's and dined on shakes and fries and watched the shoppers. Thinking about a little girl abandoned and hiding and finally rescued, on Black Friday.

How Occam Got His Name

First appeared as a serial short, as part of a blog tour in 2018.
It is written from the point of view of Occam and answers fan
questions about the origins of the were-leopard special agent.

"'Em's the biggest bobcat prints I ever seen," Wayman said.

Trace knelt, his .30-06 pointing at the sky, and angled the flashlight
to see better. He held his hand, fingers spread, over the paw print. "They're
bigger 'an my hand."

"I hope we see it." Wayman knelt beside him, his blue jeans appearing
in the circle of light. "Maybe we should come back with a raccoon trap
and catch him."

"I think this bobcat would eat us for dinner and still be hongry."

"Nah," Wayman said. "We'll jist wave our arms and jump up and down
and yell a lot. My daddy says my voice is so high that it'd scare off the devil
hisself."

Trace had to agree with that. At the Halloween carnival last year, when
a zombie clown popped up in front of them, Wayman screamed so high
the guy in the clown suit ran. It hurt everybody's ears but it was so funny
nobody cared. "I don't know, Wayman. Something about the prints bothers me. They're too big."

"Maybe one a' your daddy's demon sermons is scaring you. Trust me,
Trace." Wayman shined his flashlight into Trace's face and backed away.
"Demons ain't got paws and claws."

Trace threw up the hand holding the shotgun. "Stop that. I can't see
jack, now."

"Can't see Jill neither." Wayman laughed and ran into the night, yelling, "Come on. The meteor shower starting around midnight."

"*Idiot!* Wayman, wait! *I can't see!*"

Wayman's laughter trailed away into the dark.

"Idiot. *Idiot!*" Trace shouted into the night. "Where are you?" And he said a worse word but too soft for Wayman to hear. His daddy'd beat his butt if he ever heard about it. And Wayman had a big mouth.

Daddy was a traveling preacher, and after they'd been kicked out of Alabama for reasons he had never heard explained, they'd settled in Texas, with four Texas churches in Dickens, Ralls, Crosbyton, and Spur. Daddy and Mama parked their RV in a different town every weekend, leading hellfire-and-damnation services in homes or small churches or empty storefronts, meeting all day, every Sunday, with an occasional fourth Sunday off, and every fifth Sunday off. Those were the weekends his daddy stayed fighting drunk or passed-out drunk.

They didn't stay anywhere long, except Dickens, where they rented a small furnished house with a root cellar. It came with real beds, which was a nice change. It even had a window unit air conditioner to keep the place sorta cool. Trace liked Dickens, and he liked Wayman. Making friends was hard for the son of a plastered pickled preacher man—which is what he'd heard his daddy called once. Friends had been scarce most all his life. But Wayman was his best buddy. Wayman played pranks on him just like he played on everyone, treating him no different—like blinding him with a flashlight and then running into the night.

"Wayman!" Trace shouted. "Blast it all! Where'd you run off to?" His vision was clearing from the spots cast by the flashlight-to-the-face joke by Wayman, but not fast enough. He'd have to follow the footprints in the sandy bottom of the wash—Wayman's and the bobcat's. The cat had been this way several times, the prints overlapping one another. Bobcats were generally more scared of humans than humans were of them. But this one was bigger than normal. Way bigger than normal. *"Wayman!"*

This was a fourth Sunday, and he and Wayman had gone into the hills to camp and watch the meteor shower. And hide from his daddy's fists and his drunken sermonizing, and from Wayman's mama's boyfriend who was a little too friendly for Wayman's comfort level.

From up ahead, Wayman squealed his little-girl squeal, and Trace at least figured out what general direction his friend had run off to. "Stupid idiot." Trace trudged along the wash, casting the occasional glances up into the night sky and the millions of stars that city folk never saw. No meteors yet.

"Over here, you ass crack!" Wayman shouted.

"We'll never get back to the tent and the wagon and the bikes," Trace shouted as he trudged around the small hill. "And there ain't even a path to the top. You ever heard of rattlesnakes?"

"Come on!"

From the side of the wash, Trace heard a whistling sound and a rough vibration, kinda like a purr, like a housecat would make. A huge housecat. Probably the maker of the bobcat prints. Biggest he'd ever seen. "Dang idiot. Rattlesnakes and bobcats. *Sheesh.*" Louder, he said, "I got a gun, cat. I'll shoot you if you come at us."

"Meow!" Wayman shouted, jumping into the light of his flash.

"Dang idiot," Trace said, startled, flinching back.

"This hill right here," Wayman said, laughing. "It's got a flat top, no rocks to hide snakes and it's right beside the wash, so we can find our way back by following our own footprints."

And the bobcat prints they had seen and been trailing through the sandy bottom, but Trace didn't say that. It might sound like he was afraid, and "bein' a-feared" was "fer wussies," according to Wayman's Texan-accented accusation.

They climbed up the hill and studied the surrounding land. Just like Wayman had said, no rocks, no plants, high flat land, unappealing to snakes and other critters.

"Here," Wayman said, passing him a bottle of water. "I brung six in the bike basket, along with salt tablets in case we sweat too much. With your three water bottles, the Spam and the bread and the potato chips, we got enough water and food to last two days. And if we run out, I know how to find water most anyplace. My grampa done showed me."

Grampa Iron Mountain was pure Comanche, or so Wayman's mama said, and she had the black hair and eyes of the local tribal people. Redskins—that's what his daddy called Wayman's family when he was drunk and no one was around. Trace's mama shushed Daddy when he talked bad about people. Trace kinda thought she might like Wayman's mama and want her to be a friend. They talked about cooking sometimes. But Mama had a hard time keeping friends too, thanks to Daddy.

Daddy couldn't hide the smell of liquor on his breath on Sunday mornings, and his congregations tended to dry up and drift away after a year or two, so Preacher Oakum and his wife Miz Lizzie were always moving around. Trace had learned to make friends fast and give them up just as quick, as they moved on to find another town on a crossroads that led to still other towns that needed saving.

But Trace was tired of traveling. He liked Wayman. Wayman was the best friend he ever had. And he didn't want to leave. He was thinking about running away and hiding out when his parents moved on this next time. There were plenty of abandoned houses he could live in.

"You want it or not?" Wayman demanded, nudging his arm.

Trace took the water bottle, glad his friend knew so much about camping and the outdoors and the wilderness around them. The towns where they had lived were smaller than Satan's mercy—according to his daddy—but Trace had never spent any time in the wasteland. He opened the top and drank. Recapped it. He lay down on the small Indian blanket Wayman had brought, his hands behind his head. It brought his sweaty underarms up to his nose, but there wasn't nothing wrong with a little sweat, and nothing he could do about it in August neither.

Together, they stared up at the sky to watch the Perseid meteor show. The meteors came in bunches, shooting across the heavens like fireworks or missiles, some seeming directly overhead. One, closer than the others, blasted down in the hills to the northeast, exploding with a flash of light and a faint tremor through the ground.

They both sat up fast, eyes on the faint halo of light in the dark. "Dayum, Trace. I bet we could make us some money picking up the pieces and selling 'em." Wayman pulled a compass and shined his flashlight on it. "Got it."

Trace sighed, not wanting to tell his best and only friend that, even with the compass reading, it would be nigh to impossible to pinpoint the landing location and then even harder to find and pick up the meteor pieces. "Yep. Maybe we'll go there some day and find diamonds all over the ground."

"Space diamonds!" Wayman said. "We'll be rich."

Getting far enough away from Dickens, Texas, to see the night sky and the meteor shower wasn't hard. Wasn't like Dickens had many streetlights or nothing. The town had 280 people in it, with about as many deserted buildings as families. It was hot and miserable during the six months of winter, and he'd heard his daddy say it was hotter than Satan's anvil the other six. In August, even at night, the heat seemed to suck the life right out of him.

But the night sky made the heat and the trek worth it all. The black expanse was brilliant with stars, millions of millions, put there by the hand of God, Daddy said, put there by a Big Bang according to his teacher—who got in trouble for telling a scientific principle in a Creationist school district.

Trace kinda liked the idea of blending the two, because that would explain the light show of meteors streaking overhead. He'd called it God's Big Bang Fart. But only to Wayman, and not at home, where his daddy might use his fists to drive the devil outta his soul. Six meteors dashed across the sky, spreading out from one another as if they had broken off a bigger piece.

"God's farting again," Wayman said, laughing.

Trace laughed too and made farting sounds with his mouth.

The meteor shower was supposed to be brightest after four a.m., which was long after the moon set, but they had plans to be back at the tent and the bikes by then and it was a long hike. He wished he'd brought the cooler of chili. He was hungry and his stomach rumbled.

Mama made the best chili in the state, and she was sharing her secret chili recipe with him, trading out chores for cooking lessons. Mama—Miz Lizzie to the church members—was a saint to put up with Daddy. He'd heard one of the church ladies say so. Trace didn't know much about being a saint, but Mama could sing real pretty on Sundays, and she sure could cook.

The numbers of meteors increased, streaking across the sky, some big, some tiny, gone in an eyeblink.

About the time the silver slice of moon was setting, and the meteors were coming fast and furious, prickles started running up and down the back of Trace's neck. Maybe them rattlesnakes he'd thought about on the trip out here. Or the owner of the bobcat paw prints they had seen. Bigger than his hand.

Trace sat up, uncertain what he'd heard. Or sensed. He picked up the flashlight and his shotgun.

He flicked on his flashlight and slowly shined it around them. Rocks, sand, prickly grasses. Until his flash caught something golden and silver on the small hillock across the wash from them. Two somethings. They went away. Reappeared. He steadied his light on the golden silver things. And realized they were eyes.

"Wayman, we got a problem," Trace said softly, even though he'd broke out in a cold sweat and wanted nothing more than to run screaming into the night.

"What?"

"Remember the paw prints we saw down in the wash?"

Wayman sat up slowly. "Yeah. Bobcat. It was a big 'un."

"Well, I think it found us. And it's bigger than a bobcat."

Wayman eased around on his butt to face the direction of the beam. His voice dropped to a whisper, as if to hide their location from the cat. "It's a cat, though. Pretty big. Spotted."

"Spotted," Trace said, thinking about one particular biology class last year. "Maybe a leopard or a jaguar."

"Cowmen killed off the last jaguar from these parts in the early nineteen hundreds, according to Grampa. Ain't no leopards here 'bouts."

"Too big to be a bobcat," Trace said softly. "Bobcats ain't got them kinda spots. Should I shoot it?"

"No. If you don't kill it with the first shot," Wayman said, "it might attack from the pain. We need to get back to the camp, slow and easy. Grampa said never to run from a predator."

As he said the last words, the big cat opened its mouth and yawned, showing off big—very big—teeth. The cat licked its jaw and chuffed, as if agreeing with the statement.

"So what do we do?" Trace asked.

Wayman stood, slowly, very, *very* slowly, and Trace copied his speed. Wayman gathered up their blanket and water bottles. The cat, caught in the flashlight's beam, watched them, turning to the side from time to time, to protect its eyes from the bright light. Trace wondered if it could jump from one hillock to the next or if they were safe here on the other side of the wash.

Wayman turned on his own flash and said, "Okay. You keep your flash on the cat. I'm gonna scream."

It was good to have the warning because Wayman could scream like a little girl, a high-pitched, terrifying sound. Wayman opened his mouth, took a deep breath, and let loose.

The big cat took off like its tail was on fire and was gone.

The scream ended and Wayman sounded spooked. "Dayum, Trace. That thing was big. That was a jaguar or leopard fer sure."

Trace said nothing. His senses were frozen, his ears deadened from Wayman's ear-piercing scream, his breathing fast from fear.

"Come on, Trace. Let's get back to the tent afore it finds us again."

They clattered down the hillock to the wash below, Trace wondering how the tent would protect them from a jaguar—if that's what it was, and not a devil cat. His daddy's sermons about demons who take up the form of predators and hunt humans banged around in his skull. The Nephilim and demons with huge teeth and claws. Like the spotted thing caught in his flashlight.

As they moved along the wash, Wayman's flash picked out their path. Trace kept his moving around the hillocks to either side and along the path behind them. Once, he caught a hint of movement, but when he backtracked with the light, the thing was gone. Just like his interest in the meteor shower overhead.

Though he kept seeing imaginary bloody bodies on the sandy wash bottom, images put in his head by the demon that was hunting them, they made it back to the small tent near 82—the main road through Dickens—and made a small fire from dried wood they found in the wash. Then they zipped themselves inside. It was stupid, but the thin layer of tent fabric made Trace feel safer.

He thought he wouldn't sleep, but he did. And he woke the next morning just at dawn to find himself alone, the tent unzipped, Wayman's sleeping bag empty, but still warm. And his friend's high-pitched scream on the air.

Trace tore out of his sleeping bag and outside. Following the sound of Wayman's screams. Knowing they were different from Wayman's regular screams. This scream was real. Wayman was in danger. And he remembered the sight of the golden silver eyes caught in his flashlight's beam.

He raced down the hillock, his sneakers untied, the laces flying. Glad he'd slept in them. Not sure why he'd think about that when his friend was in trouble. Racing toward the screams. Which suddenly dropped away to a gurgling whimper. Trace stumbled on the untied laces, scratching his hand and arm in a long straight line, but picking up a stick as he righted himself. *He'd forgot his gun. Dayum. His gun . . . Daddy'd kill him for losing it.*

But he didn't go back for the shotgun.

Trace rounded the small hillock to his left. And saw the bloody mess that was his friend, stretched out on the bloody sand of the wash. The spotted cat was lying beside Wayman's weakly moving body. Trace screamed and waved his arms, racing toward the danger. He waved the stick and shouted scripture to make the demon cat go away. It wasn't a power scripture like his daddy always used in his drunken sermons, but the only thing he could think of. "Jesus wept! Jesus wept! *Jesus wept!*" Waving the stick. Screaming out his fear and rage.

The spotted cat leaped away.

Stopped. Growled at Trace. And Trace turned from Wayman and raced after the huge cat. Instead of running, the cat leaped at him. Punched-thumped-walloped down on Trace's chest, his massive cat-face hanging over Trace, bloody with the blood of his friend.

All the life and energy drained out of him. Staring into the crazed golden silver eyes. He peed his pants. Dropped the stick.

The cat bit down onto Trace's shoulder. And shook him hard.

Then it jumped away, leaving Trace. And Wayman. Alone.

Trace rolled over, his arm hanging useless, and half crawled to Wayman, lying so still on the ground. His friend's chest still struggled to move and he made a whistling sound with each breath. Trace slid his good arm under Wayman's neck and lifted his friend. "I'm here. The cat's gone. We're safe. We're safe. We're gonna be okay."

But Trace was lying. Wayman was dying. He knew it. There was so much blood. Trace had never seen what people looked like when they were dying. But most of his friend's belly was gone, leaving a gaping hole where his insides used to be. The cat had eaten into Wayman.

"Wayman. I gotcha. I ain't gonna leave you."

Wayman lifted his hand and dropped it onto Trace's arm, his fingers curling around Trace's wrist. He whispered, "Devil cat. Jist like your daddy said."

"Wayman—"

"I'm gonna be checking out God's Big Bang Fart." Wayman made a sound like crying or laughing or both. And he stopped breathing. And he died.

Trace somehow managed to get the wagon to Wayman. Somehow got the body of his best friend rolled onto it. Abandoning the tent and the bikes and even his shotgun, Trace somehow made it back to 82, pulling the wagon and the body of his friend along the dirt side of the road. Pulling the small handle. Wayman's legs dragging. The wheels bumping along. Grinding in the soil beside the road. No one passed. The main thoroughfare was empty.

Without his bike to pull the special wagon, the dirt street leading to Dickens seemed forever away. He bumped down along the road, pulling the wagon. Tripping on the laces of his shoes. By the time the sun was overhead, flies had started to gather in the ground-up meat that was his friend's belly.

He'd forgot to pick up the water. He was salt-caked and drier than a stone, walking like a demon-zombie, when a white pickup truck pulled to a stop beside him on 82. Someone started talking at him. Loud. And then more people showed up, all talking. And more cars appeared out of the hazy heat. Trace kept trying to pull the wagon with Wayman on it, back to town. And kept trying. Kept trying. His daddy stopped him.

His daddy, stinking of whiskey, started yelling, shouting scripture. Someone pushed Daddy away. A woman gave him bottles of water. Poured some over his body to cool him down.

The sheriff drove up and started asking questions. Trace tried to answer but he couldn't think straight. He was hot. Maybe feverish. He couldn't even cry for his friend. His piece-of-meat dead friend.

His mama raced up, shouting, "Trace Quaid Oakum! What have you done?" And then she saw him, touched his head, grabbed him up, saying, "Oh my God. Baby." She cussed the sheriff out and cradled Trace in her arms, calling him her baby. Forcing him to drink more water. Mama's hugs were the best thing he ever remembered feeling. Trace melted into her, his skin aching, burning up.

While she coddled him, the local men gathered rifles and shotguns and tried to pinpoint where the attack took place. Someone brought in a tracking dog and the men jogged back down 82, following his trail. Mama took him to the house they stayed at sometimes and tucked him into bed. She held his hand for a while and then she said she had to go with the church ladies to make sandwiches for the trackers, and brew up sweet tea.

Trace curled into his bed, stinking of sweat, feeling sick. Burning up and maybe dying. But he didn't care. Wayman was dead.

Eventually Mama came in to bring him some soup and noticed that he was sick. She pulled off his shirt and found the bite mark. It was all puffy and swollen by then, his arm mostly useless. Mama started hollering and the church ladies mighta seen him naked. He didn't really remember. But they put him into Mrs. Jefferies's car and they took him to the clinic in Spur.

They said it was a miracle he survived. A miracle he didn't lose use of his arm. Even more of a miracle that he was mostly healed on the day they buried Wayman. His daddy gave a ranting drunken eulogy and sermon about demons and devil cats and evil and the hero who had scared off the monster and then brought his friend home. Except Trace knew he wasn't a hero. A hero woulda saved Wayman, not let him die. But the adults kept saying different. And Wayman's mama hugged onto Trace all through the service and burial, squeezing him the whole time, crying.

When they got home, later that night, his daddy led him to the root cellar in their rented house. And showed him the cage. It had a mattress, his sleeping bag, and two water bottles, one to drink from and one to pee in. "You'll be sleeping in it for the next six weeks or so. It's for your own good, son. If the devil got into you, and you're possessed, then you put your mama and me in danger. Understand?"

Trace lifted his hand and touched his shoulder. His healed shoulder. Did devils heal? "I thought only God healed."

"If God healed you, we'll know it after the next two full moons." Daddy tilted up the bottle and drank down more whiskey, stinking of sweat and whiskey and something else. Maybe fear. Not a smell Trace had ever smelled before. "Just through the two full moons," Daddy said. "Get on in there."

Trace got in. The cage door clanged shut.

Trace slept in the cage every night for two weeks until the next full moon.

The horizon was visible through the window set high on the root cellar wall. The glow of moonrise was brightening the sky. The first rays of the full moon shone through the window.

The moment the moonlight appeared, the pain started. It was a stabbing, wrenching pain in his shoulder, like his arm was being yanked off. The torment grew. And grew. Trace got so hot he thought he might explode. Bones popped and shifted around. He grew fur. His thoughts went all muddy and confused. And Holy God it hurt so bad he prayed, but God didn't help.

That was the night of his first shift. His daddy watched the whole thing, sitting in a broken-down chair, drinking whiskey, silent.

The next morning, his daddy didn't let him out of the cage. Didn't give him clothes to replace the ones he'd torn up and peed on during that long, terrifying night. Daddy didn't give him nothing, even though he was human again and so hungry he thought he'd die. Instead, near sunset, Daddy bumped and carried the cage up the rickety stairs and outside, to the truck that smelled of dogs and cats and horse manure. And Mr. Rodrigues. It was odd how Trace knew that the smell belonged to Mr. Rodrigues. Odd but not so scary as what happened the night before.

As the moon rose, round and silver and beautiful, the transformation began again, and Trace understood. The cat that bit him was a demon. The cat bite had put the demon into him and now Trace was a demon cat. He'd be a demon cat forever.

And the world fell away.

He watched as the man who stank of whiskey, the human named Daddy, took a tray, tarnished and black, and slid it in under the bottom of the cage. It stank and it hurt. It hurt in every bone of the cat's body. He started to pace to try and get away from the tray and the pain. He paced and paced, snarling. Wanting *out*. Wanting to *eat*. Hungry. Hungry. *Hungry!*

But the human named Daddy didn't feed him. The human named Daddy drove him all night, far away. And sold him to the man at the traveling carnival. Sold him for twenty-five dollars.

"Don't never take away the tray in the bottom. Not never," the human named Daddy said.

"Why?" The carnie man spat in the dirt.

"The tray controls him. Take away the tray and he'll attack."

Cat who was once a human heard and smelled the lie. The tray was danger.

"What's its name? For the sign over the cage," the carnie man said.

"Oakum. Just Oakum."

Oakum. The cat held on to the sound of that word. His name. His name before he became a demon and the human named Daddy sold him.

The carnival man gave him a steak and Oakum tore into the meat and his belly stopped hurting.

The dawn came. The pain hit his bones and his skin and his teeth. Pain like nothing he'd ever felt before. But it passed. And the carnival man put a sign over his cage. It said, "Occam's Razor, Devil Cat."

Shiloh and the Brick

First appeared as a serial short in 2016 for the release of *Blood in Her Veins*. In the timeline, Jane is an Enforcer for Leo Pellissier.

"Yes. You are going, Shiloh Everhart Stone," Molly said, enunciating every word with pitiless determination. "You and your blood-servants. You do not have the control you need, as evidenced by your reaction yesterday."

A man had pinched Shiloh at a bar-and-grill near dawn, and she had come within a hairsbreadth of biting him. Unasked. And when her blood-servant stopped her, she nearly set the woman's hair on fire with an *inflammatur* witch working. Shiloh was a major incident waiting to happen. The girl whirled to me. "Are you going to let her do this to me, Enforcer?" Shiloh demanded.

Ohhh. Nice move with the Enforcer title. Too bad I'd seen it coming. And too bad she used it. Making me choose between witches and vamps sounded good on the surface, but calling me Enforcer decreased her possible avenues of argument and backed her into a corner she hadn't seen yet.

I shrugged. "You're a witch, as powerful as anything I've ever seen." I crossed the fingers hidden behind me. I had seen Angie Baby. So . . . liar, liar, pants on fire. "And a vamp. And you lost control. Therefore, yeah. I'm letting your aunt and uncle send you to witch training camp."

"This is so not fair," Shiloh spat.

"Thanks, Jane," Molly said, her tone nowhere near calm and reasonable. Behind her, Big Evan smiled, the expression barely visible behind his full red beard. Molly shoved her own bouncy red curls out of her face and scowled at her niece, her words still strident. "You need formal schooling. It's not an option. No witch in New Orleans can take you on to train, not with the work taking place putting together the Witch Conclave. The Charlotte coven accepted you as a student for six weeks and assured us of your safety. You. Need. Training."

"I'm not going." Shiloh stamped her foot.

I curled my lips under to keep from laughing aloud. I had never seen a vamp stamp their foot.

"And you can't make me. Right, Enforcer?"

That's what happened when you got three redheaded people, two of them witches, and one a witch-vamp, all in the same room with a Cherokee skinwalker. Trying to get them to work together to solve our problem had been difficult. Actually, impossible, so far.

I'm Jane Yellowrock. I was on my own, hunting and staking rogue vamps when I was Shiloh's age. Now I'm the Enforcer to the MOC of NOLA and, with my partners, I run Yellowrock Securities, Inc., chasing and fighting "things that go bump in the night." I can do tough. But I'd rather fight a ten-foot alligator with my bare human hands—buck naked—than deal with a teenager.

"No. They can't," I said, and I thought poisoned darts would shoot from Molly's eyes. I grinned and stood, pulling my cell. "And I can't." On the cell's face, I tapped the name Leo Pellissier, my boss and the Master of the City of New Orleans. I handed the girl the cell. "But he can."

"I'm not talking to him," Shiloh said, her eyes bleeding scarlet, her pupils dilating vamp-black.

I just laughed, the sound a little catty, a little mean, and shook my head. "Take the phone before he answers or I'll stick you under my arm and carry you to vamp HQ and watch him convince you. It won't be pretty."

Shiloh ripped the cell out of my hand and said, "What?" A moment later she scowled and added, "Sir. What, sir? It's Shiloh, sir." She turned away and hunched her shoulders. I smiled at Molly and her husband Evan. It was a fake smile but it was all I had left, and it was nicer than the one I had shown Shiloh.

Molly's niece had disappeared at age fifteen, a runaway. That same year, she had reappeared in New Orleans, in a teen shelter, just in time to be swept up by the Damours, witch-vampires who were looking for witch children to use in black-magic, blood-magic sacrifices for a big-ass spell to . . . never mind. It's convoluted. But I could still feel the chill in my bones from the day I discovered she had been taken. Soon after, Shiloh had been turned and used by vamps to accomplish their own ends.

Except for running away to New Orleans—and look how badly that had gone—Shiloh had never made a single decision in her own life. She had lived every moment at the behest of others, and she had suffered trauma. Her mother had commited murder and killed her father. Witches had abandoned the girl. Vamps had used and abused her. Her remaining family hadn't known what to do with a witch-vamp.

All that made me want to let her go, let her make this decision with her own life, let her face the consequences on her own. If she was the only one to face repercussions, I'd likely let her go. But that wasn't going to happen. If Shiloh Everhart Stone let a witch working explode, or bit a tourist, or, God help us, *both*, it would create major reverberations throughout the witch and vamp worlds. The whole country might face the results with her. And there wasn't enough of me to protect everyone.

Her eyes slowly bled from half-vamped-out to simply human, which was good. I didn't want to have to fight the girl. Despite her power, I might hurt her. And despite her freedom in the human world, and her insistence on being in control of her vampire gifts, the control of vamps as young as Shiloh was minimal.

Shiloh Everhart Stone had long straight red hair, dark eyes, and a pointy, not quite perfect nose. Her skin had that glowing, pinkish look that well-fed vamps always had. Leo had decided that a hungry witch-vamp in a training camp full of witches trying to learn their magic might be tempting fate, and so, today, she had been given a coterie of humans to feed upon every night when she woke. I thought it was a great idea, but Shiloh had dug in her heels about relocating, and when an Everhart went stubborn, it was like trying to get the moon to rotate to Mars. Not gonna happen by any power I had.

Well, except the power of Leo. He too wanted her to make her own decisions, to be grown-up and wise. He wanted her to see the wisdom of the move and agree to it. He wanted her to learn that control she so desperately lacked.

"Yes, sir, it was a mistake," Shiloh said to Leo. "But no one got hurt. I have control. I do," she said softly. Moments later, her shoulders dropped in defeat. She had sworn to Leo, she had drunk his blood and he hers. She literally couldn't say no to him. Under other circumstances I might have felt guilty for playing the blood-tie card. But not this close to the Witch Conclave.

She ended the call and handed the cell back. There were perfectly human tears in her eyes, until she set her gaze on me. Then they vanished and the familiar tilt lifted her chin again. Stubborn. "This is *so* not fair," she spat at me. "You didn't have to call him."

"You used the term Enforcer," I said, my tone still mild. "You're a vamp now. You've had lessons on the Vampira Carta and its codicils." The VC was the legal papers by which all Mithran vamps lived and died. "What happens when you use a title?"

Shiloh dropped into a chair, glared around the room, and huffed out a breath she didn't really need. "It activates the responsibilities and protocols and bindings and legal mumbo-jumbo that goes along with it." The mutinous expression finally vanished. "I should have just asked my aunt Jane."

I hid my grin and glanced at Evan, who was sitting across the room from us in Shiloh's recliner. He had claimed it upon entering and, at six and a half feet tall and well over three hundred pounds, he could sit anywhere he wanted. Even in a vamp's favorite chair. He was sipping a beer and shaking his head. I didn't have to be a mind reader to know he was thinking about his own family and how soon he'd have a teenaged daughter to deal with. A powerful teenaged witch daughter who had access to more magic than all the three witches in the room together. Big secret, that part about Angie Baby.

"Aunt Jane would defer to your witch aunt," I said.

The window next to Shiloh's head exploded inward. Something small and dark whipped across the room.

I dove for Molly and wrapped her in my arms, making a cage of my limbs as I spun across the floor and under a table, taking the weight and force of the rolling dive onto my body, on elbows and knees and spine. My braid, down and loose, caught under us and I yanked it free. "Stay put," I growled at her. My Beast was close to the surface, her cat-voice rough and coarse.

From the back of the house I heard the sound of a shotgun breach closing. The blood-servants were on the way. That left the missile up to me. I tossed my braid and shifted my body, rolling to the thing that had been thrown inside.

Glass was still flying through the room as Beast shoved me across the floor. Seeing the object as I reached for it. A brick. With a note tied on.

For freaking crap's sake.

I checked the brick with more senses—smell (no explosives), sight (no explosives). I picked it up—touch (no explosives). It was just a brick with a note, folded over, a name on the outside. Tied with twine in a neat bow. I stood, seeing a *hedge of thorns* witch ward lifting around the house. Evan had whistled it up in seconds flat, which meant it had been in place and ready to rise as needed. Pretty nifty, that.

The blood-servants stood at the doorway, a man with a shotgun leveled at me. The others with knives and a nine-millimeter and a tiny .380. All aimed at me. I set the brick down on the floor and stood. Held up my hands, trying for innocent, but that was hard for a six-foot-tall Cherokee chick so weaponed up that I looked like a walking arsenal. "Not me," I said. And then I chuffed, catlike laughter. "I come in peace."

The man gave his shotgun to the blood-servant nearest, and walked, slowly, to where Shiloh cowered, vamped out, inch-long needle fangs and sharp-as-steel talons out. She hissed at me as her witch powers gathered around her. Okay. This was bad.

To my side, Evan Trueblood was already whistling up a defensive spell to stop his niece.

The blood-servant knelt at Shiloh's side, whispering tender words and comfort. My eyes swept across the others gathered in the doorway. The man appeared to be the oldest, and certainly the most in control. But approaching a frightened, young vamp was dangerous under any circumstances. Approaching a frightened young witch-vamp was downright suicidal.

My cell rang, blaring into the sudden silence of the room. Shiloh hissed at me and her witch energies tightened around her like a purple-green shroud. Normally, at a time like this, I'd ignore it, but it was Leo's ring tone, set into my cell by my partner in Yellowrock Securities, Alex Youn-

ger, as a joke. Marilyn Manson was screaming "If I Was Your Vampire."
Not funny.

I answered, "Now is not a good time."

"You will place me on speakerphone," Leo said. It was a command,
not a request.

I tapped the cell face and Leo said, "Shiloh. My child. You will be calm."
His voice filled the room, banishing the shadows of desperation and fear
and the tingle of witch magic, filling the room with vamp compulsion and
an odd sense of peace that even I felt. "Shiloh," he repeated. "You *will be
calm.*"

Shiloh took a shuddering breath, and the blackness of her eyes decreased, the scarlet sclera fading to pink and then to white. Her fangs
schnicked back into her mouth on their tiny hinges.

I blew out my relief. Evan's spell whispered away. The group of blood-
servants took a collective breath, as if they had been holding theirs. With
the greatest of vampire formality, the man beside Shiloh said, "Do you
need blood, my mistress?"

"I . . . No," she said. "What happened?"

Shiloh's confusion was not a good sign. It spoke of rogue status. Of
vampires who lost control, draining and killing humans with the mindless
hunger of those chained in the devoveo. Of killing for the sake of killing.
And everyone in the room realized that at the same time. Even Shiloh.
None of us knew what to do about it. But none of us were vamps.

"Give my scion the note on the brick," Leo said into the odd, anxious
silence.

With a glance at the blood-servants to make sure they didn't shoot me
for following orders, I picked up the brick and pulled the tie. The note
made a *shushing* sound when I handed it, unopened, to Shiloh. Her name
was on the front in Leo's fancy calligraphy scrawl—*Shiloh Everhart Stone.*

"Read it aloud," Leo said to her, over the phone.

Shiloh opened the note and read, " 'I have granted you freedom from
the chains of the scion-lair. If, when the brick was thrown into your home-
lair, you did not react with the mindlessness of the rogue, you may go your
own way in the matter of witch training.' "

I wasn't sure how Leo had known we were having a problem with

Shiloh, but not much that happened among the vamps in his city was a secret. That he had taken the time to address the problem in advance filled me with warm fuzzies. Or as much warm fuzzies as I ever got in regard to the chief fanghead.

Human tears filled Shiloh's eyes again, but she kept reading, her voice going rough and clogged with unshed tears and shame. "If you lost control, then you will do as my Enforcer has commanded."

Leo said, "Shiloh. Did you lose control?"

The girl's shoulders drooped and she dropped her head, silken red hair sliding over her face. "Yes, Master," she whispered.

"You will obey your aunt and uncle, who know more of witch matters than I. You and the blood-servants I have sent to you will go for training. I will also send a loyal Mithran to assist you with learning a control you have claimed but have not demonstrated. You will return to me, to serve as you have so sworn. Do I have your word in this?"

"Yes, my master," she whispered.

"Good. Enforcer. Place us on privacy mode and leave the house. We have much to discuss for transporting my beloved scion to Charlotte."

I tapped the screen and looked around. Everyone was okay. No one had died. No one got drained. "Ducky," I said. I took the cell outside the house and stood on the front porch, the *hedge of thorns* ward only inches from my face. I could hear the others talking inside. I smelled the scent of human blood—or as human as blood-servants were.

I tucked the fingers of my right hand under my left armpit. It was chilly out, an early arctic front blowing down the Mississippi River basin, bringing what passed for winter in New Orleans. "You knew she was going to fight training," I said to Leo. "You knew she was going to vamp out, didn't you?"

Leo chuckled softly; the sound like liquid sex poured out through the phone and into my body. That mesmerizing thing they can do and which I had never succumbed to . . . and never would. "Yes, my Jane. I knew. It is what a good Blood Master must know. She will be docile now. She will accept her training. All will be well. I charge you to choose a Mithran from among my most loyal, and send them together to Charlotte for the duration of the Witch Conclave. She must be safe."

"Because you have plans for her." I stated.

"But of course, my Jane. I have plans for all of you." The call ended.

"Crap on crackers with toe jam," I said.

But . . . Leo had accomplished what I hadn't been able to. And him having plans that would remake everyone's life? No big surprise there. None at all.

Beast Hunts Vampire with Jane

A Short-Short from Beast's Point of View

Originally published online in 2044 as a Christmas serial and
rewritten for this publication.

Jane dressed in black dress with little skirt, with red trim, like lace of
blood. Hair in long braid hanging down back, like big-cat tail, like black
panther. On Jane's feet were shoes with tall heels. Jane was wobbly. Wearing prey clothes.

Beast watched from dark place in her mind, Beast's den. *Jane should
shift into Beast for this hunt, so Jane would be safe. Jane needs killing teeth.*

Nope, Jane thought. *This is a false hunt. Like leading predators away
from your den to protect your kits. Acting weak.*

But Jane was not weak, not silly kit, and did smart hunter thing.
Strapped killing claw to each leg, long knives for killing vampires. Shoved
silver stakes into hair. Smeared color of blood on mouth, color that said
to world, "Jane is killer. See blood of my prey."

Still . . . Beast did not like it when Jane was alpha. Did not like it when
Jane would not shift and hunt. *Shift!*

*Nope. Think of this like a shopping trip. Shopping for bad guys and tak-
ing them down.*

Beast's ears perked up. *Can eat bad guys?*

No. Gack. No eating.

Jane is mean.

Jane did not care. Stuck cross into her pocket—pouch like opossum
has, but not for young—lined with stinky metal. And I/we left Jane-den.
To go dancing. Looking like prey, but really hunter, predator, killer.

Walked to bar where band played, where humans drank strong drink
to forget pain and dance, mating rituals for lonely humans. Beast thought

humans were looking for someone to make small pack with and love. Looking for mates instead of looking for mating. Were not same thing, but humans did not know this.

Inside was loud. Was dark. Many humans danced and ate and drank much beer and alcohol. Smelled fried food and hot grease, many peppers, sweat, and alcohol. Jane stood in shadows and studied room. Then Jane moved into crowd onto dance floor. Heart rate sped; Jane smiled. Jane lifted arms and swayed, taking small steps. Head went back. Eyes closed. Jane was . . . happy.

Jane danced, moving like cat in heat, letting her scent wash through warm air, to vampire noses, who turned at tables, and from tall chairs, and watched her like prey. She looked like prey, looked weak and harmless, hiding weapons. Vampires wanted to drink from her. Jane wanted to kill them.

Band played Christmas music. *Ca-rols.* With island reggae beat. Beast liked sound.

One vampire moved across dance floor to Jane. Tall male—taller than Jane—with short red hair, sticking out like porcupine quills. Tall vampire took her hand and twirled her into dance move, pulling her under his arm.

Jane thinks he is pretty, for a vampire, skin flushed and pink from drinking much from humans.

Vampire liked her scent, pressed his nose into her neck, sniffing, breathing, heart beating. Vampire is old and drunk on blood. Naturaleza vampire, has killed to drink his fill. *Outlaw. Rogue.*

Jane smiled, and let some of Beast into her eyes. Beast helped Jane dance, cat grace and cat slink are better than primate moves, like monkey in tree. Jane moved like cat and snake, body full of promise. Vampire put his hands on Jane. She whirled away.

Vampire led Jane outside, into dark, heart beating faster. Vampire had predator movements and sex pheromones. Wanted to mate with Jane and drink her dry. Vampire pulled Jane along alley, out of buildings, under trees. I/we smelled human blood.

Jane thought, *He has killed here before. Tonight.*

Outlaw-killer-vampire must die, Beast thought back. *Will not follow law.*

Jane laughed and teased vampire—all cat now—still dancing. She slid hand under skirt. Pulled vamp-killer blade. Was ready.

Vampire vamped out. Eyes bled black and wide. Fangs clicked down, long as human finger. Vampire rushed Jane.

Jane pivoted on tall shoes, all cat balance and cat speed. Whirled, arm out, blade glittering. And took vampire head. She leaped away as body fell, vampire blood pumping out. Jane watched to make sure vampire died. Then cleaned killing claw-blade on his clothes and sheathed it. *Jane is good hunter.*

Yeah, Jane thought. *We are.*

Jane pulled cell phone and took picture of head, showing fangs, and sent it to Bruiser with note that said "Merry Christmas to me. You & Leo owe me twenty grand."

Then she sent GPS to have body picked up, and alley cleaned up.

Jane picked up vampire head and walked into night, humming song called "My Favorite Things."

"Blood drops on pavement,

And whiskers on Beastie.

Bright copper teapots and

Huge Christmas feast-ies.

Vamp-ire bodies all tied up with strings.

These are a few of my favorite things!"

Beast chuffed with laughter. *Shopping and hunting with Jane is fun. But Jane singing is like cats screaming.*

Of Cats and Cars

A Story of Beast and Cows with Trees on Heads

This short story, originally written from Edmund's point of view, was first published on my blog in 2019 (for thirty hours), and as a serialized blog tour event. It has been rewritten and extended (with more of Beast's point of view). It still fits nowhere in the existing Jane Yellowrock timeline. For the sake of argument, I am cramming it into a three-day period just after the end of the Sangre Duello between Leo Pellissier and Titus, the Emperor of the EU, and the end of *Dark Queen*. Also, after the short "Life's a Bitch and Then You Die." The timeline isn't perfect. I know that. But it is a fun story. Enjoy!

Edmund

"No. Absolutely not. I forbid it."

"But—"

"There is no way beneath heaven's sun that I will allow that . . . that . . . *cat creature* to hunt from my car. The seats are original. The carpet is original. It has never been off road and it never will." His voice rose. "She is in pristine cond—"

"That *cat creature* is your queen," Eli said, his tone cutting into the beginnings of an excellent tirade and still managing to sound laconic.

Edmund Sebastian Hartley shut his mouth. There were times when being the titular Emperor of all of Europe and the defacto (though not titular) Master of the City of New Orleans meant nothing, most often when dealing with Jane Yellowrock or her heirs and business partners, Eli and Alex Younger. He had already made arrangements to ship his prized Maserati to France, where he would join Grégoire, Blood Master of Clan Arceneau (and assorted French titles, properties, and cities) in his campaign to seize all of Europe for the Emperor of Europe—himself—and the Dark Queen of Mithrans—Jane.

The goal was to conquer the unruly, warring Blood Masters, claim their fealty, gain control over their hunting territories, and bring peace to the blood-families that had been left in limbo when Jane Yellowrock killed Titus, the former Emperor of Europe. Thanks to her, Edmund was now that titular, if moderately unwilling, Emperor. It was an empty title until he conquered the land and killed his enemies.

However, walking away from war wasn't an option, now that the European Mithrans and Naturaleza were hunting and killing humans. He could not abdicate. Leo Pellissier had made clear what the ramifications of such an abdication would mean politically and in regard to world unrest. Therefore, Ed would fight. And he would win.

Ed frowned at the puma lounging in the kitchen, her eyes on the three men gathered in the living room. She yawned, showing off her fangs, and flicked her ear tabs at him. She was a magnificent creature, lean and muscular, and he had it on good authority that those curved and serrated fangs could tear the head from a powerful blood-servant or even a vampire. Apparently, there was photographic proof.

Ed didn't know what was going on with Jane, but she hadn't been herself since Leo had been defeated. When in human shape, she was pale and withdrawn, grieving as all of them were, but there was something more, something that had sent her into *Puma concolor* form for the last two days. Normally when in mountain lion form, Jane was present. She acknowledged comments, answered questions, participated in discussion as best as the cat form allowed. At such times she called herself Beast. But not now. Two days past, she had texted him with the request to take her Beast hunting for a cow, in his car.

For a cow. In his car.

He had refused. He still was refusing. Not. In. His. Maserati.

Except that the cat creature—sans Jane—was following him around, watching him, often vocalizing loudly with clicks and whistles and mewls, like a kitten begging for milk. This dusk, he had waked from his daily sleep to find her lying on his chest, her fangs inches from his eyes, breathing cat-breath upon him. That raw-blood-and-meat stink had been the scent of his first breath of the night. Her fangs had been his first sight. Had he been alive, he would have expired on the spot. Ed had no idea how she had opened the sealed door to his newly renovated, windowless, attic sanctuary or, more likely, who had let her in, but there it was. And because Jane, in whatever form, was his Dark Queen, his hands were bound to her in fealty. Her desires were his command. *Blast and damn.*

He dropped to the leather couch, leaned at an angle to the couch back and arm, and propped his chin on his fist, staring hard to his left at the cat in the kitchen. *This is all utterly unacceptable.*

The cat rose, all killing grace and muscle, and walked to him, her very long tail moving slightly. When she was ten feet away, she leaped, landing beside him. Despite his centuries as a human-hunting vampire, he flinched.

Eli chuckled.

The cat dropped to the sofa cushion, her head fell into his lap, and she yawned again. He had a ridiculous urge to scratch her ears. She batted her eyes at him, for all the world as if she were flirting. He had no idea that mountain lions had such long eyelashes. Or perhaps only Jane's cat had them. Her golden eyes wore the loving expression of a cat who wanted something and wasn't above emotional manipulation to get it. There was no sign of Jane in the cat's eyes at all, and he wondered for a moment where Jane went when she disappeared and her cat roamed free.

The cat rubbed her jaw on his bespoke suit pants, scent-marking him and leaving behind cat hair. His tailor would be appalled. There would be no getting out the musky scent. "Stop that," he demanded. The cat rolled over and stared at him from upside down, her belly exposed. "No. I am not scratching your belly and you are not hunting in my car."

The cat mewled and began to purr, the vibration gently shaking the couch.

Ed looked at Eli, who was sitting at a table littered with pieces of weapons, smiling that almost-not-there smile. Eli seldom showed emotion, yet he was . . . *smiling.* That smile was odd enough to make Edmund think instead of react emotionally about damaging the Maserati.

The stench of solvents and oils was strong on the air when Ed took a breath to speak. "You say that Jane Yellowrock, the Dark Queen of all vampires, bargained with the cat? With my car?"

"Oh yeah," Alex Younger said from his computer-covered desk. "And the bargain that Beast wanted was to hunt in your car. The car with no head, which we're pretty sure means with the hard top off and the soft top down." He chuckled, a teenaged laugh saying clearly that he was enjoying this conversation. "Hunt a cow. In your car."

"One does not hunt cows," Ed mused, trying to think through this. "One milks them or breeds them or slaughters them for meat. They are stupid and docile. It would not be a hunt."

Eli snapped and clacked one weapon back together and dry-fired at a painting on the wall. A beautiful, extremely valuable painting of a race-horse by Edward Troye. Eli used the painting as target practice, over and over, the empty weapon clicking. Edmund closed his eyes against the sacrilege, comforting himself with the thought that at least the warrior hadn't used actual ammo.

Ed ignored the cat. She purred and rubbed the back of her head over his thigh. He ignored her some more.

The cougar rolled over and sat up, shifting her body until they were face to face, her whiskers tickling his chin. She lifted both front paws and put her forelegs around his shoulders, still purring, but she extruded her claws and pressed them into the skin of his nape, very carefully, very deliberately. Her cat-breath still smelled of bloody meat, a scent with which all Mithrans were intimately familiar, but this did nothing to stir his nightly blood appetite. Vampires did not eat the meat of their victims. *It was not done.*

Speaking to the cat, Ed said stiffly, "Even if I agreed to this insane plan, it will not be a hunt. Cows will run, terrified. They will scatter and destroy the farmer's property. They will run into the road, into the barns, across fences and ditches, bleating or mooing or whatever noise the creatures make. The undercarriage of the Maserati will be ripped out trying to go overland and my car will die within the first hundred feet. It will be an epic failure resulting in no edible cows and the destruction of my *car*."

"Not the kind of cows she wants," Eli said, placing the weapon to the side and reassembling another so fast even vampire vision could scarcely follow.

"And?" Ed said when Eli seemed unwilling to continue. "What kind of cow, then, man?" he practically shouted.

Eli gave a not-quite-there smile again. Had Edmund blinked he would have missed it.

"Beast wants to hunt cows with trees on their heads," Alex said, deadpan. His eyes were gazing at his fingers, dancing across a keyboard, nearly silent even to his vampire hearing. But there was something about his face, impish and slightly taunting.

"I beg your pardon?" Ed said.

"We think she wants to hunt longhorn cattle," Eli said, the small smile back in place in an on-and-off-again delight. Ed had a feeling that in another person, the little smile would have been a belly laugh. Eli Younger was enjoying himself.

"Or bison," Alex said.

The cat licked his cheek. It was clearly a tasting lick as opposed to a grooming lick or a loving lick, as a dog might do. If he should die, the cat would undoubtedly treat him as food. Her tongue was like sandpaper and when she licked him again, it bloody well hurt. "Stop that," he snapped.

Alex snickered.

The cat chuffed in amusement. Her purring increased in volume, the vibration so strong it reverberated where her chest rested against his. The claws pierced a little deeper.

Jane had done this. She had bargained with property she did not own—Edmund went preternaturally still.

Jane wasn't stupid. Or unfair. He had a brilliant idea. He hoped. "One cow?" he asked, meeting the golden eyes, drawing on his mesmeric abilities. He had no idea if they would even work on the cat since they didn't work on Jane, but when his Maserati was in danger, he would use all his wiles. "I have a . . . counterproposal," he said, his tone thoughtful.

The cat chuffed, her ears pricking up in interest.

"In return for not using my car for this hunt, I offer this. The hunt shall be for two bovines with . . . with trees on their heads, or bison, or even wildebeest, whichever Alex can locate to the west of New Orleans, in Texas. This proposed hunt will take place in wild country, far from humans. And, should you agree to my terms, it will occur from the back of a Hummer—a large, tall vehicle set high off the ground, and used for . . ." He hesitated, choosing phrases the cat would understand, ". . . for hunting humans in war."

The cat's ears pricked higher. Her purring stopped. She stared back at him with a predator's hungry intensity. She didn't try to tear off his face, so he continued.

"Instead of a vehicle for war, I propose a luxury Hummer, with no top. A Hummer that can go overland at speeds that will rival the longhorn or the bison or whatever. Forty-eight hours on the ranch. Forty-eight hours to hunt, though only the two animals agreed upon. No horses, no pets, no humans, no prey except the two bovines. In a Hummer."

The cat chuffed softly. She was watching him from two inches away, her whiskers moving on his cheeks, her eyes glowing with interest.

"All this will be in return for removing my car from being considered for any hunt ever again. And . . . we will also fly there and back in the Learjet," he added, "over a weekend."

The cat blinked, her long lashes dropping and opening, considering. Her golden eyes studied him as if he were a squirrel she might chase for fun. She chuffed again, harder, blowing her blood-stench breath in his face.

"That means she's interested," Eli said helpfully.

"Her interest is not enough," Ed said. "This will be a rock-solid deal, as you Americans say. A trip to Texas in the Lear, a hunt for two bovines, preferably wild, from a luxury model, modified hunting Hummer, over the course of forty-eight hours. And my car forever removed from the bargaining table."

The cat released the pinprick of her claws and tapped his neck three times.

"Three bovines? No. We don't have enough space even in the Council Chambers' freezers for that much meat and we will not be hunting simply for hunting's sake. We bring home and eat what we hunt or I will remove the offer from the table."

The cat looked at him with adoration. She liked that statement. Interesting. But then, predators were careful to protect their meat and food sources. Historically, vampires knew that problem quite well. His kind had decimated hunting ranges before, leaving human carcasses and no food sources for miles around.

The cat tapped his neck three times, insistent, pushing. As cats are wont to do.

"No. Butchering, grinding the meat, and shipping three massive long-horns or bison would be problematic. Two bovines. From the back of a Hummer. An all-night hunt with me, and then if you have not brought down two prey, an all-day hunt guided by Eli and Alex. That is my offer."

"Hey! I'm not spending all day in the hot sun in a Hummer for your hunt," Alex said.

Beast growled low, the vibration moving through Ed and the air in clear threat.

Eli chuckled. "I'm in. I'd like to bring down a meat animal or two, if we can find something interesting. I understand that some ranches in Texas cater to hunters. Maybe red stag or scimitar-horned oryx. Something with tasty steaks, that isn't on the endangered list, and is edible."

"What if Beast misses and doesn't get a cow?" Alex asked, taunting, laughing, watching them beneath his springy curls. He might be techni-cally an adult but he was still annoyingly childishly human at times. "I mean, do you have to keep hunting to find another wild cow? She might miss and then we'd be back to your car."

The cat turned her head to Alex and snarled.

"Sorry," Alex said quickly. "Right. You don't miss. My bad."

The cat tapped twice with her right paw, agreeing to the hunt, or that was Ed's interpretation.

"I think you got a deal, my man," Eli said.

She removed her claws, paws, and forelegs from Ed's neck and dropped slowly to the floor. She stretched, one of those positions used in yoga by humans, downward dog, or in this case downward cat. Casually, the *Puma concolor* strolled to Alex's table-desk where his various tablets, laptops, and paraphernalia were piled. Fast as a vampire, she struck. Knocked a stack of tablets to the floor with a clatter of breaking plastic.

"Hey! What's that for?" Alex demanded as she dropped her paw and strolled back to the kitchen. Her tail swished in satisfaction.

"I believe it was in response to impugning her valor and her skill as a hunter," Edmund said.

"Not the smartest thing you ever said, bro," Eli agreed.

"Dang cat," Alex grumbled under his breath as he dropped to the floor in a squat and picked through the broken electronics. But Ed heard the irritation and so did the cat. She looked entirely too pleased with herself.

"Alex, would you be so kind as to search your databases for a ranch I might lease or rent for two days? No other guests on the premises. One vampire-worthy guesthouse. One with wild longhorn cattle, bison, or wildebeest, and whatever Eli desires to hunt?"

Alex looked up from his position on the floor and grimaced. "And I guess you want me to make the reservations and find you a Hummer she can jump out of to hunt? And then make sure the Lear is ready to fly and get you a pilot and a flight crew? What am I? Your personal tour reservations staff?"

"No," Edmund said, hiding his amusement. "You pointed out that the cat creature is the Dark Queen. You are the business partner to the Dark Queen. And she wants to go hunting."

Alex muttered again, cursing under his breath. Edmund smiled, the motion barely there, and pulled his cell phone to finalize shipping his Maserati to France. He had just successfully negotiated a contract with a predator who could kill a vampire. How much harder could it be to negotiate with the warring Masters of the Cities of Europe as their Emperor?

Then he looked down. His handmade shirt and bespoke pants were covered in cougar fur.

Scowling, Ed rose, crossed the room without looking at the cat, and climbed the stairs to his rooms to shower and dress in clean clothing. He stank of cat.

Beast

Beast breathed out. Chuffed. Had left much hair and scent on Edmund. Had claimed Edmund. Watched as Ed walked upstairs. Loved Ed. Loved Ed more-than-five. Wanted Ed as mate. Ed and Bruiser and Grégoire. But Jane would have only Bruiser. Humans were strange. But . . . Beast thought hard thoughts, while lapping water from good china bowl. Hard thoughts said Jane was skinwalker too. Skinwalkers were strange like humans.

Beast did not have three mates, but Beast was happy. Had hunted and played with Ed-not-mate like prey. Was best kind of love. Had gotten two prey-meat-animals instead of one. Had gotten fancy war-car for hunt.

Beast had played with Ed like mouser-cat with toy on floor. Beast had won. Was glad.

Jane *could* be mad that Beast got better bargain. Beast did not care. Beast was best hunter and would hunt cows with trees on head.

Beast looked up steps, up to Learjet-machine, one-two-three and more-than-five steps. Could see air between steps. Human male was at door to Lear, high above.

Beast did not want to fly. Wanted to be on ground with paws in Texas dirt. But had to fly to put paws in Texas dirt. If had to fly, then Learjet-machine was best, not Jane helo with noise and stupid wings on top. Learjet-machine was better than Jane helo. Lear had leather everywhere, skins of prey to sit on.

Beast chuffed and gathered body close. Leaped from ground up high. Landed inside Lear-door, on Lear-floor.

Human male at plane-door made mouse-squeak as Beast landed beside him. Smelled of fear and sweat and a little of urine.

Beast chuffed. Was good that human understood Beast was best hunter. Walked inside belly of plane, long thick tail swaying. Found and lapped at large water bowl. Smelled at small refrigerator. Ed and Jane's Learjet-machine smelled of Jane and dead cow skin on chairs and fresh cow roast. Was good Learjet-machine. Beast padded to big chairs and climbed into dead-cow-skin-chair smelling of Jane. Put head down. Closed eyes. Yawned. Smelled Edmund and Eli and Alex come into plane. Smelled irritation of Ed and laughter of Eli. Was good smells. Went to sleep.

Edmund

Their hunting group landed at the San Antonio International Airport after dark had fallen. They were escorted through back hallways so no one would panic seeing a cougar walking uncaged and free and "start a stampede." Those were the words used by the airport low-level flunky of security when Edmund greased the way forward with a single large bill. He had brought a goodly number of them for just such purposes. Mesmerism was easier, but also illegal.

The cat paced beside him through the back hallways, her head at his right knee, her curious, golden eyes taking in everything. Her nose also taking in everything, including the crotch of the man who led them through the back hallways. The horrible cat chuffed in amusement as the man leaped away, squeaking. That required another large bill.

The driver of the luxury, topless Hummer with its elevated rows of seats had also been less than sanguine at the sight of Beast's fangs, and had nearly swallowed his wad of tobacco. It had taken a much smaller bill and only a slight pull with his vampire abilities to calm the man and implant a suggestion that the puma was actually a large dog, for him to become agreeable. And talkative. Some humans, including "Bronco Sam," were easy to sway. And there were no cameras to suggest that he had used his gifts on a human.

Bronco Sam was a grizzled older cowboy who walked with a limp from an injury, and who was likely hired for his good-ol'-boy attitude, his Western cowboy attire, the "chaw" as Alex called it, and his stories. They secured their luggage to the back of the flat bed of the Hummer and took places inside. The cat raced to the top seat and sat, the queen of her world, seeing everything, excited and delighted and her pelt hairs standing up high. Ed took the second row of seats, Alex beside him. Eli claimed the shotgun seat, Bronco having no idea that real weapons were involved with "shotgun" seat and secreted upon Eli's person.

Chattering at the top of his lungs to be heard over the engine and the wind noise, Bronco drove them out of town, into the countryside. Edmund had forgotten how stunning the night sky was when city lights fell behind them, the stars a wash of brilliance above, the bloated orb of the moon on the horizon. He breathed in the night air of desert country. It was spicy with trees and plants he couldn't identify and rich with the scent of life—rattlesnakes, rats, lizards by the hundreds, insects, rabbits, and farther away, the scent of larger prey, animals he had no name for except bovine, goat, pig, and, more faint, predator cat, perhaps bobcat or lynx. Though he had traveled far, he had never been to this part of the States, preferring the cities and their well-stocked hunting grounds, human culture, museums and music and theater.

But this . . . this was a sensory overload of a different sort. He felt his body relaxing as all the tension of war plans, travel plans to Europe, the pressure of schedules and conflict and meetings and duels began to slip away. He lounged back in his seat, and he didn't even worry when the cat rested her chin on his shoulder, purring, getting cat hair all over his suit coat. Her whiskers tickled his neck, just over his carotid, the exact place where his first master had bitten and turned him. She couldn't know that that spot, electric and tender, would stir old memories, old joy and old pain. She chuffed out a sighing sound and made a soft mewl.

Almost unwilling, he reached back and up and . . . scratched the space between the cat's ears. Her purring increased in volume. Her scent reached his nose despite the wind. Her purrs fell silent and he realized she had fallen asleep, her head on his shoulder.

Something old and half-forgotten turned over in his chest. Sad. Broken. And human.

Beast

Beast leaned against Edmund. Scent of Ed was all over Beast. Scent of Beast was all over Ed. Beast loved Ed. Beast did not love Bronco Sam. Bronco talked. Bronco talked all time. Beast was not sure that Bronco took breaths between words. Bronco was stringy and hard and smelled of chemicals and tobacco and alcohol that Eli called whiskey. Bronco would not taste good, but Beast might hunt Bronco anyway to make Bronco stop talking.

Ed lifted hand. He touched Beast.

Beast went still.

Ed fingers groomed Beast head between ears like mate. Scratched deep. Beast felt . . . strange feelings. What Jane called peace. Beast was safe, like kit at the teat. Like Beast in den in high rock face. Beast closed eyes. Beast slept.

Edmund

"The Circle III Hunting Ranch outside San Antonio is family owned by the current generation of Iverses," Bronco Sam said, "but it was founded by Charles Ivers. He was a well-educated man, good-lookin', charmin', traveling from Maine to see the Wild West and make his fortune. He stopped in San Antonio where he met the exotic, beautiful, beloved, only child of Hector Casillas, a wealthy Mexican businessman, who specialized in banking, acquiring gold, and selling weapons to the Mexicans and the Americans both." Bronco idled the Hummer in the middle of the road so they could stare through the iron fence down the long straight drive to the white-painted two-story home illuminated with landscaping lights. There were several outbuildings and log cabins just beyond the house, and horses in the pastures to either side of the drive.

The smells of hay, feed, manure, and horse came to Ed's nose, awakening a forgotten longing in him. The smell of bovines and other, less familiar creatures were carried on the night air. Beast woke and sat up tall, sniffing and curious, quivering with interest. Ed put up a hand to touch the cat's paw in restraint. "Not now," he murmured. "Not yet."

The cat chuffed and made a *yawrllll* sound. Somehow, he understood the noise to be both discontent and agreement.

"Charles Ivers, that city slicker, fell in love and promptly married Olivia Casillas, who bore him three sons," Bronco said, "giving the older Casillas a happy, joy-filled later life watching his grandsons grow. When Olivia's father passed and the two Iverses inherited her father's fortune, they purchased this land. And in 1849, not long after Texas became a state, the Circle III cattle brand and ranch were born. The O stands for *Olivia*, and the *Is* in the center of the circle stand for the three Ivers sons. A love story to last the generations."

"Mmmm," Ed said. He understood the tale to be about a charismatic and beguiling young man who had found a way to acquire a fortune with nothing but charm. Ed had known many such men over the centuries. He had even been such a man from time to time and wealthy woman to wealthy woman. The scent of horse increased on a swirling wind and the sound of horse hooves on the air. Soft equine snorts followed as they caught his scent and the scent of the predator cat at his shoulder. He asked, "Would you inquire of your employer about the possibility of a moonlight ride?"

Eli tilted his head in surprise at Edmund, who merely smiled. It had been decades since Edmund had ridden, but why not? He had forty-eight hours here before he was neck-deep in duels and the arcane rules and politesse of his own kind. Why not enjoy this mess Jane Yellowrock had gotten them into? Money talked and he had paid an unreasonable fortune for five-star service.

"Make that two of us," Eli said. Then he grinned. "Prissy boy here will need a prissy English saddle, Bronco, and a prissy flashy horse. I'd like a good, sturdy, neck-reining cow pony."

"You ride?" Edmund asked, surprised.

"I ride. I spent six months on horseback in-country once upon a time, tracking down a gang of bad hombres." Eli chuckled and the sound was cold and harsh. "Uncle Sam's finest know all sorts of things, Prissy Boy."

"Are you challenging me for some reason," Ed asked mildly, "or just for fun?"

Eli grinned, a sudden wild light in his eyes. "We can call it fun. For starters."

The gate opened with the touch of a button and the Hummer turned down the drive.

"I can arrange a ride," Bronco said, his tone cautious and his words guarded.

"Good," Eli said. "We can be ready fast."

"Hmmm," Edmund said, curious why Eli goaded him. And then he remembered. Men of war often pushed one another. Goaded, provoked, and annoyed one another. A peculiar sort of comradery-of-war. Was Eli's badgering that sort of . . . bonding? Of friendship? And, dear God, did he want to befriend this man? Ed's mind and body went still, considering the ramifications of such a comradeship.

The Hummer drove on.

Alex had rented one of the log cabin cottages to the back of the house. Bronco dropped them off—and the cat jumped to the ground in a single leap—to freshen up while Bronco proceeded on to the main house to inform the boss that the guests would like to begin their stay with a moonlight ride. As the Hummer rolled away into the night, Edmund watched as the cat stretched into impossible positions and breathed in the night air with that sucking sound she made. She chuffed, raced to Edmund, rose onto her hind legs, and shoved him to the earth. He landed with a soft *whomp* and an exhale of surprise. She jumped atop him, her front paws on Ed's chest, her back paws on his abdomen, digging in, getting dust all over his suit.

"Damn it all to—" He stopped. Her face leaned in to his. Nose to nose. Her irises glowed a soft yellow with a pupillary silver sheen in the blackness of the night. Ed discovered that he didn't really care if he was dusty and dirty. Who would dare to take offense? Besides, he could afford a dozen new suits if he so wished. He was the Emperor of the European Mithrans.

The realization hit him hard.

He was the Emperor of the European Mithrans.

Leo Pellissier had plotted, contrived, and schemed for this, to get Edmund into this position, as a last-ditch maneuver should the Master of the City of New Orleans die. And then . . . then Leo had died, his head attached by a thread of skin. And he had been buried in the blood of his enemies. Not blood freely given, but blood drained from the unwilling. His . . . his friend was buried.

Tears gathered in Ed's eyes and wild grief swamped through his chest, a flood, a torrent of anguish. His friend was dead and buried. There was a million-to-one chance he could ever come back, and if he did, if Leo Pellissier rose as a twice-dead, he would not be the vampire he once was. Revenant . . . mindless killing machine.

As if she felt his pain, Beast patted his cheek with one paw, the way she might a kitten. She chuffed into his face, licked his cheek with that sandpaper-harsh tongue. She stepped from his body and trotted into the darkness. Ed assumed she knew she had created this maelstrom within him, was satisfied, and was now getting the lay of the land. *Damn cats.* "Don't kill anything tonight, Cat," he called. "Our official hunt begins at dusk tomorrow." In the distance he heard another chuff, but she was gone.

Beast

Leaving Edmund on ground in dirt, Beast loped into night. Loved Edmund, but Edmund needing teaching, like foolish kit. Edmund was important vampire with many powers. But Beast was best hunter. Beast could still teach Ed.

Smells swirled on night-wind. Dust from ground lifted in dust devils, swirling and whirling. Beast watched dust devils caper over land like kits, silver and blue and green and many-more-than-five colors of gray. Sniffed, pulling air in over tongue and scent sacs in what Jane called flehmen response, a sucking dry noise, smells full of promise of hunt.

Smells of familiar deer and strange deer and . . . and strange cows. And . . . *bison*. Beast pelt lifted in sharp points. Beast crouched. Bellycrawled to small hillock. Night vision was silver and sharp as Beast crested hillock to see.

Bison everywhere.

Everywhere!

Beast tightened. Pulled claws inside claw-sheaths. Pulled paws under self, tight, ready to leap or run or hide or kill. Watched bison. Smelled bison. Beast lay on warm stone and stared down into low land full of bison.

Many, many-more-than-five bison. Smell of bison filled nose. Male bison with no sex parts. Female bison ready to mate. And one bull bison, ready to fight for mating rights.

Beast watched. Pelt high. Ears perked. Night deepened. Darkened.

Bison male mated with females. Many females. Was noisy and earth moved beneath Beast belly. Females were stupid to share bison bull. Should be other way. Should be many bulls to fight over every female. This was why Beast was hunter predator, and bison were prey.

Beast crept, and then ran, to check on Edmund and Eli and Alex.

Edmund

Ed stepped into the cabin, his hand-cobbled, calf-leather dress shoes tapping on the dark-stained wood floors. The log house was two stories, with the main living area open to the high rafters and dormers to let in the light by day and the view of the stars by night. As advertised, the cabin had fifteen hundred square feet of living space, all the outer walls composed of logs, all the inner walls rustic reclaimed barn wood. On one wall, there was a huge, stone-cased, wood-burning fireplace with a bison head centered over it. A wood-burning stove stood in the corner, the shape old-fashioned enough that he felt the familiar tendrils of history wrap around him.

The open living space was filled with old furniture. Not antiques, nothing from a civilized time, but just old furniture, all with a Wild West flair, not a single piece more than a 100, 150 years old. He might have laughed. *He* was older than that.

Old rifles hung, wired to the walls, too high to remove without a ladder and wire cutters. There were American tribal blankets on the upstairs railing, an old saddle draped over a board extending from the balcony, and of course, the ubiquitous antler chandeliers. There were sepia-tinted photographs of gunslingers and Western cities. The jars in a glass-fronted mini-cabinet had once been used in a pharmacy. Heavy stoneware—hand-turned mugs, plates, and bowls—were stacked next to cobalt blue glasses from a department store in tall, glass-fronted cabinets. Inexpensive, but clean and neat and beautiful.

The bedroom on the lower level had steel shutters on the widows with heavy draperies for a vampire's daytime sleeping schedule, and a thumb-turning deadbolt on the inside of the bedroom for personal security.

He walked into the vampire room to find Alex already there, his tablets spread over the bed.

"Dibs," the Kid said.

Ed merely looked at him. Drawing upon the smallest hint of his power, silent, deadly. Cold as an arctic wind. He let his eyes bleed scarlet and his pupils widen. He kept his fangs in place. They weren't needed. All that was required for the moment was the reminder that he was in charge. That he was the predator.

Alex had been obnoxious and bossy and acting out, as Jane might have said. So he stared, holding Alex's gaze, leaking power. Reminding the youngster that there was a pecking order. Or a feeding order. And Ed had brought no blood-servants to feed upon.

Alex broke into a sweat. His lips parted. He stepped back. He gathered up his tablets. "It was a joke, dude," he muttered, practically jogging from the room.

"Was it?" Edmund asked, his voice carrying, yet soft as a whispered snarl. He heard the Kid swallow and held in a chuckle. Humans were so easy to manipulate.

Ed opened his suitcase and dumped his belongings on the bed. Stared at the denim jeans that erupted from his suitcase. The button shirts. He hadn't packed these. They were *plaid*. He hadn't worn plaid since visiting his mother's clan in Scotland. He hated plaid. But . . .

When in Rome, eat pasta. When on a southwestern hunting ranch . . . Something that might have been the stirring of excitement warmed him. He closed his door.

Ed slid from his dusty jacket, folded it carefully, and laid it on the foot of the bed. He undressed and showered fast in the small but elegant marble bath, and redressed in his small-clothes before studying and touching the blue jeans and the shirt. Both were softer than expected. He pulled on wool socks, the new jeans, and the plaid shirt that belonged to no clan at all, machine woven in shades of green that crossed at angles, signifying nothing. He ran his hand up the thighs and the arms, accustoming himself to the cloth. Stretched to put on his leather belt. He had packed none of these clothes and he wondered which of the Youngers had removed his clothing and replaced them with . . . this. This gaudy Western wear.

He looked at himself in the brass-backed mirror on the back of the door. He looked taller than he knew himself to be. Leaner. Perhaps even meaner. More powerful, and he was powerful enough.

Suddenly, he understood why Jane Yellowrock wore garish clothes and acted the country oaf before her vampire betters. There was power in the barbarian attire, the barbarian actions. Power and danger. Excitement raced through him again.

Standing on the wood floor in garishly patterned wool socks, he considered the bed.

Centered on the mattress was a shipping box. As instructed by him, it had been placed there by their host when it arrived. The boots within had been flown in and delivered to the ranch. The brand was chosen in honor of Jane, a tribute, as it were.

He slid the shipping box across the Matelassé spread and opened it. And then the inner Lucchese box.

Inside were a pair of black, low-heeled riding boots. Ed lifted them out and held them to the lamplight. The scent of leather filled the room, rich and aromatic and very expensive. Being off-the-shelf, they were not his usual bespoke footwear, but they *were* handmade, snip-toed.

The artisanship was excellent.

And . . . he had never worn footwear made from crocodile belly.

New experiences were rare for a Mithran of his age.

He gripped the tabs and slid the boots on. Stamped once with each foot. Not bad. Not bad at all. He regarded himself in the mirror once more. "Prissy boy?" he murmured to himself. "We'll see about that."

He stepped from the room, the new boots not quite silent on the wood floors, and stopped by the kitchen. The space was spotless and, like the bath, ultra-modern in contrast to the rest of the tourist-trap cabin. He checked the brand of coffee, found it acceptable, and the year of the wine in the wine fridge. It wasn't quite to his usual tastes but it wasn't Mogen David either. He could stand it. He opened a bottle of red. Poured himself a glass in the department store glasses. Sipped and drank.

Different.

Not horrible.

Interesting . . .

When he entered the living space again, Eli was waiting. The former Ranger was dressed similarly to him, except his boots were old and well-worn. Slung low on his hips was a double-holster gun belt. Not a weapons harness. A gun belt. Made from leather. There were six-shooters in each holster.

Ed smiled slightly. "I haven't seen a .45-caliber centerfire Colt Single Action Army pistol in decades. Won't the long barrel be difficult in the saddle?"

"Never bothered me before," Eli said. "You know guns?"

"I know weapons from certain eras."

Eli removed the weapon on his left, opened the cylindrical magazine to reveal a full load, and passed it to Ed. The weapon was old, heavier than modern weapons, and this one had been reconditioned.

"The gun that won the West," Edmund murmured, his finger on the trigger guard, checking the load, "by killing bad hombres and the native people wholesale." He clicked the barrel shut and checked the Peacemaker's sights. "Nice. Though I never did care for a revolver. Give me a rifle any day."

"We hunting tonight?" Eli asked.

Ed shrugged and moved to the door. "If you wish. I think I'll simply enjoy the ride, however. Once one has hunted human on horseback, little else seems to compare."

Eli went still as a hunting cat.

Ed smiled. Eli and Alex wanted to play games. It had been a long time since anyone except Leo had baited him. He found it oddly enjoyable to pull their tails. He went on. "Though that was a century and a half before you were born, Eli, and was a hunt of vengeance and judgment well earned."

He opened the outer door and called over his shoulder to Alex, "Stay out of my room unless you are offering to be my meal, Alex." The Kid, who had been about to enter again, turned and walked away. "You will also not play silly human games like short-sheeting my bed without facing the consequences. And take a shower. Please. You reek."

Eli chuckled. "You're a lot like Jane, you know that?"

"Mmmm," Ed said, stepping outside, off the porch, and around the log cabin to the back.

From there, he could hear voices and the stamping of horses' hooves. A light brightened a small barn and four horses standing inside a covered fenced corral. Three of the horses stood patiently; one danced, edgy, tense. His night vision was far better than a human's, and the prancing mare drew him. She was young, buff with pale brownish dapples and a darker buff-colored mane and tail. Unlike his usual preferences, she wasn't a big horse, standing barely fifteen hands, one inch, but she was regal and fiery and her spirit called to him.

He crossed the space between them slowly, at an angle, his head turned slightly to the side, not staring at her with a predator's gaze. But she caught his scent and snorted, stamping, prancing, smelling hunter, a scent that meant, to her mind, meat-eater. And likely smelling the cat creature on the air as well. He was glad he had rinsed off in the shower, to remove the cat-predator stink. The cat scent on him might have sent her over the edge. He moved slowly, stopping often, and realized that Eli was watching him from the cabin, and so was Bronco Sam, standing at the barn door, a saddle in his arms. Their host, a small man with a large belly, stood with Bronco. There was a sense of ownership and entitlement, a razor-sharp attentiveness about him.

None of their weapons smelled of silver load, so Edmund ignored them all, his entire concentration on stalking and winning the skittish mare. He would ride this mare.

It took a good fifteen minutes, but he got close enough to breathe at her, and he was glad he had fed well before leaving New Orleans. His breath was warm, not the cold of the grave. And he smelled of red wine, not blood. She stamped and snorted, tossing her mane. She set one eye on him, the white showing all around as was common with the Appaloosa breed. When their eyes met, he sent out a tendril of compulsion and murmured, "Hello there, lovely. You are beautiful, yes you are."

She pricked her ears and tilted her head, just a little. Attracted, though not yet captivated.

He moved toward her without raising his hands. His upper arm finally touched her. She stilled, breathing in his scent, and his compulsion wrapped around her. Slowly, she settled. He offered her a sugar cube that he had taken from the kitchen coffee set. He held out his other hand to Bronco, smelling what he needed next. "Carrot."

A carrot was placed into his hand and he offered the treat. She chomped through it, her teeth white and strong. Less than ten years of age, more than five. A good age for a riding horse. She took the other half of the carrot and tossed her head, getting it into her teeth. When she had chomped it down, she leaned her head in and breathed on him again. He leaned back and breathed on her. They stood together for perhaps half a minute before she tossed her head, nudging him back.

"What does she like best?" he asked, still without taking his eyes from the mare.

"Hard peppermint candy," Bronco replied. The grizzled man held out a candy, already free of the crinkly noisy wrapper. Ed took it and offered it to her. She lipped it off his palm and crunched it, blowing and snorting and making soft sounds of pleasure. He held out his hand to Bronco and the old man gave him a handful.

"I reckon this means you wanna ride her," the un-introduced man said. "I usually ride Ginny. She's a mite much for most riders."

"Not for me," Ed said softly. "Saddle her. With a *prissy* saddle." He smiled. "An Australian cattle saddle would be my preference, if you have one." Ginny bumped him again and he gave her another peppermint, which she cracked between her strong teeth. He stroked her broad face and grinned widely, turning to the unidentified man, their host and the owner of the ranch, according to the website photographs. Ed sent a small hint of compulsion into the man as their eyes met. The man stopped. Still as a statue, caught in Ed's mesmeric gifts.

"You mean the funny saddle with the thigh supports that stick up in front?" Bronco asked from behind him, though it was clear the cattle hand knew fully well what kind of saddle Ed had requested.

"If possible." Speaking softly, Ed told them his seat size.

"Not sure we have that exact size but we'll have something." Bronco limped into the back of the tack room.

"Charles Ivers the Fifth," the small, potbellied man said proudly, and stuck out his hand, all Texan graciousness.

Ed took the hard, work-calloused palm and said, "Edmund Hartley. Ginny and I are going to be the best of friends." Ed released Ivers's hand and petted her neck. The mare bumped him affectionately.

The man to his side didn't like that the mare was being affectionate to Ed. The scent of jealousy, sharp and bitter, cut the air.

Ed didn't care what the man liked or didn't.

He was the Emperor of the Europeans. He would ride this mare. And before this night was done, if he wanted her, this mare would be his own. And her name was no longer Ginny. It was *Genevieve*.

Beast

Beast watched Ed and restless mare from low hillock. Her own cat scent was swept away by wind. The mare, young and eager enough to prance, could not smell her. Ed was happy, the odd scent of joy bright as moonlight on the wind. Beast watched and was happy that Ed was happy. Happy was good word. He rode prey animal and mare danced beneath him. Beast followed, pawpawpaw, watching Ed and mare. They were like one mind and one body, prancing down dirt road into far reaches of the ranch.

Beast followed, racing from hillock to hillock, as if chasing prey but . . . Edmund was not prey. Edmund was Edmund. Better than prey. Better than many others. Beast loved Edmund.

Edmund

Genevieve was his. He had just purchased her for a fortune from the potbellied Ivers, a handshake deal that Ed would hold the man to, though the rancher was not happy at the sale. He liked the little mare, but he liked money more, a fact that confounded the human and left him angry at the loss of his prize, despite the pretty penny that she brought.

Joy like a river at flood-tide filled Edmund. He rode, exuberant. The mare beneath gamboled. Ivers grumbled and sweated and hated the vampire on *his* mare. Ed didn't care. There was no scent of silver on the night wind. No scent of enemies. He was in no danger. They rode on into the dark of night, the remembered stars sparkling from horizon to horizon.

The moon set and, for the humans, the night grew darker than the armpit of hell, a fact that Bronco repeated again and again, but they were on a dirt road, easy for Ed to see. Eli dropped low-light-vision headgear over his eyes, gear Ed was fairly certain had not been on his person when they left the cabin. And despite the complaints at the now-moonless ride, the rancher and Bronco were comfortable anywhere on the property, which was good since the ranch comprised forty thousand acres. It was not the largest ranch in Texas (which came in at more than nine hundred thousand acres) but big enough for the average human to get lost in should someone determine to leave them in the wilderness.

Ed and Eli, were, of course, far too adept and experienced for such a possibility, but their host and their guide did not know that, and both of the unknown humans knew that he was a vampire. It was not beyond the realm of possibility that the two were vamp-haters and wanted him captured for his blood or dead—not that his blood would do them any good beyond capturing their minds for his use. But they did not know his power or their danger. And Edmund was not one to be taken, should that be their intent.

It was a delightful conundrum. It was the possibility of a battle, and battle was not his usual desire. Perhaps he was more prepared for the fight for Europe than he had thought.

He settled into the gait of the mare beneath him. She was smooth and easy and perfect. It had been many years since he sat a horse, and he loved Genevieve. Loved her fire and her spirit and her desire to please her rider, even without compulsion. Despite the time of year—midwinter—the night was warm, and the mare beneath him was excited, full of piss and vinegar, which was a term Bronco had used. It fit.

Edmund determined to adopt it. Jane Yellowrock was full of piss and vinegar too. Perhaps he would use the term on her when she was human-shaped again. He could almost see her expression as he said the words. It would be wonderful. Perhaps even . . . fun.

Even as he thought that, the mare snorted and sidestepped, her hooves skipping and darting. He kept his seat. By a hair. He caught the scent of Jane on the air. Or, rather, the scent of her Cat. No wonder the mare was salty. A cougar on the night wind and a vampire on her back. It was a near miracle she hadn't bolted.

He sent another wave of compulsion through to the mare. She settled.

Genevieve was warmed up and Ed took the lead, putting her through her paces. He hadn't known that only a few Appaloosas were gaited horses, but he was in luck with Genevieve. The lovely, dappled mare slid into a slow pace that was smooth as silk, like riding the clouds. She hadn't been trained to jump or race, being used solely as Ivers's personal mount and bred for a foal for her excellent bloodline. She was mature but with a lot of sass. Ed was deeply in love.

Beast

Beast watched Edmund and three riders. Four in all, one for each toe pad. Edmund and horse danced. Beast loved Ed. Would like to eat horse. But Beast thought Ed would say no. Beast chuffed with disgust and padded into night. Beast was learning land. Claiming land. Had found scat of bobcat, of fox. Dry scent of rattlesnake. Had left scat and spray in many places.

Beast stopped. Smelled something new.

Tilted nose to wind, sniffed. Pulled in air over tongue and roof of mouth, flehmen response, to smell smells. Was . . . cow with trees on head. What Eli called long-horn-cattle!

Long-horn bulls. Together. Should not be together. Long-horn bulls were stupid. Were angry. Beast raced and raced and stopped fast. Saw long-horns. Two bulls inside fences, but . . . too close. Fences were stupid. Bulls had smelled each other on strange wind. They raced at one another, even in the night.

They knocked down fences.

Hit! Horns locked. Bulls snorting, angry. Smell of testosterone was hot on air. They hit and hit again. A third bull joined fight. Gored the bigger bull. Smell of blood rose.

Beast tail twitched with excitement.

Was fight!

Was fun!

Beast quivered with hunting joy.

Bison in far field caught scent and snorted and rammed and called.

Beast heard sound of horses on air, sound of men shouting. Smelled Eli and Edmund. Beast chuffed. Watched as two humans who put bulls too close in stupid fences tried to stop fight. Was funny. Beast chuffed and chuffed. Eli and Edmund laughter reached Beast on night air. Loved Eli and Edmund.

Then air swirled and Beast smelled new thing.

Beast sniffed and sniffed, pulling in scent over tongue and over scent sacs in top of mouth. Used new gift had stolen from ugly-dog-good-nose.

Scent was not there in part of brain Beast had taken from dog. Scent was new thing. New kind of bull.

Ed had said new word. Wil-de-beast. Beast had thought Ed was talking about Beast, but . . . but maybe Ed was giving Beast a gift.

Moving into wind, Beast trotted, followed scent. Scent of new bull grew strong. Belly-crawled over low flat hill.

Beast saw many, many-more-than-five big black cows with curled trees on head. *Wil-de-beasts.* Beast began to circle, learning new cows' hunting grounds. Learning where bull was. Learning where fences were. Where road was. Learning high ground and low ground. Wil-de-beasts!

Edmund

The sun was a bruised purpled red on the western horizon, the sky to the east that dark blue of twilight. Ed remembered the first time he had woken so early, able to see, for the first time in decades, the last vestiges of daylight that had been denied him when he was turned. The sight had left him with an elation so great he had wept, and when the light had been stolen by night, that joy had been followed by an utter devastation that lasted for another decade. The depression had been so dark and deep that it made King David's biblical miry pit sound like an afternoon frolic.

Many vampires did not last through the melancholy of sun-loss. Many walked into the sun and burned to a crisp, for the opportunity to see it one last time. Ed had survived, and now he stared at the plum and amethyst clouds, watching as the night crept in and killed the sky's brilliance. Ed took a breath he didn't need and walked to the Hummer.

Bronco Sam stood beside the big vehicle, his hat in his hand, his jaw working on a wad of chewing tobacco. "Thank you for this nighttime hunt," Ed said, catching the man's eyes and holding his gaze. He wrapped the cattle hand's mind, tying him in the silken threads of power. Most vampires, both Mithran and Naturaleza, could thoroughly bind a human for only a few moments, the gift useful for obtaining a first meal. For most of his kind, a full binding required blood meals and vampire saliva in the donor's blood. Better, the vampire's blood as an exchange. Ed could bind much more easily, with just his eyes and his power and his smile. His master had changed him and then later cursed him for that smile. Ed had simply learned how to use it.

"Do you remember the acreage where we found the wild, 'mean-as-snakes-on-fire' longhorn bulls?" he asked.

Bronco nodded, his movements slow. He spat into the dirt. Chewed for a bit. "I don't know why Ivers bought 'em," he said at last. "They're too old to make good eatin' except you grind up the meat for burgers. Too dangerous to put 'em in with the regular herd. And one of 'em was hurt last night. Took a horn to the flank, up into the belly. Vet's done seen him." He shook his head. "Might make it. Might not. Mean-as-snakes-on-fire," he repeated to himself and Ed. "Meanest, stupidest bulls I ever did see. They got no use at all except to eat, shit, gore each other, fu—ah, screw—sorry 'bout that—and tear up pasture and fencing."

"You will follow us into the countryside on horseback. Back to the mean-as-snakes bulls."

"Mean-as-snakes on fire," Bronco corrected.

"Mean-as-snakes-on-fire," Ed agreed, his mesmerism deepening, tightening. "You will stampede the mean-as-snakes-on-fire bulls right at the Hummer. When they are running, you will depart until I need you again."

"That's a stupid way to hunt. But you paid the man."

"I did."

Bronco limped to his cow pony, which was already saddled, and swung into the saddle. Without another word, he and the horse rode into the darkness.

"That was creepy," Alex said from the small porch of the log cabin. "When did you drink from him?"

"Never," Eli said shortly, his eyes on Ed, calculating, disgruntled, suspicious. He leaped in and started the Hummer, and the huge engine filled the air with its diesel roar. Over the sound of the roar, he continued. "That was like Onorio power on steroids. I've never seen anyone, including Leo, do that so fast and so totally."

Ed raised a hand, grabbed the passenger-side roll bar, and swung himself up and into the passenger seat. The shotgun seat. He didn't look at Eli, but he could feel the man's glower. The former Ranger was dressed all in charcoal camo and was armed to the teeth. His scent was hostile and dangerous. Ed liked it. "It's a small but useful gift."

"Useful, right. That gift is why Leo picked you as his emperor. Isn't it?"

The tone was even more aggressive than the scent. Eli had been itching for a fight for some time, though Ed wasn't certain exactly why. He had decided on the reason being the loss of Leo, though there might be more to it. The military man hadn't confided in him. "It played a part."

"How often do you use it?" Eli asked, the sound almost too soft to be heard over the engine, even with Mithran ears.

"I don't mesmerize my friends."

"That doesn't tell me a damn thing."

Ed looked at Eli. "You may not be *my* friend, but I am *your* friend." His tone became more acerbic. "Now please put away the weapon you have aimed at my heart and let's take Jane's cat creature to hunt cows with trees on their heads."

Eli didn't put the weapon away.

Ed assumed the conversation wasn't finished. He leaned back in his leather bucket seat and stretched an arm toward his adversary and friend. This turned him so his chest made a larger target to the weapon. "Silver ammo?" he asked, nonchalant.

"Yes."

"Good. If you ever shoot me with anything less," Ed said, still just as casually, "I'll have plenty of time to rip off your head."

"As long as we have that cleared up. Friend."

Ed's small smile grew.

"If I ever think you're using that gift on me, I'll—"

"You'll behead me as I sleep." Edmund smiled slightly. "Yes. I know." The weapon vanished.

"You people are crazy," Alex said from the front porch.

Neither of them disagreed.

"No way am I letting you two nutcases go off together without me."

Carrying a large box, Alex climbed into the Hummer and took the seat directly behind Ed, leaving the higher bench seat behind him empty. They all buckled in. This ride was likely to be jarring.

Jane's cat appeared from the shadows at the edge of the cabin. She walked to the front porch and lapped at the water in the bucket Eli had placed there. She drank and drank. When she was done, she licked her jaw, her eyes on them in the dim light of the small bulb over the door, her pelt buff and tan and darker gold.

The cat gathered herself and leaped over twenty-five feet across and more than ten feet up, landing in the Hummer's elevated backseat. Alex made a sound worthy of a toddler. The cat chuffed and settled on the higher chair, like the cat queen she was. She batted the back of Alex's head.

"Ow." He rubbed his curls and said, "Stop that. Go, before she draws blood."

Eli glared at him before positioning his low-light headgear in place. He pulled away, lights off, following Bronco Sam's horse to the first pasture gate.

Beast

Beast sniffed air, smelling cows. Smelling manure and blood and . . . smelling bulls with trees on head. Pulled paws in tight. Nose in air, sniffing.

Will hunt with male human and vampire.

Beast had never hunted with adult males. Had always chased almost-adult-juvenile males from litter. Had hunted only with juvenile and fully adult female pumas. But never males. Human males acted like juvenile male pumas. Posturing. Beast had claws to stop that.

Beast wondered if she would have to swat humans. Beast chuffed with laughter.

Edmund

Softly, just for Bronco's ears, Edmund said, "Now."

In a single instant, the night erupted.

Bronco Sam dug his heels into the cow pony's sides, fired his pistol into the air, and yipped a Texas yell. He raced toward the longhorn bull, his high-pitched "Yiyiyiyiyiyiyi" shrill in the night.

Eli hit the horn. Hit the lights.

And the puma screamed.

The bull's head came up.

The massive bull leaped, whirled in midair, and thundered away.

All in perhaps a half second.

Eli whipped the wheel and followed overland. He guided the Hummer on the trail of the bull. They bounced as hard as the bull himself. Eli pulled beside it. The big bull rammed the sidewall. The vehicle—built to withstand roadside bombs—rocked on its oversized tires.

The bull darted away. The cat leaped. In the headlights, Ed watched as she landed on the bull's back. Dug in with claws and fangs. Snarling. The bull sprinted and bucked and whipped his body, a nearly boneless, snaking, corkscrew movement, hooves flying. He vanished into the night and down a ridge, the panther on his back.

Eli slowed the vehicle and rolled to a stop. The engine went silent. Edmund released his death grips on the roll bar and what Eli called an "oh-shit handle." He was fairly certain he had bent them both. He was breathing hard, his heart pounding. It had been . . . *exhilarating.*

Alex opened the box on his lap, revealing a small drone, complete with camera. His computer screen came on, illuminating the Hummer seats. In seconds, he had the drone in the air, but it was too dark for him to see much even with the low-light camera it carried, and he grumbled beneath his breath, cursing in words he never used in front of Jane. Or in front of him, for that matter. Oddly that too made Edmund feel happy. Accepted among the men.

Bronco Sam came trotting back down the dirt road on his cow pony, the man hooting and hollering in glee. When he reached the Hummer, Bronco pulled out a flask and drank deeply, the scent of cheap bourbon on the air. He twisted in his seat, both legs on one side of the horse, and the cow pony leaned a hip onto the Hummer too in what looked like old habit.

The night sounds returned, the fight between bull and puma in the distance, the bull roaring with fury and pain. The puma snarling and hissing and making angry cat noises that had no name in human language.

The bull screamed and blew breath, snorting hard. The cat went silent. Then, so did the bull. Stillness settled on the land.

Edmund chuckled. It was a true laugh, not something any vampire experienced often. True laughter was something left over from being human, and it reminded all vampires that though they had gained power, they had lost something vital as well. He turned to Eli, still laughing. "Thank you. Thank you for this trip, for this experience. I am in your debt."

Eli started at the sight of the smile and the sound of laughter. His eyes narrowed.

"Hey," Alex said. "What about me. I made all the arrangements."

Edmund smiled back at the human boy. "And I thank you as well. This has been . . . not precisely delightful. But . . . something I have not ever felt before, or not in a long, long time."

Alex scowled, so like Jane Yellowrock that the sight of it surprised Edmund. The boy grumbled, "It was something new. Something you never did before. And it involved fighting and blood. Of course you like it. You're a frickin' fanghead."

Edmund's bright laughter sounded again, human, so very human. And exultant. "Yes. Yes. I am indeed."

The two humans stared at him in surprise.

"I am all that," he explained. "But I am also a man out in the wilderness, in the night, with friends, a mountain lion, a cowboy, and a cow pony, on an adventure. And I thank you."

"Friends?" Eli said, still uneasy but better. Then the human warrior smiled. "Yeah. You keep your mesmerism to yourself, so affirmative. Friends. You're welcome."

In the distance, the bull fight grew loud again, the death throes going on and on, weaker and weaker. Finally, even that sound fell still.

Sam offered them his flask. Eli declined for them all and sipped espresso from a small insulated mug. "Can't see shit," Alex said.

"Language," Eli warned softly. "You say that where Beast can hear, she might swat you."

"Yeah, whatever. Beast probably pulled the bull into a depression or under an overhang. I can't even find them on infrared." Disgruntled, Alex recalled the drone and put it away. The computer screen went dark.

Bronco Sam said, "You folks do know that the meat on that bull is gonna be hard as jerky. Animal that runs and feels fear? Meat's ruined."

"Yes," Eli said. "We'll have it all ground for hamburger."

Bronco tilted his flask into the air. "That's a lotta barbeque. Feel free to invite me. I got a pepper sauce recipe that'll roast your eyebrows off."

Edmund had no idea if that was a good thing, but Eli seemed pleased.

The wind freshened. The night deepened. Ed leaned back in his seat and watched the stars overhead, brighter so far from city lights, remembering when the night had always been this dark, the stars this bright, before electricity and the brilliance of humans. There was little he missed about the past, hating the stench of sewage, the lack of fresh water, the smells of unwashed bodies, the sight of starvation, the sounds and stench of illness and pain, the remembered agony of losing loved ones so easily to whooping cough, measles, the flu. Back then even vampire blood was often not enough to save the sick and dying. The past was dark and full of grief. But the stars in the night sky . . . that he missed.

Twenty minutes later the cat leaped from the darkness into the high backseat. Alex yelped. Ed hid a smile. He had known by the scent of hot, fresh blood that she was coming. "Did you eat your fill?" Ed asked her placidly.

She yawned, showing off her white fangs and bloodied muzzle before beginning to groom off the blood.

"Is the bull where we can find it?" Eli asked.

The cat turned her head to the right of the vehicle and Eli started the engine. She stepped over the middle seat and stood with her paws on Eli's chair back, nudging him in the right direction. They found the dead bull in a small depression beneath a rock overhang, and Eli and Bronco applied the Hummer's winch to drag the two-thousand-pound bovine to the vehicle and up onto the flat ramp in back. The bull's weight rocked the Hummer hard.

The puma dropped down over the bull and sniffed all over it. In the beam of a small flashlight, the men studied the longhorn bull. There was relatively little blood or gore. The cat—Beast, as the Youngers called her—had dug in her claws and fangs on the bull's shoulders and the back of his neck, letting him run and buck and tire. Then she had, somehow, gotten in front of him and gripped his throat. She had held on until he suffocated enough to be rendered unconscious. And then she had torn out his throat and eaten her fill from his belly.

Sam said, laconic, "Yup. That meat's good for nothing but ground burger. I foresee a lot a barbeques in your future."

Beast

Beast chuffed at the sight of her kill. *Is good kill. Is big prey. Bull with trees on head. Big bull with big trees on head. Was good chase and good hunt and good kill.* Beast was happy like Ed was happy. Was good feeling.

Beast wanted more.

Edmund

The six-hundred-plus-pound wildebeest bull was much smaller but much faster, and no less dramatic. The wildebeest herd was asleep when they located it. They got into position, turned so the prevailing winds worked to their advantage. Beast chuffed and panted in excitement. They waited for some time as Bronco trotted into the darkness and got into position.

Eli sipped another espresso. The Kid complained under his breath that it was taking too long. But when Bronco fired his pistol into the air and yodeled his patented yell, the Kid flinched. The wildebeest scattered, confused, panicked. All but the old bull. He put his head down and charged Bronco.

Sam galloped into the night. Without headgear to help him see and guide the pony. It was a very dangerous move, over uneven terrain. The horse might trip or step into a hole and fall and roll. Break a leg. Kill Bronco.

"There!" Edmund pointed, shouting. "Eli?"

"Got it." Eli spun the Hummer's wheel and hit the lights. Tried to cut off the bull.

The puma leaped to its back. A half a second later she was bucked off. The bull went after her. The cat leaped, twisted madly in midair, and landed on his back again. This time she got her teeth and claws into him. He bucked and threw his head. He twisted into impossible positions, most of them in midair, the fight caught in the lights of the Hummer.

Alex had his cell camera out.

Eli brought the Hummer to a stop and the fighting pair fought and roared and screamed. Then they thundered off, the cat, Beast, now hanging on to the bull's haunches. Alex already had the drone in the air, and here the land was flatter; he was able to keep the camera on their trail. The fight was long and violent. The four men watched the battle on the small screen, the fighting pair a bright green in the drone's camera. When it was finally over, Beast tore into the bull's belly and feasted while they guided the Hummer close enough to winch the bull in.

After the hunt, Beast was happy and covered in blood, smiling and showing her killing fangs, chuffing with happiness, and that was all that mattered. They had enough burger-worthy meat to last in the Council Chambers' freezers for the next year, the cat was pleased, and their bargain was satisfied.

Most importantly Edmund's Maserati was safe.

Edmund

Forty-eight hours after they landed in San Antonio, the Lear touched down again in New Orleans. That night, Ed tossed his jeans and his ugly plaid shirt into the hamper and donned his new suit for the flight to France. But, just this once, he refused the proper footwear. He pulled on, instead, the Lucchese boots. Wearing footwear approved by the Dark Queen, he left his attic rooms and slipped down the stairs of the Yellowrock Clan Home. In minutes he would board the Lear again for France and the battles awaiting him there. He'd made certain his swords were properly packed. His blades. His silver stakes, weapons most Mithrans could not wield without burning their flesh on the metal.

He didn't want to leave. He had no desire for this conquest of Europe.

But he understood the reasons for it, and he also understood his own worth. He was the only person who might, possibly, conquer the fighting clans.

Beast

Beast watched Edmund walk into living room. Beast rose to four paws and stalked to Ed. Edmund shook Eli hand. Shook Alex hand. Men and vampire talked. Silly human words.

Beast moved to Ed and pressed with head to thigh. Wound around Ed legs. Rubbing and scent-marking Ed. Got much Beast-hair on Ed.

"Good lord. You damned cat," Ed said, laughing human laugh. "You've ruined another suit."

Beast chuffed with laughter. Ed belonged to Beast. Beast loved Ed.

Beast Hunts Pie-bald Deer

Beast story of Hunt. Beast talks to Reader Humans in Beast point of view. First published in 2019 on Beast's fan page, and now with increased word count.

Reader Humans who read and watch with Beast must be quiet or Beast will swipe with paw, Beast thinks. *Will hit Reader Humans with claws inside claw sheaths. Will not draw blood. But will knock Reader Human over.*

Beast chuffed quietly, thinking of picture of Reader Humans rolling down long hill. *Is funny.*

Start of Beast Story

Day was sunny and cool. Beast was happy. Beast crouched in tree over small creek. Beast must tell Reader Humans about hunt. Talks to Reader Humans. *This is Hunt! Deer come to creek to drink when thirsty, when summer has been dry and hot. Beast is patient hunter. Beast is best hunter.*

Human Readers were still quiet. *This is good.*

Beast went to water that Writer calls runnel. Beast sat for many hours over small creek.

Deer came to creek. Three does with four young. Number is more-than-five. Beast can count to five. Is best number. Deer smelled good. Deer smelled of meat and rut and all things good.

But no males with trees on heads were with herd and Beast does not kill does. *Females breed, and mean more meat. Beast only kills male deer.*

Beast thinks. *Is hard thing to think.* But . . . *Will tell Reader Humans about male deer. Is easy to tell are males.*

Males (in fall cool) grow trees on heads and smell of rut-sex-stink. Males in rut-stink are stupid. Males run at cars and at other males. Are stupid-stupid-stupid. No males were in this group what Writer calls herd.

Beast did not hunt. Beast watched does and young. All wandered away through trees.

Sun began to set, making sky color of fire.

Beast needed water.

Jumped, leaped through trees and over neighbor fence. Was small fence, only good to keep in small, hairy, old dogs with stinky rotten teeth. Easy for Beast to jump. Landed inside fence. No silly old dogs were here. No yap-yap-yap to annoy Beast. *Is good no stupid dogs.*

Drank from Neighbor Human pool for swimming. Tasted terrible. *Neighbor Human is stupid to drink from pool.*

Beast saw bird-water-bowl on short tree. Beast put front paws on bowl and drank from bird-water-bowl. Was good water. Beast left scat and sprayed around bird-water-bowl to show thanks to good water.

And to claim good water.

Beast thought about water and bird-water-bowl. Beast scat will also scare stupid little dogs. Beast chuffed in laughter, then leaped over short stupid fence into trees. Walked pawpawpaw across branches to Writer house and jumped onto RV. RV was tall. Was warm. Beast went to sleep.

Last twilight. *This is time of day when sun is gone but sky is still light.* Writer was laughing. Says, "Other writer wrote famous books about Twilight."

Beast thought, *But was no Beast so other books do not matter. This is Beast story.*

Writer nodded. Was human motion that said Writer understood. Or agreed. Or was afraid. Human nod meant many things.

Beast was perched on Writer RV. *Is tall truck with house inside. Top of RV is good place for Beast to rest.*

Was lying, belly down, on top of RV. Smelled deer on wind.

Smell made Beast mouth water. Beast licked jaw and muzzle. Small herd came into Writer yard to eat. All females and yearlings. Ate leaves off tree called mulberry. Deer liked mulberry leaves. Ate many while Beast watched, mothers teaching young to eat leaves.

Herd is too small to take young. Must wait. Must be patient.

But . . .

Am hungry. Am starving. Have not hunted for many days.

Writer was laughing harder. Writer said, "Beast is melodramatic. You ate yesterday."

BUT WAS NOT DEER! AM STARVING.

Watched deer. Deer Beast could not eat. But . . . smelled male deer, called buck, on wind. Many bucks.

Ears pricked. Smelled with flehmen response, mouth open, with *scree* of sound. *THREE BUCKS!* Beast gathered paws beneath body.

Bucks raced into yard! Chasing females!

Females ran fast, away. Yearlings raced into trees to hide.

Beast leaped to ground. Smell of fear and terror and deer-rut was strong. Beast chased along ground to bigger trees. Leaped high and raced on branches. Spotted male deer. Jumped to ground and ran! Was long race.

Last male deer was small buck. Had small horns. Had odd white spots on pelt. Beast crept along branch and watched small buck.

Beast pulled paws and legs in close, watching. Was strange buck.

Writer said, "That buck is called piebald, which means brown with patches of white. Or even spotted white all over. But with brown eyes. Piebald deer are beautiful."

Beast had seen such strange deer, but did not have name for pelt-color until now. *Pie-bald.* Beast had seen pie. Was messy human-food with no meat.

Was messy deer.

Pie-bald buck was alone. Separated from male herd, alone for first time since birth. Was young. Was afraid. Beast gathered paws close.

Writer said, "Stop. Leave piebald alone!"

Beast leaped. Landed on Pie-bald back. Dug in with fangs and claws. Pie-bald ran.

Was good fight. Was good feast. Writer was silent. *Good.* Was Beast story.

Jane Tracks Down Miz A

A Short Short Story

The original version of this short-short went to a single winner for a charity auction. Except for the winner, no one has ever seen this vignette, and the ending has been altered. Its place in the timeline is uncertain.

"What kind of flower do you take to a recuperating blood-servant?" I asked the clerk. She looked at me like my question was nutso, but maybe it was the weapons that made her eyes go round. Except during Mardi Gras and Halloween, when my gear looked like a costume, the M4 strapped at my spine made some people nervous. Others reacted to the stakes and the blades. Whatever it was, she scuttled away.

Woman is prey, my Beast thought at me. *Smells of fear.*

I was a vampire hunter by inclination, training, and trade, but tracking down old and injured blood-servants was one of my least favorite hunts. Old blood-servants were wily and had had decades to pick up all sorts of martial arts moves and sometimes had weapons I wasn't expecting. Even the little old lady blood-servants, like the one I was looking for.

Miz A had disappeared after a bloody fight at Katie's Ladies, not long after I got to New Orleans. She had been badly injured, maybe even maimed, and I honestly thought she might have died. Then, yesterday, I got word that she was alive.

Miz A was over two hundred years old, and the words that had been whispered in my ear—literally—had said she was healing very slowly. Too slowly. Something was wrong.

The old woman had been injured on my watch. That made her my responsibility and I hadn't made an effort to find her. I was feeling guilty enough to go into a grocery store and buy flowers, which I had never done before, but there was a first time for everything. I stood over the limited display, debating on roses, which reminded me of funerals and filled my nose with a sweetness that made me sneeze, or daisies and mums, which downright stank. To avoid the funeral floral overtones, I plucked a dripping, stinking bouquet of daisies and mums and carried them to checkout. Then I had to figure out how to carry the flowers on the Harley. I bruised the petals, stuffing them into one of Bitsa's saddlebags, and knew the reek was going to linger inside.

Stinky plant, Beast thought at me. *Why Jane not give catnip?*

I'm not sure what effect catnip has on humans or bloodsuckers.

Beast sniffed in derision. I wasn't a flowers kinda gal.

Just after dusk, I pulled up in front of the two-story house just outside the Garden District. It was painted a pale pink with turquoise shutters and a deeper-toned peacock door. There were window boxes above big elephant ear plants and some kind of striped, low-growing leafy things in shades of yellows and greens. Baskets hung near the front stoop, long tendril-y stems tipped with bright pink flowers. The place was pretty and kinda froufrou. I retrieved the grocery-store flowers and knocked on the door. Weirdly it opened. But no one was there. The house was dark inside, and felt empty.

"Come in, dear," a quavery voice called.

I took a breath, another, smelling . . . one familiar vampire and one old-lady, human-ish blood-servant, a little on the moldy side, the scents mingled and tangled together. I scented no other beings, vamp or human, on the premises. I loosed an ash wood stake and pulled it free, tucking it into the bouquet. And entered the house.

I flipped switches as I moved through the house, turning on lights. The place was decorated in Early American Doily. There were crocheted doilies everywhere, on every chair, every tabletop, every square inch of space, and on top of them were more doilies, stacked. There were also knickknacks from the 1920s and 1930s: toys, little car models, train models, dolls, stuffed bears, and box-style cameras. Hundreds of them. Not a speck of dust rested on anything. I figured it must take a full-time housekeeper to keep the place this clean.

A faint light and even fainter tinkling came from the back of the house, on the first floor. I stepped into the overstuffed room. Sitting in a rocking chair, dressed in her usual blacks, was Miz A, crocheting. Her hands moved swiftly, too swiftly, too surely. And the tinkling sound I heard came from her, a *clink, clink, clink* with every move of her hands.

On her wrists were handcuffs. The handcuffs were attached to a chain that wrapped around her and attached to the back wall of the house.

Miz A was physically bound. Not mentally, as most blood-servants, but chained.

Slowly she raised her head and looked at me.

Her eyes were wide black pupils in bloody sclera. And as she smiled, I heard a tiny click, but no needle-thin fangs snapped down. Her mouth stayed human. "Did you come to feed me, my dear? I'm so hungry."

"Holy crap," I whispered.

"It was unexpected."

I flinched, as I whirled, just a bit, pulling the stake.

Breath caught in my throat, I stood there, flatfooted, crushing the flowers in one hand, the stake in the other.

Katie Fonteneau was coming down from the second floor, her long silky dress making soft *shushing* sounds. Her ash-blond brows raised together in amusement. "Do you think you can stake me in my own lair?"

I slammed the stake back into the sheath with the others. "My apologies for"—I rolled my hand in the air, searching for the right word—"my general stupidity?"

Katie offered a vamp smile, which is to say, not a human one, and in the doily-covered house it was kinda creepy.

"What was unexpected?"

Katie took the flowers from my other hand and placed them in a pink glass vase, then added water from a pitcher near Miz A, who was clinking steadily as a new doily formed in her hands. "She was too old to survive her wounds. She was given too much blood trying to bring life back into her body, blood she could not process." Katie moved a stack of doilies and placed the vase on a tiny table near Miz A. She stroked the old woman's scraggly hair and twisted loose strands into her messy bun. "My darling Amorette was too old."

Miz A looked up at her and said, "Did you come to feed me, my dear? I'm so hungry."

Katie smiled slightly, her hand stroking. "Despite her partial fangs and desire for blood, she is neither vampire nor blood-servant. She is not Onorio. Amorette is, perhaps, hanging in the balance, neither human nor Mithran, and not yet one of the long-chained." Katie looked up at me. "I begged for the Mercy Blade, but he says Amorette is not his charge and will not be for a decade. Leo—" Sudden tears gathered at her eyes, pinkish red. "My Leo says I erred when I tried to heal her. I gave her too much. I—" She stopped. Turned slowly to me, captured my eyes with hers. I felt her pull, her power. It wrapped around me. I stepped back. She whispered. "Yooouuu. You will do this for me."

"Did you come to feed me, my dear? I'm so hungry."

Beast pressed down on my brain, her claws sharp as knives. The mesmerism snapped and broke.

"I will do what?" I asked.

Frustration flashed through Katie's eyes. "You will tell me how to fix my dear old friend. How to help her."

I looked from Katie to Amorette. *Okay.* That was not what I'd expected after her comment about the Mercy Blade.

"Did you come to feed me, my dear? I'm so hungry."

"Katie, when humans get old, sometimes they get a disease of the brain called dementia. Many of those are perfectly content and happy as long as they are well cared for. You're caring for her, right? Feeding her? Cleaning her? Bringing her company to socialize?"

"Yes. But this does not fix her brain. All she wants is to make her lace things and drink."

More blood might fix Miz A, I thought. More blood might make her fully vampire. And perhaps fully rogue.

"Did you come to feed me, my dear? I'm so hungry."

Katie slit her wrist with a tiny knife and held it to Miz A's mouth. The not-human, not-vampire dropped her needle, took Katie's wrist in her hands, and drank. When she was done, she released the vampire's undead wrist and picked up her doily. "Thank you, my dear."

"Miz A?" I asked. "Are you happy?"

"Of course I am happy." She patted Katie's hand. "I have my dear Katherine. I need nothing else."

Katie looked at me with wide eyes. "She has never said those words before."

"You saved her because you loved her. So you can love her longer, feed her regularly, and maybe your blood will continue to heal her. For starters, take off the chains and bring her old-lady blood-servants to visit with. There have to be some somewhere. Did she like games? Painting? Poetry? Anything that might stimulate her and draw her away from the doilies?"

"Scrabble. She liked to play a word game called Scrabble."

"So get some humans in to play Scrabble with her." I thought a moment, and added, "And I'll get Amy Lynn Brown to feed her. That might help." Amy was a Mithran vampire with a rare and potent blood that brought young vamps out of the devoveo, the ten years of madness vamps went through when first turned. She might help Miz A, stuck between vamp and human.

"Yes," Katie said quickly. "I have heard of this Mithran. Thank you. If she helps, I will be in your debt. I will owe you a boon."

"Sure. Whatever." I backed out of the room. Hope was all I could give Katie, and that was more than humans ever had when faced with the decline of an elder. Hope was a fragile gift.

Glad I hadn't had to . . . do anything, I left the house, and Katie, and the woman she loved like a mother.

Anzu, Duba, Beast

First published in *WERE-*, an anthology from Zombies Need Brains (2016). It is in the timeline somewhere before Jane becomes the Dark Queen.

The note read "Jane, We will hunt. Ready yourself. We leave after dusk, Gee."

I hated orders. But I owed Girrard DiMercy—the vampires' Mercy Blade—a hunt, which he had won from me in return for information. Gee had a good memory, but his timing sucked.

I flicked the note against the fingers of my other hand, thinking. With vamps and their playthings, you have to be one step ahead, and thinking things through had proved better than attacking first and asking questions later.

Gee expected me to shift into something like a hawk or an owl and hunt at his side, while he shifted into the thing he really was under layers of glamour. If that happened, he'd set all the parameters and I'd be little dog to his big dog—earth bird to his Anzu. So far as I knew, the feathered Anzus were not native to Earth and had once been worshipped as storm gods. Big honking storm gods with claws, wings, a raptor's beak, and a bad attitude.

"Does Leo know about this invitation?" I asked, crumpling the note. Leo was the fanghead-vampire Master of the City of New Orleans and my boss. Gee's boss too, in a way.

The blood-servant-messenger's face broke into a smile that said I had asked a question he could answer. "Yes, ma'am. He knows. My master said, 'May your hunt be bloody. May you rend and eat the flesh of your prey.'"

"Well, crap." I had plans. I was spending a four-day weekend with my sorta-boyfriend, eating and sleeping and everything my heart and body desired, in bed. Plans. And the following Tuesday, I was flying to Asheville, North Carolina, to spend a few days with my BFF Molly, to see the ultrasound of her baby, the one where the doc tells if it's a boy or a girl. And then I was gonna pick up my Harley, Bitsa, from the repair shop in Charlotte. Finally. Big plans. Leo liked jerking my chain, and he would feel just peachy messing with my life.

But . . . it was only Wednesday. The hunt we bargained was for twenty-four hours. I should be back by Thursday night. Friday morning at the latest. I'd still have a few days to myself and my honeybunch, Bruiser. Plus Gee didn't know that I had aces up my sleeve. Well not exactly aces. More like jokers, both of them wild, cards that didn't belong in the deck of cards the Mercy Blade expected to deal. "Hmmm," I said.

The helpful human said, "Mr. DiMercy and the Master of the City have requested the courtesy of a reply."

"Did they, now. Well, tell them I said this." I shut the door in the servant's face. Turned the lock. Pulled my official cell phone, the Kevlar-cased one that allowed the Master of the City to track me, listen in on me, and read all my texts. It was daytime and he was probably in bed, but no way could I just take this. Vamps had a thing for pecking order. I couldn't refuse the invitation, but I was neither blood in Leo's fangs nor at the bottom of the suckhead hierarchy. I was the Enforcer to the MOC. This required more finesse than my usual hammer-and-machete style of retort.

I scrolled for Leo's number. It was listed under Chief Fanghead.

As a skinwalker—a supernatural being who can shape-shift into animals, provided I have enough genetic material to work with—I've actually flown, and not just in planes. But Gee might not know that. A familiarity with flight was my first wild joker.

Deep in the darks of my mind, my Beast huffed. *Eat order from Gee*, she thought at me. Beast didn't like it when I took the form of an animal other than hers—the *Puma concolor*—the mountain lion. She especially didn't like flying.

We made a promise, I thought back at her. I wandered to my room as I punched Leo's number.

Promises are stupid human things. We are Beast. Eat note.

Beast is opinionated, with a mind and feelings of her own. I had pulled her soul into my body in an act of accidental black magic when I was five years old, while fighting for my life. That was back in the eighteen hundreds. Skinwalkers, even the two-souled, can live a long time.

The cell trilled the first ring. Thinking that I would balk at the order, Leo would keep me waiting.

My second wild joker was a blue feather. Not so long ago, I came upon the glamoured body of a slain Anzu. She had looked perfectly human, albeit dead, except for the bright blue feathers on the floor around her body, downy and fluffy, catching the air currents and waving at me as if alive.

I hadn't intended to take a feather. I had forgotten I had stolen one. I'm guessing that Beast did it while I wasn't looking, a theft she had accomplished using my hands while my mind was occupied with more important things, which is scary in all sorts of ways. I hadn't discovered the feather until much later, in my collection of magical trinkets, but had never used it because taking the form of a sentient being was one of the darkest kinds of evil. Black magic. Unless I had permission. "Jane." Leo answered my call. "You have refused Girrard's invitation."

"Nope. But I need to talk to Sabina." Sabina was the woo-woo priestess of the Mithran-Vamps and she lived in the vampire cemetery. I'd need permission to enter.

There was a long pause, and I was sure Leo's brain was clicking through all the possibilities of why I'd need to talk to the eldest of the local Mithrans. "One moment."

A much longer pause later, I heard the sounds of movement and the *shush* of fabrics and soft-voiced instructions. The ambient noise changed and I knew I was being put on speakerphone, which made no sense. Until a voice spoke. "I am here," Sabina said.

I blinked and opened my mouth. Closed it. This saved me hours of afternoon traveling across the Mississippi and back. But I had to do this right. I drew on the scraps of vamp etiquette I had learned in my time as Leo's Enforcer and said, "Sabina Delgado y Aguilera, outclan priestess of the Mithrans, keeper of the sacred grounds, keeper of the Blood Cross, arbiter of disputes, deliverer of judgment, I have a question and . . . uh . . . and I wish you to determine if the path I wish to take is one of sin."

"If I say it is sin, will you take another path, my child?"

"Yes."

"Speak."

I took a deep breath. "I want to know if it's black magic for a skinwalker to shift into the same kind of creature as Gee."

The silence on the other end of the connection was total. And then, in the background, Leo laughed. It was one of those vampire laughs, the kind that writers and producers and other creators of fiction got right. Seductive, warm, enticing, like heated silk sliding across my skin. A laugh that reminds you vamps are predators, built to seduce and charm before they kill. The liquid notes cut off in midpeal, interrupted by a gasp of surprise or pain.

"You wish to know if this will turn you to the path of *u'tlun'ta*," Sabina said, "the evil your kind becomes when they eat of sentient flesh."

Chills raced over me. *U'tlun'ta* was what my kind became when we got old and went insane and started eating people. "Pretty much, yes."

"Is the Anzu alive, and will you eat her flesh?"

"No!" I looked at the blank screen in revulsion, put the cell back to my ear, and said, "No. She's dead and I didn't kill her."

"What do you use for the snake that resides in the heart of all beasts?"

The words Sabina used froze me for several heartbeats. They were skinwalker words, for a skinwalker concept. "A feather," I whispered.

"With this action, you walk the sharp edge of a blade between light and dark. You do not cross that edge into darkness, but if you slip, you may bleed."

"I'll try not to slip."

The call went dead. I dropped to my mattress. I had no idea if I'd be able to shift into an Anzu. No idea if there was enough genetic material in the core of the feather to allow me to shift. No idea if Gee would kill me at first sight. Or, for that matter, how much an Anzu weighed. Even though I'm a magical creature, I am still bound by the law of conservation of mass-energy. Taking on extra mass or leaving part of myself behind is dangerous. Flying by the seat of my pants never got any easier. No winged pun intended.

Stepping around piles of clothes and boots, junk mail, and a small stack of the *Times-Picayune*, I picked up my gobag and shook the grindy-low out of the folds. The neon green, kitten-sized thing spat at me and showed her steel claws. "Stop that," I scolded. She wrinkled her nose at me and leaped to my shoulder. Grindys kill were-creatures. It's their mission. This one liked nesting in my clothes. Absently, I patted her, and she cooed at me, nuzzling under my ear.

I packed a special gobag with a change of clothes, lightweight shoes, and my cell phone. I laid out the weapons candidates and then weeded them down, ending with a nine-millimeter, extra mags, six stakes: three ash wood, three sterling. And one vamp-killer—a steel-edged, long-bladed, silver-plated knife created especially for beheading vampires.

It's what I did, or had done, prior to taking the gig as Leo's Enforcer. I'd been a rogue-vamp hunter. And no way was I leaving home without the tools of my trade.

Packed, I left my room and skidded to a stop. My business partners were standing in the foyer just in front of my bedroom door. Alex Younger had a mulish set to his jaw, though at nineteen, he pretty much wore that expression all the time. Eli Younger, the elder Younger, stood with arms crossed, a speculative gleam in his eyes. I handed him the note.

He unclumped it, read the three sentences, and some infinitesimal hint of tension in his face relaxed. "Payback's a bitch," he said, giving the note back. And I wasn't sure who was getting paid back: me for making a bargain, or Gee for enforcing it. "I guess you won't be needing us?"

I shouldered my gobag. "I have no idea where we'll fly for this hunt, but Gee said something about elk or moose when this first came up, so I'm guessing somewhere far north."

Elk? Moose? Beast perked up. *Mooses and elks are bigger than cows?*

Pretty much, I thought back at her.

Do not eat note.

I chuckled and passed the grindy to Alex. To both of them I said, "Start your vacation early. Go play video games. Take in a movie, go visit Sylvia, start a new board game. Whatever. I'm sure I'll be somewhere way off, where there aren't many people. And then I have plans."

"Fly for this hunt?" Eli quoted me.

"Yeah," I said, going for casual. "Thought I'd try to shift into an Anzu."

Things took place behind Eli's eyes, things too fast to catch, but the tension was back, hiding beneath the skin of his face. "Watch yourself," he said, heading up the stairs to pack a bag. "It's hunting season in some northern states and it would ruin my weekend if you got shot out of the sky. I'd have to go find your body. Track down and kill whoever shot you. Spend the rest of my life in jail. Totally not in my long-term plans."

"What my bro said." Alex tossed me a box wrapped in brown paper and tied with twine. I caught it as he continued, "But my game's online, so I'll be here. Keep your official cell on, and wear that." He pointed at the box. "I can track you anytime you're within range of a tower or within range of a satellite, which should be nearly universal coverage these days. If you stay too long in one place, I'll assume you're in trouble and send Captain America." He thumbed at his brother.

Sunset had freshly bruised the skies. I was in the backyard, holding the Anzu feather, sitting on chilled boulders, naked except for my gobag (full of clothes, weapons, and equipment) and the necklaces around my neck. My gold nugget necklace and the new tracking necklace—looking like gold, but much more useful—and my gobag were extra loose. I took several slow breaths. Concentrated on my heartbeat. Let my shoulders droop. The first stars came out as the sky darkened. I dropped into a meditative state, reached down into the tip of the blue feather, into the snake that lives at the center of all creatures: the double helix of DNA, as understood by the Cherokee of my own time. My skinwalker magics rose, vibrant, luminous, the silver and gray of the Gray Between. I dropped deeper, into the dried flesh at the base of the feather.

Anzu genetic structure unfolded before me.

The DNA wasn't a double helix, common to Earth creatures. It was a tangled mass of strands, spun in circles, glowing like glass, pale blue and green light. One ovoid spot in the slowly spinning circle was denser and darker. It opened its eyes and looked at me. Unfolded slowly. The genetic structure was a snake, holding its own tail in its mouth. Ouroboros, the name came to me. The ouroboros focused on me, in the Gray Between, a place where energy and mass are one.

The snake opened its mouth. Let go of its tail. And struck. Before I could jerk away, snake fangs pierced me. Pain shot through me as if I had been hit with a Taser. I screamed. Bones bent. Darkness took me, blazing and icy.

I woke. The night was cool, humid, strangely scented. Chemical stinks of exhaust, gasoline, diesel fuel, coffee, food, and hot grease were familiar, but sights and sounds were different. The world was orange and silver, my vision so intense it was like looking through a scope, each line of light and shadow vibrant and intense. Something moved. My eyes found it instantly. Even in the dark, I could see individual hairs on a small mouse, hunting along the brick wall, hear its nails click on the concrete.

The music from a club several streets over was a booming din that hurt my ears. The house band's off-key rendition of "One Way Out" would have made the Allman Brothers cringe. A motorcycle engine in the distance was cutting out. Cars motored through the French Quarter. A jet overhead slowed, descending for landing.

I lifted my arms and my right fingers brushed the wall nearest, ten feet away. I jerked back, rolled to my feet, and looked around, my head swiveling and turning; I had shifted shape. A warbling sigh sounded in my throat as I took myself in.

I was blue and scarlet and some sort of glowing color that might only be seen in ultraviolet. The glowing feathers were up under my wings and on my belly. A darker version overlay the tips of flight feathers and tail feathers, glowing with black-light intensity to my bird eyes. My feet were long, with clawed toes, ten inches from back claw to longest toe claw, with glowing orange skin over knobby joints. My beak was pointed and curved, a vicious hook on the end. It matched my orange legs. I spread my wings again, carefully, inspecting sapphire flight feathers, with a band of scarlet near my shoulder and another on the back of my neck—which I could see with the head-swiveling thing I could do. I had a twenty-foot wingspan. I shivered, settling my feathers, and I could feel each one as it found its place. I was freaking gorgeous. I also wasn't hungry, which was a change from all my other shape-shifts. Usually I had to fuel my shifts with prodigious amounts of food, but something about the soft-lit magic trembling along my wings suggested that I had pulled the energy from elsewhere.

Beast can kill many mooses with claws and strong beak, she thought.

My hearing grew clearer, sharper. People were talking everywhere. A whiteout of noise.

In the house, I heard Eli speak, his voice soft and dangerous. "Bro." My head tilted that way. "You go out there and I'll deck you."

"But it's been an hour. Aren't you worried about her?"

"No." But there was the sound of a lie in the single word. Aw. Eli was concerned about me. I should razz him for it.

But . . . I was shaped wrong to go inside. I was shaped wrong to open a door. I imagined raising my huge foot and trying to grip the doorknob. I laughed at the vision, the sound warbling, unexpectedly loud. The back door opened on the last note. "Jane?"

I froze. But . . . parrots could talk. I warbled again, trying to say hello. It came out a rippling trill. As Eli and the Kid raced out, I tried again, and this time, there were words mixed into the warble. "Thish ish warble warble intersh-ting."

"Janie?" Alex asked.

"Babe?" Eli asked. And he started laughing.

I lifted a clawed foot and said, very distinctly, if slowly, "Crack your skull like walnut."

Eli shut up, but there was still laughter on his face. The Kid went back inside where I could hear him laughing his head off saying, "Big bird. Big blue bird. Holy shit." Laughing so hard he couldn't breathe.

I narrowed my eyes at Eli.

"Babe. I know you could crack my skull like a nut. But you're also funny-looking."

I swiped at him with my wing, which banged into the porch support with a *thump* that freaking hurt. I warbled a word that I never would have spoken in English. Which made Eli laugh harder. Midlaugh he drew a weapon and injected a round into the chamber. Aimed at me. I ducked. But he didn't fire.

Air whooshed down. Nearly knocked me off my perch on the cracked boulders. A foreign warble, an interrogative, carried on the air as I regained my balance. I turned to see an Anzu, smaller than my hundred forty-five pounds but a far brighter blue, alight on the brick wall surrounding the backyard.

He gleamed in my bird vision, ultraviolet blues and purples and a shocking ruby at shoulders and throat. He smelled like feathers, heat, and the down we line our nests with. He settled his feathers and cooed.

"Gee?" I managed.

"Jane? How have you . . . ?" His words wisped, warbling but crisp and clear.

"Ummm. I had a feather." The consonants sounded like sharp *tocks*, but it was understandable. Sorta.

"You took a feather from Urggggllllaaammmaaah's body." He tilted his head. "Did you ask her consent?"

"She was kinda dead. So I asked Sabina. She said it was okay."

"Did she?" Gee considered that. "This is acceptable to me. Come. We must hurry or our prey will escape us."

I cocked my head at my partner. "I'll call when I'm back." He nodded. I hunched down and leaped, hopping to the top of the brick fence surrounding the backyard. It was easier than I had expected.

"'Tis only the launch that is difficult," Gee said, trilling what might have been laughter, expecting me to face-plant. He threw himself into the air.

I know the glory of soaring, wingtips splayed, tail feathers twisting in subtle harmony with updrafts. And how to land, wings tilting just so, feathering down into a controlled fall with flight-feather positional changes and wing angle alterations, the variation slowing the descent, carrying me to a perch.

I gathered myself and dropped down until my knobby toes touched my breastbone, a position I might achieve in human form—if I broke my legs first. I leaped and threw out my arms. Wings. Air caught beneath me and I beat down. The long wingtips hit the earth and brushed brick before I managed a second stroke. And then I was lifting, wind in my face, air heavy, full of moisture. I tucked my feet, caught a rising thermal over the street, hot asphalt stink in my lungs. Beat downward again and again.

Below me, New Orleans glittered like diamonds, the Mississippi a black snake slithering through. I caught a second thermal and soared upward, Gee just ahead. I adjusted my flight position to his left, which decreased my wind resistance, things I knew by instinct and genetics. We rose higher, leaving the earth behind. Intermixed below us I could see circles and triangles in all the colors of the rainbow and long lines of something blue below the surface.

In this form, I could see magic far better than I could in human or

Beast-form. It was the magic of full circles and smaller workings. The long blue lines beneath the surface were . . . ley lines. I had never seen them like this. They were so beautiful they made my soul ache.

Anzu is good, Beast thought at me, sniffing the air. *Like Anzu.*

I cooed back at her.

I had no idea where we were going and I didn't care as my wings carried me, untiring, across the darkness of the world. Hours passed.

After midnight, Gee descended toward the faint lights of a small township. In the distance, ley lines glowed bright. They seemed like a nexus of some sort, a snarled clump of earth magics. I knew next to nothing about ley lines but they looked dangerous. Overloaded. As we spiraled down, they fell from view and I smelled freshwater lakes and streams, the richness of untouched earth and uncut forests, stone, crude oil, and much more faintly, the stink of old blood.

The scent grew stronger. A lot of old blood. And the stink of were, species unknown. It was a type I had never scented before. Not wolf, not big-cat, something more musky, though the scent was overpowered, fading even as we flew by.

Gee circled and dove, alighting on the edge of a house roof. I landed atop an abandoned car. The huge ranch house was in a clearing, at the end of a long empty road, the sharp piney scent of trees all around, trying to overcome the stink of vampire and human blood. The battle was at least a month old, the season having frozen, melted, and washed most of it away. What was left was the stench of fury, desperation, fear, and death.

I remembered Leo's words, quoted by the blood-servant who had delivered my invitation. "May your hunt be bloody. May you rend and eat the flesh of your prey."

Leo had known what Gee was taking me to hunt. "Well, crap," I said.

Gee trilled with mocking laughter.

Beast, who had been remarkably silent, growled to me, *Jane should have eaten note.*

I squatted down on the hood, chest to toes, and fluffed my feathers against the cold, trying to piece together the battle. My Anzu night vision picked out the entire house as if it was day, not darkest night, dried body fluids glowing as if they were under a black light.

The attackers came in through the front door, through the front windows, through the garage doors at the back, like a home invasion on steroids. The damage looked as if battering rams had been used, huge holes punched right through the thin wood of the garage door, the front door knocked off its hinges, the frame shattered. I leaped to the front door and leaned inside.

The fight had been bloody, but the invaders hadn't used guns. All the gunfire destruction was from the back wall and hallway, toward the entrances and windows. At least five vamps and ten humans had died in the parts of the house I could see. And so far as my senses could tell me, not one of the attackers had been injured. I still couldn't identify the species of were, their scent hidden beneath the gruesome stinks of death.

There were no bodies. They had been carried off and buried or burned. But the crime scene hadn't been worked up. There was no crime scene tape, no sharp smell of fingerprint powder, no carpet taken up for analysis. The house hadn't been cleaned. Something was really wrong here.

"You coulda warned me to bring a coat," I grumbled as we trudged down an unpaved road, pea gravel crunching beneath my thin-soled shoes. Suddenly, just bam, the road became paved, for no reason, but it was easier to walk, so I wasn't griping. I crossed my arms over my chest and hugged myself for warmth. Gee seemed unaffected by the cold, but glamour and shape-shifting were very different things. I was cold and starving. He wasn't. "Where are we? It's still fall and there's freaking snow on the ground."

Gee drawled, "We have alighted in Foleyet, little goddess, a tiny hamlet in Ontario, Canada."

"I'm not a goddess," I said by rote. I checked my cell. Nothing. Nada. No bars. *Ducky. Just freaking ducky.*

Gee turned off the road and around an abandoned building, the windows boarded over. The back door opened before us, light pouring into the night. The herbal stink of vamp and the rancid smell of old blood boiled out. I dropped my arms, leaped back a dozen feet. When I landed, I was holding a silver stake and a vamp-killer. Gee laughed, sly, mocking.

Holding the door was a vamp, a tribal woman, black-haired, black-eyed, tall and lean, similar to my own six feet of height and build, but she was utterly gorgeous. "It's our honor to receive the Enforcer of the Master of the City of New Orleans," the vamp said. "Why do you draw weapons?"

I slammed my weapons back into the sheaths. "Because I wasn't informed I would be meeting with Mithrans," I said, catching up with Gee. "Your species likes to play games." And I stuck out my foot, neatly tripping Gee over his own feet and mine, feeling better when Gee landed face first in the hard dirt and dusting of snow. "His kind does too. My apologies," I said to her. I drew on my training and said, "Additional apologies for my scent. It's considered a provocation by many Mithrans and that's unintentional." I took the two stairs and stopped in the doorway.

The woman leaned out and sniffed delicately before backing inside, her hands indicating welcome. "Namida Blackburn, of Clan Blackburn. We'd been told you smelled of predator, but all I detect is wind and storm clouds."

Interesting. "No insult was intended with the weapons," I said. I turned around and shut the door in Gee's face. My big-cat liked to play games too. Grinning, I faced Namida. "How may the Enforcer of the MOC of New Orleans assist you?"

The problem was simple, and not. Something were-tainted had attacked the local vamps, every full moon night for the last three months. In multiple attacks, three blood-families, vamps and their humans, had been decimated in remote areas, killed, eaten. The MOC of New York had declined to assist. The MOC of Toronto had declined to assist. The MOCs of Chicago, Montreal, and Minneapolis had declined. In desperation, the local vamps had contracted (for an outrageous sum) the werewolf clan of Wisconsin. The wolves had flown in, taken one sniff, returned the down payment, and flown out. The Montana wolf clan hadn't returned calls. The local law and the Royal Canadian Mounted Police had declined to assist, calling it a suckhead problem.

I could see why. The photos of what, in my part of the world, would have been crime scenes were horrible, and I had seen some pretty horrible stuff in my time. "I'm not familiar with many were-creatures. What do you speculate?"

"If it was a natural creature, then I'd say a small, deformed brown bear." She shuffled the photos and showed me a clear print, one in a pool of dried blood. "Eh. The claws are too long and wide but the paw shape is bear. They grow to a thousand pounds. This one's four hundred?" she guessed.

I frowned and pulled the borrowed flannel shirt and down vest tighter across me, swirling the caramel-apple-flavored moonshine she had poured for me. Moonshine was the drink of choice here, not New Orleans tea or coffee. "It smelled like were," I murmured, "but even at four hundred pounds, the mass-to-energy ratio is off for the average human-to-were conversion." And then things came together: the magical fuel for the shift to Anzu, the timing of this hunt. The sight of the twisted ley lines we had seen in the air. Magic here was messed up. So were physics. So were the weres. "Well, dang," I muttered.

"What?" she asked.

I waved it away. "Nothing. Leo wanted it taken care of, so I'll take care of it," I said, sipping the moonshine and finishing off the pile of smoked elk meat and fresh bread. It had assuaged the hunger from my shift. Anzu magic only worked to fuel the shift one way, and I had eaten enough for four humans, but Namida didn't begrudge my caloric needs. "I'm on salary. What does Leo get out of this deal?"

"We align with him." The words were spare, without emotion.

"Uh-huh." Namida and Leo had negotiated under the vamp system of parley, kinda like a peace treaty with the white man, with just about that much fairness. I'm Cherokee, so I know how "fair" works. "Fine. I'll need stuff, to include clothes, weapons, food, maps, and something that carries the weres' scent. Leo will reimburse you for my supplies."

Namida's eyebrows went up in amused surprise.

I canted my head, wearing a half smile. "He sent me in return for your loyalty. I say he pays for expenses. In the long run, you might have gotten the worst part of the bargain. Of course, if I get killed on this gig, then I got the worst part." I checked my cell phone, which displayed local time, so I'd acquired a signal at some point. I still had hours before dawn. If I was lucky, I'd find the weres' hidey-hole before morning, shift, and come back in my human form and shut them down. Nights were long this time of year.

"Thanks for the meal." I handed her my partial list of weapons, and her eyebrows went up again. Yeah. It was a lot. But if I could hit the were-creatures with fragmentation grenades, or their hidey-hole with the C-4,

I'd injure them enough to take them down, no matter how big they were. And I wasn't too particular about bringing in paranormal killers of humans alive and uninjured.

"Gee, you can come in," I said, without raising my voice.

The back door opened and Gee DiMercy minced in. He looked like a twenty-one-year-old Mediterranean man, delicate and pretty in the shadows, until he got a good look at our hostess and suddenly morphed into something older and harder. The shift looked like a trick of the light, but I knew better. Light didn't make you suddenly six inches taller and give you a three-day beard. Gee was now a black-haired, blue-eyed warrior, tough and elegant all at once, the kind of man who can track, shoot, and dress an elk without breaking a sweat, and dance a gavotte at a black-tie soiree in the evening.

"Madam," he said, taking her hand and bending over it in European old-world charm. "I am Girrard DiMercy. You are Namida? You are as beautiful as your name. Star Dancer, yes?"

The vampire tilted her head, amusement sparkling in her black eyes, with a hint of interest. "You speak Ojibwe?"

"Sadly, no. But I knew a Chippewa woman by that name, many seasons past. She was lovely, but never so lovely as you."

Namida laughed and looked at me. "I see why you tripped him." She slid her hand from Gee's. "Kill the things that are killing my people and you have my permission to court me, little misericord. Until then, you two need to get cracking, eh?" Namida went to the far corner of the abandoned room and brought back a plastic baggie. The closer she got to us the worse the stink. She held it out. "One of my people managed to hurt the attackers. These are three samples of blood that aren't human or Mithran. Good luck." With that, she walked past us and out the back. She paused there, one hand on the door, and said to us, "I'll have all this stuff"—she waved my list in the air—"by dawn." She closed the door behind her.

Gee stared after her, a hand on his chest, and murmured, "I am in love."

"Uh-huh." I pushed him to the door. Outside, Namida was gone, the night even colder. I opened the baggie and stuck it beneath his nose. Gee nearly threw up, but now we both had the scent. I placed the baggie beneath a rock on the top step. Between retches, he managed to say, "Duba. Kerit."

Using a cell phone provided by Namida, I wiki'd it and discovered that the Duba kerit was a cryptid, a creature never proved to be alive, also called Ngoloko, Nandi, Chimosit, and other less pronounceable names. It was a half-bear, half-hyena, and it was carnivorous, vicious, and nearly impossible to kill, except with silver. It also ate the brains of its victims—so, zombie were-bear-hyenas. Bears were solitary except for mothers and cubs, and hyenas lived in groups, making our prey an improbable were-hybrid. One that stank and scared the crap out of Gee. Just ducky. But we had its scent. Anzu had a great sense of smell and were able to follow a scent over very, very, *very* long distances. We walked out of town and I made Gee turn his back so I could strip, repack my gobag, and shift again. Back on the wing, we soared over Foleyet in widening circles. A snowstorm blew in, ice stinging my eyes. I discovered that I had nictitating membranes and the discomfort eased.

Within an hour, a hundred miles from Foyelet, we caught the scent of the were-Duba. Heard screaming. Gunshots—two shotgun blasts.

I tilted my head down and folded my wings.

"Jane! No!" Gee shrilled.

I dove at the surface. The piercing wind whistled sharp. Lights below were blurred by snow and driving wind. A dozen rounds sounded from semiautomatic handguns. I smelled the stench of blood, human, and Duba. The smell of wood smoke.

The screams cut off.

A large log cabin came into view, metal roof, smoking fireplaces, backyard fenced with tall planks. Cars inside the yard. Children's toys. A green-and-blue swing set.

I landed hard. The gobag slammed forward. My body rocked with momentum, wings slashing out to catch my fall. My wing hit something. Duba. It was holding a human head in its claws. It dropped the head and charged.

In the moment of attack, everything slowed, a thick, gluey bending of time: The falling snowflakes sluggish. The spin of the head the Duba had been chewing, its long, blond, bloody hair in a whirl, bearded face with two-inch fangs. True dead. My own body still tilting. My chest hitting the ground. The thing in midleap, hyena jaw and ears, bear nose and shoulders, hyena forelegs and bear back, paws a mix of the two. Bloody snout. Black-spotted tongue. Huge.

Scent and sight of a child in the broken window, her face filled with fear and fury. Smoking gun in her hands. The stink of silvershot in the were-blood.

The Duba's mouth opened, roaring. It leaped toward me.

I'd have died. But Gee hit the earth running, in human form, swords drawn. He attacked. Time crashed back over me. A tsunami of sound. The swords of the Mercy Blade whirled into the arcane forms of the vampire Spanish Circle—La Destreza. The attacking Duba flipped to the side in midleap and landed near me. Already bleeding. The swords were a cage of death that cut and cut and cut. The Duba bled, the silvered blades like acid in the wounds. The stink of silver and Duba blood filled the small area. The Duba screamed in fury.

Other Duba raced from the house into the black night, carrying various body parts. Dinner. One turned and looked back at us, roared. The reverberation beat on my ears like a bass drum.

I caught my balance and screamed an Anzu challenge.

Stupid. Stupid, stupid, *stupid*. Like I could fight in this form.

The Duba who had screamed raced toward me. I folded my wings and slid between two of the parked cars. And thought about my human form. So very different from the form of the Anzu, so banal and ordinary and ...

Prey, Beast thought at me. She took over the shift and forced me away, a clawed paw on my mind.

Bones shifted and broke and slid and cracked into place. Muscle reformed. Feathers became pelt. Beast screamed our challenge.

Leaped to the top of nearest car, long tail spinning for balance. Saw Duba attack Gee from behind. His head in her claws. She was mammal, and carried milk for young in long teats. The male that Gee had fought was dead on the ground. It had been her mate. Duba female was killing Gee.

Beast leaped again, rotating body and tail. Stretching out front claws. Landed on top of female Duba. Bit her head. Blood was hot and stinky. Like meat of old possum on hot road, long dead. Killing teeth scraped skull, holding. Reached around and sank claws into Duba throat. Ripped with claws, tearing and shredding flesh of throat. Blood flew. Duba let go of Gee. Mercy Blade fell. Bloody heap of flesh.

You can kill the Duba or help Gee, Jane thought. *Not both.*

Female Duba shook self like dog in water and raced for broken wood of hole in fence, black night beyond. Beast sank claws in. Duba leaped. Jagged spines of bloody wood bit into Beast flesh at shoulders and back. Should let go. But twisted forelegs in moves had seen Gee's sword make, claws biting deep.

Duba fell. Beast tore into throat, savaging flesh. Tore off Duba head. Spine cracking. Carried it to lighted side of fence. Raced to Gee. Dropped head. Gee blood everywhere. Gee could not heal self of injury. Needed Jane. Needed hands and—

"I got this."

Whirled. Paws and claws out, head down. Snarled. Saw little girl who stood at window. Little girl holding gun and rags and . . . with fangs. *Is not child.* Was small vampire female.

"Don't make me shoot you, eh?" She held up gun. Pointed at Beast. Beast snarled. Looked to Gee. Growled. "Go change shape," she ordered. "I talked to Namida Blackburn, so I'm unimpressed with the display of teeth. Go." She shooed with hands as if to send a kit out to play in grass. Beast snarled again and walked back to cars. Changed.

I was shaking badly, hunger pulling up through my body. It felt as if someone had reached into me, grabbed the soles of my feet, and pulled me inside out. But eating would have to wait. There were injured here, piled among the dead. And not enough saving hands. Using supplies given to me by the small vamp, working with those less injured, I bandaged and applied pressure, squeezed bags of fluid, forcing saline into the living, trying to stabilize blood pressure. It had been a long time since my emergency medicine class, and my skills were rusty. But the humans here were skilled, and together we kept the less horribly wounded alive until a vampire could feed them, heal the wounded with their blood or saliva. It was messy.

Dawn came before we could finish and I helped the vamps, their humans, and a badly wounded Gee into the narrow stair leading to the lair beneath the cabin. They would spend the day drinking from one another to heal. Seeing a vamp's lair was a rarity, usually a sign of great trust, but this time it fell under the category of emergency. I was alone when I closed the hatch beneath the kitchen table and heard the bolts ram home.

"Just me and the bodies," I said. Which was bad. Vampires who couldn't be saved had to be killed true dead or risk rising as revenants— mindless eating machines akin to Hollywood's worst zombies. That meant they had to be beheaded or burned to ash in the sun, thankfully not a job I had signed up for. I called Namida. She was old and powerful enough to be able to answer the phone after dawn, tell me where I was (at the Johnson Clan Home, which gave me nothing but a name, though every little bit helped). She promised human assistance and cleanup via heli-copter, which was pretty cool.

There were four tiny silver linings to the night: no one had died in the kitchen, the kitchen was fully stocked with meats of all kinds, the stove was hot, and so was the shower water.

I was gone by the time the helo showed up. I saw it through the low-lying clouds as I circled the Johnson clan holdings and found the scent I was chasing. The Duba. I beat my wings and followed the stink. I found their den a hundred miles or so from Foleyet. It wasn't far as the Anzu flew, but the den was underground. According to the Internet there were no mines in the area, but the opening into the low hillside looked like an old mine, ancient timbers shoring up the entrance, iron rails leading in, the area denuded of trees, spotted with rusted vehicles, buildings in disrepair. The site, whatever it was, had been empty for a long time. I circled, looking for two things—a back entrance and signs of magic. I spotted them both instantly. There were three back entrances, all stinking of Duba and death and broken magic. The mine centered on the crisscrossed ley lines, the jumbled, twisted energies I had seen earlier. It was a place of intense earth magics, where normal—assuming there was a normal—were-creatures had been altered, possibly on the cellular level, by the concentrated, warped energies.

Bad place, Beast thought at me. *Do not go in.*

Good advice, I thought back. The last time I went into a mine I nearly died. That wasn't happening again, especially into a mine flooded with sick magic.

Nothing about this hunt was proving easy. I flew back to the Johnson cabin, shifted, dressed, and checked my cell. I had a signal and placed a call to Alex Younger back home, set the GPS system in the new necklace to broadcast my position, and ate again. Around me, humans carried out the last rites offered to the vamps they served. It was bloody. Messy. Their grief awful.

I was tired. Too tired. Shifting so many times was using up reserves I didn't have and eating up more calories than I could take in, even with Anzu magic fueling half the changes. In human form, I ate. And ate. When I could talk, I questioned the visiting humans and found that Namida had sent what I needed. She had also sent a special human, Masie, who had mad skills with explosive weapons. Handy, that.

Leaving the others burying the dead and cleaning up, we two flew to the mine again, this time on the helo they had come in, the craft loaded with explosives. At each of the three back entrances, Masie set explosives, enough C-4 to bring down the tunnels and maybe half the mapped cave. The rumble and slam of explosive might was satisfying and properly climactic, dirt, smoke, and debris flying, the ground vibrating like a drum. There was no way to know if Masie had saved us the trouble of killing the weres. Not yet. We'd have to wait until dark. So we set up cameras at the remaining front entrance to track activity and took the helo back again.

At sunset, Gee and I landed at the mine and shifted shape. This time I had sufficient clothes, borrowed from the Johnson clan and smelling of vampire and unfamiliar humans, but better than the cold I'd have been otherwise.

"You found the den," Gee said, when I came out from behind a dilapidated building. He sounded surprised, which was mildly insulting. Deep inside, Beast hissed at him.

I said, "Yeah. Their den is a mine that angles into those ley lines we saw, which are twisted and knotted like a snarl of yarn. The energies coiled there are where I figure the Duba came from in the first place. Some werecreature holed up inside and was changed by the magics down to the genetic level. That change was passed along to the bitten progeny."

"Ah," he said, excitement lacing his words. "We will hunt them in the mine?" I could smell anticipation on him.

"Not exactly," I hedged. I would fulfill my deal with the Anzu to the letter and not one iota more. My plan was down and dirty but effective, and did not include exposing him or me to the gene-altering energies. Or an underground hunt.

"What do you mean, 'not exactly,' little goddess?" he asked, suspicion in his tone and body posture.

"Ummm . . . that?"

His scent underwent a distinct change at the sound of a helo, the blades cutting the air with a deep thrum. "What have you done?" he asked.

I didn't answer, but I didn't let him from my sight either.

"You steal the hunt from our bargain?"

The helo dropped through the cloud cover and hovered twenty feet overhead, the downdraft beating the ground, the thunder of the engine like a thousand drums. This was a big mother of a bird. From the fuselage, something dropped, stretched out in the air, and landed, softly as a hunting big cat. And then raced inside the mine. Gee hissed. I laughed.

"This was to be *our* hunt," he said.

"We hunted." When he started to object I said, "We flew. We tracked. You killed one. I killed one. I have officially completed my part of our agreement. We. Are. Done."

From the mine entrance I heard screams and yowls and sounds that might emerge from a hellpit.

His voice toneless, knowing I wasn't to be moved on this, Gee said, "There is no honor in this battle."

"No," I acknowledged, my voice as dry as his. "No honor at all."

"Why, then?"

"They bit humans. Those humans will likely become were-Duba. Were-Duba are worse than werewolves. Insane. Violent. Once they shift, they'll be killed." I frowned at the mine pit. "By their loved ones. Besides, hunting were-creatures has never been the job of a Mercy Blade or an Enforcer. It's the job of a grindylow and by the sounds, she's doing just fine."

Gee said, "When first we met, I thought you foolish, inept, and too gullible to work for the Master of the City. But you have grown shrewd, crafty as a cat in your dealings with the Mithrans." It didn't sound like a compliment but I didn't react. He looked up at the sky. "There are still moose and elk to be hunted and eaten, and a night of flying before us. Shall we?"

I looked at the mine and back to him. "Let me slip into something more appropriate." As the sounds of death echoed up from the mine and the last rays of sunset streaked the sky purple, I slid into the shadows, stripped, stuffed my clothes into the gobag, and found the shape of the blue-feathered Anzu. With the Mercy Blade on my tail feathers, I streaked for the sky.

Eighteen Sixty

A Prequel from Ayatas FireWind
from the World of Jane Yellowrock

First published in *The Weird Wild West*, an anthology (2015).
This short story takes place in 1860, and is written from the
point of view of Ayatas FireWind.

The *yunega* with the hairy face was feeding dry palo verde sticks to the
fire. The snap and spit of fresh wood was lost to the distance, but the smoke
rose and carried on the scant breeze, hot and tangy to Ayatas's cat-nose.
The cowboys he had been following had stopped early for the night, making camp at a watering hole to rest the horses and let the cattle drink and
graze. The watering hole and the small crick that carried the spring water
into the desert were muddy now with the deep prints of cattle and filthy
with cow and horse droppings, and man piss. *Ama*—the water—was no
longer drinkable.

Yunega always ruined *ama*. It was part of what they were, like a wolf
howled and bison grazed, white man ruined water. Always. *Lisi*, his grandmother, told him, "Never live downstream of a *yunega*. You will drink
their shit." And the old woman had laughed. He wondered if *Lisi* still
laughed today. He hadn't seen her since the dreams sent him into the
sunset, to find the wildfire wind he saw in his visions.

His stomach cramped with hunger, and he pressed down on it with
his mind. His people were accustomed to hunger. They did not allow it to
rule them, no matter how strong it became. He pressed his paws into the
stone ledge and his claws came out, white and pointed and sharper than
the claws of the panther that his father and his grandmother had most
often shifted into. Jaguar claws were better for what he had planned this
night. Jaguar speed and strength, jaguar jaws and killing teeth. Jaguar

scent that the horses and cattle would recognize and fear. Jaguar that was stronger in every way than the puma of his father's clan. That panther that had failed his father at the last and allowed him to die.

Down below, the small fire had caught, the flames a tight blaze in a ring of rocks. The white men were making biscuits in a tin pan, and heating beans that smelled sour. White men ate bad food and were often sick. It was beyond his understanding how a people who were so stupid had lived so long and conquered his own people, the *Tsalagi*, the Cherokee. *Lisi* said it was because his own people had been unwise and let them share the land. If his ancestors had simply killed them all, their lives would have been much better today, and they would still have their tribal lands in the green mountains.

The Black cowboys, *gvnagei*, took care of the horses and piled the saddles around the fire. They put the horses' legs into twisted rope hobbles, so that they could graze without getting away. This would make his job much easier. He chuffed with pleasure, the sound too soft to carry. His scent was downwind of them, and the grazing prey did not know they were stalked.

The day darkened and the cattle lowed, the sound plaintive and lonely. The sunset was a red smear on the western sky. The scarlet light was hard to see in his cat form—it was much easier to see greens and blues and the silver of gray—but he knew it was there. The western sky was always bloody here in the barren hills of the place *yunega* called Arizona.

He had been following the cowboys and their cattle for seven days now, and they were far enough into the desert to be at a good place for his ambush. They set a watch, a *gvnagei* on a hillock, but he was young and never looked into the hills around him. This was stupid, as Apache were known to raid here. Apache and Ayatas.

The men below him laughed and talked, the strange sounds carried on the nearly still air. Black men and white men, in two small groups, working the cattle but not working them together. Divided by tribe and skin color and *yunega* false superiority. *Lisi* had said the white man would eventually stumble and fall on his pride, but Ayatas had not seen signs of that, at all. He had believed her when he was a child, but *Lisi* had gotten foolish in her old age.

Back then, when he was a boy, living with her, he had been called *Nvdayeli Tlivdatsi*, or, as the white man would say, Nantahala Panther, but the Nantahala River was a thing of memory, lost to his people since the *yunega* sent them from their tribal lands into the territories. Panther had been his clan name and his father's beast. But the panthers had been hunted by the *yunega* until they were no more, in the mountains of their first home, and the *Tsalagi* had been driven away, in broken treaty, by lie-speakers of the *yunega* government. His childhood names were words of sadness and grief, and he had changed them after his spirit walk. He now called himself *Ayatas Nvgitsvle* or FireWind, for the raging fires he saw in his dreams. He had left *Lisi*'s house and searched for the winds for years but still had not found them.

Instead, he had been chased and shot at by *yunega* and by many of the tribes he had come across. The Apaches were the worst, and the best. They were fierce and they might stop the white men. If they killed him and yet destroyed the white man, he could die happy.

But on his search, he had found a dead jaguar, shot by a *yunega*, beheaded and skinned, for sale to fur traders. The carcass had been three days old and stinking. But Ayatas had defleshed the feet bones and boiled them clean, and added the toe bones to his bone necklace. Now he could become jaguar any time he wanted, anytime he could bear the pain and hunger of shifting and walking in the skin of the beast.

Along the tops of the hills, the wind picked up, the tingle of magic brushing along his spotted pelt. He chuffed, his whiskers moving as he scented the magic in the air, his ear tabs flitting. The woman was right on time. That was another thing he had found, the white woman with hair the color of the sunset. She called herself Everhart, which he had translated into Forever Heart, or *Igohidv Adonvdo*. Or perhaps she had meant Forever Deer, which would be *Igohidv Awi*, but sounded stupid. Deer were prey. The woman was not. The woman had magic, though different from his, and different from the magic of the shaman of his clan. She called herself a witch. She did things that she called workings. And she was his. His *lisi* would have wanted him to find a girl of the *Tsalagi*, but he had *Igohidv*, his Forever woman. This was much better.

As the magics grew, the wind picked up and whirled, making the leaves of the tree whisper, making the white man's fire dance. On the hillside, the *gvnagei* lookout stood up and stared out over the open space. His eyes tracked the wind, moving back and forth, as if he too felt the magic. But Ayatas knew that humans could not feel the magic of his Forever woman, and that no men of her tribe had magic. The *gvnagei* shielded his eyes from the last of the dying sunlight and focused in on the ledge where Ayatas lay.

Perhaps he was wrong. This man might have different, dangerous magic.

The wind shifted and the smoke whirled and swept into the cowboys' eyes. Sparks flew and swirled among the leaves in the tree. It was drought season and any small sparks were a danger. He saw the tree catch fire; even from so far away, he could hear the *whoosh* as it caught and blazed. The men screamed and began to pick up camp, moving away. Ayatas chuffed with laughter. The smoke swirled again and careened among the horses, carrying sparks that bit and stung. They were too small to do real harm, but the pinprick fires hurt like a cowboy's spiked rowels and the horses threw up their heads and snorted, lashing their tails. One whin-nied, its eyes rolling white. The others picked up its fear. One began to buck and lost its footing in the twisted ropes that tied the horses. It fell, screaming.

The wind whirled faster, up along the ledge where Ayatas lay, picking up his scent before whirling down into the gulch. The smell of jaguar and fire reached the cattle, and the mindless beasts stomped and lowered their heads, rolled their eyes, seeking out the dangers.

The *gvnagei* lookout pulled his gun, a six-shooter, and stared right at Ayatas's ledge. But the man was too far away for a reasonable shot. He would have done better to have a rifle like the one that Ayatas had taken from the dead body of an Apache who had challenged him to combat.

Ayatas pushed up to a sitting position, certain that he was now hidden in the shadows of the falling sunset. Below him, in the growing darkness, the white men were fighting to keep the horses calm. The cattle stomped. A mother was nudged away from her calf and she bellowed a warning. She raced up a short rise and lowered her head. With one horn, she gored a steer in the back. Two other steers jumped and hopped on four feet, bouncing in fear at the confrontation. Dust rose and added to the shadows. He growled, the sound coming from deep in his chest.

The cattle started bucking, the delicious scent of their fear growing fast.

They split, one group galloping into the sunset. The other beginning a constricted, spiraling race that grew tighter and tighter as the panicking cattle followed the circling female, frantically searching for her calf. Ayatas raised his head and called, the vibration sending the cattle into a frenzy, stomping hooves and goring horns. The smell of blood and panic rose on his woman's magic wind. Ayatas licked his jaws in hunger.

He called again and raced down the cliff, his spots hiding his movement. A gunshot sounded. Men screamed. Horses screamed. On the wind, Ayatas heard his woman's laughter.

He leaped down twenty feet, as *yunega* would calculate it, and landed with his front paws together, pushing off with his back paws as they touched down. He leaped on a young steer, his weight driving it to its knees. He caught its windpipe between his fangs and clamped down. Instantly the steer's back legs buckled and it fell. Ayatas dragged him into the small cave he had prepared before the white men arrived. Concealed behind brush, it had remained hidden. The steer struggled feebly and tried to get up. Ayatas held tight, and the steer flopped over. He held the killing bite for longer, to make certain that his dinner was dead. Then he ripped out its throat and gulped down its blood, his hunger, carefully held in check, instantly freed. He gorged on the soft tissue and blood, eating until the pain he had been fighting dissipated. He needed to eat more, much more, but his woman's magic called to him and he raced out of the small depression in the rock.

In the gathering dark and confusion, he saw that several horses had broken their hobbles and raced into the night. A group of men on the other horses raced after the cattle. The white men would chase the larger cattle group first. Ayatas followed two horses, the man part of him herding them toward his woman.

When the moon was full overhead, throwing black and white shadows, he chased them into the small arroyo where she had camped. His woman caught them with her song. She gentled them, as she had him. And she led them all to water.

Later, he followed his own trail back to the small cavern and pulled his kill out of the bushes and deeper into the desert. He ate. In the morning, he would carry the carcass back to the woman and shift back to human. Together, they would butcher and smoke the rest of the meat and then they would ride on, looking for the wildfire winds of his dreams.

Wolves Howling in the Night

A Story of Ayatas FireWind

First published in *Lawless Lands: Tales from the Weird Frontier*, an anthology from Falstaff Books (2017). Time: 1879.

Ayatas touched his horse's flank with a heel and guided him closer to the mount ridden by Etsi, his Everhart woman. They had been on the trail for days in the summer heat, with limited water, only enough for them and their mounts to drink sparingly. They had run out of even that twelve miles on the south side of Eagle Tail Mount and Dry Wash, which lived up to its name. The summer sun had baked the land dry. If they did not reach the town of Agua Caliente by nightfall, their plight would become desperate, yet Etsi still laughed, saying she smelled ripe, her scent as strong on the air as his own.

The town they hoped to reach had abundant water, enough to have a bakery, saloons, a laundry, a livery, a feed-and-seed shop, a half-dozen seamstresses, a school run by a woman from back east, and two dry-goods stores. The newsletter they had read when they shared a campfire with a wagon train said that an inn was being built in Agua Caliente, "with a bathhouse," as Etsi kept reminding him, a bathhouse with hot water that rose from the ground, from hot springs. Etsi would get a hot tub-bath with soap, as her own people, the *yunega*, the white men, bathed.

He would wash out back with the other people of color—the Mexicans, Africans, and Indians—though Ayatas might prefer to bathe in the Gila River, near the town, if *Indian* meant Apache or Pah-Ute. The *Tsalagi* and Western tribes did not make peace together, and fighting would anger Etsi. His red-headed woman's temper was hot like fire, and his heart had ached the few times she had turned her anger toward him.

Tonight, Etsi would sleep in a real bed, and Ayatas would bed down with the horses or out in the night, under the stars, knowing that if she called him with her magic, he would hear the sound of her summons on the wind.

Beneath him, the horse stepped higher and his head came up, moving better than the tired beast had all day. "I smell smoke," Ayatas said. "And water."

"Hallelujah and praise the Lord," Etsi said, her voice hoarse. She tied the small pouch of *dalonige'i* into her skirt to hide it. White men traded for gold, gave news for gold, stole land for gold, killed for gold. She was wise to keep it out of sight.

Together, as the sun slid into the scarlet west, they studied the town from a small rise. Agua Caliente was mostly low adobe houses and buildings, a few stone-built ones, and some dried-brick buildings, all flat-roofed and mud colored. Wood smoke billowed in low waves down the main street, curling and mixing with the dust clouds. Horses and mules, saddled or loaded with packs, stood, tied to hitching posts here and there. A scrawny, short-legged dog trotted down the street, her teats dragging on the dirt. A wagon rolled out of town. A Mexican woman with a white head scarf and dark skirts carried a heavy bundle into an alley and disappeared. The sound of a piano plinking and men singing echoed down the street.

They let the horses have their heads, and the tired animals moved down toward the town. The noise got louder. Dogs barked. Chickens ran across the main road and under a bakery. There was much shouting from laborers, still working in the town, using the last light in the cool of evening. He spotted stonemasons, bricklayers, adobe plasterers, and tile layers constructing the inn that would make the town great and bring in more white people. And drive out more tribal people and people of color. The walls were rising, arches appearing where windows and doors would go. Heavy beams were in place to hold the roof. The wind spun and changed direction, bringing the smell of the town to them.

The horses found a spill of water and a clay-lined pool outside the bathhouse. The puddle stank of soap, white men, and sulfur, but the mounts drank with desperation. "Son of a witch on a switch," Etsi muttered. "I forgot how noisy and stinky towns are." The stench of outhouses, saloons, fires burning, and food cooking was overpowering after so long in the wild.

"White men always stink," he said, keeping his own thirst at bay until he could get Etsi and the horses to safety.

"Yes. Well. Don't forget," Etsi said, her tone telling him more than she realized, speaking of pain and long-held anger. "It's only a game we play to keep you safe."

Ayatas grunted. The game claimed that he was her servant instead of her man. That he worked for gold instead of searching for his dreams. But Ayatas would pretend many things to keep Etsi, which meant My Love in the tongue of The People, safe. His red-haired woman, who had gone by many names as they traveled, was possessed of a fiery nature, changeable as the wind, and was constantly searching out danger. She had been born Salandre Everhart, but when she ran away with him, she had changed her name to *Igohidv Adonvdo*, or Forever Heart, in *Tsalagi*. Now, after many years of travel and adventures, his fire woman used a different name in each town, but she was always and forever his Everhart woman, and Etsi.

He pulled the horses away before they could take in enough to grow sick and jumped back into the sheepskin saddle. The mounts knew they would be fed now and trotted on into the town and up to the sheriff's office. The man with the badge waited, his guns in clear view, an old hunting rifle in his arms, and a six-gun at his hip. They reined in the mounts in front of the man, and Etsi slid from the saddle to the ground. She groaned with pain on landing in the dusty street, knees stiff from all day in the heat, on horseback. Ayatas landed behind her, silent.

"Good evening, Sheriff," she said, approaching him and smoothing her skirts. His Everhart woman did not offer her hand, but the sheriff looked pointedly at her left hand and the thin gold band that could be seen beneath her dirty gloves. "I'm Mrs. Everhart, reporter for the *Arizona Daily Star*, out of Tucson."

"A woman reporter?" The sheriff spat, the stink of tobacco strong on the air. He transferred his sharp gaze to Ayatas. "Women can't work for newspapers. That your young buck? He don't look like Apache or Ute."

"He is Cherokee, from back east," Etsi said with asperity, "and he's my guide. And women most certainly can be reporters. Watch your tongue, young man. You may be sheriff, but you are not above manners."

Etsi was no longer a girl, but a woman now, sharp-tongued and stern, and she knew how to stop men from showing disrespect. They had been together since 1860, and she had grown more fiery with each passing year.

The sheriff laughed, the sound like sand scouring rock in a low wind, and when he spoke, it was with a tone of insult and amusement. "Manners. Yes, ma'am. I'll mind my manners." Before Etsi could respond he added, "You looking to take the baths and find a bed, Old Missus Smith can help you. Your guide'll have to sleep in the stables with the other animals or outside the city. We don't risk our scalps letting Injuns stay inside after sundown."

"You have nothing to fear from my guide, Sheriff."

"I ain't a-feared a' no redskin."

"Hmmm." Her tone suggested that he lied. The sheriff's eyes narrowed. Etsi continued, "I'm sure he'd rather be as far from the white man as he can get. If you'll direct me to the boardinghouse and the baths and point my guide to the livery?"

The man with the tin star on his chest gave directions. Etsi turned to Ayatas and gave him six small coins, saying things she did not need to say, to appease the sheriff and to fulfill their roles. "Aya, take the horses to the livery and purchase their care. See if they will also feed you and let you sleep there. If not, go to the back door of the bakery and buy some dinner, and then bed down outside the gates."

Ayatas took the coins and nodded. "Yes, ma'am. Thank you, ma'am." Gathering the reins, he led the mounts down the street, following the scent of manure and hay more than the lawman's directions. With his predator's senses, he could feel several pairs of eyes on him as he walked, so he kept his shoulders slumped and his head down as befit the station of servant instead of the warrior and skinwalker he was, a beaten man instead of a man of much power and magic. It galled him. But the white-man world was not kind to people of color.

He had spent much of his youth in the Blue Holly clan house, under the thumb of his *uni lisi*, grandmother of many children, in the Indian Land of the Western Cherokee. He had hated being with the women in the summer or winter houses, but with no father, and with the obstinacy of his grandmother, he had no one to take him in among the older men. Until his *uni lisi* taught him to shift into an animal when he was fifteen and he had learned to dance. Then he had many offers to join the hunters and many offers of marriage from the women, but he had refused them all. He had changed his name to *Ayatas Nvgitsvle*, or FireWind, for the raging fires he saw in his dreams.

"Pride," *uni lisi* had said. "Foolish and stubborn pride."

"Dreams," he had responded. "Dreams of fire and wind and magic," such as his people had long ago lost to the white man. He had left the Indian Land.

At the livery, the white man and his two half-white sons sold him two stalls and enough feed for three days. They helped him to brush down the mounts, check their feet, and untangle their wind-tossed manes. One of the boys was good with animals, discovering a swollen place on the cannon bone of Etsi's mount. The older man applied an herbal liniment and wrapped the limb. Ayatas gave the boy great praise. White men needed praise to feel worthy. *Tsalagi* warriors needed no such words to know their worth.

The man and his sons gave him permission to sleep in the hayloft, sold him a meal of dried meat and cold beans, and sent Ayatas to the back of the bathhouse, as he had suspected. His bath consisted of a bucket of water he poured over himself, a sliver of soap in hand. It cost a penny, but the water was clean and pure and still hot from the springs.

As he dried off, Ayatas heard two white men talking within the men's private room of the bathhouse. They talked about a bird that was to be sold. He thought nothing of it, except that the dove would be in need of cleansing, which he thought was strange. Etsi would likely understand and would explain it all to him, and perhaps in the telling, she would find a good story to write for the newspapers back east, for his Etsi was a newspaper reporter as she had claimed.

Smelling much better, dressed in his clean canvas pants, wool socks, and a cotton shirt, Ayatas bedded down in the small loft. Tonight he slept on layered sleep rolls and blankets and his serape, atop fresh hay. His pillow was his scarf, his gun and skinwalker necklace by his hand.

He slept well until about three a.m., when a noise woke him, the squeal and creak of a buckboard with a wheel that rubbed, needing a wheelwright. Above the rubbing he heard a woman's muffled sobs. The sound of a ringing slap. The woman fell silent.

Ayatas rose and secured his clothing, hiding his weapons, tying his moccasins. He crept down from the loft to the stall where his own mount slept, standing, head low, at the window that looked out onto the street. A wagon rolled by, a white man driving, two white men, a Mexican, and a Black man in the bed. A woman was propped on a feed sack, her hands tied, her mouth tied with a gag. In the bright light of the moon, he could see that she had been beaten. Some of her clothing had been torn away.

Abuse of women was a foreign thing among the *Tsalagi*. Had a man tried that on *uni lisi* or *elisi*, his mother, the women would have removed the parts that made him a man and put him to work in the fields. But Ayatas knew that white men were often cruel to women.

The buckboard rolled on, and Ayatas thought on what he should do. His Everhart woman would have intervened, even at the risk to her own life, believing that her magic could protect her from anything. It was hard to keep her safe from her own actions, but he could not keep this from her even to keep her safe.

Ayatas secured his long hair, rolled out the window, and landed silently on the dirt. Keeping to the shadows, he followed the buckboard to the biggest saloon. Etsi had taught him to read and write, and the sign over the door read PEACOCK SALOON. The words FARO and DANCEHALL were beneath it. Faro was a card game. Dancehall meant that women danced with men and then pleasured them for money, though the women seldom got to keep much of their earnings. It was a hard life, and the women died young and sickly. And . . . the women were called soiled doves.

Ayatas recalled the conversation between the men in the bathhouse, the words about a bird that was to be sold and the dove that would be in need of cleansing. Were these men selling the woman to the saloon owner? Slavery was now illegal, but women were often kept as sex slaves, and the law did nothing to stop it. Ayatas remembered the sheriff and his insulting tone to Etsi.

The buckboard stopped in the street. Ayatas climbed the rickety stairs of a building nearby and crawled across the flat roof to the next building, and then to the Peacock. He heard the sound of coins clinking. Gold made a dull sound, silver clinking sharply. The woman was crying behind her gag, making a single sound over and over. He thought it might be "No, no, no . . ."

He spotted an open shutter on the back wall of the saloon and dropped from the roof to the ground. There was no glass here to bar the way or to stop a breeze from cooling. Ayatas raced to the window and vaulted inside, landing on the dusty wood floor in the dark. Silent. The smell of alcohol assaulted his nostrils, a sneeze threatened, but he forced the urge away, staying crouched, allowing his eyes to adjust. Gray shapes resolved out of the dark—large whiskey and beer barrels, a side of smoked hog hanging from a hook overhead, bags of flour and cornmeal. He was in a storage room. Still stealthy, he moved through the room and out the door to find himself behind the bar in the saloon's main room, the barkeep asleep on a blanket on the floor, snoring.

Ayatas crawled to the opening and studied the main room of the saloon, which was lit with two lamps, one on either side. A piano was on one wall. Rough-hewn round tables made from broken wagon wheels with boards atop them were everywhere. Stools and a few chairs were scattered. A small stage took up the space beneath the stairs to the upper floor. On it stood a man, part Mexican, wearing a fancy suit and two guns on his hips. There was an air of ownership about him, the saloon owner, surely. He watched as the two white men carried the bound woman up the stairs. She was kicking, fighting, screaming behind the gag. Ayatas could not help her. He remained in place, watching, learning the room the woman was placed in—room seven at the hall's end. The white men carried her in and shut the door. The sound of blows and muffled crying followed.

The other men were each poured a shot of whiskey by the saloon owner, who said, "Turner, you sure—"

"I'm sure." Turner was slim with a curling blond mustache and blond hair slicked back. His clothing was expensive, his boots shiny. He pulled two cigars, offering one to the saloon owner, and snipped off the ends with a small silver clipper. The two men lit their cigars from a taper placed in the flame of the nearest lamp.

"If you want her back," the saloon owner said, "I'll make sure she comes away a more contrite and pliable female. The women sold through this house are valued up north and eager to pleasure a man."

Turner said, "I've had enough of her sass. And her money's mine now, so I don't need her. According to the sheriff, law's on my side."

Turner was the man who had held the buckboard reins. Ayatas studied him the way he studied prey when he was a jaguar. Turner had delicate hands, uncalloused with rounded nails. He was dressed in city clothing, the kind Ayatas had seen in San Francisco, worn by the wealthy. This man had taken his wife's property, her gold, and had sold her into abuse.

The saloon owner was part Mexican, a handsome man with a pock-marked face. He had grown wealthy on the labor of women slaves. Ayatas had heard the words himself. He would tell his Everhart woman. They would decide what to do.

Ayatas stayed for an hour, listening to the men talk. Long enough to learn the name of the stolen ranch. Carleton's Buckeye Springs Ranch. When the men left, Ayatas tried to get into room seven, but the door was locked and he did not have a key. So he disappeared into the shadows, following the buckboard to the ranch. It was only three miles away, a short run.

Dawn came quickly, and Ayatas had already checked the horses when the liveryman and his sons arrived. The sore place on the leg of Etsi's mount was better, the heat pulled out by the liniment. The horses' piss smelled healthy, and their eyes were bright despite the days with low water rations. The liveryman began shoveling out the stalls, giving the horses hay, feed, and fresh water. Knowing that the mounts were cared for, Ayatas wrapped his scarf around his waist to help hide the weapon he wore strapped to his leg and went in search of the inn. His Everhart woman was still asleep, so he left word with the small Mexican child who came to the door, and sought out the bakery. He approached the back door and knocked.

A large woman came to the door and looked him over, head to foot. Her skin was white; her lips were full and fleshy. She smelled of wood smoke, sweat, and sourdough, and she mopped her face with an apron she pulled up. It was already warm in the desert air, and the heat in the room where she toiled was stifling from the wood-burning stove and oven. She dropped the apron and heaved a breath. "Not Apache. Not Ute. What are you?"

"I am a man."

The white woman blew out a breath. "A traveling storyteller, full of comedy. What tribe, injun?"

"*Tsalagi* or *Chelokay*. Cherokee as you might say the tribal name."

"Long as you ain't Apache, I don't care who you are. Apache killed my father when we first came out west." She waited, as if to give him time to think and speak. Ayatas shrugged with his shoulders as the whites did. White men had claimed and invaded lands that belonged to others. The people who lived there had fought back. People on both sides died. The white man was winning that war. There was nothing else to say, and the white woman would not understand his reasoning. Those who grieved seldom did.

"You want food?" she asked gruffly. "I got fresh loaves coming out of the oven shortly. Fifty cents for a fresh wheat loaf. Yesterday's bread is half that, and I got one left. Dime for a square of cornmeal." She held out her fingers in a square to show him the size. "I can toast the bread, and I got eggs I can skillet-cook, mix 'em up with yesterday's beans, five cents for three."

"Your prices are low."

"I charge three times that for the ranch hands." She pulled off her kerchief and finger-combed her hair. It was gray and wet with sweat. She leaned against the jamb of the door, resting. "Ranch hands pay more for my cooking. People like you eat cheap."

People like him. Nonwhites, so long as they were not Apache. Or perhaps men of any race who had bathed and were not drunk. Ayatas tilted his head, wanting clarification. "You charge more to feed a white man?"

"Cowboys are always drunk and causing trouble, so they pay more. You have a problem with that, I can charge you more too."

"No." Ayatas waved one hand between them, as if to wave away the smoke of a fire. "Cornmeal bread and three eggs with beans. Yesterday's, please." He pulled the necessary change from a pocket that held little and gave the coins to the baker.

"Coming up."

"Thank you, baker of bread."

"Name's Mrs. Lamont." She shut the door in his face.

Ayatas sat on the stoop to wait and to think about women and their power in the world. They were often weak because of childbirth and because of the blood they shed each month to bring life. But when they were no longer burdened with children, they were stronger than any man. The baker, Mrs. Lamont, ran the only place for many miles where the men of the land could go to buy bread. The baker would be a woman with influence and power in the town, even though the male leaders would not know it. His mother and his grandmother had been such women of power. He had been gone from Indian Territory many years. He did not know if they still lived, but he remembered the lessons he had learned at their feet.

The door opened and Mrs. Lamont handed him a tin plate wrapped in a frayed cloth. Ayatas took the offered food and bowed his head. "Thank you, Mrs. Lamont."

"Leave the cloth on the hook by the door and the plate on the step when you're done. The chickens'll peck it clean." She shut the door, and Ayatas sat back on the stoop. He ate with his fingers, and the food was delicious, filled with salt and spices and red peppers. When he was done, he wiped his hands clean on the cloth, hung it on the hook, and placed the pan on the stoop. As soon as he did, four laying hens and a small rooster raced out from beneath the house and attacked it, pecking at each other as often as at his leavings.

Hunger satisfied, Ayatas decided to look over the town. It was the biggest place he and his fire woman had been to since they went to San Francisco. He had been lost there. Surrounded by wealth and filth, amazing things to buy, countless new things to eat, many different ways to live, and dead men lying in the streets. He never wanted to go back. He and Etsi stuck to the smaller settlements where she could gather information and send it to the newspaper that paid her half pennies for the words she sent in. The stone-and-adobe town of Agua Caliente was small and cleaner than most places white men lived. Someone here knew how to build a decent latrine, and the abundance of hot water meant clean people and clean clothing. The hot springs meant wealth would come.

A prospector riding a mule, leading a heavily laden donkey, passed him at a slow walk, tin pans tied to the pack on long tethers, clanking softly. A woman wearing a starched blouse beneath a well-mended waistcoat and full skirts swept by him, carrying a satchel. A cowhand lay in a pool of vomit in a small alley, his pockets turned out. Three children passed, faces clean, clothes mostly so, metal lunch tins dangling, heading for school. He passed the church, its shutters closed; the saloons, which stank of piss, alcohol, and vomit; the site of the inn, walls rising as stonemasons and bricklayers were already at work, trying to get as much of the day's construction completed as they could before it became too hot to labor. They would sleep in the heat and return to work in the cool of evening.

He had the layout of the town in his mind, a mental map that told him where the wealth was, where the power was, and where the poor and the victims were. He returned to the inn and sat in the street to wait, as was expected of people of his race. Fortunately, a small screwbean mesquite tree had grown up, and it cast some shade.

"Are you sleeping, Aya?"

"Dreaming of you, my *Igohidv Adonvdo*." Ayatas didn't open his eyes but let a small smile cross his face.

"And if I had not been alone and you had been overheard?"

"The white men in this town would have dropped me into tar and then rolled me in the feathers of Mrs. Lamont's chickens. I would have shifted into my jaguar to heal. And then I would have killed them all." He opened his eyes and smiled up at her. Her face was no longer as taut as when he first met her, her eyes not quite so brilliant blue, her hair not so fiery, but she was the most beautiful woman he had ever seen. Though she always wore a hat, her face was tanned and lines fanned out from her eyes. She smelled clean again, and her hair was down in a long braid. "Beautiful woman, such torture would have been worth this single vision," he murmured.

"Oh, pish." But she blushed like the girl he remembered. "Come. Walk with me. What have you discovered? The wind told me you have been out and about for half the night."

Her magic was the power of the air, and it would have told her. Ayatas stood, his body long and lean, lithe as the day he left the tribal lands. He took his place a little behind her, his hands behind his back. Etsi wore her dark blue dress and matching short jacket with a white shirt. She carried a matching dark blue parasol and wore a wide brimmed hat against the sun. Her gloves had been washed overnight and were nearly white again. Her leather shoes scuffed the earth, and her skirts swung with the motion of her strong legs. She smelled of the blue flowers she loved, lavender.

Etsi said that barring accident, she was likely to live to one hundred years of age, which meant that if he could keep her safe, they might be together for many years. While he . . . Skinwalkers didn't age as others did. He still looked like a young man of twenty years.

Speaking softly, he told her about the men at the baths. About the captive woman and her vile husband. He described the Peacock Saloon and the location of room seven. He shared about Mrs. Lamont. About the workers and the inn. Described the ranch and the town to her.

"Dreadful," she murmured when he was done. "But it will make a wonderful story."

His Everhart woman sent in stories of the Wild West to the newspapers of the east, using the name E.V.R. Hart, stories that were a strange mixture of truth and lies and were called fiction. When the newspapers published her stories, Etsi made much money. E.V.R. Hart had been approached by a publisher about writing a novel set in the Wild West, and she had begun the story. His best memories were the two of them at the fire at night, while she read the day's words aloud.

"Did you hear the name of the rancher's wife?" she asked.

"He called her Amandine. His name was Jessup Turner."

"Interesting names for the owner of Carleton's Buckeye Springs Ranch. I postulate that Amandine's father owned the ranch, and when he died, he willed it to his daughter. And when she married, the husband assumed ownership. Let's take a walk out toward the ranch before the sun is too hot so that I might visit my dear old friend Amandine. Then perhaps I'll stop by Mrs. Lamont's bakery and ask some questions."

"Perhaps," Ayatas said, amused.

"You have your gun?"

"It is strapped to my leg inside my pants, hidden beneath my shirt and scarf." Ayatas wore his shirt outside his pants in the *Tsalagi* warrior way, tied with a scarf that could double as a turban, and could be tied about his neck when he shifted shape, so he might carry his clothing to dress in when he shifted back. Today, he wore boots, which they had purchased in San Francisco, but his moccasins were tied in his scarf, and his skinwalker necklace was tied around his neck, strung with the teeth and bones of predators. Should he need to shift, to fight, or heal, he could choose from among several big cats, a gray wolf, and a large boar. He preferred the jaguar. The cats were strong and swift, though rare in the desert. As they walked, the heat continued to rise, and sweat trickled down his spine and darkened Etsi's clothes.

It was near ten a.m. when they reached Carleton's Buckeye Springs Ranch. The house was long and lean, with thick adobe and stone walls and narrow windows that kept out the heat. There were arches in the Spanish style around the wraparound tiled porch and plants in large clay pots. He called to the house, and when the door was opened, he stepped into the shade and passed the small child the business card of his Everhart woman. The card summoned a small, pretty, dark-skinned woman in an apron who told them that Mr. Turner was out on the range.

Etsi pulled on her magic.

A small dry whirlwind sprang up, bright and hot, and entered the house. A moment later Etsi's words and magic had convinced the house-keeper that she was an expected visitor. The girl told Etsi a tale of woe about the troubles of the ranch as she let them into the coolness to wait.

A man took a fast horse to find Mr. Turner while the maid brought tea to the study where Etsi insisted she be allowed to wait. Ayatas was given a metal cup of water and sat on the cool floor in front of the closed study door, the place a man of his color and race would be expected to wait. In reality, he was his Everhart woman's lookout and guard while she searched the office and desk for important papers and evidence of Amandine's past.

A little over an hour later, he heard horse hooves coming at speed. He scratched on the door. Etsi opened it a crack and said, "This man is a rascal and a scoundrel. I think he'll make a wonderful story for back east. I'm ready to bring him down," she said.

"You will be cautious," he murmured as the sound of boots rang on the front tile stoop.

"I most certainly will not."

Ayatas sighed. Etsi made a harrumphing sound and closed the door. Moments later, the man who had sold his wife entered and stomped to the back of the house to wash up and to use foul language to the pretty house-keeper. And to hit her. Ayatas placed his hand on the hilt of his knife, ready to help the woman, but Turner slammed a door and stomped toward the study, Etsi's business card in his hand. The white man ignored him as trash. It galled Ayatas when fools thought him unworthy of notice, but it was a useful tool.

The door opened, and Turner started to speak, but Etsi demanded, "You will tell me where my dear friend Amandine is, Mr. Jessup Turner, and you will tell me this instant."

"Who the bloody blazes are you, and what kind of woman works for a newspaper?" He spun the card across the room, like a stone tapping across water.

Ayatas caught the door with one hand and slid inside, into the shadows behind a chair. The door closed softly on its own. The room was dim, but his eyes had adjusted. Turner's eyes had not, or he would not be still standing in the room. Several strands of Etsi's hair had come free from her bun and from beneath her hat, and they spun in the wrath of her magics, a slow tornado about her head.

A cool breeze blew through the room, carrying the smell and tingle of power. "Amandine and I met when she attended San Francisco Girls' High School. Now that I am out of mourning for my dear departed husband"—her voice trembled as if she had begun to cry—"I was invited to visit her and her father at their ranch, to do a story on the daily life of a young female rancher. And as my publisher's own daughter went to school with her, he was most eager to send me. As of our last correspondence, all was arranged. However, I arrive and poor Mr. Carleton is dead and buried, and Amandine is both married and missing, all in a matter of two months." She lifted a hand as if to wipe away a tear. "All my . . . wealth is no protection against the vicissitudes of life and fate." The power of compulsion surged through the room. "You must tell me what has happened," she finished.

Ayatas smiled into the shadows. She had told the man that her whereabouts were known to the wealthy back east, and that she had wealth of her own, yet was foolish enough to travel into dangerous territory. His fire woman appeared to be in need of protection. A victim. Which she was not nor ever would be. She also acted young and the man did not look beyond her words to the woman's face or the underlying steel.

"My dear Mrs. Everhart, my heart breaks to tell you that my father-in-law died only last month after a horse fell on him. It was most unexpected and sad for us all. Yet yesterday's news has proven much worse. Please be seated." He indicated the leather sofa where Etsi had been sitting, and when she sat again, he sat beside her and took her hand. Ayatas gripped his knife at the man's presumption, though Etsi did not indicate that she needed his help.

"There is no good nor kind way to speak the news," Turner said. "Amandine and her personal servant rode out into the desert to bring me a picnic dinner yesterday. She never returned. I and all of my men have been out searching for her, all night and all day. All we found was a dead horse and a place of struggle. I fear a mountain lion or a small band of Ute or Apache may have taken her."

"Oh. Oh no! What did the sheriff say to the attack? We saw him in town last night. He wasn't leading a search? This is truly dreadful. You must tell me more!"

Ayatas smiled and listened as the man wove a tale of lies, and what his fire woman called seduction—his words leading her to trust when there was nothing to trust at all. As they talked, Ayatas slipped from the room and learned the layout of the house. He found the room where Turner slept. He found the location of the ranch's gun collection. He discovered that the housemaid was covered in bruises and cried softly in a tiny crevice of a room at the back of the house. He controlled his rage. Wrath would help no one.

It was the hottest part of the day when Turner offered Etsi a small repast and left the room to order a bowl of fresh greens, a loaf of bread, and a bottle of wine to be brought to the study. Ayatas slipped inside, and Etsi whispered, "He thinks I am a fool, to be drugged." Her expression was stern, and he knew she feared the food would contain the peyote mushroom or opium.

"You have never been a fool, my fire woman." Quickly he ducked back out and into the shadows. Turner and the housemaid came and went, leaving the door open. Turner continued his seduction, but Etsi ate little, drank only water, and, as soon as the meal was over, insisted that she and her guide would walk back to town. Turner countered, equally insistent, that he drive them back. Etsi agreed.

The buckboard was brought around, and Turner helped Etsi up to the seat. They rode back to town on the bench seat. Ayatas sat on the back of the wagon, staring into the distance, planning how he would kill the man who sought to woo his woman.

"Is she still in room seven?"

Ayatas dropped his chin in the *Tsalagi* way. The scent of Turner's wife had come out of the window, along with the scent of opium. She had been drugged. The two of them would free her before the sun set. And kill her husband by morning.

"Where is the sheriff?" Etsi asked, her voice low so that Mrs. Smith, if she came back from her errand early, would not know that she had a man in her room.

"The sheriff and the dead man are at the ranch."

"Ayatas," she protested, laughter in her voice. "Dead man. Really. Here. Help me into the boots."

"They drink and play cards," Ayatas said, inserting the boot hooks in the leather loops. "In the morning, they will tell you that the ranch hands found what was left of the body and brought it in. They think you will not know the difference between the bones of a deer and the bones of a woman if there is no head."

"Of course. Women are uniformly stupid and gullible. And when not, then easily bruised and forced. Pull." She stood and Ayatas lifted the metal hooks against her weight until her left foot slipped in and then the right, snug. Etsi was dressed in dark gray and black, men's breeches and riding boots, black shirt, and a scarf over her hair and face. She wore a small gun at her waist and a knife at her thigh. He had taught her to fight. She was not a warrior, but she was capable. And she had magic.

"Is Mrs. Lamont still at the bakery?" Two hours past, they had talked to Mrs. Lamont, telling her the story of Amandine. The baker did not want to believe that Turner had sold his wife to the saloon, the sheriff assisting, claiming that no white man would do such a thing. But she had been convinced and would help with the rescue and then care for Amandine through the night.

He dropped his head in agreement again, but this time his fire woman gripped his chin and pulled him to her. "What we do is good." Her kiss was heated, and she laughed low in her throat. Long minutes later, they were sprawled on the narrow bed, her shirt unbuttoned and his discarded. She whispered, "We'll be late if we keep this up."

"I do not care," he growled.

She smiled and trailed her finger across his brow and down his cheek. "We will save her and fix things and then we will leave this place for the wild lands. Just us two beneath the stars, the wolves howling in the night."

"You will write your story while I hunt."

"And we will indulge ourselves beneath the moon."

"You are my fire woman."

"You are my beautiful man." She drew his long black braid through her fingers and kissed him before standing. "Work before pleasure."

In the heat of day, they had prepared for the night, gathering a ladder, ropes, a blanket, and medical supplies. Their horses were saddled, needing only the girths tightened to be ready for a fast race out of town.

At the back of the saloon, they waited for dusk to fall and Mrs. Lamont to take action. They did not expect the noise that followed.

Women screamed, shouted, and guns were fired. Men shouted. Footsteps thundered. Etsi's eyes went wide. "Go!" she whispered.

Ayatas raised the ladder to the window of number seven and ground the legs into the dirt to secure it. He raced for the window of the storeroom. Dove inside. His last sight of his woman was her rounded form climbing the ladder.

He came up in the dark and raised the scarf over his face to hide his identity. Pulled his knife and his six-shooter. He raced from the storeroom into the saloon. And he nearly stopped dead.

Mrs. Lamont and Mrs. Smith stood shoulder to shoulder with the schoolteacher and a man in a black robe. A priest. The women held guns on the saloon owner and three other men. "Shoot them! Shoot them!" the owner shouted. But the men with him could not decide what to do.

The priest shouted, "You have dishonored women! Repent!"

Ayatas sped up the stairs, his moccasins silent, his passage unnoticed by any but Mrs. Lamont. The gray-haired woman tilted her head at him, shouldered her shotgun, and shouted at the saloon owner, "We've heard that your doves are here against their wills! Drugged! Abused!"

Ayatas reached the far room and turned the knob. There were two locks, and he had no key. He tightened his grip on the darkened bronze knob and drew on his skinwalker strength. The first lock broke inside with a harsh snap. The other lock was unsecured. He put a shoulder to the door and slipped into the dark.

Amandine was deeply drugged, tied to the bed, her breaths shallow, her face bruised and streaked with tears. Her scent was sick and broken. But he knew a woman could survive many horrible things and become strong again. His mother had survived, and no one called her a victim.

Etsi had cut the bonds on the woman and used the ropes to tie the blanket over her. Together they lifted Amandine up and over his shoulder. Etsi adjusted both their scarves so no hair and only their eyes would show. Ayatas drew his weapon with his free hand. Etsi drew her gun and the knife at her thigh. She raced from the room and down the stairs. He followed into the bright lights and the shouting and the sound of gunfire.

Halfway down, the saloon owner spotted them and raised his gun to fire. Etsi paused, aimed, and shot him. The saloon owner stumbled, screaming, a spot of blood on his chest beginning to spread. The smooth action, the lack of twice-thinking her actions, brought fierce happiness to Ayatas. But the owner was not dead. He lifted his gun again and this time aimed at the women gathered in front of him. He fired.

Mrs. Smith fell. Mrs. Lamont raised her shotgun and fired. His head blew back, blood and brains hitting the wall behind him. The saloon owner dropped. The other three men dashed away.

Ayatas and Etsi carried Amandine into the early night. Hoofbeats galloped away, one sounding lame already. "They'll go for the sheriff and the ranch," Etsi said. "Let's get Amandine to safety." They took her to the bakery. No one was there, but the door was open. Gently, Ayatas placed the unconscious woman on the small bed in the corner.

"We owe you."

Etsi whirled, aiming at the door. But it was Mrs. Lamont. Etsi lowered the weapon.

"We all knew there were too many young women disappearing, most as they passed through. The sheriff blamed it on Apache, or panthers, or jaguars. Once a raiding party of Comanche, though Agua Caliente is a mighty long ways from their territory. And no young men disappeared.

We—the women—knew something was wrong. But we didn't know what to do, not until you came."

"You'll care for her?" Etsi asked.

"All of them." Mrs. Lamont sat in the only chair, beside Amandine. "There's five other young women. Been abused something awful. We'll take care of them. Give them a place to stay."

"The sheriff?" Etsi asked.

"Oh. I have a feeling he'll disappear." Her tone was cunning, her expression amused. "Mrs. Smith is securing his rooms and the jail cell, making certain it's all locked up. One of us will stay there all night. If he ever shows up again, the sheriff's out of a job. But you, well, you best hurry if you want to . . . finish your night's work."

"Thank you," Etsi said. "We couldn't have done this without you."

"And we *wouldn't* have done it without you."

Ayatas and Etsi sped to the livery and within seconds were trotting out of town, warming up the horses. As soon as they safely could, they gave the mounts their heads and leaned forward, across the saddle horns, into the night wind.

They passed a man leading a horse. It was limping. Ayatas wanted to shoot the man for abusing the animal. Perhaps on the way back. They passed a second horse, this one lying on the ground, grunting with pain. His leg was broken. They rode past. Ayatas would come back and put the animal out of its misery. They ran for half a mile and walked the animals for half a mile. The lights of the ranch house came into view.

Ayatas and Etsi slowed their mounts. The horses were sweating and blowing, and Ayatas worried about the cannon bone on Etsi's mount, but the horse wasn't limping, not yet. Maybe they hadn't damaged the horse. Through the night air came the sound of shouting and then silence. "The other rider got here just now." Etsi sounded sad. "They'll all ride in together, too many for just us to stop. And I doubt the town's women will have the gumption to face down a well-armed group of men."

But Ayatas knew men. The sheriff and Turner would not wait for the ranch hands to gather. They would believe that the two of them could handle the town's women. He slid from his mount and gave the reins to

Etsi. "Take the mounts into the brush. I will shift into jaguar. I will herd the horses as they leave the ranch. Spook them. I will take one, you the other."

She looped the reins to her saddle. "Be careful."

" 'I most certainly will not,' " he quoted her.

Etsi laughed like the young girl he fell in love with nearly two decades before. She led the horses into the brush. Ayatas stripped off his clothing and tied it in his scarf, securing the weapons so they would be at hand when he shifted back. Naked, he tied the scarf around his neck, leaving the fetish necklace in place, pulling the heavy bundle uncomfortably tight. Then he sat and called upon the snake in the center of all things, calling upon the life-force of the jaguar in the bones of the fierce beast. He was not moon-called, but it was easier to shift into another shape when *gauwatlvyi* was full. It was only two days to *Guyequoni*—the Ripe Corn Moon of the month the white man called July. His shift was fast and painless.

Ayatas raced to the middle of the street when horses came at a run. Tilted his ear tabs, finding their speed and location with his cat-ears. He squatted, leaving fresh piss in the middle of the street. Then he leaped thirty feet to the top of a pile of boulders and crouched. Waiting. As the horses passed at a hard run, bright silver-green in his cat-night-vision, he growled, the sound rising. He screamed out his big-cat-howl, a chuff of territory claiming, a bellow of sound.

The horses screamed and leaped to the side, shying as they passed over his piss. One tucked its head and began to buck. The other raced off the road. The man on the bucking horse cursed, lost his stirrups, and then the horn. He was tossed high. He landed. The cursing stopped. The horse bucked its way into the night. The man on the ground groaned.

The wind began to rush, fiery with magic. In the distance, Ayatas heard a man scream.

Ayatas trotted to the man, facedown on the ground. It was the sheriff. Ayatas hungered after his shift. It took energy to feed his shape-changing magic. He sniffed the man. He bled. He was injured prey. Ayatas leaned and blew on the sheriff's neck, growling. The sheriff screamed and tried to pull his gun. Ayatas caught the man in his claws. Flipped him over. Pounced on his chest. The man screamed again. Ayatas chuffed with laughter.

"Stop playing with your food, Aya," Etsi said. Hungrily, Ayatas tore into the sheriff's throat. The man died, bleeding out on the dirt, gasping wetly for his last breath. Ayatas sank his fangs into the dead sheriff's liver. He ate enough to appease the cramping in his own belly. He ripped out the heart and both kidneys, eating voraciously. Had he eaten of a human while in human form, he would have endangered his skinwalker energies, but as a predator cat, he was free from such fears.

Full, he strolled away, leaving many tracks in the blood and in the dirt of the road. In the darkness, he shifted back to human form and dressed. The attack had taken perhaps ten minutes in the white man's time.

He and his Everhart woman rode on to the ranch and alerted the ranch hands, who were gathering their gear in preparation to follow their boss into town. "Hello the house!" she called as they neared the bunkhouse. "There's a dead man in the road!"

At dawn, a very tired Ayatas and Etsi were in the saloon, sitting at a table in the dark beneath the stairs, sharing a pot of coffee. Etsi was writing her story, a sheaf of paper at her elbow, with pen and inkwell. They were watching and listening to what his Everhart woman called a ruckus.

Two dead men were lying on tables pushed together in the center of the saloon. The rest of the space was taken up by men, drinking and arguing and staying as far away from the women as they could. Because the women were angry and the men were rightfully afraid. The women were being led by Mrs. Smith, formidable even when wounded. All carried loaded weapons. The men had been disarmed.

A mob of armed angry women was a frightful thing to observe, unless one had been raised under the heel of *uni lisi* and *elisi*. Nothing was more frightening than those two in a rage. Ayatas sipped his coffee. It had been served in his own tin cup, to keep his filth from contaminating the cups used by the whites. Ayatas found it amusing and thought that before he left, he might shift into jaguar again and piss into all the cups.

The hands from Carleton's Buckeye Springs Ranch were all drunk. Other ranchers from the surrounding area stomped the horse manure off their boots and entered, only to be disarmed, surprise on their faces at the sight of women holding them at bay with guns.

The men claimed to be worried about the safety of their stock and children, most likely in that order. The undertaker, aware of his audience, measured the bodies for caskets. The doctor (who cut hair and shaved men at the bathhouse) was studying the wounds. He stood and tucked his thumbs into his vest lapels and pronounced, "These men are dead! The new owner of Carleton's died by a broken neck fallin' offa horse. The sheriff died by a broken leg that left him game to a . . ." He raised his voice. "To a marauding mountain lion."

"We need to track down that mountain lion and shoot it," a stranger said.

"No!" Mrs. Lamont shouted. The room quieted. "No one will be leaving this saloon until justice is served."

Amandine walked slowly into the saloon, and the place went as silent as the dead men. She stood straight, her bruises purpled and scarlet. She looked around the room as the other women moved to cover the exits with their bodies and their guns.

"You all know me," Amandine said. "You know that I was married fast to a man who appeared to be all that was ever in a girl's dreams. Then my father died, and it was proved to me that the man I thought loved me was a flimflam man. Now he is dead. According to my father's will, the ranch is mine. Is that understood?"

The men around her nodded. Two men edged toward the doors.

Mrs. Lamont aimed at them. "I can fire twice before you get out and I won't feel bad for shooting you in the backs."

They stopped.

"My husband sold me two nights past to Ramon Vicente, the owner of the saloon." Several of the men in the group leaned in to study her face. "He and two of my former ranch hands abused my body and my person. Vicente is dead. The ranch hands who abused me are Jimmy Jon Akers and Slim Tubbers."

The two men bolted. Mrs. Lamont raised her shotgun and coldcocked one. The other was tripped. One woman sat on him, another beat his head against the floor. A third kicked his side so hard the snap of broken ribs could be heard across the room. Etsi laughed. She was taking notes as fast as her pen could flow across the paper.

"I have witnesses. I call the reporter, Mrs. Everhart, and the baker, Mrs. Lamont, to speak to the truth of my statement."

Etsi stood and told the story of the night Amandine had been brought into town, telling it as if she had been the witness. She told about finding Amandine and setting her free. About riding out to the ranch. His forever woman was a wonderful storyteller.

"The two men tried to get away," Etsi said. "You saw them. They abused the body of a woman. Where I come from that means either a neutering or a hanging."

Ayatas did not think the men would neuter the rapists. But one did pull out a length of rope and start braiding.

Satisfied, Etsi motioned for Ayatas to follow, and they left the saloon.

That night, under the stars, Etsi read him the story called "Savior of the Doves." It was wonderful. And then she fell into his arms on their layered bedrolls and they loved together beneath the nearly full moon, as they always had, as they always would. If he could keep his Everhart woman safe.

Death and the Fashionista

First published in *The Death of All Things*, an anthology (2017). This story takes place just after Molly found her death magics, in the Yellowrock timeline.

The sun was setting when I slipped out of the house and over to the pile of boulders jutting on the crest of the hill. Sitting on the boulders gave me a clear view of the skyline in every direction, of the mountains that arched high and the valley that fell low, bright with the lights of Asheville. Of the moon rising and the few early stars glittering, of the last of the sunset in the west, a scarlet reminder of the day.

If I turned my head, I could see inside my home, the lights glimmering through the windows, my children at the table with their father. The TV's muted laugh track sounded, stagnant and repetitive.

I ran my hands through the herbs planted around the boulders in the rock garden, releasing the scent of rosemary, basil, thyme, and chives, and pulled my ratty house sweater close against the autumn chill. Night birds called. Something crashed in the underbrush. But I was paying attention to one thing only—the forest I had killed.

I stared at the bare trees, bark sloughing off, revealing the pale wood beneath, limbs broken and pointing at the sky. Pointing at me as if in judgment. The accusation of death. Everything alive there had given itself to the pull of my new and unwanted death magics; the cursed gift had destroyed every blade of grass, every tree, vine, bird, lizard, snake, deer, squirrel. Everything.

With my native earth magics I had blessed and nursed that woods for years, bringing the trees from saplings to full grown and healthy, and then I had killed it all in a slow attrition of leaking death. Since that time I had managed to encourage a honeysuckle vine to grow there. One vine. A few blades of scrub grass. Nothing else.

I came out here often to remind myself of the dangers of my cursed magics. To remember that if I didn't tamp down my curse-gift, strangle it, I might kill something more precious than the woods. If I let go, I might kill my husband. My children.

The power was seductive, forbidden. With it I would curse and kill, withering the land and bringing death to the ones I loved.

I massaged my belly and the baby who resided there, a magic user of undisputed power but unidentified future abilities, and I shivered. Night in the heights of the Appalachian Mountains was cold. Or maybe fear made me tremble. That was always possible. Death and fear rode the same horse and, for witches, pregnancy came with the likelihood of peril and sorrow.

As if in answer to my thoughts, the baby kicked. At the same instant, I heard the clop of hooves, two horses, iron shoes on the asphalt road. I opened a *seeing* working. The outer ward was still active, still in place, a pale reddish ring of protection around the house and grounds. A stronger one surrounded just the house. Double wards were difficult to maintain, but with Big Evan's and my magic combined, not impossible.

The back door opened and Angie poked out her head. "Mama!" she whispered, the word magically amplified by her will and desire. "Company's coming."

At her side, EJ, her little brother, stuck out his head. "Com'pee com'n."

They couldn't have heard the horses' hooves, not with the TV on, but Angie was a dangerously strong witch. The clopping grew louder. Closer. I climbed to the ground. "Who?"

"Don't know his name," Angie said. "But the lady is Sally."

"Sauwee," EJ repeated.

"My angel says she's a 'piece a work.' What's a piece a work? And he says, 'Death is the Truth and the Lie. And Death can be cheated.' My angel's confusing, Mama."

Confusing. Yeah. And the warning made about as much sense as anything else ever said to my daughter by a supposedly celestial being—which was no sense at all. I clenched my sweater tighter across my chest and rounded belly. "That's it?"

Angie tilted her head. "Yep. Cheating's wrong, right, Mama?"

"Right. Take EJ back inside. Tell Daddy what you told me." Angie took

her brother's hand and closed the door. I walked around the house to
the front, to the darkness at the edge of the driveway, and the sound of
horse hooves, getting closer. Cue scary music, I thought.

The outer ward dinged smartly and juddered as horses turned into the
drive and stopped.

The security lights came on, illuminating a man on a . . . a yellow horse.
A heavy warhorse in daffodil yellow, its coat gleaming, its feathers, mane,
and tail a brilliant white. The man atop the gelding wore black: a leather
jacket and pants, Western boots, black saddle, while his flowing hair
matched the horse's white mane. The man was gorgeous and color coor-
dinated, like something out of an airbrushed Ralph Lauren ad.

Beside the yellow horse was a blood bay mare, a woman on the mare's
back, her clothing matching the red horse: scarlet moto jacket, leather
pants, boots that came to midthigh, matching riding gloves, and lipstick.
Her scarlet hair was piled high in an eighties style. She carried a red leather
handbag slung over the Western saddle horn, the kind of pricey handbag
my sisters loved. Sally and the man were improbable, ill matched, and
doing a poor job of aping human. When paranormals came calling, it meant
trouble.

Something gleamed on the sole of the man's boot, darkly glowing,
reflecting the silver moon. A taint of hellfire and brimstone. The man had
been walking where he shouldn't. These two were far more dangerous
than they looked.

When she saw me, the woman on the blood bay mare laughed. It was
the sound of bones dancing, of dead bodies floating on still water, of ravens
on a battlefield, laughter that ruined her harmless eighties style statement.
Terror skittered up and down my spine at the sound and the thoughts
stimulated by her laughter. I dropped my arms and put back my shoulders.
Holding my comfy, shabby sweater closed was not saying good things
about my self-confidence.

The woman in red looked me over and lifted her eyebrows, mocking.
"You're not what I expected, Molly Megan Everhart-Trueblood." She had
a caustic high-class Southern accent, maybe Georgia. Rich, old-money
Atlanta. Servants, cotillions, and finishing-school money. "Such a tacky
cardigan."

"What's it to you, Sally?" I said.

The woman's gaze razored in on me, and when she spoke, the words went rough and sharp, like broken glass, her silly eighties façade cracking. "How do you know my name?"

I didn't answer. "What do you want, Sally? And who's your pal?" I glanced at the man. His face was pale, his eyes the bright white of the moon.

I heard the front door open, and Big Evan's air sorcery lifted my hair. We had created the wards to allow him access to air currents and weather outside the magical protections. He whistled a long note and the security lights brightened about a hundred percent. The two uninvited visitors turned aside, blinking. "I asked you a question," I said to the woman.

"Two," the man said. "You asked her two questions. Specificity is vital to such as we."

I tilted my head slightly. "Fine. I asked two questions. I still haven't received replies."

Behind me, Big Evan's whistling trilled. A harsh wind sprang up and blew back Sally's scarlet locks, whirling, playing havoc with the mounts' manes and tails, wrapping the man's hair around his face. The chilled breeze fluffed my own red curls. The heavy animals danced from hoof to hoof.

The woman sniffed, scenting the magic, and focused on my hubby standing on the porch. "You know my name," Sally said, sitting forward in the saddle and gathering her reins into one hand, "but you don't know his?" She flicked a thumb at the man.

Her question and change in posture sent more fear skittering across me, and I had no idea why. She swirled the fingers of her free hand, amassing power, curling it into her palm. In response, Evan started to hum. The ward began to glow a pale red at the corner of my witchy-eyed vision. My eardrums fluttered as if the barometric pressure had changed with a fast-moving weather front. Sally's magic spread around her in a slow spiral. I had no idea what she was, or what her gift was, but she was powerful. Fear skittered up my spine like baby spiders hunting.

I wanted to gather my own power, my earth magics, which were still available to me, but death magics taunted, whispering of the brimstone on the man's boot. So easy to blast these unwelcome visitors and be done. *So easy*, it whispered. *Just reach and out crush the threat.*

But death magic was powerful, a nuclear arsenal compared to the slow, life-giving energies of my earth magics. I might use it—but at the risk of destroying everything. My earth magics were weaker but came with a much lower price.

I shoved down the desire to rip the visitors apart and said, "All I know about you two is that Death is the Truth and the Lie. And you are a piece of work, Sally."

The magic in Sally's hand tangled, fell to the ground, a reaction I felt as much as saw. Eyeing me the way a cat eyed a goldfish in its bowl, Sally said, "No one insults a Death."

"It isn't an insult if it's the truth." I pressed my small advantage, repeating, very carefully, as if in some mild warning or threat, "What. Do you want. Sally. And who is your pal?"

The pretty man smiled. "I am Death come riding, one of Seven am I. Not youngest nor eldest, Death of Magic, I cry. Untested, unconquered, waiting beyond the veil. Till a ruby-haired lass calls, 'Death Magic, Avail!'"

Riddles. I hated riddles.

Sally said, "You know what your sister thinks about prophecies."

"Death of War is tired," the man said, his eyes on me. "What she wants will soon be unimportant. It's my time to rule."

I narrowed my eyes at the two, absorbing and dissecting the riddle and the banter. I had red hair; so did my child. There was no way I'd avail myself of death magics. "Death of Magic. Death of War. Titles, not names." It wasn't sneering, it was stalling so Evan could finish whistling up his working. I added, poking the bear only a little, "Death of Magic sounds like a Marvel Comics character."

Evan chortled on a breath and went back to whistling softly. In the sky clouds started to build. "Do you kill all magic or everyone who has magic? Either way, you die too, and no one left alive likes you much."

Sally said, "Death of Magic has come to offer you a bargain and assistance."

I said, "Not interested. Not now, not ever." A cat interrogative sounded. KitKit mewled, winding around my ankles, her tail looping, a steady caress.

"A pet," Sally sneered. "I expected more of you."

KitKit leaped at the ward, claws spread, ears back, fangs showing. She hit and screamed a challenge, sticking to the magics for just a moment. The blood bay bolted. The yellow gelding sat back on his haunches, nearly unseating the man. Sally used her entire body to regain control of her mount and Death lunged forward, his arms around his horse's neck. Kit-Kit slid and dropped to the ground. I laughed as my non-familiar cat sat, lifting her back leg to clean her nether regions, bored. "Name," I said, taking my cue from the cat and sounding jaded. When neither answered, I said, "Come," to the cat and turned my back on the uninvited visitors. The man growled at my pointed insult. I kept walking, KitKit loping in front of me. Big Evan's eyes were on me, my husband not questioning my decision to toy with predators, but offering support and protection. In the distance, I heard the howl of wind. KitKit raced inside.

I climbed the steps and stood beside Big Evan, his bulk and height dwarfing me. I took his hand, his magic surrounding me, surrounding us. Rising, humming with power. My earth magics responded and the ward, the upgraded *hedge of thorns* 2.0, was glowing so brightly red now that any witch could have seen it even without a *seeing* working. Even a human could have seen it.

"Tell me," Big Evan said.

"Brimstone on his boot."

My husband muttered an imprecation. The two looked silly. They weren't. Outside, the wind grew stronger.

The man had dismounted and was standing before the ward, hair and clothing blowing in Evan's wind, his arm up, his palm open, flat. He placed it on the ward. A single loud *dong* rang, the warning of protection. He pressed, his power creating a prism of hues, iridescent blacks, like oil on ink. The ward *gonged* again, deeper, heavier. The wind whipped. The black iridescence of his attack spread, the shape of the hand growing, as if he claimed the ward.

Behind him, the horses moved restively, hooves dancing in distress. The wind blasted across them. Sally fought to keep control and slid to the ground, to hold the reins close to their heads.

I watched as *hedge of thorns* energies coalesced at the bottom boundary, where they entered the ground. The red haze of the ward grew thick and bisected the black energies with a sizzle of power, like scarlet lightning. Death's attack fractured across the dome of energies and fell apart, our ward still strong.

Death jumped back, eyes wide. The wind fell, leaving the world silent and still. Death studied our working. I turned my back on him again and slipped past Big Evan, almost into the house.

Death of Magic shouted, "Sam! My name is Sam! And your children are in danger!"

My belly twisted and the baby kicked. Right on my spine. I nearly fell to my knees, but there was no way I was going to appear weak in front of an enemy. I caught myself on the jamb and turned around slowly. "What threatens my family?" I growled—the tone of a mother when her child is endangered.

Death said, "A demon newly freed from the inner circle of hell has scented you and your bloodline. Your children have gifts too strong to be contained in mere mortal bodies. They will die at the hands of the demon and it will eat the children's souls. I know this. I am Death of Magic. But I can save them from the demon's attack. For a price. A small price."

Death of Magic was either a very bad negotiator or he wasn't the brightest bulb in the chandelier. Or both. But stupid people could be dangerous. Deadly even.

"Save us for a price? Did you think an earth witch might miss the brimstone on your boots? You set this deception in play to barter for your own needs." He had said it was his time to rule. He wanted power. I stepped back to the lawn and began to pull the energies of the earth up through the ground. Taking just a fraction of a fraction of life-force from every living thing for a hundred miles.

"Oh shit," Sally said. "I told you this wasn't going to work."

"Molly," Evan said, a gentle warning in his tone. "Be careful. His name is Death. What if this is what he wants?" Meaning, what if they wanted me to get mad, lose my temper, and pull on death magics. *Right.*

"I've got this," I whispered, thinking, *All life. Only life.* But I broke out in a sweat, hot and stinking in the night air, straining to hold on to my earth magics and keep the death magics at bay. But . . . death magics would destroy this threat so easily.

Sam vaulted into the saddle, watching me across the intervening space.

"Sam?" Sally warned.

"Molly?" Evan asked, in nearly the same tone.

"They need to know we're not without claws." I shaped the magic of life into a spear point, a knapped and wicked-sharp weapon. I pulled Evan's magic behind it, like a shaft, to give it distance and force. And I focused on the being that threatened my children. "Now," I whispered.

Big Evan dropped the outer ward. In the same instant I threw the gift of life. It shot through the air. Toward Death. The point pierced Death's chest.

Sam fell off his horse.

Through the hole in the ward, something entered. Something dark and cold and seeking destruction. It saw me. It saw my death magics. It saw my blood. The blood demon spread its claws, a cobra hood expanding around its black light face. It snapped the hood closed, opened its mouth, rocketed at me. Aiming for my belly and the child within.

"Sam!" Sally shouted. "Don't!"

"Stop," Sam said from the ground, a hand out.

The demon stopped, hanging in midair, a foot from me. I backed slowly up the stairs, and through the inner ward on the house itself. The magics composed of the life-force of Evan and me, woven together, slid around me and snapped into place.

Evan followed. The magics sealed behind him too, leaving the demon just beyond our door. Evan turned out the inside lights and we fell together, holding each other. I was shaking, sweating a greasy film of fear, sick to my stomach, pressing gently on the baby with both hands. We stood in the dark, Evan's arms around me, and watched through the windows. I laid my head against my husband. "I messed up," I whispered, my voice barely a breath of fear. "I just wanted to make him go away. Mess with his pride a little."

"I agreed with showing a little power. Get him to back off," he said. "I didn't sense the blood demon either."

"Sam?" Sally asked, leaning around the yellow horse. "You okay, Sammy Boy?"

"I'm hurt."

"What kind of hurt?" Sally asked.

"I'm green."

"Gre—" Sally interrupted herself as Sam walked around his mount and up to the *hedge of thorns.* "Shit, Sam." She pulled a cell phone from her big purse, aimed it, and took a couple of shots of her partner.

"Stop that!" he yelled at her, just as a toddler might to his nanny. To the house, he shouted, "What have you done to me, witch?" He was still pretty, but now he had green scales, like a snake, and brown hair like dried vines. There were leaves unfurling from his hairline, darker than his scales, and daffodils bloomed from one arm and the right side of his head. Earth magics at work, though the working wasn't designed to last long. "Make it stop!" he shouted to me, panic in his voice. Yeah. A child. Death of Magic was a grown-up child, pampered, spoiled, and not overly bright.

Sally put away her cell, giving me a glimpse of a silver zippered kit of some kind and what I could have sworn was a hair dryer in the red bag. "Sorry, Sam. But it's part of my job. Your daddy will be pissed."

"You tell Death of Flood about this and I'll rip out your eyeballs."

"Yeah, yeah, yeah, whatever. We talked about the demon getting free but you said you could hold it. I told you this was a stupid plan to get close to the witch. Can you get the demon back?"

"No. My gift is . . . wrong, now."

"How wrong?" Her tone went jagged again.

"When I call the demon nothing happens."

"And if you just let it go?" she asked.

"It'll kill all the Everhart-Truebloods and steal their magic. And then it'll come after me."

My shaking worsened.

"Well, shit. You really screwed up. Again," she said.

Death of Magic stared at the snakelike blood demon hanging in the air. "I . . . I . . ."

Sally shook her head and to the house shouted, "Little problem out here."

Little problem. The idiot went to the circles of hell, let loose a blood demon, attacked my house, and set the blood demon on my family. If the demon got free, the result would be even worse than if I had used my death magics—everyone I loved would be dead, their souls sucked into the demon, giving him power. And I still didn't know what Death wanted. I'd have cried except that the demon whipped his head to me and writhed in the air. Sam, if he ever had control of the demon he had summoned, was about to lose it.

"Sam . . ." Sally warned.

"I—I—I—" He stopped, swallowed.

My hubby whistled, the note low and vibrating, like air blowing over a jug. The demon's motion stuttered to a stop. It began to back up, slowly, and out though the hole my magic spear had made. The instant it was on the street, the hole snapped closed. The ward was unsteady, weak, but better than nothing.

I risked a look around and spotted the children on the sofa, sound asleep. In a *seeing* working, I followed Evan's blue magics tying our babies into slumber with a rope of our own gifts. It was hasty but powerful work, their own burgeoning magics reinforcing the working. Death wanted to use them for some purpose of his own, but if we died, our magics would augment the bindings and the tiny ward around them. The demon could get to them through their blood, but Death couldn't get to the children now. Half the threat beaten. "Good work. What should we do about flower boy, his nanny, and his demon?"

"Fear," Evan said, his lips scarcely moving, his long red beard shaking slightly. "That's Sally's job, Sally's title. For which info you may thank your sisters."

I spotted my cell phone in his shirt pocket. "Is it on speaker?"

Evan whistled a soft note. "Two-way speaker now."

Cia said from Evan's pocket, "We're both on the way, ETA seven minutes. Faster if Liz wasn't a wuss driver."

"Not a wuss. Just want to arrive in one piece on mountain roads," Liz said.

Boadicea and Elizabeth Everhart—Cia and Liz—were twins, and excellent researchers of witch oral tradition. The twins were the babies of the family, fearless, gorgeous, and always trying spells they shouldn't.

Cia was a moon witch, nearly powerless at the new or sickle moon; Liz was a stone witch, weak from nearly dying, crushed beneath a boulder in a fight with a demon. "Okay. What can you tell us?" I asked.

"The Deaths are an obscure legend tied into oral witch history," Liz said, her voice tinny over the cell. "There was the first Death, Death of Eden, and his only son, the second Death—Death of Floods. The legends say Death of Floods has seven children: Death of Starvation, Death of Plague, Death of Childbirth, Death of Age, Death of Misfortune, Death of War, and Death of Magic, who hasn't used his power since the end of the Burning Times."

The Burning Times was also called the Roman Catholic Inquisition. So many witches had been killed that our race nearly died out. I stared into the dark and the two standing before the outer ward.

"The Deaths each rule over a form of human death," Cia said, "except the Death of Eden and the Death of Floods, both of whom retired after they harvested millions all at once. In Flood's case, according to oral tradition, only eight people escaped."

"Noah, his family, and his animals," Liz said.

"So what do we do?" I asked.

Outside, the demon quivered. What might have been a tail whipped hard, hitting the outer ward. The ward emitted a deep and panicked *dong*, before Death of Magic got the demon in hand again. At the moment we were fine. But if that thing got loose, this could go bad, fast.

"I think we have to invite Death of Magic inside the outer ward," Evan said, "and use his power to help bind the demon. Then we have to kick Death's ass."

I shook my head, not liking that idea at all. But not seeing any alternatives.

"Do we have time to draw up a contract?" Cia asked.

"Would a Death honor a contract?" Liz asked.

"Death can be cheated," I whispered. "That's what Angie said."

"If a witch cheats on a contract, the threefold repercussions are bad. So instead of a contract, we plan on cheating Death and just fly it," Evan whispered back, miming throwing a paper airplane.

"Good by me," I muttered. Raising my voice, I called out, "Death of Magic, and Fear. If you come in peace, you are welcome inside the outer ward."

"We come in peace," Sally said. "Can I come in and use your powder room? That wind played havoc with my hairdo."

"Hairdo?" Cia said. "What century is she from?"

"The eighties, from the looks of her," Liz said. "Evan sent us pics."

"She has an Hermès bag," I said.

"Oh. My new best bud, then."

I called back to Fear. "Pee in the woods. We'll drop the outer ward and you'll walk in. Leave the horses on the other side. "

Fear blew out a breath and pulled hobbles from her bag. She strapped each of the horses' front legs together, leaving the mounts unable to travel far.

I contemplated the demon again. It had big teeth, gleaming talons, a long tail and scales, but without the dragon charm. And mad, mad eyes in a shade of burning purple tinged with emerald. There was no bargaining with demons. No negotiation. There was also no way to kill them. They were immortal. We'd bind it back to hell or die trying. Even a Death couldn't kill a demon.

Sally and daffodil-blooming-Death stood at the edge of the outer ward, Sam staring at the demon, his brow covered with sweat, his hands trembling. The demon shifted, and a stench of burning sulfur trailed into the air.

Evan said, "I'll handle the inner ward. Liz, Cia, when you get here, take over the temporary bindings on the demon. Molly, you figure out how to bind that thing."

I nodded, the gesture shaky. My sisters agreed. I heard the hum of a Subaru climbing the hill and caught a flash of car lights through the trees.

"Offer them tea. Put the kettle on," Evan said, giving me something to do to keep me from worrying as I tried to figure out how to save us. Busy hands and all that.

I went to the kitchen and started the electric kettle because it was faster than regular heat on the AGA stove. I heard them still talking as I worked, getting out a strainer for the teapot and a good strong black tea. There would be no nodding off tonight.

"A tea party," Liz said, "with Death and Fear and a demon, oh my . . ."

"Alice in Wonderland meets the Wizard of Oz," Cia said.

Liz said, "Evan, your house wards are sparking."

"I see your car," Evan said.

As I put tea together, I also gathered necessities from my kitchen: the *silver spoon* working I kept in the kitchen for emergencies, quickly powering it with the rosemary plant I'd killed and then brought back to life. Long story. But the important thing was that now the plant seemed to be able to store a lot more earth power than it should. And . . . the solution came to me. I broke off one needle-shaped leaf and tucked it into a pocket. "Thank you," I murmured to the plant.

"Getting ready to drop the outer ward, ladies," Evan said. "You drive straight in. On three. One. Two. Three."

I felt the ward fall, the magics lashing back through the ground and through my bones. It stole my breath and froze my chest. The magics twisted and curled into the inner ward, reinforcing it. It was so heavy now that air and weather wouldn't pass through. Once I got out of the house, there might be no getting back inside until Evan dropped the ward.

Putting a hand on my baby bump, I said a *protection* working over my unborn child. Though I didn't pray often, I added a prayer to seal the working and then whispered, "Hayyel, I could use some backup on this one." Angie's angel didn't respond. I heard the Subaru rolling into the drive, over the lawn, and up to the door. My sisters had driven between the unwanted visitors and us. Smart. The car engine died and the doors opened. I forced myself to keep moving, keep thinking, and got out mugs.

Cia called, "Lasso is working, in place on tail end."

Liz said, "Lasso on head. We need something stronger for its teeth and claws." Louder she added, "Hey, Death. Get off your ass and lend a hand here."

Cia shouted, "Fear, pull something out of that fancy bag and tie off its tail. It's getting free."

"I don't do magic," Sally said. "I do hair and fashion and terror. And Fear of Death."

"Well, the fashion is seriously out of date," Cia said. "Big hair hasn't been around since the eighties and Peg Bundy. If you can't help, then get the hell out of my way."

"Witches. So snarky," Sally said. But her eyes hinted at her ire and dread. They coiled together on the night wind like asps, stinging. She was attacking us all. I fought the fear she caused and breathed my way through it.

"Liz, can you pull from the rocks beneath the earth?" Cia asked.

"I can try, but I'm limited when I'm not touching them."

I poured water over tea leaves. The aroma of tea rose, soothing. I stirred the leaves with the silver spoon, the stored working moving from spoon to the tea. "You can draw from the boulders in the rock garden, Liz. They will help some, as they trail underground where their magic is untouched by air and rain."

Softly, Evan said, "Mol? You need to see this."

I set the oversized teapot on the tray with mugs, linens, silver, sugar, and cream, and carried it to the front. I felt better having done something, even something so simple as tea. I placed the tray on the table near the door and took Evan's hand. The ward on the house zinged through me, and I realized he had it looping through his own body. It was a dangerous tactic, but it also gave him total control over the energies and the maths of the ward, allowing me in and out more easily than I had feared. It wasn't something I could do while pregnant without harming my child. I squeezed his hand.

His voice rumbled in his barrel chest. "You know I'd never let you out of this house if I could do it myself," he said. "I'm good but I can't protect the kids, hold the wards, and dispose of a demon that wants your blood."

"I know. Of the two jobs, the one you left for me is safer for the kicker." I patted my belly. "And Cia and Liz and I can work a triangle inside the existing outer circle. What did you want me to see?"

"Their lasso working."

With my *seeing* working, I focused on the magics my sisters were using to blind the demon. "Ohhh," I breathed. "It's tinted with the same shade of energies as the stuff on Sam's boots."

"Yeah. They've been messing with something dark. Not enough to coat their souls or tint their auras, but enough to bring them more power than they ever had before. You be careful." He paused before adding, "I love you to the moon and back."

"I love you most of all," I said. It was a way of saying good-bye. I laid my head on his arm for a moment, took a deep breath, and stood away. Giving him a mug, I picked up the tray, took a steadying breath, and pushed through the ward. The magics coated my body and hair and pulled through me like electric taffy. The energies were attuned to me, and usually walking through wasn't a problem, but there was so much energy coiling through it now, far more than it was designed to hold. And it all looped through Big Evan, which was the only reason I could get through. Dangerous for my husband, but we'd deal with any repercussions later.

I opened the back hatch of the Subaru and set the tray down inside. Poured tea into mugs. Carried mugs to each of my sisters, then to Death of Magic, who looked like he needed the entire pot. Sam was shaking with exertion and drained the mug in a single gulp. I studied the shape and form of his *snare* working, the incantation holding the demon. It was vastly different from a witch *lasso* working, but there were enough similarities for me to harness my workings to it. "Stabilize your working and then get out of the way," I said. "And I'll need your Tony Lamas."

"I'm not giving you my boots," Death said.

"I'll buy you another pair, Sammy-pie," Sally said. She was standing at the back of the Subaru, drinking a cup of tea, one I hadn't offered her. I gave her a sunny smile, which seemed to startle her. "Just give the little witch what she wants," she said. "I have to be back across the veil by dawn. I'm doing one of the Waters' hair at ten, and I need at least some beauty sleep."

"Hope you don't give her broccoli hair like yours," Liz snarked.

Sally snarled and stared daggers at my sister, but nothing happened. A look of surprise and then horror crossed Sally's face. My lips twitched as she looked down into the mug she had drained. Looked back at my sisters. She snapped her fingers. Neither witch sister showed the slightest bit of fear. I felt my own lingering terror lift too, and my smile took on a measure of satisfaction. The scarlet-haired sidekick's power had been neutered. Well, that's what you get when you take a mug that was never offered to you. The quick little *happiness* working from the silver spoon had been for me, Evan, my sisters, and Death, to negate our fears. That same working had stopped it at the source. Sally wasn't used to feeling fortunate.

Fear-Fettered slammed her expensive bag on the back of the Subaru and pulled out a makeup kit, a brush, and a mirror that was way too large to actually fit within the confines of the bag, and started to make herself presentable after all the wind. I got a good look inside and there were also three knives with crosshatched hilts and two semiautomatic handguns. The brush was spelled and the mirror was a scrying surface. Sally, the Fear of Death, was a fashionista killer. I hadn't forgotten they were here after my children. I gave Evan a significant look, mimed putting a purse over my shoulder and mouthed, *Her bag.* He nodded.

"Boots," I said to Sam, holding out a hand.

Death of Magic sat on the ground and pulled off his boots, the smell of the sweat of Death strong on the air. As he was yanking off the expensive footwear, I took over his *lasso* working and wove the threads of my own earth magics into it, and into my sisters' power, securing the *lasso*. Death's magics felt warm, slippery, unstable in my hands. Foreign. The power in the magics skidded up my hands and wrists to my arms, enveloping my own cursed gift. It was a yearning, a wooing, a siren song of desire to join my gift with his magics. To . . . to become a Death myself.

Not Death of Magic. But Death of All. All humans. All plants. All animals. To do to the entire world what I had done to the hillside nearby. My mouth went dry with horror. If I lost control . . . if I let it ride me . . . I'd kill. I'd be a Death and my own fear would have won.

Sally looked at me and then at Death. "Oh, Sam. It wasn't the kids. It was her."

I understood. This was what Sam had wanted. Death magics. Not my children. They had thought the kids were the carriers. They had intended to trick us into helping them trap the demon, allowing them in close, so they could get at the death magics.

But my daughter's guardian angel had said I could trick Death. I shook my head, trying to force my earth magics to the forefront of my mind, to satisfy my magical needs. I accepted Death's boots, the brimstone and darkness on his sole shining bright. Brighter than the moon. The brimstone picked up my own curse. Pulled on my curse. The boots glowed.

"Mol?" Cia asked. "What's happening?"

"Nothing," I lied, jerking my attention away from the evidence of darkness. I had to end this quickly. "Binding?"

"*Blood of angels*," Liz said, naming the working. "Places, everyone."

Holding the temporary bindings, I moved to the north. Cia walked to a position sixty degrees to my left, close beneath the moon, now high in the sky. Liz took the third place. We spread the energies we were working into the full one hundred eighty degrees of the equilateral triangle. Then we backed away, spinning the magics out until we touched the permanent circle of the outer trench, and sat—not so easy when a baby was in the way.

I pulled out the rosemary needle-leaf and placed it between my knees. Cia and Liz each placed their elemental focal between their knees. Cia invoked the circle: *"Dùin."* It was Scottish Gaelic. The circle rose around us, enclosing the half-bound demon, Death and Fear, and three Everhart sisters, but excluding my home, husband, and children. Everything I held dear was safe. Except my sisters. I mouthed my thanks to them and got a wink from Cia and a nod from Liz.

"Faoi dhraíocht," Cia said. *Bound by a spell.* Her hands braided the energies, twisting, pulling, sliding them through her fingers.

"Hhí ceangal na gcúig gcaol air," Liz said. *He is bound hand and foot.* She plaited the energies she held with her twin's. They grew bright, a lovely blue and lavender tinted with paler pinks. The demon screamed, his howl full of anger and pathos and thwarted desire.

A cheangal, I thought, calling on my daughter's angel. I wove my death energies—no. I wove my earth energies and Death's own energies in with my sisters'. *You said I could cheat death,* I thought to Hayyel.

I gathered Death's magics, magic he had passed to me freely with his boots, into my own and tied them to the single rosemary leaf. I scraped the brimstone off Death's boot; at the same time I wiped sweat from the inside onto my fingertips. I rubbed the darkness and the sweat together and took up the weaving, letting the magics pull through the mixture. I wove the dark energies and the sweat of Death's foot into the binding mix. Softly, I said the words *"Mallachd dha! Mallachd dha! Mallachd dha!"* three times. *Curse him, to hell with him* in the language of my mother's mother's people.

Death stood up fast. His eyes blazed with golden light. He glowed. Ravens began to call, the crowing of blackbirds out of place at this hour, screeching, screaming.

Fear reached into her Hermès bag and pulled two weapons, the slides *schnicking* into place as she chambered rounds. She aimed the weapons at me. Big Evan laughed, the sound all wrong, too deep, too heavy. The *hedge of thorns* on the house shivered and flashed a nearly black and sapphire blue. The weapons didn't fire.

Sam stretched out his hand to me. To the death magics he had come for. The death magics he wanted to steal to rule. I said a final time, *"Mallachd dha!"*

Death screamed, his cry like that of the ravens. Sally, Fear of Death, screamed with him. Their wails rose, a crescendo that cracked across the air and made the boulders out back shift and slide in a grinding tumble. Fear and Death both vanished.

The demon wailed and screeched, writhing against the bindings. It began to stretch and twist and pull, the power of brimstone dragging the demon after them in a long twirling trail of dark energies. It vanished. With it went all the power in the equilateral triangle, then in the outer circle. Our own magics snapped back painfully. Liz and Cia swore at the sting.

There was only the final echo of the ravens. Silence settled upon the night.

I slid sideways and lay on the chilled ground.

Cia stood. So did Liz. Big Evan dropped the house ward and was by my side faster than he should have been able to move. He picked me up as if I weighed no more than his daughter and carried me inside. Liz and Cia gathered up the Hermès bag, the weapons, and led the horses to the backyard and grass to eat.

My sisters and my husband fed me tea and microwaved soup while they drank Evan's best single malt. The Everharts helped Evan unwind my babies from the *sleepy time* working and put them to bed. It was too late for the girls to make the trek back down the mountain, so they crashed on the oversized couches in Evan's man cave. I curled up in my husband's arms in the bed we shared.

"Your magic is different," Big Evan said. "It's cooler. Less barbed than before."

"I think . . . I think I figured out that death magics belong in hell," I said. "I think I channeled them, well, most of them, there."

"Temptation to use them is gone?" he rumbled.

I let my mouth pull into a wide smile. "Yeah. Your turn. Your magics feel different too. Hotter. More barbed."

Evan nodded, his beard tickling my shoulder. "I never wanted to kill anything before, not with my magic. But this time, with you and the baby and the kids . . ." He stopped, his breathing ragged. "This time I wanted to hurt them. I wanted them to be dead and gone forever. It's still roiling under my skin."

I nestled closer. "Part of that is the nature of Fear of Death. It'll go away soon enough. But if you can't sleep, the baby's nursery needs another coat of paint."

Evan chuckled. "Later. Tonight, I just want to hold you." He kissed the top of my head.

"Cia and Liz got Sally's bag and everything in it."

Evan sighed. "More trouble. But that's a problem for another day."

"They got sucked into hell with the demon. We cheated Death," I said.

"And Fear. Nothing wrong with cheating the bastards. It's what life does every day."

That's my hubs. Full of wisdom. And strength. And all good things. "Night," I whispered.

"Good health and happiness. From now on," Evan whispered. I smiled into the dark. It was the Everhart blessing. And it was good.

My Dark Knight

First published in *Temporally Deactivated*, an anthology from
Zombies Need Brains (2017). In the Yellowrock timeline, it
occurs just after Angie Baby started calling Jane "Ant" Jane.

She waved her hand in front of Mama and Daddy's open doorway, pushing a little of her magic into the working. It wasn't what Mama called
elegant but it *was* strong. They wouldn't wake up or hear her. She sneaked
down the short stairs into the den, setting her toes and then her whole
foot carefully on each step. Once on the solid icy flooring, she inched
forward, past the unlit Christmas tree and the few wrapped presents.
Around the reclining sofa.

Mama had left her cell on the table beside Daddy's spot and there
wouldn't be a better time to make her call. Even EJ was deeply asl—

"Hey, Sissy."

Angelina made a little squeaking sound and stopped with a jerk. The
glare of an extra-bright flashlight hit her in the face. "Turn that off," she
whispered. The light went out and Angie blinked against the blindness
from the glare. She used a *seeing* working and spotted her baby brother
cuddled under a blanket in Daddy's spot. He was a wriggling mass of blue
and gold and purple magics, bound with Mama's greens and Daddy's
yellows. EJ giggled at her and she frowned at him, trying for Ant
Jane's mighty scowl. "You're a son of a witch on a switch." Which were
Mama's swear words. And Mama would threaten to spank her if she heard
her say that. Mama said witch words had power, Angie's words especially.
But EJ was a *paaaaaain.*

Her baby brother giggled.

"How did you know I was up?" she demanded.

"You's magic was singin'."

"Magic doesn't sing. It sparkles."

"Sings. And the magic from the woods is singin' louder. It hu'ts my ea'us."

Angie moved to the window and looked up the small hill behind the house. The woods were dead-dead, not just winter dead. Mama had killed all the trees and bushes by accident and they were gonna take a long time to regenerate. Yet her brother was right. The pale glowing magic that had been in the woods all day was sparkling brighter. Way brighter. It was a big magic, yet Mama and Daddy said nothing was there. For some reason, they couldn't see it and they had refused to listen to her.

She could call Ant Cia and Ant Liz or Gramma to come deal with it. Or she could call Ant Jane. She was undecided.

"It sings like a wolfie and a bird and the bells in the church."

Angie turned to her brother who had joined her at the window, dragging his blanket. They had waked George and KitKit. The basset hound and not-a-familiar-cat joined them at the window. George growled, a deep menacing vibration. KitKit hissed and arched her back. "A wolf?" Angie asked her brother.

He nodded, his head moving hard up and down, his bright red hair catching glints from the working on the hillside. "Yup. And a bird and bells."

They had just attended a bell service for Christmas and EJ had loved the bell choir. Now, to him, everything sounded like bells.

Angie said softly, "It shines the color of a were-creature. That might make it an animal." She frowned at the hillside. "A paranormal animal-person Mama can't see, maybe a were-creature, or like Ant Jane." Were-creatures could only be the were-creature that bit them. Ant Jane was a Cherokee skinwalker and she could be any shape she wanted. But it wasn't her.

If Angie called her Witchy Ants for help, and if it was were-magic, they could get bit. Her brother could get bit. He stood beside her, a corner of his blanket in his mouth, his blue eyes staring up at her in the dark. He was kinda stupid but Mama and Daddy liked him so she had to take care of him, him and the new baby on the way.

She dragged her eyes back to the hillside. The magic on the hill didn't move like an animal. It moved in a line and a clump. Daddy would say it moved like chaos. Daddy was big into chaos. The sparkles were witchy, the colors were-creature, but the size of the magic was wrong for a move-able witch ward or glamour and wrong for a were-creature. Mama said it wasn't there at all, so it wasn't witch magic.

She studied her own magic, zinging through her blood, knowing she needed someone close by, someone strong, to deal with the strange not-witch magic. There were only a few she trusted, and her magic told her that Ant Jane was too far away. Her Dark Knight, Edmund, was vampire strong and when she thought about him, the magic in her blood got brighter. He was nearby.

She retrieved her mama's cell, returned to the window, and punched in the security code. She looked through the contact list for Edmund, the vampire she'd sworn a blood oath to. She had wanted him to be her fian-cée, but when he swore his blood oath and fealty, he didn't promise to marry her. He swore "to the Everharts and Truebloods . . . I shall protect your children and your children's children unto the laying down of my own undeath." He had included her whole family, which was how he be-came their protector. The mystical bond wasn't what she wanted, but it was good enough until she grew up and convinced him to marry her.

She was just about to touch the call button when EJ said, "Sissy? Its bells is comin' c'oser to the house. If it's a animal, it can get in the ward."

She found the glow in the dead trees on the hillside. Fear shot through her, a bright sizzle of her own red-gold magic. The line-and-clump magic *was* closer, and brighter. It was directly outside the ward that protected the house and grounds. This wasn't good. The *hedge of thorns* was built to allow Ant Jane to get in. If a Big Bad Ugly had figured that out and had a way to use that one weakness, they were in trouble. She had to make her parents understand. Still holding the phone, she grabbed EJ, his blanket, and the flashlight, and hauled him across the TV room toward her parents' bedroom. The critters followed, KitKit meowing.

She made a fist at the entrance of the bedroom and envisioned the power she had stretched over her parents' sleep. "Wake up," she said. The magic flashed red-gold, a sizzle of light, and rushed back into her, popping like a rubber band and covering her with a copper-pink glow. "Ow! Mama! Daddy!" she shouted.

In the dark, Mama rolled over. "Kids? What are you doing up at this hour?"

And then the ward made a gong, GONG, *GONG!* Daddy sat up, still asleep, one arm waving in the air, his other reaching for his flute. Mama raced clumsily to the window and threw open the drapes, looking up the hill, holding her baby bump. Bright light blasted in. Mama said a very bad word, followed by, "Evan, what *is* that thing?"

Her little brother's hands covered his ears. "It's louder! Bad bells hu'ts my ea'us."

Angie pulled EJ closer, under her arm, standing in the doorway. She heard nothing now that the gonging had stopped, because her magic didn't work that way, but there were the dazzling, angry lights of an attack. "I told you it was out there," she accused her parents as Mama and Daddy poured magic into the wards. The thing on the hill started gonging again, which everyone could hear, louder and louder. It threw lights at the ward. Hammering on it. The ward began to hum and echo, brighter and brighter.

EJ cried in pain. KitKit leaped onto the bed, her eyes on Mama, stalking her across the mattress. George tangled into EJ's blanket, underfoot.

Mama screamed, "I don't see anything!"

"Me neither," Daddy said. "But the ward is fracturing."

The foreign magic was beating a way through. That shouldn't be possible. If it busted the ward, there would be an explosion. They could all die. Unless they dropped the ward and just let the attackers in.

"Evan!" Mama shouted over the magical noise. Terrified.

"Angie," Daddy yelled. "Make a ward. The strongest one you can. *Now!*"

Angie breathed in hard, shocked. Mama and Daddy didn't know she could do big magic.

"Do it! Use all you got. I know you can," Daddy shouted. He blew a long, piercing note full of magic on his flute, creating a personal ward for Mama. He was red-faced and breathless. Mama was panting.

Using her hands and her power, Angie pulled the bindings off EJ, her parents' confining magic tangling around her, sticking to her fingers. Beneath the bindings, EJ's magic glowed a soft purple with sparkling green lights.

"Ohhh," he said. "That feels good."

Daddy's music filled the room, the notes full of power. The *hedge of thorns* shivered. Mama's magic went black as a cave, so dark it sucked all light out of the air, her death magics like a cloud around her. They were

wild raw magics and every time she used them she risked losing control
and killing them all. Now they had two ways to die.

EJ's eyes got big. "Sissy, I'm sca'aed."

"Me too." Scared because her ward would protect her and EJ, but it
wouldn't stop the thing on the hill or stop Mama from using death magics, and the ward Daddy wrapped around Mama was unfamiliar. Daddy
stumbled, sweating, his magic sputtering as he started a personal ward
for himself. To EJ, Angie said, "I learned how to do this in magic camp."
Which wasn't entirely a lie. "You trust me?"

EJ threw his arms around her waist, knocking them to the floor, George
under her knees. Angie reached inside and found her magic. She looped
and twisted it with EJ's. Carefully, she imagined a circle around them,
over them, and under them, like being in the middle of a beach ball. Daddy
said to make it strong, so she thought about the *hedge of thorns* and the
magic of heaven. Angel magic glowed brighter than any magic anywhere.
It was the strongest magic she had ever seen. Maybe she could . . . Angie
reached out and pushed the world aside, just a little. Angel magic glowed
out from the other side, blinding bright.

The *gonging* was so loud EJ screamed, his head in her middle. Tears
raced down Angie's face, burning. Daddy's magic went louder too, as he
snapped a pale yellow ward in place over himself.

Mama's magic went pure black. It hit the new, yellow ward.

KitKit leaped, claws out, cat-screaming, for Mama.

Angie pulled the angel magic into hers and said softly, "Safe."

Edmund Hartley wiped the blood off his sword with a square of chamois.
The injured scion bowed and limped off the circle, into the crowd. The
silence was absolute, Mithrans in the stands not breathing, not moving,
not even blinking, a sign of respect. Humans in a similar situation would
have been applauding and screaming, stamping their feet. Vampires were
far more courteous and elegant in their appreciation. His host, Lincoln
Shaddock of Clan Shaddock, inclined his head in approval at the demon-
stration of La Destreza, the Mithran form of swordplay.

Addressing the Mithrans in the stands, Edmund said, "The moves, in
order." He placed his feet in proper position and lifted his weapon. "Alle—"

His cell phone rang, the emergency tone.

Edmund snapped his fingers. The assistant scion raced to his side with the cell. Edmund swiped the screen and was about to say *Yes, Molly*, but instantly he knew this wasn't Molly. A prescient fear sang down his spine and through his veins, as if his blood boiled. As if he was being summoned, his bond commanded. "Angelina?"

"My Dark Knight. We have troubles," the little girl said, sounding nearly vampire formal. She took a breath that sounded full of tears. "Come save us. Hurry!" She pulled on the bond between them, a sharp twanging pain.

Edmund tossed his sword to the scion and raced from the sparring chambers with a pop of displaced air. As he passed his host, he murmured, "The Everhart-Trueblood place is under attack. Call the family." Back into the cell, sounding calm even as he sped through the night to his car, he said, "Angelina, are you in danger?"

"No. Because EJ and me is under a strong personal ward. But Mama and Daddy's in their bedroom and they aren't moving." She whispered, "I'm afraid."

Dead? Pray God they aren't dead. He sprinted down the drive to his vehicle, everything to his sides appearing as unmoving blurs. Dread and fear swelled inside him, as strong as the thirst for blood, but when he spoke, his voice was calm. "I'm on the way. Tell me what happened. Tell me what you see." He leaped into his Thunderbird Maserati, the top open to the night's chill. Roared the car to life and hit the gas. The 1957 prototype leaped off the bald mountain and down the drive, Edmund shifting gears through the icy streets toward the Everhart-Trueblood home.

"Our ward was being attacked from the hill in back of the house. Daddy said to make a small *hedge*, as strong as I could, for EJ and me. I started making it. Daddy made one for Mama. Then he started one for himself. Then Mama's magics—" Her words cut off.

Ed had access to intel on all the paranormals in the territory. Molly Everhart's death magics were one of many secrets to which he was privy. Carefully, Ed said, "I know about the death magics, Angie. It's okay."

She sobbed hard, as if a weight had been taken from her. "Okay. Everything happened at once, Edmund. Mama's death magics shot out. Daddy started his ward. I got our *hedge* up and it's really strong. But now everything's stopped, even the glowing thing in back of the house."

"Explain 'stopped.'" He took a turn too fast and black ice swept him into a fishtail. Wind blew through the convertible. If fear hadn't taken up residence in his heart, it would have been exhilarating.

"Daddy's glow got dim and the gonging on the ward stopped. Mama's standing at the window with her arms out and her magics stopped like a cloud. KitKit's hanging in the air in the middle of a jump. Daddy fell and his head is bleeding everywhere."

A stray thought presented itself. "How did you know I was close?" he asked. Driving one-handed, Edmund swerved around a truck, hitting seventy on the coiling roads outside Asheville. Up into the hills that surrounded the city.

"I felt you in my blood."

Shock moved through him. Angelina Everhart-Trueblood should not be able to sense him. She was not a Mithran, not his scion, not . . . not anything that should permit a mental or mystical connection. Their connection was a bond of fealty, not a bond in the Mithran vampire way, yet he had felt a command through that bond, a *calling*. What had the little girl done with his sworn word?

He swerved around two slower cars and took a turn too fast. Angelina was a double-X-gened witch, having received the witch trait from both her father and her mother. Double-X-genes were rare, he knew of only a half dozen in the Americas. Over the connection, he heard panting. Angie was powerful. And terrified.

"I'm only a few minutes away, Angelina. Tell me about"—his mind went blank for a moment—"about the dog. Where is he? Will . . . will he bite me?" he asked, to give her something to focus on.

"No. George is under the *hedge* with us."

"Tell me about him."

"George is my basset hound and Mr. Shaddock gave him to me. I'm teaching him to fetch, but his legs are short and he keeps tripping over his ears. George. Not Mr. Shaddock." Edmund smiled and she kept talking as he negotiated the hills and the snaky roads. He pulled up to the house, braking hard to miss the *hedge* that glowed red over the house and grounds, clearly visible to Mithran eyes. A warning to his kind to stay away. Oddly, it was bright enough that even humans could see it tonight, bright enough to cast a reddish shadow. Faster than human, he slid his weapon from the glove box and leaped from the car, dashing into the shadows, away from the beacon of car lights, leaving them shining to attract a predator's attention, should they not all be "stopped."

As Angie talked his ear off, he studied the witch ward, shining into the night. There were shadow groups in the human government and human military, and many less-than-savory characters from the underbelly of society, who wanted witch children. They were in high demand in the magical slavery market. He had no idea what he could be facing. Fear made his pupils expand fully; his fangs clicked down on their hinges.

He would protect this family.

"I am here, Angie. I'm going to scout the edges of the *hedge*, up the hill. I need to end our call to be silent. I'll call you right back. Is that acceptable?"

"Okay, Edmund. I saw your car lights. Bye."

Edmund turned off his cell and pocketed it. He moved around the side of the property, wishing he had kept a change of shoes in the Maserati. The soles of his Italian leather La Destreza shoes were useless for an inaudible reconnoiter. He made his way to the back of the property and saw a shimmer of brighter light there, mostly yellow with striations of blue, purple, red, and hints of green, oddly static-looking. Inside the glow were two forms, a man and a woman, both wearing night camouflage. The two were indeed "stopped," like mannequins, as if they were frozen outside of time in a . . . a temporal distortion.

The woman knelt, facing away from the man, wearing a dual ocular headset, a matte black sniper rifle in her arms, aiming back up the hill. Her hip pressed the man's and the point of contact glowed silver. The man leaned against the *hedge of thorns*, a small device in both hands, pressed against the energies, emitting the prism of light. He wore dark glasses against the glare.

The colored light was odd, wavy, spotty, broken, as if it was no longer moving, but hard, stationary, plasticized. Whatever had stopped the people had stopped light too, or slowed it to something visible. Edmund thought back to Angie's description of creating her small, strong ward. Was it possible that she had tied it to the outer *hedge* and to her mother's death magics? If so, this temporal anomaly could be unstable.

It had been centuries since he felt the cold, but it crawled up his spine on icy feet now.

He sent his senses searching up the hill where the woman was aiming. There was no glow of undeath, no sound or scent of life except for small animals and a distant herd of deer. Yet the magic of death clung to the land and he had an instinctive revulsion to the dregs of power that had depleted the hillside of life. Fear clung there, as if the death magics cast by Angie's mother still had the power to drain him.

Retrieving his cell phone, he took dozens of photographs under various filters of the couple and the device they used. He sent them to his military and tech security team, texted the situation, and asked for input.

He had no idea what might happen if he reached into the light or touched the couple who had attacked the ward. Edmund chose a stick from the dead forest and touched it to the rainbow of light. The stick passed through easily. Gently, he slipped it forward, through the stopped magics, to inspect the man's pockets, lifting a lapel, poking at pouches on his military-style pants. All were empty, but a faint silver glow appeared at the point of contact each time the stick touched him. The same glow appeared when he inspected the woman, growing brighter each time. It seemed cautionary and he stepped away, tossing the stick uphill, completing his circuit of the large *hedge of thorns*, back to the car. He turned off the headlights, slid the weapon into the waistband of his dress slacks, strode to the *hedge*, and called Angie on his cell.

When she answered, he said, "Angelina, let down your personal *hedge*, please, and come to the front of the house."

"Ummm. I tried." She sounded mortified. "I can't make it go away."

"We's stuck!" EJ chirped in the background. "And I gotta peepee!"

"Angie, do a *seeing* working and tell me if you detect a thread of your magics tying your small ward to the *hedge of thorns* around your home."

She whispered over the cell connection, "Ohhhh. I tied them together."

The Everhart witches had devised numerous wards based on the original *blood-hedge* of protection. Because few of them had to be recharged, he presumed they were either solar charged or ley line powered, though they never volunteered such information. The outer ward wouldn't simply stop at dawn, wear thin, or die off. It had to be turned off, as if with a switch.

"Edmund, it's worse," she whispered again. "My protection ward has tails. One goes to the back of the house. Somehow, I tied my ward to the magic that was breaking through the *hedge*. And . . . oh no. It's tangled in Mama's death magics and to angel magic too."

"Angel?" The little witch must have created a ley line feedback loop, powering it with even more energy than Angie possessed herself. If it broke, would the children enter the temporal distortion, blow up the house and parents and themselves, or perhaps send time-warped space and death magics out like shrapnel?

"Whoot!" Angie shouted, and he jerked the cell away from his head. Vampire ears were not made for the shrill tones produced by a witch child's vocal cords. "I got it! I can't make it go away but I can move it. Me and EJ are scooting to the front door."

"Angelina, wait. Take some pictures of your father and mother and send them to me."

"Okay." He heard clicks, followed by grunting and dragging sounds and the chuffing whine of an unhappy dog. The front door opened and he saw the children through a red-gold ward of energies as they came down the steps and along the drive. The children were beneath a low-lying, moveable ward, the upper dome of which was just high enough to allow them to sit up. "I'm hanging up so I can push," Angie said. The call ended and Edmund studied the photos she had texted. Her parents did appear frozen.

Ed felt the power of more witches as two cars climbed the hill to the house, one a half mile behind the first. The Everhart twins had arrived and another witch followed. The first vehicle stopped, the engine went silent, and the ginger-haired identical Everharts joined him at the *hedge*.

"Oh dear," Cia said quietly, the taste of a *seeing* working on the air as they studied the frozen ward. "I had hoped Shaddock was mistaken about an emergency."

Puffing with exertion, the children reached the *hedge*. "Hey, Ant Liz and Ant Cia," EJ said, waving. Angie straightened her nightclothes and made sure her brother and the dog were wrapped in the blanket they had dragged with them, patting the basset hound and her brother equally.

Liz raked short red hair back from her face and said, "EJ. Angie, is there some reason you called a vampire instead of family?" Her tone was carefully calm, but a defensive scowl lit Angie's face, one so like her mother's that Edmund smiled.

"The attack isn't witch magic," Angie said, her tone unapologetic. "It's animal or something else and I didn't want you to get bit by a werewolf or something."

"Big teefs to eat you with!" EJ said happily.

"Ah," Liz said, still composed. "Next time, please call us too."

"Yes, ma'am," Angie said, but she transferred her antagonism to the vehicle parking beside theirs. "Who's that?"

"Melodie?" Cia called in surprise as a dark-haired witch emerged from the car.

"Mama said not to talk to people I don't know."

"Angie," Liz said sharply. "Manners." But Angie's scowl grew worse as the third witch approached.

Melodie said, "I'm sure the child has been through a lot tonight. I'm Melodie Joy Custer-Luckett from the Custer witch clan, Angie. I'm renting a room from your aunt Elizabeth while I finish a course at the university." She added, "I was studying late and saw you rush off, Liz. I'm a paramedic. I thought I should follow."

Angie regarded the three women, her mouth turned down. Edmund prepared himself for what she might say.

Angie's suspicion remained but she said, "It's a pleasure to meet you, Miz Melodie."

She elbowed her brother and he pulled a slobbery finger out of his mouth to say, "Pweasure meet you." And stuck his finger back in his mouth.

"Edmund," the little girl said, her formal tenor returning, "Ant Liz, Ant Cia, Miz Melodie, we must break the ward and save my mama and my daddy. And KitKit."

"Breaking an Everhart ward will be difficult," Melodie said.

Liz and Cia nodded, but Angie's eyes narrowed at Melodie's words. Edmund had come to trust the child's discernment. His senses went on alert.

There was nothing obviously wrong with her, but Angie didn't like the strange witch being here.

"Sissy, I havta peepee," EJ whispered. "And I'm hungwy and cold."

"We'll be free soon," Angie said, hoping she wasn't lying. She wrapped George in the blanket too, to give EJ some heat. George promptly fell asleep, drooling on EJ's leg.

The grown-ups discussed the "situation," as they called it, and looked at the pictures she had sent Edmund. Ant Liz said, "Tell me what happened, Angie Baby, and very carefully, walk me through what you did to make such a strong ward."

"I messed up," she admitted. Angie described what had happened, emphasizing the colors of the magical working and EJ piping in with its sound—a drum beating slowly.

"You twined the magics together," Ant Cia said, her tone worried, one hand smoothing her braid over her shoulder.

"Yes," Angie said. "It's what Mama and Daddy do to our magics when they bind 'em so we can't use 'em."

"And you can see the magics? The energies they use to bind you?" Miz Melodie asked.

"It's why it's so easy to get out. But this is different. Mama and Daddy and KitKit are all frozen."

Ant Liz asked the others, "Could she have triggered a temporal disengagement?"

"Or a temporal deactivation," Cia said.

Which sounded very bad.

Melodie said, "Temporal . . . You Everharts are an interesting bunch."

"I gotta peepee!" EJ said, holding his private parts. "I gotta peepee noooow!"

"First thing, then," Ant Liz said, giving him her usual fond expression, "is to get my favorite nephew out of the protection ward so he can go potty."

Ant Liz never looked at *her* that way. No one ever looked at her that way except Ant Jane. She should have called Ant Jane. "He's your *only* nephew," Angie said crossly. "And I gotta use the bathroom too."

"Alrighty then," Ant Cia said, unwinding a ball of string and starting to trace a protective circle.

EJ muttered, "Hold it. Hold it. Hold it. Hold it. Sissy, I gotta go *now*!"

"You'll need three of us. Where do you want me?" Miz Melodie asked Liz.

"North is here," Ant Liz said, taking that position, "so each of you to the sides in a triangle pattern." In seconds the witches were sitting and closed the circle, the powers flaring into place with a flash of light.

"Oh my . . ." Miz Melodie said, staring at the small ward, then up over the *hedge of thorns* that covered the house. "I've never seen anything like this. Do you Everharts do this kind of"—her hand made little circles in the air—"working often?"

"No. But there's always a first time," Ant Liz said, sounding grim. "I've never seen one so tangled. Cia, Melodie, can you determine the first step?"

"The strand from the top of the *hedge*, perhaps?" Cia said. "Except we'd never get to it."

"No. But Angelina can reach her end. Angie," Melodie said, studying the energy patterns. "Do you see the energy strand trailing from the *hedge*, one you twined into your smaller ward?"

She meant the glowing yellow strand. "Yes," Angie said.

Miz Melodie said, "Good girl. Reach up to where it touches the top of your portable circle and, gently, tweak it loose."

She trusted her ants but something felt wrong. Angie frowned and looked at Edmund, who nodded slightly. Scowling, Angie reached up and tapped the top of her ward, plucking at the yellow strand of energy, un-weaving it with her fingers, colors and sparks shifting in the air. As she pulled the tail of the thread loose, the *hedge* overhead shivered and shook, throwing a light show of sparks and flickers of color.

Edmund watched the three witches. The Custer witch kept glancing at him and he wondered why, beyond the general hatred most witches har-bored for Mithrans. He smelled nothing leaking from her pores. Betrayal and ambush had a foul scent in humans and witches. However, Angie still frowned at her. "Question," Edmund said mildly, watching Melodie. "If the small ward falls, won't the children be caught in the same temporal displacement as their parents?"

"Angie, stop!" Liz said.

Angie's fingers stopped moving. Carefully, holding as still as a Mithran, she turned wide eyes to her aunts.

For an instant, Melodie's lips flattened. Her pores emitted the sour stink of frustration, hot on the night air. She lowered her head and schooled her expression to concern, but he was Mithran. Even had he not caught the facial expression in the dark, he would not have missed the spike of scent change.

Edmund said, "If Angie peels away the power she is drawing from the *hedge of thorns*, might that also destabilize the entire ward, resulting in a release of energy?"

Cia sucked in a breath of shock. "We could have blown up the entire hillside."

"We'd have been fine under our own circle," Liz said, "but at the very least Ed would have been toast and the kids would have been stuck or killed."

"I gotta peepee! I gotta peepee *now*!"

"Elizabeth," Edmund said. "What would happen if the children simply pushed their small ward through the larger one?"

"We'd have . . . I don't know. Cia?"

"I gotta peepee!"

"I think . . . the smaller ward would peel away and the kids would be free?" Cia said. "But—"

"Good. We're coming through," Angie said.

"No!" both twins shouted.

Angie touched the edge of her protective shield against the outer ward. It stuck. It didn't explode or make a light show or—

"I gotta peepee! I gotta peepee! I gotta *peepee*!" EJ's voice shrilled.

Angie shoved the small shield hard against the larger one. It took both hands, her arms, body, and toes pushing. The edge pressed through and she and EJ and George followed. Nobody died. The small ward did not peel away or explode. It was too strong. Stronger than the house ward. Angie was proud but her ants looked mad. "What?"

"You disobeyed us," Liz said.

"I been studying the wards and how the energies worked. I figured it would be okay."

"*I gotta peepee!*"

Angie pulled on the yellow thread of energies and her small shield made a strange cracking noise, like bubble wrap popping. It fell in a shower of sparks. EJ jumped upright, his feet tangling in the blanket; he nearly fell. Edmund caught EJ and carried him behind a tree.

"I get to peepee on the tree? Sissy, I get to peepee on a tree!"

Edmund stepped back around the tree looking amused.

Angie brushed off her hands and said, "He is such a *paaaaaain*." But magic was stirring.

In a really fast move, Miz Melodie raised her hands, broke the circle, and shot at Edmund. With a gun.

Several things happened at once. Edmund said a bad word and dove back on top of EJ. Ant Liz threw a *wyrd* working at Miz Melodie. Edmund popped beside George and her, picked them up, and raced behind the tree where EJ was hunkered down, moving so fast her hair flew out in a wave. Edmund looked dangerous, the way Ant Jane looked dangerous. It made her feel better, even as more gunshots rang out from Miz Melodie. Edmund plopped them on the ground, saying, "Angelina. Stay. Behind. The tree."

"Why?" But it suddenly didn't seem important and he was gone anyway. Angelina petted George, who was too lazy to care that they had been hidden in the dark, and then petted EJ, who snuggled up against her muttering sleepily about wanting a hamburger. Thankfully the blanket was warm and the smell of little-boy pee wasn't too terrible. But the sounds were strange and . . . Angie realized that Edmund had used vampire compulsion on her. Which was *so* not fair. She broke the compulsion and duck-walked around the tree to see better.

Edmund watched as the twins zapped, tackled, then restrained the now unconscious Melodie with plastic ties they mysteriously had on their persons. Everhart witches never ceased to delight him.

As snowflakes began to float down, Liz asked, "Why would she shoot you?"

Edmund gave a small smile. "Perhaps I was the greater threat. Take me down and then take down the less powerful witches."

Liz gave a very unladylike snort of derision, which he quite liked. "Greater threat? I don't think so. We were prepared, you weren't. And what good would it do to take *us* down?"

"I assume that this particular witch is working with the humans attacking the ward," Edmund said. "There have been tales of black ops government groups and even of private armies kidnapping witches for personal use."

Liz glanced up at Ed as she secured the unconscious witch's ankles. "Fangheads too. Witches for the power, bloodsuckers for the blood."

A faint sound caught his attention and Edmund whirled. "Movement cresting the hillside. The two back there may have backup."

"Melodie's gunfire alerted them," Liz said. "Damn."

"Keep the children safe," Ed said, and disappeared with a soft pop.

Liz made a fierce face that Angie had never seen before. It matched Edmund's. "Give no quarter," she shouted.

Angie didn't know why attackers would want quarters. Dollar bills were way better. Her ants grabbed EJ, George, and her, and raced behind their car, before setting up a protective, *warming* working. EJ rolled over and George drooled on EJ's back.

The *warming* working thawed Angie and she lay down, trying to figure out what she had done to freeze time. The stopped energies spiraled up to the high center of the *hedge*'s dome like whirls on a multicolored candy cane. She had torn through to the angel place and taken energy from there. Heaven had been bright as the sun, those energies and the utter black of her mother's death magics tangled in a messy ball at the *hedge* top. It looked like something KitKit made when she got into Gramma's yarn basket.

Angie sighed. She had really messed up. The problem was the combination of heaven and death. They'd met and entwined when they should have canceled each other out. A small yellow strand was dangling from the very top of the dome. On the other side of the ball of magics was a lightless strand of death. Right *there*. Not that she could reach either.

The death magic strand wiggled slightly and grew just a little. Nothing else moved. Somehow, Angie knew that was bad.

From high on the hillside came the sound of gunfire. Then someone screamed, abruptly cut off. Edmund's fury leaked through their bond before the connection disappeared. Her Dark Knight had the Big Bad Ugly.

Edmund carefully wiped the blood from his lips and licked the fang marks from the human's throat. He now knew who the attackers were, how many there were, how well they were armed, and what they wanted. He tucked the enemy's weapons into his pockets, shouldered the man's body, and jogged down the hill, his victim's heart beating fast and arrhythmically from blood loss.

Movement at the Everhart-Trueblood back door caught his eye. Evan, Angie's father, was on his knees, pushing his protective ward down the steps, his eyes wide, his face and beard bloody, shirtless body pale with shock. Angie had said her father was bleeding everywhere and Edmund realized that meant the male witch had not been caught in the temporal dislocation.

"Evan," he said, as he approached the *hedge of thorns*.

"My children?" Evan gasped.

"Safe."

The big man seemed to reshape with relief. Ed dropped his dinner at the *hedge* wall. Evan was huffing when he got there, fresh blood trickling from a nasty head wound, probably concussed. He fell to his backside, breathing heavily, as he pulled on sweats. "Update me."

Edmund told him everything, including how Angie had pushed her ward through the *hedge*, and watched as Evan tried it, successfully ramming his small protective ward through. He dropped the tattered ward and staggered to the glowing protuberance of the *hedge* energies where the two humans were frozen in time. "They were . . . going to kill us."

"Yes."

"I'm not a violent man," Evan said, his face twisting with fury. "But . . ."

"They will not trouble you again," Edmund said gently. "My military and tech team are analyzing the people and the device. They will be dealt with."

"Good." Mixed scents of self-loathing and satisfaction came from Trueblood, tart and acerbic. "What did he tell you?" Evan gestured toward the human at Ed's feet.

"He is with a group called DTP. Death to Paranormals. Starting with the Everhart-Trueblood family. There are two more warriors and two 'suits' over the hill in a van. We must assume they will be along presently."

Gunfire rang out. Pain seared along Edmund's side and in his right chest.

He fell. The witch dropped too.

———————

Gunshots. From the hill. Angie broke the *warming* ward and reset it, leaving EJ and George safe and asleep. She scrambled around the car and froze at the sight of Ant Liz and Ant Cia on the ground, twitching beneath an *attack* working that writhed like red snakes. Miz Melodie struggled to get loose from the straps on her ankles. Angie wasn't good with delicate spells, so she just raised her hands and hit the evil witch with *sleep*. That one she knew real good. Miz Melodie fell over.

She ran to her ants and studied the *attack* working trapping them. It was solid and squiggly at the same time, like jail bars hit with lightning. The electricity made her ants shake. Ant Liz was turning blue. She had been injured once and her lungs were bad. She could die. Angie didn't have long.

She took a deep breath, pinpointed the nearby ley line, and shoved her hands into the *attack* working. It punched her like . . . like something awful. She shook. Bit her tongue and tasted blood. But she directed the *attack* working down into the ley line, draining it. The blackness of night shrank her vision. It had never happened before, but she was pretty sure she was passing out.

Edmund sped up the hill and tackled the shooter. The sniper's rifle skittered off the boulders, breaking the scope, firing a final shot into the sky. With a furious, vicious twist, Edmund broke the shooter's neck at C5. His own wounds were painful, though not life-threatening. To heal himself he fed, reading the man's thoughts. Verified that three others waited on the far side of the hill. He carried the still-breathing human, racing back to heal the witch. But Evan had wrapped himself in a protective ward and had not been shot. Ed dropped to his backside beside the big man, calling Lincoln Shaddock. It was past time to request reinforcements.

Angie scowled as Daddy said, "We don't have good options, Angie. You, Little Evan, and I will go home with your aunts and we'll try tomorrow—"

"No." She crossed her arms over her chest just like Daddy did when he was putting his foot down. "Mama's death magics are growing. They'll kill her and the baby by morning." Daddy looked weird, the way he had when a rattlesnake found its way into the backyard and Angie killed it with a hoe. She had been four. "We have to stop it now."

"None of us knows how, Angie," Daddy said softly.

"I do." She pointed up. "We have to find a way to get up there and unravel the knot of death and heaven." Daddy didn't reply. He just shook his head.

Edmund said he had a 'cussion. Whatever that was. Edmund also said Mr. Shaddock was taking care of the bad guys on the other side of the hill. She didn't want them taken care of, she wanted them dead, but no one asked her.

"The top of the *hedge* is twenty feet above the roofline," Edmund said. He rested his hand on the ward and the frozen *hedge* only buzzed. "The *hedge of thorns* feels slightly warm, with a faint vibration. I can leap and climb to the top, provided the *hedge* is as solid at the top as here."

"Even if you got up there, over the house, in the air," Liz said, her voice rough and hoarse, "even if the *hedge* held your weight and didn't fry you like bacon, you aren't a witch. You can't unravel the working."

"Hell," her twin said, "I don't think *we* could."

"The *hedge* won't hold more than two hundred pounds," Daddy said.

"I can do it," Angie said.

"No, Angie. You can't," Liz said.

"That isn't happening," Daddy agreed.

"In a moment of panic," Edmund said, "Angelina merged all of these energies. I fear that if this temporal deactivation explodes, time-warped-space and broken death magics might destroy the surrounding area. Might perhaps result in worse consequences."

Liz cursed. Daddy looked mad.

Angie said, "Edmund can carry me up the *hedge*. I can pull the threads through and unravel all but the last strands. Then we can slide back down with me holding them. On the ground, I can pull them. The *hedge* and the temporal thing should fall." She tilted her head, watching her family, her red-gold curls sliding to the side.

Edmund said, "You figured that out on your own?"

She sighed. "Somebody hadda. It's my fault."

"You didn't do this on purpose, Angie Baby," Cia said. "If your mama hadn't drawn on the death magics, they wouldn't have been there to get tangled up in your shield."

"If Mama hadn't used them, then EJ and me woulda watched Mama and Daddy die."

Daddy sucked in a horrified breath.

Edmund said, "As viewed from a military perspective rather than a personal one, Angie is correct. It will take all of us to stop this, and only Angelina can untangle the energies."

Daddy started to argue, but he stopped, staring at Edmund. "You swore to protect my family."

"Even to my undeath. Yes."

Cia said, "Angie needs food and water first." She brought a bottle of water and a banana from her car, along with EJ's blanket. Angie ate and drank and went behind the tree where EJ had peed. When she was done, Edmund held out a hand and Angie placed her small, cold one into his.

Edmund adjusted Angie on his back, wrapped her arms around his neck, her legs around his waist. "Hang on tightly." She did. It was a good thing Mithrans didn't need to breathe. He stepped back several yards, toed off his ruined shoes, reached for the gift of speed that was part of his nature, and raced at the *hedge*. Displaced air popped. Toes digging into the frozen energies, he sped up the side of the *hedge*. At the top of the massive ward, he stopped and swung Angie off his back, sitting her on the slightly curved dome, the blanket around her.

Wide-eyed, she said, "Can we run like that when I'm not scared and cold?"

He chuckled. "If we succeed, Angelina, I will take you on a full moon run. For now, can you untangle the magics?"

She pressed her fingers against the top of the ward where the energies of the original *hedge* had been drawn up like a balloon and sealed. She pressed through the energies, her tiny fingers weaving, or perhaps unweaving. She mimed pulling a strand up and up and had to stand to continue. He steadied her to keep her from slipping, and still she pulled the invisible energy strand through the small opening she had made. She tossed it and began another.

An hour passed.

He had to restrain himself from looking toward the east. There was no sun protection here and though he would give his life for the Everharts, to burn up in front of Angie might scar her. Undoubtedly, it would be painful for him as well.

Another hour passed and sunrise had begun to tint the sky gray when Angelina sat back from the opening, leaning against his legs in exhaustion. She held her hands in front of her, as if she held reins, and he saw flashes of light and pulses of power in them, though there was nothing tangible to focus on.

"I'm done," she said. "Being an Everhart is hard."

"Why is that?"

"We have to save the world sometimes. Like Ant Jane."

"Ah. That is indeed a heavy burden. Do you have the strands you want?"

"I have two. I can't ride down on your back." She looked up at him and her cheeks dimpled. "You can carry me like a bride!"

"Oh, Angelina."

Her dimples slid into an expression he could only call grief. "We're never gonna get married, are we?"

"It is unlikely," he said gently, helping her to stand.

"I woulda made a beautiful bride."

Edmund choked back a laugh and lifted her into his arms. "Coming down," he shouted, and leaped. His bare feet caught the surface, skidding along the frozen energy like snow skiing. He dropping to his backside when the angle became too great to maintain balance. They hit the ground in a run.

"Twenty minutes until sunrise," Liz said. "Cutting it close, fanghead."

Ed said to Angie, "Give me one minute to get in back to take out the time-frozen humans. Then I want you to say, 'One, two, *three*,' and yank the strands of magic on three." He looked up. "Cia and Liz will rush in the moment the magic falls and help your mother. Evan, you'll have to carry Angie to safety. Are you up to it?"

"Yeah. I can do that." But Edmund wasn't certain. He looked as if he'd topple in a slow breeze.

"On three," Ed said again. "I'll hear you."

Angie nodded.

———

Angie said, "One, two, *three!*" She jerked the last strands from the time-space deactivation. The *hedge of thorns* shrieked. It fell.

Daddy picked her up and carried her away from the screeching energies and the sparks and the lightning power that burned her skin. He placed her in the front seat of Edmund's car with George and EJ and left her there.

She heard shouting. Heard her mother crying. And then Edmund was back, bloody and fanged, inside with them, raising the convertible roof. His fangs clicked closed and he turned on the engine and the heat. Softly, he said, "You did it, Angelina. I'm proud."

Angie began to shiver. She had fixed the mistake she made. A moment later, Angie threw up. All over Edmund's expensive leather upholstery. And Edmund.

Edmund sat with Big Evan at the bar of Shaddock's barbeque restaurant. The big witch was aptly named, a mountain of a man who had just finished a mountain of ribs and brisket and side dishes. He wiped his mouth, taking extra pains with the sauce on his beard, and said, "How'd you get Angie to stop wanting to marry you?"

Edmund stopped a smile. Such a union would have been the very worst possibility to a witch father. "She has recognized the implausibility of such a mating. She matured considerably when she accidentally endangered her family with her magics. And those of your wife. She recognizes the responsibility of heritage and family and witch clan. Your daughter is an impressive child."

"She's scary is what she is. How'm I gonna keep her from doing something like this again?"

"You will talk to her."

"Not bind her magics?"

Edmund smiled and drank his beer. It had a hoppy, sharp taste, citrusy and tart. "She sees magical energies without the need for a *seeing* working, making her capable of undoing your magics. She is powerful and that power deserves respect, rather than fear." Ed placed a fifty on the counter. "I am yours to command, Evan Trueblood. Call me. Especially if there's another temporal deactivation. This was . . . interesting." With Mithran grace, Edmund departed.

Bound into Darkness

A Novella

First published in *Dirty Deeds,* an anthology from Pen and Page Publishing (2024). It takes place sometime between books 13 and 14 of the Jane Yellowrock series.

CHAPTER ONE

Liz

Liz Everhart finished the email, tucked her cell into a back pocket of her jeans, ignored the weird buzz of blood-curse taint that still pulled at her flesh, and tried to decide who she wanted to call for backup on this gig. Finding a lost dog sounded easy on the surface, but it could involve hiking up and down mountain ridges, maybe camping overnight, and then hauling a seventy-pound, possibly wounded dog back to civilization. That wasn't something she wanted to do alone. Liz dialed her twin, Cia, and discovered she was spending the weekend with her boyfriend, so help on that quarter was out. Her other sisters were covering the family business, Seven Sassy Sisters' Herb Shop and Café. That left asking Jane Yellowrock, who she didn't particularly like, and who was way too busy being some big hoo-ha in the vampire world. Or she could ask the man who had been avoiding her for weeks. Yeah. *Him.* She thought about being rejected again. Or, not so much rejected as suddenly, inexplicably ignored.

Staring out over the vineyard, watching her older sister, Molly, work, she remembered the various comments he'd made a month ago, ones that suggested he was now totally disinterested. She didn't know what had happened, except that he'd been in some pretty dangerous situations protecting Jane Yellowrock. Maybe he really thought the danger to "civilians," as he called people who were not part of Yellowrock's vampire-human-witch clan, was too great for her to handle.

Come to think of it, his apparent disinterest had come almost immediately after her bout with viral pneumonia. He'd been there for her while she recuperated, then he'd pulled back. *Son of a witch! That was it.* Because she'd nearly died, he thought she couldn't keep up with the danger. If she hadn't caught him looking at her a couple of times, she would have believed he'd changed his mind about them being together and become oblivious to her. He thought she was *weak*, which might be worse. *Stupid man.*

Down the hill, Molly stretched hard and blew out. She'd been hired to talk to the vines to help them grow. Molly was an earth witch and, when she talked to plants, she actively pushed her earth magic into the soil, into the roots, encouraging them to good health, to seek out proper nutrients. She gave them a boost of life. Liz wasn't an earth witch like Molly, but even she could tell the land here was well cared for, happy, and productive, in part due to Molly "talking to the vines." Yellowrock and her consort, George Dumas, should have a good crop come harvest time. Aaaand she was wasting time.

Liz trudged back up the terraced incline to the big inn where the Yellowrock Clan wine label originated, and which housed the Yellowrock Clan itself: a mixed para clan that did crazy stuff trying to keep the human-versus-para war from erupting here like it had in other parts of the world. *Politics.* Liz hated politics. Wasn't real fond of vamps. But Yellowrock's adopted clan-brother, Eli Younger, the man who had been avoiding her, lived here. That ornery man made it worth the trip from Asheville.

It wasn't a hard climb, but Liz was huffing by the time she got to the house. It was early fall and the humidity, even in the hills above Asheville, was at 80 percent with temps near ninety. And while Liz's lungs were better, thanks to witch healing, they were permanently damaged from the trauma that resulted when her now-deceased elder sister Evangelina dropped a boulder on her in a magical fight over a demon. She had nearly died. Her other sisters had saved her from instant death. Yellowrock had made sure she had vamp blood to sip to speed the healing. But even with continued healing blood and *healing* workings, along with her niece's prayers, trauma was trauma.

Then the virus struck. Pneumonia had sucked. There were days when

Liz still fought her way through every exertion, breath by breath. Which was why she needed a partner to locate and retrieve the lost dog. Standing on the front porch, she pulled her red hair up in a tail and secured it off her neck with an elastic hair tie before going inside.

When the door closed behind her, Liz stood and just breathed the cool AC air for a while, letting her sweat evaporate, listening to the placement of voices, the various positioning of people. No vamps, thanks to the daylight, but George Dumas was talking to Big Evan, Molly's husband, in the kitchen ahead and to the right. Her niece and nephew, Angie and EJ, were playing a game somewhere, one that involved a lot of stomping, thumping, shouting, and screaming a single word over and over. A werewolf—one stuck in wolf form, which had always been unnerving—was panting from her left. Keys were clacking from the office area where Alex, Eli's brother, was working. Music came from upstairs. Jane had been dancing a lot lately, working on moves and trying to get control of some facet of her magic.

Two particularly loud screams pierced the air. She heard Eli's soft voice say, "Good. Excellent foot placement, EJ. Great arm position, Angie. Again."

More dual screams pierced the air. The kids weren't playing a game. They were taking a lesson in self-defense.

Liz didn't get teary often. But knowing that Eli—big bad Army Ranger warrior injured in one of the Middle East wars, tough as nails, emotional as a stone—was teaching her niece and nephew some form of martial arts, did the trick. Both kids had been through a lot. And Eli. *Damn.* Eli was just about as perfect a human being as she knew. She wanted to be part of his life and he'd drawn away because she might be weak? That made sense. He probably didn't want or need anyone else to care about, plan for, or to worry about right now. But his eyes, those dark eyes, they still followed her when he thought she wasn't looking.

Blinking away the stupid tears, Liz wandered closer to the workout room, where the screams were ear-piercing. Something like, "Hah! Hah!" For the one martial art she was familiar with, practitioners often shouted "Kia. Kia!" But she knew that Eli practiced a military form of MMA—mixed martial arts—a combo of forms, so maybe that was the difference.

Besides being Jane Yellowrock's adopted brother, Eli was her second-in-command in charge of mundane munitions and tactics, defensive measures, all that fighting stuff, because of the vamp war. The Everharts were part of that war, having been attacked and having homes burned.

His back was turned when she leaned against the wide-cased opening to the workout area. He was demonstrating a move that might be useful if an attacker or kidnapper tried to come at them. They knew from personal experience that they could be picked up and tossed around like sacks of potatoes, but combined with the magic they were technically too young to have—according to all the witch-lore Liz knew—knowing this stuff could make them safer. One more weapon in their arsenal. And they looked adorable in their little white workout suits.

She crossed her arms to indicate she was no threat. When Eli turned around, he didn't flinch or jerk, but his eyes landed on her instantly. A bare half second of recognition and evaluation before moving on. He finished the form with the kids, walked them through a series of stretches and breathing techniques for a few minutes, and said, "Okay. Y'all go take off your doboks and put on your play clothes. Your aunt Lizzie wants to talk."

She narrowed her eyes at him. No one called her Lizzie.

The kids bowed ceremoniously, and said together, "Thank you, Captain America!" They whirled to see her in the doorway and rushed at her, squealing. They threw their arms around her. Together they shouted, "Hey, Ant Lizzie!"

She frowned at him and tousled their red hair. They released her and sped away, bare feet pounding. *"Lizzie?"* She hated that name.

A minuscule smile touched his mouth as he started across the floor space toward her. "Lizzie. It fits you."

"Uh-huh. Like Captain America, Marvel superhero, fits you. Wanna go camping?"

Eli stopped.

Oh. There it was. That spark of interest in his eyes.

"I could do some camping," he said cautiously.

"Not just to relax," Liz said. "Maybe a hard hike too. I have a job. Tracking down a missing dog."

"You're asking me to work with you." And there it was, gone again. Shoot. She should have asked just for camping.

"I'm asking you to accompany me on a hike into the gorgeous mountains between Morton Overlook and Morton Tunnel, and down toward the gorge if necessary, to the Appalachian Trail." She had just described some of the most rugged, unmarked hiking areas off U.S. Route 441. Eli did not look impressed. That expression probably scared off most women. Liz wasn't most women. Liz was a stone witch, of the Everhart witch family. She stared at him. Waiting.

"Just the two of us," he said.

"Yes. To find the missing dog of a friend of a friend. It ran off after a car accident, but it has a magical *tracking* working on its collar. I'm expected to pick up the tracking fob at the hospital before we leave. The dog may still be near the accident site. Or it may have run off and be farther down the gorge. And it may be injured, in which case we'd have to carry it out."

"Overnight."

Something warm and heated flushed through her. "Like I said, we might get lucky"—she paused deliberately—"and find Rover on the side of the road, waiting for us. Or we might have to walk down and get a ride at the bottom. I'll split my fee with you."

That faint almost-but-not-quite smile reappeared. "Rover?"

She smiled back. "I didn't name him. I'm far more clever and imaginative than that." *Yeah. Mull that one over, Captain America.*

"When do we leave?"

"I don't have my sleeping bag here. It's back at my house."

"I have enough gear for both of us."

Liz didn't know if that was a double entendre or not, but she could hope. "Food?"

"I'll take care of it," he said. "I can be ready in twenty. You got hiking shoes?"

"In the car," she said.

"Meet you out front."

Eli moved away. She'd never been able to describe his walk. It wasn't a saunter. It wasn't pretty like a glide. It was economical and efficient with a sense of purpose. She shook herself awake from the image of his butt walking away from her naked and left the house to check in with Molly, who was finished with the land-working gig. Her sis was breathing hard and a little milk had leaked around the nursing cups and through her nursing bra.

"Thanks for the gig," Liz called, waiting beside her Subaru.

"God, I hate this heat. It's September, not the middle of freaking summer," Molly griped. "You got a job? What job?"

"I just got a job from a member of the Ainsworth witch clan. Woman named Golda Ainsworth Holcomb. She used your name."

Molly shrugged and trudged onto the porch, where she dropped to the steps in the shade and fanned herself. Her red curls waved in the hand-breeze. She leaned against a massive stone column and said, "Everyone wants an Everhart these days. But *son of a witch on a switch*," she swore, witch-style, "I'm getting too old for this."

"Dumas is paying you a fortune. You'd have taken this gig if you had to push yourself around with a walker."

"True. And with the house nearly finished, I need extra money to complete the furnishings. Top of the line all the way." In a part of the ongoing para war, Molly's house had been the target of arson, a magical firebombing, and had burned to the ground, even with the *hedge of thorns* ward protecting it. Since Yellowrock's enemies had done the firebombing, Molly and her family were rebuilding and staying at the inn free of charge until they could go to their new home. "What kind of gig?" Moll asked, closing her eyes and fanning herself.

Liz said, "Looking for a lost dog." Casually, she added, "Eli and I are going together. It"—she paused deliberately—"may take until tomorrow, so if I'm not back tonight don't get worried."

Molly smiled. "Finally got him to agree to another date, did you?"

"A job. We'll see if it turns into a date."

Her sister's smile widened. "Hmmm. Have fun." There was a lot of emphasis on the word *fun*. "I'm going to shower and feed Cassy. Later, sis." Molly grunted to her feet and went inside, closing the enormous carved door.

Liz walked down the steps to her vehicle and put on her hiking shoes.

When Eli appeared, he tossed a lightweight titanium-framed backpack into the open Subaru hatch. "Can you fit your gear inside?" he asked. There were two sleeping bags in vacuum-sealed plastic strapped to the top, and when she looked inside, she counted twelve dehydrated meals, three packets of salmon, several bags of nuts, a tiny French press, a bag of coffee, and a lightweight, deep-sided fry pan. She transferred her essentials from her overnight bag to a zippered travel bag and tucked the bag into a roomy pocket of the backpack. She added a pair of birdwatching binoculars, a lighter and a bag of corn chips for starting a fire, and her battery stone, which held a magical charge to fill her other amulets if necessary. She slung it on and adjusted the straps. She could manage this, even wearing and carrying all the amulets and the battery, which added eight pounds to her overall load.

She looked Eli over. He was carrying a much larger backpack by the straps, and his appeared full. And strapped with tools. And heavy. "You're carrying the water," she guessed. And then she saw the weapons. He had a shotgun in some kind of sling, a semiautomatic handgun in a thigh rig on his right, a silver-plated vamp-killer sheathed on his left, and a machete attached to the backpack. And there was a hunting knife peeking out of a sheath on his belt.

"Going bear hunting, Captain America?"

"Protection from possible werewolves."

"There haven't been any seen around here in months."

His expression didn't change. His body position didn't change.

Liz tilted her head and raised her brows in an expression that said *whatever*, and shrugged out of the backpack, now carrying it with both straps slung over one shoulder. "My car or yours?"

"Mine."

She grabbed her walking stick, a fifty-five-inch-tall, hand-carved stick she'd used for years.

"No weapons?" he asked.

Liz touched her necklace. It was forty-two inches of large polished nuggets, several carved rock beads, three silver amulets, and her grandmother's wedding ring. The metals had been charged by a metal witch. Each stone and amulet contained a different working. The necklace was heavy, but it was her best defense, especially when used in conjunction with the big-mama power sink, a fist-sized hunk of granite she'd added to her travel bag essentials. She could use it to draw raw power straight from any partially buried boulder she could find. She slid the nuggets between her fingers and made sure the clasp was tightly closed. When she released that catch, it allowed all the stones to slide free, to be put together in a different configuration, or for independent magical purposes.

Eli snorted delicately. It wasn't quite derision, but he clearly wasn't impressed.

"Uh-huh," Liz said, amused at the goading. "We'll see."

Eli

Lizzie was cute, touching her necklace, challenging him. He had never cared a thing for redheads, until Sylvia, and he'd thought Syl was a one-off. He didn't really want another one in his life. And if she hadn't nearly died in the hospital recently, he'd still be interested. Still was interested. But he knew his lifestyle. He couldn't put anyone else in jeopardy again. It was bad enough that Alex was always in danger, but he was teaching his younger brother how to shoot, how to take a fall and come back fighting. The kid was putting on muscle and he had the hand-eye coordination of a natural shooter. Jane was fighting all comers, dancing, and in the best shape in ages. The kids were coming along.

Liz was . . . Liz had nearly died. She might never be able to take care of herself, certainly not in a fight. He'd seen too many abused women in the war. He couldn't stand to see such a thing again, especially not to Lizzie. Never to Lizzie.

Yet here she was, planning to go off into the mountains alone. He couldn't let her do something stupid like that. Maybe she could handle a hike and a lost dog fine. And maybe she'd fall off a cliff or get bitten by a rogue werewolf—not that there had been reports, but still, it could happen—or turned by a rogue vamp, and he'd hate himself for not going along to keep her safe. Images of her in danger flitted through his mind. *Son of a bitch.*

He closed the hatch of her Subaru and placed their gear in the back hatch of his SUV, locking the weapons in the gun safe that was bolted into the floor and stowing their equipment in the new mesh partitions. He opened his door, got in, strapped in, and saw from the corner of his eye that Liz did the same.

The vehicle had been in the sun all day and it was stuffy hot. He pressed the start button, adjusted the necessary temps and mirrors, and lowered the windows so the AC could blow the hot air out. He liked the way Lizzie smelled. Like vanilla and stone.

He backed out, reminding himself that the next step in security measures involved building a garage for the armored vehicles Jane traveled in. His POV—personally owned vehicle—didn't fall into that category. He wanted it out where it was ready to go at any moment.

Vanilla and stone.

He raised the windows and shut that thought off.

"We need to stop at Mission Hospital on Biltmore Avenue to pick up the locator fob," she said. "Golda is meeting me in the lobby."

"Roger that." He tapped a button on the steering wheel and gave a voice command. "Call Chewy's cell."

"S'up, Hoss?" Chewy answered.

"One passenger and I need a ride from the Mingo Falls campground to a vehicle accident site between Morton Overlook and the tunnel. Then provide vehicle cover while we hunt for a lost dog. If the dog isn't found onsite, we'll need pickup at a GPS to be determined later."

"ETA to Mingo?"

"Sixty mikes."

"Roger, out." The call ended.

Liz asked, "Just like that?"

He raised his brows and looked the question at her.

"You called a guy and he shows up? No questions? No story? No convincing? And why the campground at Mingo? And what's a mike?"

"Yes to the first question. No to the next three, and a mike is a minute." He glanced at her. "Military jargon. If Chewy hadn't been available, I had a plan B." Plans B through G, not that he needed to say that. Always having a plan had kept him alive too many times to ditch that way of life now. "If we leave a car on the side of the road overnight, it'll be stripped or impounded by morning. So we have a ride from Mingo to the accident site and a pickup near any GPS I name. Chewy knows the trails like the back of his hand and has any wheeled equipment we need for an exfil." He'd also arranged to have the helo on standby if they needed emergency evac and had left orders with Alex on which wildlife and game and rescue groups to notify should there be complications. Plans A through G with options and alternatives.

"Oh. Right." She tugged on her ponytail, scowling.

He could tell she hadn't thought that part through. He resisted a smile. *Cute.*

Vanilla and stone.

He was well and truly screwed.

CHAPTER TWO

Liz

They stopped at Mission Hospital on Biltmore Avenue and Eli let her out to circle the block while she talked to the client. Liz texted Golda that she was out front and a woman sitting in a wheelchair inside waved her in. Liz went through the standard protocol for entering a hospital, put on her mask, and walked toward Golda, who was sitting in a wheelchair in the waiting room. She passed two other patients, both wearing white hospital bands, and both being wheeled outside to waiting cars. Golda must be waiting on her ride.

The witch was wearing a mask and had a leg up, the lower leg wrapped thickly in wide Ace bandages and purple sticky wrap. Her arm was in a sling and there was dried blood matted in her hair. It was an odd color for dried blood, but the yellow-brown stains around it said a wound had been cleaned with that nasty Betadine stuff. It had clearly colored her hair and the blood. Oddly, she smelled sweet, not the sickly scent of bruised and damaged flesh.

"I'm Liz Everhart."

"I know." Golda handed her a little silver box. Golda wasn't much for chitchat. She launched into instructions. "Inside there's a quartz crystal about three inches long on a split ring. It has a limited range of three miles and only has enough power to last twenty-four hours once you open the box. Don't open the box until you get to the accident site. He's a seventy-pound rescue and looks like a German shepherd–chocolate lab mix. He'll come to anyone who calls him. Please find Rover." She put her head down and sniffled. "I miss him. And I'm so worried he's hurt."

Liz shoved the rectangular box into her front pocket. "And when I find him? If he's hurt, what vet do I take him to? And do you want him boarded?"

"The closest vet or veterinary hospital. And they can board him. I'll be out in three days and can claim him then." She extended a padded envelope. "There's a picture of Rover inside, his favorite doggie chew, a package of dried roast beef, his leash, and—" She stopped. "And two thousand dollars."

Liz's eyebrows went up. "That's more than we agreed on."

"It's also a down payment on vet bills and boarding. Your reputation says you're honest and reputable. Just . . . please find him and get him to help."

"I'll do my best. How do I get in touch when I find Rover?"

"My cell was destroyed in the accident. You'll have to email me, the same way I reached you. My tablet is my constant companion." She patted a small device at her side, nested in a wheelchair pocket.

"I can do that and tell you which vet he's at. Hope you feel better."

"I'll feel better as soon as Rover is safe."

"Yes, ma'am." Liz dinged Eli's cell and walked out the door, dropping the mask in the special biohazard can at the entrance.

When Eli pulled up, she got in the SUV and he eased back into traffic. Liz opened the envelope. It had all the things in it Golda had said. She counted out the twenty hundred-dollar bills.

"Is half of that mine?"

"No." She ruffled the bills and shoved them back in the envelope. "You get half a grand. The rest is for the vet bills and boarding."

"So why are you frowning."

"I don't know. Something's odd."

"Odd as in we abort and go get a steak? Or odd as in we continue on, eat dinner in the mosquitoes and humidity, and hope snakes don't crawl into your sleeping bag."

"I'm not scared of snakes," she said thoughtfully. "And I don't have a feeling we should take the money back and quit. I don't know what I'm feeling. Something."

"Burger before we leave civilization?" he asked.

"I thought you only ate healthy."

"I occasionally do stupid things. And enjoy them."

Liz wanted to say *Am I a stupid thing you might still want to do?* But she kept her mouth shut and smiled very, *very* slightly. Two could play the guessing game. Liz had heard Eli's last girlfriend had been a redhead, but otherwise, very different from her—a law enforcement officer who loved coffee and firearms. Liz didn't drink much coffee, didn't need firearms, and could take care of herself just fine without them. Liz just wanted things back like they had been. That meant admitting she hadn't thought about parking and give kudos where they were due.

"I hadn't thought about where I could safely leave the Subaru overnight when I took the gig. I guess I planned to leave my car on the side of the road when I hiked in. That was stupid. Thanks." She had planned on Eli carrying the seventy-pound dog out overland and hadn't thought about much else.

"You were hoping to find the dog close by," he said mildly.

"Yeah. Still am. But scared dogs can run for hours. The crystal has a range of three miles. Rover could be anywhere."

Thereafter they rode in silence, though Liz did look at his hands often. Dark skinned. Strange calluses, probably from weapons practice and fighting, a few white hairline scars, likely from the explosion that nearly killed him in Afghanistan. He was wearing a short-sleeved T-shirt, camo pants with lots of pockets that bulged with stuff, and hiking boots that bore a strong resemblance to combat boots. She was wearing thin, water-wicking, water-resistant hiking pants and a tank top, and had stuffed a thin, lightweight jacket in the pocket of essentials. Eli's wardrobe looked sturdy and hers looked like she was out for a walk with the kiddos. She wondered if she had brought the right clothes. Or the right anything. But she figured she had brought the right man. Eli Younger looked like he could handle anything she couldn't, and she had more magic in her necklace than most other witches.

Liz

Sometime later . . .

Their driver from Mingo Falls was the taciturn vet named Chewy who called Eli "Hoss." Chewy was a white guy with a beard thick enough for eagles to nest in, never looked at her, spit tobacco juice into a foam cup every few minutes, and played Merle Haggard over Eli's sound system at earsplitting levels. When he pulled over on 441 at the obvious signs of a very recent car crash—skid marks, a bumper and car door still lying in the trees—Chewy looked up and down the road and said, "Position of this vehicle gives you adequate room to maneuver. Leave the doors open."

Liz got out and started calling for Rover. Eli slung a small day pack around his shoulder, pulled out a pair of fancy binoculars, and began to scan the surrounding area.

"What does your locator fob say?" Eli asked.

She pulled the small box out, opened it, and simply stopped. The crystal inside nearly took her breath away. It was a quartz crystal in its natural form, clear as diamond, but with slight magnification properties. "Wow." She touched it and felt the faintest sizzle of energy inside. That energy pulled her hard off the road in a direction where the land fell off downhill fast. Like it was the end of the world. Liz clipped the crystal on its split ring to a carabiner on her belt and pointed downhill. "That way. 'Second star to the right.'"

"'And straight on till morning.'" Eli finished the quote while checking their position on an old-fashioned compass.

Liz grinned but said nothing. Either he was a *Star Trek* fan, a *Peter Pan* fan, or he'd been watching movies with the kids. Liz was betting on the latter.

"Any idea of distance, or are we just gonna whistle and call Rover all day?" The words bordered on snark, but his tone was relaxed and calmer than she'd heard it in weeks.

As a stone witch, Liz might be able to get something more specific than

Golda's "within three miles." She closed her eyes and concentrated. She smiled, then frowned. "About a mile, down the hill, that way, and moving away from us." She pointed, getting a flash of the blood-curse taint still on her skin. She dropped her arm. At least it had never gotten any worse.

Eli gave a faint grunt that could have meant anything and began removing their gear from his SUV. Liz slid into the straps of the backpack, hung her own binoculars around her neck, took her walking stick in one hand, and by the time she was done, Eli was fully kitted out in his guns and blades and heavy pack. Dang. That was fast. "All clear?" he asked Chewy.

Chewy looked over his shoulder and said, "All clear. Get out of sight before I pull off. Black man with guns. Be careful."

"Always am. We'll be out of sight in two mikes."

"Call when you need exfil, Hoss," the old vet said.

They shut the SUV hatch and doors. "Let's get out of sight," Eli said, "Chewy's right. Black man with guns is considered a clear and present danger, especially in backwoods North Carolina."

"Unless you're with Yellowrock."

"Being with her makes things easier and harder." He didn't elaborate. She didn't ask. They started downhill, walking in the path of the car that had gone over the railing, taking out the thick underbrush that grew near the road. And down. And way down, fast, for about thirty feet until it flattened out just a bit.

When they were out of sight from the road, Chewy pulled away and they were on their own. Eli stopped again and took in the location of the mountain peaks, compared their location to a topo map on his cell before pocketing the cell. He asked, "Does your magical crystal see an exact trail, or does it just show what direction the dog is now and which way to go."

"I don't—" She stopped. "Let me try something." She lifted the crystal with her left hand, touched a blue-and-green chrysocolla bead on her necklace with her right hand, and opened a *seeing* working. The magic stored inside the crystal pointed off to the left and directly down. "Nice. Okay. The workings are compatible. No direct trail, just a location and current movement. A mile that way as the crow flies, moving parallel to the bottom of the gorge, but slower than before and still away from us."

"How did that just work?" he asked.

"I used a *seeing* working to follow the magic tying the crystal to the amulet on the dog."

"So not something a mundane could use." His tone was asking for clarification of a supposition.

Liz frowned slightly. "On your own? Without a witch? Maybe. With some modifications and an additional amulet or two." Or with a witch and physical contact. Like holding hands. "I'll think about it."

Eli put away his toys and led the way down. And down. And *down*. She had to grab trees to stop wild careening slips that would have sent her rolling like a ball. She had to stab her walking stick into the ground and use it like a lever to hold herself in place. She was noisy and breathless, while Eli moved almost silently, was alert to everything around them and above them, and stepped downhill with his usual economy. He might as well have been on flat land. It was disgusting.

He never looked at her, but somehow she knew he was aware of her every noisy move. When her hand missed a tree, he caught her lower arm and swung her to the right into a bigger tree. She leaned against it and just breathed for a bit, but it was hot and muggy and even with the elevation, gnats and no-see-ums were everywhere. One flew into her eye, and as if that was a command, others flew into her mouth. Which started a coughing fit, her eyes watering. She held up a finger and the gnat finally flushed out, but the damage to her lungs made her coughing last longer than she wanted. Between racking coughs, she risked a look at Eli. He didn't look worried or pitying, which helped mitigate the awkwardness of what felt like a terrible weakness. When the fit passed, Liz dug into the backpack pocket and pulled out a hat with netting, her sunglasses, and the jacket, and reapplied sunscreen with bug repellent. The last coughs passed while she dressed.

Eli asked, "You got a respiratory inhaler?"

"Yeah. And a dozen healing charms." She pointed to her necklace. "The orange ones are for things like broken bones and major lacerations. If for some reason you need to activate one for either of us, put a little of the injured person's blood or saliva on it and wrap it in place over the area. Or drop one into a wound before you bandage it. They're easy for a doc to

feel if they need to be removed later. If I need to use one for my breathing"—
she pointed to three purple ones—"I'll put one in my mouth like a lozenge.
But I'm okay for now."

Eli gave a spare nod and turned back to look out over the terrain.

Liz breathed. And wondered if this gig was worth the money.

CHAPTER THREE

Eli

From midway down the hill, he called the damn dog, even though the
mutt was clearly a hard hike away. He watched for movement of scrub at
dog height in the general direction she'd pointed, and he called and whistled, while keeping an eye on Lizzie, giving her a chance to rest. Her
breathing leveled out quickly enough that he knew she wasn't in distress.
She had handled the terrain better than he'd expected. He'd heard about
the boulder falling on her, crushing her chest cavity. Her own sister had
done that. And she'd survived.

He called out again, "Rover! Here, boy! Rooooover!" Stupid name for
a damn dog. To Lizzie he said, "You ready to move on?"

"If that's a euphemism for dying, then nope. If it's referring to the fact
that the earth disappears about twenty feet that way"—she gestured to
the line ahead where the earth vanished—"then sure. That looks really
easy. Like a stroll in the park. Or maybe like falling off a cliff."

He chuckled and passed her a pair of lightweight fingerless gloves.
"They'll fit a little large, and your fingertips will stick out the end, but
they'll help your grip on the trees and your walking stick."

"Thank you."

"Meanwhile, that's called a horizon line," he said, one arm indicating
the straight line just ahead where the earth did indeed vanish. There was
nothing beyond it but mountains, and those were on the other side of the
gorge. "And a horizon line isn't always a bad thing," he added, voice calm.

"Uh-huh. Sure. Tell me another one."

Liz seemed better. And she had an inhaler. And the purple beads. Yeah. Witch shit.

Liz

The land dropped off ahead.

"Meanwhile, that's called a horizon line," he said. "And a horizon line isn't always a bad thing."

"Uh-huh. Sure. Tell me another one," she said as she joined him.

He added, "It just means the drop gets steeper. You climb?"

"Not much," Liz said, hating the fact that she'd taken this *stupid* job. She could have invited him to dinner or camping on the edge of Yellowrock Clan vineyard property. "I took a rappelling course once, but it's been a few years."

"Chewy says there's a ledge at fifty feet. If I rig you up, can you drop down or do we take the longer, flatter way?"

Liz inspected the crystal again and checked the position of the sun. *Oh fun.* She was falling off a mountain at the end of a rope. She said, "I can drop down."

Eli didn't argue. He spent a while picking out the best line, strapped her into a harness, and described the landing site, which was fifty-five feet below. Liz didn't say that her longest drop was closer to twenty-five. Or less. "After that," he said, "there's a ledge and, according to Chewy, what looks like an animal trail off to the west. Things should be easier after we set down."

His hands roamed her butt, waist, groin area, and abdomen, cinching the harness tighter. It was totally professional, and not the least handsy. She wasn't sure how some guys got the whole "proper way to touch a woman without coming off creepy" thing, but Eli had it down pat.

He walked her through how to lower herself safely and what to do at the bottom. "Take off the harness, yell when you're safe, and shout for me to pull up the gear. Sit tight and wait for the gear to drop down with the backpacks. Unhook them. Then, sit again and wait for me."

"Okay."

"Watch where you put your hands and feet on the way down. Rattlers might be nesting in the crevices."

"Oh. Whoopie."

"Want to turn back? If so, let's do it now. Chewy says once we get down to the ledge, it'll be a lot harder to get back to the road."

Liz looked at his face, which was noncommittal, not giving her a clue which way he thought she should choose. But her lungs felt better after the short rest. "I have a soft spot for lost dogs. I got this."

He repeated his instructions and strapped her walking stick to her pack. Liz took a breath, blew it out, turned her back to the mountains on the far side of the gorge, and started walking down the not-quite-vertical drop. A few feet in, her confidence grew, and she pushed off with her feet, dropping a short distance before stopping her fall, over and over, her eyes scanning for snakes, her hands picking up the muscle memory of her last rappel.

The ledge was just where it was supposed to be. No snakes were anywhere in sight and getting out of the harness wasn't impossible. "I'm down. Harness is ready," she shouted. The harness moved swiftly up, and Liz sat down, taking in the vista. The earth fell away, the trees were still bright with summer, the wind whispered through the forest like the breath of the Earth itself. Molly would have broken into tears at the sight of so much life and peace and so much amazing *green*.

The gear came down, tied with knots Liz didn't know how to undo. It took a while to figure out how they worked before she could shout for him to pull it up. She tucked her walking stick under her arm and went back to the view. Eli landed near her. She heard him putting away gear, his harness, all the climbing stuff. He sat near her and offered her a bottle of water. She took it and drank. It was warm, but she needed the moisture. "This view alone is worth this gig," she said.

"Pretty amazing."

When the water was nearly gone, Liz went into the bushes and used her portable urinal, rinsing it with the bottle's last drops of water. Eli went the other way and, she assumed, did the same, but without a female urinal. Then they started down the animal path. And down, and down.

An hour later, breathing hard but feeling better than she had in a long time, she leaned against a handy tree and said, "I'm pretty sure a mountain goat made this path."

Eli burst out laughing, stopped, and looked at her over his shoulder. "You don't talk much for an Everhart."

"I can be chatty. But Cia is the talker. I'm the silent twin."

"Why did you ask me to work with you on this gig?"

That came out of left field. But if he wanted direct, she could be direct. As long as she didn't look him in the eyes while she was being candid. "I like you. I thought you liked me. Then I got sick and you backed off like I had the plague. Which I did, sorta. I hoped spending the day together might let us see if there's anything left between us. Falling off a mountain and maybe ending up in a splatter of blood and broken bones seemed the best option at the time."

Eli laughed again. It was a good laugh. He didn't do it often. Maybe hanging with the kids had brought out a softer side of him. "You rethinking that strategy now?" he asked.

She pulled off her hat and scratched her sweaty scalp, thinking. She redid her ponytail, this time hanging it out of the small hole in back. "Not really. Angie Baby and EJ called you Captain America. They're right. And this is fun, in a hot, sweaty, hard-to-breathe, muscle-wrenching, exhausting kind of way."

There was a lot left unsaid in that exchange, but she'd take what she could get. He grinned at her and something warmed again in her middle, which reminded her. She dug in a pocket and handed him a tiny reddish stone. "I forgot. Raw hematite. It's spelled to make ticks think you're made of rock. Next time I'll see if I can make one to repel snakes, spiders, and these gnats, which my lotion does nothing to combat." She waved at the gnats again swarming her face.

Eli took the small rough stone and tucked it into the chest pocket of his T-shirt before starting back along the pseudo-trail. They crossed a runnel of water. When her foot landed on the other side, the odd itchy feeling of the blood-curse taint hit her. Hard. She stopped, activated her *seeing* working again, and stared around. Eli didn't look back, but his hand went to his gun at his right thigh. "What?" he asked, sotto voce.

"Not something I can explain. Just this itchy feeling I get whenever something evil is close by or is watching me."

"Evil."

"Yeah. I don't *see* anything, but something's not right."

"Your dog crystal is glowing."

Liz looked down at the crystal, and in her *seeing* working, it glowed red. In her normal human eyesight it was pale pink.

"Your dog crystal is *glowing*," he repeated, pushing her behind a tree, his eyes still searching for mundane threats, "at the same time you get an itchy feeling about evil. I don't like coincidences. What do you know about the woman who hired you?"

Not much, Liz thought, her mind ranging through possibilities she hadn't considered before. "She was . . . She claimed to be Golda Ainsworth Holcomb, from the Ainsworth witch family. They've been in this country since the eighteen hundreds, are allied with three covens that I know of, and have a solid rep. She sent an email, referencing my sister who doesn't remember her, but Moll is well known everywhere, so she might have heard her talking about me and that I supplement my income with the occasional magical investigation."

Liz looked at the crystal again and saw that the energies were still pointing well over a half mile away. They had been trekking hard, but mostly downhill, not horizontal. "But . . . I had a vague feeling at the hospital that something wasn't right. Never could put my finger on it. Let me think." Liz slid down the tree she was leaning on and closed her eyes, trying to recall every word, every gesture.

"Holy crap," she whispered. "Golda wasn't wearing—I can't say *wasn't*. But I don't remember seeing a hospital bracelet on her wrist. And . . . she smelled wrong." She looked up at Eli. "Golda had a head wound, broken bones. And she smelled sweet. Vaguely like jelly."

Softly, Eli said, "People with wounds don't smell sweet. Shock and trauma to the body release toxins into the blood, and even after the flesh is stitched back up, they sweat out the stink. It can take days for the smell to go away."

"She had blood in her hair. It was hours old and it was still reddish, like pinkish red."

"Shouldn't have been. Should have been brownish red. Unless the accident tossed jelly into her hair. Maybe she had groceries in the car."

"Could be. That could also account for the sweet smell." Liz brightened and stood. "That makes a lot of sense, but I think I'll call the hospital and ask to be put through to her room."

"Not likely," Eli said. "We've been out of a service area for an hour." He pointed down the trail and then up. "Maybe by the time we get to that low peak we'll have service. Not in this crevice." He checked his watch and the compass. "We should start climbing soon, and be there in two hours, barring any forced detours." Without looking back at her he added, "You're breathing hard."

"Exertion. My pulmonologist says I healed up great, but that I have to breathe hard all the time to force my lungs to work. I've begun to run and walk, but not on inclines like these. The pulmonologist calls it rehab, but he means torture."

"Rehab sucks."

"Oh yeah." She followed him along the trail and toward the peak where they might get cell service. Or not.

Eli

He made the trek up and down the terrain as easy as possible, making sure her hands were in place on the next tree or outcropping, her walking stick was properly positioned, and her feet were secure before he moved on. But he didn't hover. It wasn't in his nature to take over other people's jobs, and the witch had set this up.

At the top of the small hill, he made sure she was okay—as in still breathing and not in clinical distress—and took out his binoculars and compass. He took a fix on the surrounding hills, inspecting what he could see of the folds of the land leading down. There was a signal here and so he took another look at the topo maps on his cell. He couldn't see it from this vantage, but there was a flat place about halfway down that would make a good campsite. Looked like maybe a water feature.

Looking at the nearby hills again, he spotted a cellular tower or three and took another reading on the compass. He set his kit down and removed a battery-powered, solar-backup Wi-Fi system. He figured about eight feet up on the tree would work. He handed Lizzie a bottle of water. "When you get your breath back, we have a signal," he said.

Liz

Liz was fit and in good shape for a woman with leftover lung damage, but at the top of the peak she dropped the backpack, fell flat on the ground, drank another bottle of water, and poured the last drizzles over her face through the netting of her hat. Her chest was heaving, her heart was pounding, she was wet with sweat, and if she didn't have Toto to find, she might just lie there and die, toes curling up like the Wicked Witch of the East.

Most witches hated it, but early on, before she understood the social impact of the film, *The Wizard of Oz* had been one of her favorite childhood movies, especially the flying monkeys. At age four, she'd wanted a flying monkey as a pet so bad she'd cried when her mother brought her a puppy. She pulled off the hot sweaty hat and searched out Eli.

He was staring out over the surrounding area with a pair of good-quality binoculars. A full minute or three later, her breathing finally settled into an even pattern, one without the rasp of extreme exertion, and Liz sat up. Her jacket was full of twigs, seeds, leaves, and forest-floor junk. Her hands were blistered even through the gloves from grabbing tree trunks to ease her way down and pull herself uphill, and her fingernails were grubby from all of the above. Her walking stick was dark from dirt.

Eli handed her a bottle of water and she drank it down fast with a murmured word of thanks. He made a little grunting sound of acknowledgment and told her they had a cell signal. When her mouth wasn't so dry, Liz dialed the hospital and put her cell on speaker so Eli could hear. He was getting ready to do something with some kind of gizmo, but he stopped to listen.

It was a newsworthy and unsurprising conversation with the hospital operator. The woman informed her that she could not be put through to

Golda. Either confidentiality concerns had kicked in or there was no such patient as Golda Ainsworth Holcomb.

When she ended the call, Eli asked, "Shall I get Alex to do some digging on her?" Alex was Eli's brother, the younger Younger, a kid with a police record for hacking, a degree on the way from Tulane, and a job as the number one IT guy for the Dark Queen. If anyone could find where Golda was, what she wanted, and anything she might be hiding, it was Alex. He could probably dig up dirt on Saint Peter.

"Please," she said. "Molly will have all the info on the Ainsworth clan. Make sure Golda is really Golda."

"You didn't check before you took the job?"

There was no censure in his tone, but she wanted to bristle anyway. "I had a photo from last year on a witch website. I compared when I saw her in the hospital. She had put on a few pounds, but then so have I."

Eli grunted again and called his brother. The phone call was just like the man: efficient, spare, and devoid of all but the most basic of details.

When all the phone calls were done, Eli, moving with grace and ease of breath that she envied right now, sat beside her. After a while, he asked, "Why would someone give you two K cash, up front, and a magical thing-amabob, and send you out into the wild? Where's the dog now? Assuming there is a dog? Assuming we're actually on its trail. We've seen no tracks, no dog scat."

Liz reached to her waist and unclipped the carabiner, holding the crystal up to the light. There was hardly any magic in the quartz anymore, which was surprising, since it was supposed to have a twenty-four-hour charge, but the little power still present indicated a location down the far side of the ridge they had just climbed, into a ravine that led to the bottom of the gorge.

She pointed downhill and said, "It's moved toward us a bit. Maybe half a mile away as the crow flies, but way back down the mountain, on the other side of the ridge."

"And your evil-sense?"

"I'm not feeling anything now," she said, "except a case of sore muscles."

He nodded and stood, grabbing the gizmo he had been fiddling with. She watched as Eli climbed a low tree, attaching the device to it about eight feet off the ground. It had a black wand that he pointed down the hill, and other parts that he was careful to align according to his compass.

While he worked, so did she. Sliding the backpack straps free, Liz retrieved her battery stone—what she called the chunk of granite that carried stored energy like a battery—and placed the crystal on it to re-charge. The dog was still in the same general area, so she put the quartz back in the silver box to preserve the refurbished energy levels.

He swung down from the tree and alighted in a bent-kneed, soft land-ing. All he needed was the shield.

"There's a runnel of water and a good campsite about two hours away," Eli said. "I just installed a portable Wi-Fi system pointing downhill and up toward the towers behind us and the other side of the gorge. It might give us some access to the outside world. You up for another couple hours of rehab?" He grinned suddenly and it was blinding, lighting his entire face.

Her heart skipped a beat or seven at the sight.

He added, "I'll see if I can massage the soreness out of your muscles after we get camp set up."

For the first time since she got sick, she saw a wicked little twinkle in his dark eyes. He just had to wait until she was slick with sweat, smelled like a dockhand, and was so tired she could barely move. The man was an idiot.

CHAPTER FOUR

Eli

There was no trail. He checked all around, even up into the trees for overhead threats. The tree canopy was both too high and too low to allow him a direct line of sight down, but this was no different from a hundred other ops or training exercises where he'd been dropped in, given an objective, and expected to find his way out.

Except for Lizzie. She had been athletic enough before the battle that had nearly killed her, but not being able to breathe deeply put definite restrictions on the amount and type of exercise she could do. She should probably be lifting weights and stretching, maybe some MMA, and swimming for her cardio. Not running, not yet. No matter what her pulmonologist said.

He wondered how insulted she would be if he suggested a workout regimen for her. That might be one of the things that civilian women got pissy about, thinking he was talking about weight or being out of shape. He thought she looked good with the few extra pounds she'd put on. All in the right places. But again—not something he could say to a woman. A buddy would get it without all the angst. But a woman? He blew out a breath. Best to keep his mouth shut.

Just ahead and down, between them and the campsite, was a stand of laurel, thick and impenetrable. Too wide to go around. Laurel was a low-growing plant, most never getting more than fifteen feet in height, with big leaves and twisted branches. They grew in stands so dense they were a bugger to get around and through. But they provided good cover from airborne predators, which meant animals liked them. All sorts of critters denned and slept in the cover, and there were often trails down to water. He was optimistic he could find an animal trail that led in the general direction of the campsite. Again, he checked everything around and over them. He checked his cell. They still had a signal thanks to the WI-FI in the tree. He had a feeling it would disappear as he traversed the downward ridge covered with the laurel.

He hated to break up the buddy system they had going, but looking at the alternatives, that might be the best bet, short term.

"Stay here a bit," he said, dropping his pack and detaching the day pack to secure around his waist. He repositioned the thigh rig for ease of movement, left the vamp-killer behind, pulled the machete for left-hand use, and positioned the shotgun on its tactical sling with an extended mag of standard ammo. Nothing beat the Origin-12 semiautomatic shotgun for these conditions. He texted her Chewy's number and said, "I'll scout ahead and see if I can find an animal trail to widen."

"You don't have to tell me twice." She sat down and leaned back against the backpack and bedrolls. "I'll just take a nap, right here." She closed her eyes and sighed.

He studied her for a moment, her eyes closed, not breathing quite so hard, and a slight smile on her face. Yeah. She looked good. She looked healthy. And she smelled like vanilla and stone.

God help him. He did not need another redhead in his life. "If for some reason I don't come back, or you hear a lot of gunfire, open a ward over yourself and call the number on the text you just got. Chewy'll find you and get you out."

She opened one eye, rolled a little to her side, and scooted her bottom against the dirt to sit up and remove her backpack all at once. "And why would there be gunfire or why would you not come back?"

"You're the one with a sense of evil and a bad feeling. I'm just prepping for your worst-case scenario."

She waved a hand in the air and said, "Everything feels fine now. These hills are full of magical hotspots. I'll set a short-term *hedge of thorns* to be safe. Go whack some weeds, Captain America. I need a nap."

Without another word, he crouched and entered the laurel grove. Within seconds she was lost to sight. It was another world under here, the ground oddly powdery dry, with micro-runnels of erosion everywhere. When it rained, the laurel leaves and the plants' natural shape acted like overlapping umbrellas, directing the rain down onto the roots, but they also blocked the sun, which meant little to no undergrowth, just the twisted limbs. He whacked a path toward a likely spot, about a hundred feet away. Hot, sweaty, miserable work. But he found an animal trail, just as he had expected. He explored down and down and then climbed back to Lizzie. There was one section where she might need a belaying rope, just in case, but overall, it wasn't a terrible descent.

Liz

The laurel thicket was torturous simply because she couldn't stand upright much, and her thighs and back were not in shape for the crouched posture Eli seemed to find so easy. The belay rope down had given her a sense of security, and the one time she did slip, her walking stick stopped her downward progression before the rope did, which increased her confidence a lot.

They reached the holler with the little runnel of water faster than expected, and since it was mostly downhill, and since the day had cooled off as the sun dropped behind the ridges, Liz was a lot less sweaty, and a lot more comfortable. Eli picked out a flat space for camping, strung their food in a tree so bears couldn't get it, and disappeared upstream into the brush for a "little recon," as he put it, his shotgun at the ready. His last words to her were "If I don't come back—"

"Stop," she interrupted, this time holding up a hand. "I know. If you disappear or I hear gunfire, call Chewy, open a ward, and sit tight until the helpless little woman can be saved. Got it. Now go do your recon before I throw a rock at you and it explodes."

"You have exploding rocks?"

"Not with me but I know how to make 'em. Meanwhile"—she hefted a small stone in mock threat—"this stone witch has really good aim. So stop hovering."

"I don't hover," Eli said with a grin. He turned and slid into the trees.

"Yes, you do," Liz muttered to herself. She studied the campsite and spotted a half-buried ring of stones with about a ten-foot diameter, maybe the remains of a firepit seating area. Or maybe a witch circle. She walked to the stones and touched one. No latent magic was present, just normal ambient magic in the stones. The stones were worn and smoothed; it had been campfire seating, but it had been ages, maybe a century, since it had been used even for that. She scuffed debris away and discovered that with a little work there was a depression in the center for the ancient firepit. Using a little mixed tool on Eli's pack that was part small shovel, she dug a narrow circular trench around the small depression, then carried smaller weather-worn and broken rocks to line the trench. She was sweating again, but voilà, she had a multi-use firepit. She made sure the rocks were all touching in both rings, not that she expected to need two witch circles, but one never knew, and Liz was always prepared. She wedged smaller rocks into the crevices between the larger rocks and placed her hands on the largest stone, testing the circles for power connection. Her magic slid around both rings and back to her. Perfect.

She gathered firewood and arranged a campfire, kindling piled properly, ready to ignite. She then cleared all the brush in the camping area away to contain any sparks from the fire and tossed the bedrolls to the side. Before Eli got back, she relieved herself in the bushes. But she really, *really* needed a bath.

When Eli returned, he was wearing a fresh T-shirt and his buzz cut looked suspiciously damp. He eyeballed the campsite, gave it a scant nod, and said, "There's a pool of water upstream about fifty yards. Deep as sin, cold enough to puck—make you feel better."

She grinned at his word choice alteration and asked, "Bath deep?"

"No bottom I felt. Clean and cold. I scouted around and it seems safe enough, if you can open a ward over the pool."

A bath would be perfect. She tossed him his gloves with a casual "Can do. Thanks."

"Shout 'A-Okay' when you get there."

"A-Okay. I can do that." She grabbed her travel bag and battery stone and headed upstream. Liz reached the small trickle of water splashing over mossy rocks; a tree canopy high overhead cut out the heat. The temps dropped dramatically, and a cool mist filled the air. Using her walking stick, Liz began to trudge upstream. Which was uphill. Of course. Everything seemed to be uphill or vertically downhill today. Her thighs were burning, and her calves were like rocks.

Oddly, her lungs felt better than they had in a long while, but if Eli had to carry her out of the gorge because her leg muscles locked up, things were going to get dicey. Water splashed louder ahead, and she pulled herself up on a tree, climbing up its roots as if they were stairs. She edged around it to see a narrow, crystal-clear, bouncing, ten-foot falls splashing into a pool. "Oh my stars and stones," she murmured.

The pool was a good twelve-foot oval with mossy-green covered rocks everywhere, ferns leaning over the pool, and roots trailing into it. She carefully made her way around the next tree to a small, flat place, one surrounded by bracken and overarching laurel, and with damp scuffs in the dirt made by Eli's boots. She plopped onto the ground and just breathed as the effect of the day's hiking and this last little climb leached away in the clean air. It was shadowy beneath the laurel, chilled and wet; droplets fell on her face and hands. She sighed in something close to peace. She shouted, "I'm A-Okay! Opening a ward now!"

"Good!" Eli shouted back. He sounded a lot closer than she expected, as if he had followed her to make sure she made it. A now-familiar warmth filled her. *Interested.* And camping overnight. And . . . *Oh yeah.*

Her breathing eased out completely and she laid a hand on a half-buried rock. There was power in the stone, a lot of power. She pulled her hand back, trying to figure out why there was so much power here. It was way more stored energy than should be in the stones, as if someone used this place as a power sink. Except she was absolutely certain no one had been here in a very long time. There was no indication that power had been tapped and siphoned from the site in decades. Maybe centuries. Maybe ever . . .

That meant that a previously unknown ley line might run beneath the ground here. Except that was impossible. There were no unmarked ley lines in this area, all of them having been mapped by witches over the centuries, and, before the Europeans came, by tribal shamans and medicine men and women of power. But this *felt* like ley line power. More importantly, it felt like untapped, unused ley line power.

Liz took off her necklace and placed it and the battery stone on a powerful, flat rock. She set the amulets to draw energy through the stone in a slow trickle. She removed the crystal from its silver box, checked to see where the dog was, and placed it to recharge too, setting its box into a pocket. Carefully, because she was afraid of energy backlash, she drew only on the stones she was attuned to and opened an old-fashioned, protective ward around the pool. It was wider than her usual ward, but the rocks accommodated the simple working easily. She shouted to Eli, "Ward is set."

"Good to know," he called back, still sounding too close. "Heading back to camp. Yell when you're ready to head back if it's too dark."

She looked at the trees overhead and, though it was quickly growing darker, decided she had nearly half an hour of workable light left. She pulled off her boots and stripped, grabbed the small squirt bottle of Everhart homemade biodegradable soap from her travel kit, and slid into the pool. "Ooooh my God," she murmured, and dunked her head. The water was deep, with no bottom she could touch, and Eli was right, it was cold. Very cold. She shivered, stretched her back and shoulders, and began to bathe. "Best bath ever," she whispered as she dunked her head again and washed the day's sweat and twigs and leaves out of her hair, her toes holding on to roots. She tossed the squirt bottle back to the small clearing.

For a final rinse, she dove deep, searching for the bottom. At ten feet, the light cut off. The water went from cold to icy. There was a small glow at the surface at the splash of the waterfall and just above it. It was so pale she wouldn't have seen it had the daylight been any brighter.

She kicked in the water, her red hair in a horse-mane-twirl around her as she approached. The glow started about two feet below the waterline and rose up high behind the falls, not seen in the last of the daylight on the surface. It was a green phosphorescence, a dim light in the dark and above her. She swam closer and saw glowing moss on the rocks below the surface behind where the water splashed, the glow leading up to the surface behind the waterfall. Glowing phosphorescent moss. Molly would have gone nuts over the sight. Liz rose to the surface and touched a rock, feeling for danger or evil or anything not right. It had to be the node of the ley line. Ley lines were safe. If she brought word about an untapped ley line to her sisters, it would give them untold power. She caught three breaths before dropping down again and swimming slowly under the falls, closer to the pale light.

The phosphorescence was in a ring with a center that was darker than night. She surfaced in the shallow mouth of a narrow cave, the falls cascading over her, and grabbed the lip of the cave opening, her hands still underwater on the moss. She kicked to stay upright in the water.

The cave was about ten by twelve, composed of solid rock. Not smooth stone, like from water seepage through limestone, but jagged and sharp, as if created by a rock fall long ago. The roof was a solid layer of rock, as were the two sides and the back wall. The wall where she held herself was smooth too, but the rocks inside, on the floor, were broken, splintered, shattered rock, as was the area to either side of her. It appeared that the cave had once been completely enclosed on four sides, and the wall at the waterfall had caved in. The glowing moss covered everything, even the broken rock, which suggested that the front wall had shattered some time ago. Years? A few decades?

The stone beneath her hand was even more powerful than the rock on the surface of the ground had been. The rock beneath her seemed to reach up inside her and share its power.

She pulled herself up and sat, her butt still in the water, on a mossy smooth rock and placed both hands, palms down, on the stones. Power, amazing power, was stored in the stone. Power of the earth, stored in the cave itself, power that seeped into her body, healing her muscles, helping her to breathe better than since Evangelina had used her own power against her and crushed her with a boulder.

Liz would have expected it to feel cold inside the cave, what with water evaporation and being underground, but it was improbably warm. Not steamy, though she wasn't chilled, even being naked and wet. When her breath was totally smoothed out, she swiveled her legs inside and stood, stepping into the cave. The roof was eight or nine feet tall. The interior was lit all around with the phosphorescent moss. It was like a playground of energy for a stone witch. Water slid down the stones everywhere, between the tiny phosphorescent mosses covering every surface. It made soft trickling sounds like a high-pitched percussion instrument, groundwater weeping down from rains above. The lower-pitched sound of the falls just behind her was a deeper thrum with splashy midrange notes. The sounds of water everywhere were magnified, echoing like music in a grand hall.

Tears that might have been joy or peace came to her eyes and she blinked them away, not wanting to miss a thing. Peace flowed through her. A calm she had never experienced. Inebriating and yet serene.

For Liz, keeping her witch power locked down had been a necessity all her life. When she was a kid, some people still considered witches to be uniformly evil, and losing control meant proving them right. Losing control meant exposure and being ostracized by friends. With the name Everhart, people already knew she came from a witch family, so they were always watching her and her sisters, watching for the slightest error. She had learned early on to not give in to anger at the taunts of bullies, to not fight back with her magic. She had held herself aloof, her power deeply locked down, as all witches did.

But this much power all around her, flowing into the soles of her feet, into her lungs with each breath, gently pressing on those internal walls, was urging that locked-down-something inside her to give way, to open up, to accept all the energies around her. To be free. She laughed, a sputtering sound that echoed through the cave.

Her body filled with the power. More and more. Without an amulet, using just raw power, she opened a *seeing* working, a witch working that let her see energy. She had never opened one before without an amulet to direct the energies. The power all around glowed richly into her, around her, beneath her, and she realized she had to be standing directly over that ley line. An unmapped, untapped ley line.

"Holy . . ." she whispered. "Holy, holy, *holy* . . ."

Placing her feet carefully between sharper rocks littering the cave floor, she moved deeper inside. Her eyes adjusted to the dim green light, and she saw, at the back, a small area of cave floor that was without stone. It looked like a puddle of mud. Quicksand? The groundwater had to go somewhere, and maybe not all of it ran out into the pool. At the very back of the cave was a different mass, one not covered with moss, yet, in her *seeing* working, it glowed brighter than the rocks with ley line energies. She eased closer. It looked like a bundle of sticks.

And then she saw the skull.

CHAPTER FIVE

Eli

Eli positioned the wire cooking rack over the surprisingly efficient pile of kindling. Liz had used the old seating ring he'd noticed and created a firepit in the center, placing the stack of larger deadfall logs to the side of the inner ring. It looked like enough to make it through the night. He checked the leaf canopy overhead. It was far enough above to be safe from sparks, there had been rain two days ago, and there was no burning ban in place. Liz had also cleaned up the campsite so there wouldn't be unintended fire. Not bad for a weak witch with no survival skills. He wasn't sure what he felt about that, except maybe satisfied. Relieved. Something. And she'd been totally safe under a portable magical *hedge* when he had to leave her on the trail. Even he didn't have a *hedge* in his arsenal.

He got a fire going using her lighter and the kindling, poured water to heat in his camping pan, and set bottles of water out. He added two dehydrated dinners and foil packages of salmon and nuts. He placed his weapons within easy reach and laid out the bedrolls. Not close enough that it looked like he was expecting anything.

But.

Yeah. But.

Eli preferred women who liked guns. Even Jane, with all her magic, used and appreciated mundane weapons and trained hard to keep up her proficiency levels. Liz found guns amusing, saying it was because she had defensive and offensive weapons he didn't. He'd never seen her display any magical weapons and he had to admit to a certain amount of curiosity.

The military had been trying to get covens to work with them for decades, but except for a few covens that charged fortunes to create anti-magic-spell armor, and a rare outlier witch misfit with delusions of grandeur, they hadn't been very successful. Hitler had done better, but he'd been willing to use methods to secure cooperation that Uncle Sam hadn't. Sooo. What did Lizzie have that he didn't know about?

Her amusement and that vagueness made her intriguing.

He squatted over the fire and rearranged the kindling, adding a larger piece of log. He then pulled his machete and used it to cut up one of the longer deadfalls she had dragged over. He placed it on the pit, the splintered end in the flames, the longer end hanging over the rock edge, to be pushed closer to the flames as needed. The burning wood smelled good. He leaned back on his bedroll and drank a bottle of water. Tonight he would need to bring water from the waterfall, purify it, and refill the bottles, but for now he was content to wait.

Without losing any of the situational awareness that active combat had provided him, he closed his eyes.

Liz

It was a partially mummified human corpse, bones showing through. It was propped upright by a small circle of stones, knees high, as if in the fetal position, and was bound with rotted vines and rotted, braided ropes. The skeleton had black hair in a long braid that lay across its shoulder beside a necklace of stone beads. The skeleton was held together with a rotting plant material, cloth, and a strange belt or chain that appeared to be made of metal plates with odd tabs holding them together. The metal was old and pitted. By the light of the moss and the ley line, and with her *seeing* working, she could tell it was heavily coated with verdigris. That made it copper.

An ancient skeleton bound with copper was not something that belonged here, and it should have fallen apart ages ago. She touched a nearby rock and felt with her magic through the rocks until her stone magic touched the bones. Ancient, *ancient* bones. Far older than she expected. Thousands of years they had sat here, in this wet, dark place. And yet they weren't rotted through to dust. That meant magic had been a part of its burial.

There had been a copper age in the Americas between 4000 and 2000 BCE, mined from somewhere up north. But even at its height, copper had been extremely valuable and rare, especially here in the Appalachians. The copper miners up north had been tribal people who had mined the ore, smelted it into purity using a method long lost to the ages, and made implements out of it. They'd been up near the Great Lakes. Maybe Upper Michigan? This copper had likely been traded for a lifetime of valuables. And it was buried here, with a skeleton that had sat here for millennia.

Out of the top of the skull was another piece of copper, this one like a narrow ax blade. She edged closer, avoiding the mud puddle. Yeah. It was an ax blade. It vaguely reminded her of the ancient ax carried by the mummified man from the Alps. Ötzi.

Liz breathed out a laugh and breathed in power. So much power passing into her through the air and the soles of her feet, until she felt a little light-headed. Drunk. Power, this much power, was a drug to witches. Liz knew that, had been taught that, but saying no to the power felt . . . wrong. And stupid. And . . .

This was what she was *supposed* to feel like. This wonderful. This powerful.

The copper sticking out of the skull had no handle, but she spotted the rotting stick resting on the mummy's shoulder. That suggested that the ax had pierced the skull and been driven deep. And left there. The fact that some ancient tribal people had left the ax behind, a treasure to the ancients, meant it was supposed to stay there. In place. Like a sacrifice or something.

Her fingers itched to touch the ax. She rubbed fingers and thumbs together. They tingled. Her *seeing* working strengthened all on its own. She stepped carefully closer.

She had a feeling she wasn't supposed to touch it, but the copper glowed. It called to her. She passed around the mud puddle, into arm's reach of the skeleton. Gently, she reached out to touch the ax. Just a fingertip. The metal was frigid, cold enough to burn. She yanked back her hand and stepped away.

Her heel touched the very edge of the mud puddle.

The ax fell through the skull and landed inside the skull, behind the jaw and teeth.

Red light blasted up from the mud, so bright it blinded her. Liz shut off the *seeing* working and stepped away, fast, bruising her instep. Bumping, grazing her knee on a rock. Pain shocked through her, clearing her head.

The mud burped. A single expulsion of air. *No.* Of gas. It smelled like sulfur. Like brimstone.

A second bubble erupted. Sulfur and old ashes and the fetid stink of death. "Oh. Hell." She looked back at the skeleton. The chain glowed. The ax glowed. She looked down at her body. Her skin glowed where the blood-curse rested just below the surface.

She had just messed up. Bad. She raced to the cave opening and faced back inside. The floor of the cave was littered with broken rocks. The front wall had once kept all intruders out, hiding the cave. It had once been a solid chamber. Like a prison.

A rumbling vibrated through her feet. Her skin glowed with the blood-curse magic.

Something was coming. Something big. Something bad.

She had to fix this.

Liz pulled on the ley line, drawing the power into herself. Placing her palms on the rocks near the cave opening, she pushed the energy back out of her body, fast, hard, through the rocks and into the chain that bound the skeleton, everywhere the copper touched the rocks. Shoving the power into the metal hurt. Her energies weren't usually compatible with refined copper, but there was so much power. *So* much. It felt far easier than it should have been. She pushed and pushed. Knotting the ley line power into strands that she tied over the copper and into the rocks.

The mud was bubbling around the edges.

The vibrations got harder. Earthquake . . . except not. It was something much worse. The ley line power popped free of the binding she was attempting. Liz stepped back toward the water.

The rocks holding the copper-wrapped skeleton shook and slid to the side. And into the mud. As they tumbled away, she saw the hands and feet of the skeleton, dozens of tiny bones. They fell apart as she watched. The skeleton rocked. It fell forward. And toppled into the mud.

Eli

The earth rumbled. Eli sat up fast. He had been in earthquakes, the kind caused by plates of the Earth sliding around, the kind caused by a volcano erupting, the kind caused by mudslides. This felt like that, the low deep, muted rumble of rocks and mud sweeping everything in their path.

Liz was at the pool. If a mudslide came down the hillside, it would take the path of least resistance: down the runnel.

Without even looking, he grabbed the gear he might need and sprinted back to the pool.

Liz

She cursed. Panting in the sulfur gases, growing desperate for oxygen. Unable to look away. Unable to leave. Knowing what she had done. Knowing what was happening and unable to fix her stupid, foolish mistake.

The bones lay there for a moment, on top of the mud puddle. The mud bubbled harder, even in the center, little plops of sound that shoved gas up, creating holes and suction that began to draw the skeleton down. Heat was mixed in with the reek. Liz covered her mouth and nose. The stench was dangerous. She was breathing too fast and not feeling any better. The stench had displaced the air in the cave, and she wasn't getting oxygen.

The skeleton sank into the mud. A moment later, something rose from the mud, something like a tree trunk, if trees were made of mud. Mud and bone. Long bones stuck out the top, bumpy joints pointing to the cave roof. Embedded in the mud were smaller bones, the toe and finger bones. No copper was visible.

Liz took another step back. The step caught its attention. It leaned in toward her. She froze, except for her desperate breathing and the sudden, urgent need to cough. The mud bent away and then it flung part of itself at her.

A ball of mud and debris hit her in the face. Like muddy slime, it covered her face and hair and down her naked body. It covered her nose and eyes and mouth. And it tried to get inside. Shoving up into her nostrils, trying to slip past her lips. She couldn't see. If she tried to take a breath, the thing would be inside her. And she had no breath left at all.

She drew all the power she had, all the power she could access. She threw it at the mud thing. It screamed like an animal. Something exploded out from it. It hit her in the chest. Slid down her arms, over the blood-curse remnants. Pain shocked through her.

A third mud bomb hit her. The force threw her back.

Like a rag doll, she flew back through the waterfall, flailing, taking with her the mud, a rock she caught in one hand, and a small bit of bone that had been in the mud bomb. She landed in the water. Her head above the surface for a moment.

She fought with all her magic, wrapping herself in the ley line. Desperate for a breath. She dunked under. Rose back up. Threw more raw energy.

Mud hit her again.

And something . . . happened.

CHAPTER SIX

Eli

She wasn't in the pool. Her boots, clothes, her walking stick, her rock necklace were laid out. A squeeze bottle of homemade soap from her family business was on top of her small pack. He waited. She wasn't swimming. She didn't resurface. With a touch he discovered that the protective *hedge* was still in place. He couldn't get to the pool, but . . . it hadn't been a heavy ward, like a *hedge of thorns* put in place by a full coven of witches. Had some sort of ward-resistant paranormal creature gotten to her?

Was Lizzie dead?

He should have been here.

His heart rate sped then slowed as he shoved his own reactions away.

The earthquake passed. There was no sign of a mudslide. At least not yet. Maybe a mining company or a quarry had set off a charge nearby, but he didn't think so. It hadn't felt like the effect of drilled charges, of dynamite. Plus, there wasn't a lot of mining permitted this close to the Blue Ridge Parkway.

At the risk of screwing up his night vision, Eli closed one eye, clicked on his tactical flashlight, and searched the ground with the other eye. Something had splashed up a lot of water. His instant conclusion was that something had taken Liz, but there were no footprints. He scanned the water patterns, turned off his light, and closed his eyes. Counted to twenty, listening.

Eli had only been halfway joking when he explained why he carried the weapons he did. Not many things in life scared him. Not vamps, not witches, not Janie, not even dying. But being bitten by were-creatures scared the living hell out of him.

He'd quartered the area before his bath and gotten a good lay of the land. The water patterns on the ground suggested a northeast trajectory, some creature that could leap far, carrying a full-grown woman, without her screaming or fighting. He moved out, silent as death.

Liz

In total darkness, Liz opened her eyes, as if from a dream, lungs burning for air. There was no sense of up or down. Panic rising, she blew bubbles, following them by feel as they tickled across her, showing her the way up. She rotated her body, kicked, and swam to the surface, which brightened slightly above her. When she breached, her breath exploded out. She sucked in fresh air and a little water and started coughing. Her skin was pebbled with cold, teeth chattering. Her hands were so cold she couldn't grab the roots to pull herself to the surface. It took three tries, and when she landed on the ground, she was shaking so badly she had trouble not curling into a ball and expiring on the spot.

In the dark of deep dusk, she reached for her amulets. Blistered her fingertips.

Her amulets were all scalding hot. In the distance, Eli shouted her name. She tried to reply but the coughing worsened. She picked up her walking stick and banged it against the tree. She doubted he heard her, and she was too weak to bang harder.

She dropped the stick. Her lungs felt full and heavy, and the air that moved through them felt thick as slime.

Shaking, coughing, she pulled on her only pair of clean underpants and a clean tank top. Struggled back into her dirty jeans. There was no way to get her socks and hiking boots on. She was shaking too badly. Her breath was mostly coughing. Her hands ached and burned, and when she ran her fingertips across her knuckles, they were bruised, the skin torn as if she had been fighting. Fresh blood trickled out.

But she didn't remember what she had been fighting. She wasn't even certain when she got into the pool.

She slid her arms into the jacket. In her pocket, the silver box was too hot to touch, and she smelled burning nylon. She held it away from her body. She put the amulet necklace on over her head, over the jacket hood, and stuck the battery stone into the pocket on the other side, away from the silver box and the amulet she scraped back inside. Her amulets were odd-feeling where she touched them, and she didn't know why.

Head wound? Liz touched her head and her hand came away sticky.

Okay. That made sense. She had banged her head on something and had lost some time. And nearly drowned. Still coughing, she carried her boots, socks, and the rest of her gear, and moved around the tree.

It was nearly full night, but Eli must have heard her coughing because he appeared out of the dark. "Found her." He ended a call. "Where the hell have you been?" he asked. "I was just here."

"I don't know," she managed between coughing and shaking so hard her teeth rattled. "Boots."

"How can you not know—" As if realizing questions were counterproductive, he stopped. "Drop the ward."

Liz touched the small stone and deactivated the protection. Eli squatted and helped her feet into her socks and boots. Not an easy task with the shivers. He hoisted her to her feet and put her walking stick in her left hand and an arm under her right shoulder. That left his right hand free, and he carried the shotgun in it. For once, she was happy to have a mundane weapon on hand and someone who could use it.

Half carrying her, Eli got her back to the campsite and the fire. "You're hypothermic," he said, sitting her on a sleeping bag that he dragged close to the fire. He sat behind her and folded his legs around her before wrapping another sleeping bag around them both. Eventually, her coughing eased, and her lungs felt clear. She wondered if she had taken in more than the drop of water at the surface. Maybe she had taken in a lot of water while deep under.

Eli gave her a scrap of cloth. "Handkerchief. Blow."

Liz blew and something gross came out of her nose. "Oh, yuck." She blew several more times, coughed hard for a while, and when the coughing spell passed, she dropped her wet head against his shoulder.

"What happened," Eli asked, his mouth beside her ear.

"How long?" she asked, the two words bringing on another coughing fit.

"You left the campsite at twenty oh-two," he said when the racking coughs passed. "At twenty thirty-two, I went after you. You weren't at the pool, though your things were there. I started quartering the area. At twenty forty-seven, I heard you coughing, back at the pool. What. Happened."

"I don't know. I'm guessing I banged my head somehow." She touched her head and Eli turned her to see. "Either that or I was underwater for thirty minutes or so."

Eli's arms tightened around her, a fast hug, or maybe shock. Her coughing started again, now sounding wet, like pneumonia, and he bent her forward over his left thigh, hitting her back with his open palm in upward thrusts, as if to dislodge something in her airway. Her cough worsened. Long racking sounds. She coughed up water. A lot of water. And something gross. Out of nowhere, she vomited. He seemed to be expecting that and slapped her back with enough force to help her expel the water and gunk from her stomach and lungs. The coughing fit went on too long, and when there was a short break in the coughing, Eli somehow found the three purple healing stones on her necklace and placed all three between her lips.

That helped dramatically. When she could breathe again, he butt-walked them and the sleeping bags away from the gross pool of mucoid muddy water and rolled her back into his lap. He wiped her face. Her shivers went from shaking to bone rattling. Her amulets blazed hot again. She pulled her pocket away, and when Eli realized that the silver box was scorching the fabric, he opened a short-bladed folding knife and cut the pocket out. The box and the burned cloth landed with a hollow thump on the ground.

The instant it landed, the flames in the firepit roared high.

Eli cradled her and rolled them in a half-backward somersault, away from the firepit, his arms and legs cushioning her, the sleeping bags flying. He folded her up in the bags again and grabbed an expandable plastic water container. Tossed its contents on the flames. They blazed higher. Steam rose. "What was that?"

"Opposing magic systems. The elements exploded when they collided."

Liz touched the blue-and-green beads on her necklace and cast a *see-ing* working. The flames were dark with something odd, something she hadn't seen before. She pulled up a sleeve and looked at her arms. The blood-curse was sooty black beneath her skin, tracing up along her magic.

Beneath her butt, the earth rocked.

"Earthquake," Eli said. "Or mudslide." The flames from their fire ignited the leaves twenty feet overhead.

Something was wrong. The smell of brimstone filled the clearing.

The horrible feeling Liz had been carrying for months intensified, a buzzing vibration that brought on a bout of nausea. Her flesh went gray and bruised-looking in her *seeing* working; the blood-curse taint darkened. Her neck burned as the amulet necklace went hot again. All her protections activated at once. A memory came at her, like being hit with a club. "It's not an earthquake," she whispered. "It's not a mudslide. It's a . . . a fire demon."

Eli

The logs on the fire erupted again. Heat and magic blasted out. Eli ducked. Cradling Lizzie. Fire hit him. He threw himself away from her, rolling as his shirt flamed and smoked. Instantly, he was on his feet in a crouch. Weapons in hand. Shotgun and vamp-killer.

The fire went out. In the pit, in the leaves overhead. Utter darkness descended. The smell from the fire smelled odd. Brimstone. Very softly he said, "Fuck. Me."

The pain was like all first-degree burns. Hurt like a mother, but ignorable. He made a fist, stretched. Everything worked. It hadn't burned deep like thermite and it wasn't exothermic like sodium. He'd live.

He quartered the campsite. Wished he'd brought some lenses. FLIR would be handy right now. When he was sure there was no immediate threat, he went back to Lizzie and squatted on the ground beside her. "Can we outrun it? What will it take to kill it? Talk to me."

Liz

"Hang on." Liz blinked against her human vision of fire-bleached retinas. All she had for the moment was the *seeing* working. With it, she spotted a muddy blast of energy, brown and orange and gray as death, approaching from upstream. From the pool.

She had never seen energies exactly like this, yet she recognized what it was in the sooty ocher of her flesh. She had no memory of it, but she knew she'd just fought the approaching energies, those demonic magics, somehow. And . . . underwater. In the pool. Either she'd won that battle or she'd gotten away. She needed to remember how, because however she got away might save them now.

A flash of memory returned as the brimstone smoke of the firepit burned her nose. A green glow. A glimpse of darkness. A struggle. There had been a small cave at the pool, behind and underneath the narrow falls. This thing, this demon . . . had it been in the cave? Had it tried to take her over? She remembered a struggle, a breathless, desperate struggle.

Later she'd coughed and vomited it out. That meant she had fought this approaching demon off, but somehow it had caused her to forget. Maybe the gunk up her nose had contained a *forget-me* working? Or the head injury. She touched her head again. It was swollen, it hurt to the touch, and a trickle of fresh blood was running down her forehead.

And . . .

There had been a ley line. The demon had been bound into the ley line. That was the only thing that made sense.

She touched her head again, fingering the gash on top of the goose-egg lump. She had bled from her knuckles. This thing wasn't a blood demon. It didn't fit any of the old grimoires or the old tales, but all demons could track through blood. And this one was coming.

"Lizzie," Eli demanded.

"Demon," she said again. The word brought on a coughing fit. "Your weapons won't touch it."

Eli pulled his cell. Said into it, "Alex. Demon. Exfil if possible to my GPS. Backup if not. Roger that." To Liz he asked, "Where?"

"Close. Coming."

Eli circled the campsite. His shotgun ready to fire. "How long?"

"No time." Liz made it to her knees. Eli pulled her upright. She grabbed Eli's wrist and the well-charged battery stone. She stumbled across the firepit stones, inside the circle.

"What the hell?" Eli asked.

"Circle," she said.

"Got it." Eli stamped out the last of the hot ash, silent, effective. He placed the shotgun on the ground outside the stones, stepped back out, and grabbed up a bedroll, his handgun, and knives.

As he worked, she dropped to her knees again, one hand on the ring of stones. Felt on her necklace for a piece of green marble shaped like a pig.

Eli scooped up the silver box. Stepped back inside the circle.

From the direction of the pool, but much closer to the campsite, a flame appeared through the trees. A torch. A ball of fire. It rose with a *whoosh*, a blazing conflagration. A dead tree exploded with flame. It shot up to the heavens.

"Oh, that's not good," Liz said.

"Do you have a portable *hedge of thorns*?"

"Yes. But it won't keep out air. Or temperature changes."

Eli discovered another thing he was afraid of: roasting to death.

She pressed the stone to bring up the *hedge of thorns* working, a protective barrier. The sparks were all out. He placed everything on the dirt and reached for the shotgun and his backpack. "No!" she shouted.

The magic shot eight feet high and closed on top like a knotted balloon. It went a foot deep into the earth and stopped. Eli cursed again, with vulgar ingenuity that might have made her laugh if she hadn't been so terrified.

Her newly charged amulets were enough to make a strong *hedge of thorns*, but the power stored in them wasn't enough to keep a *hedge* up until morning, not against a demon. She needed to have charged a boulder for days to have enough stored power to protect against a demon all night. She needed a full coven. Or a priest. She had nothing. Worse, the firepit rocks were nestled on the ground a long way from the ley line. She needed that ley line. She wiped her hand across her head wound and wiped her blood onto the rocks. The *hedge* glowed brighter but until she saw what form the demon had taken, she didn't know if it would be enough. She touched her head. The blood there was drying and would already leave a scar. Damn vanity.

"I need a knife," she said.

Eli clicked on his flashlight. In the beam, she saw him open the short-bladed folding knife he had used to cut her pocket. He placed it hilt first into her palm.

Liz pricked her finger, too deeply, too long. She cursed. The blade was *sharp*.

Eli half yanked up her wrist and demanded, "How much blood do you need? A body full?"

"I opened a *hedge of thorns*. Protection from the demon. But we need more power, and fast." She yanked against his grip and snarled, "Let me work." He let her go.

On her knees, she crawled around the outer circle of stones, rearranging them, pulling all the inner circle of stones into the outer ring, wedging them in place, making certain they all touched one another. She wiped her blood on each rock to strengthen the working. She had planned both circles of rocks when she created the firepit. Just in case she needed something. But she hadn't planned for a demon. Especially a fire demon wrapped in mud. If that kind of demonic entity even existed. "Son of a witch," she muttered, her heart pounding.

Liz looked at the center of the inner circle. There was something like burned mud in there.

Eli—Captain America—carried all the things that went bang and was always ready with a weapon. She carried around less mundane weapons and was prepared for . . . Okay. Not equipped for *this*. But she had made certain that all the rocks in the circle were touching.

When she looked back at him, Eli was holding his handgun in one hand and a vamp-killer blade in the other. Staring at the shotgun and their backpacks only feet away. "Drop the *hedge*. I need my weapons," he said.

"If I drop it, it'll come back up at lesser power. If you fire that gun or cut with that knife, the *hedge of thorns* working goes down."

In the light from his flash, his body looked taut, tense, ready for anything. And it was so useless. No weapon he had would even scratch a demon.

"I don't see anything," he said, his voice now a whisper. "Except a sparkle here and there from the *hedge*. Where's the demon?"

"It's that way." She pointed. "It crawled up from the pool. It's here."

CHAPTER SEVEN

Eli

The bushes moved. Eli angled his flash into the area. Smoke blossomed up from the leaves before vanishing in wisps. A . . . thing . . . walked into the clearing. It was six feet tall, bipedal with short-stocky legs, and built like the Michelin Tire Man, except it had at least three arms like tree trunks and no head. Bones stuck out everywhere, presumably human bones, with a fully articulated hand in the center of its chest, a femur poking up at the shoulder, and rib bones pressing outward where its liver would have been if it had been human. It had no eyes, no visible ears or nose. No mouth. Other than bones, it seemed composed of mud, sticks, and leaves it had picked up on its way here. The wood and greenery was smoking and curling in the heat. The thing stopped, as if letting them look.

Eli's flash settled on the only color on the thing—a flash of red near the hand bones. "Blood, shaped like a fist." He dropped his flash to Lizzie's hands and the torn skin of her knuckles. "You did that. Good punch."

Lizzie's face underwent a dozen emotions. She said, "There's a cave beneath the falls. And a skeleton, partially mummified. We . . . we fought. I think that, when I socked him, I used all the stone power in the cave. It didn't stop him. It didn't even slow him down. He covered my face, my nose and mouth, with mud so I couldn't breathe."

"How did you get away?" Eli murmured.

The memory came clear. "I touched a boulder that's connected to a ley line. The demon let me go, and I fell into the pool. Most of the mud washed away. The rest I gagged up on the ground."

"According to the Book of Enoch, demons are the souls of the children of fallen angels. Why's it made of mud?"

"I don't know. Maybe the demon spirit is bound up in the bones? When the skeleton fell into the mud it may have been able to incorporate that into its body?" Lizzie shivered, shaking her head.

The demon walked forward. Not a shamble, not a stride, more as if its legs were different lengths, giving it an uneven stagger. Right up to the *hedge of thorns.*

"I think I can share what I'm seeing," she said. Eli held down his hand, wanting to see what Liz saw. Without looking, she took his hand. Her fingers were icy.

In the *seeing* working, the mud thing was blazing with power, orange and a sick green, and pulsating pockets of pitch black. The bones glowed an oily black too. The mud demon leaned close to the *hedge*, only inches away from Eli's face. His fingers twitched toward his weapon. Counterproductive. But the urge was hard to ignore.

The demon had no eyes, but Eli knew the thing was looking at him, seeing him, all of him, every failure, every mistake, every bad decision. The sense of wrong, of danger, of evil washed over him. Eli had never seen anything like this, never felt anything like this. Fight and flight were at war in him, and he struggled to keep his breath steady and his heart rate low.

Eli looked down at the witch. In her own working, she glowed a soft red, like heated stones. The energies in her necklace were burning fast and hot against her skin. She lifted her free hand and adjusted them so they rested on her jacket. He looked back at the thing he had no weapons to fight.

The . . . mud-and-bone demon was a good enough description. The mud-and-bone demon lifted one of its arms, which ended in a flattened-off stump the size and shape of a dinner plate. It placed the stump against the *hedge*, and it flamed bright red as it fought the unique, dark energies. The thing pushed against the *hedge* and instead of being burned, the mud bubbled a little but was otherwise unharmed by the energies. That shouldn't be possible. The thing pulled the round, plate-shaped limb away. A long thin bone pressed forward, protruding from the limb's center. It was splintered on the end, maybe part of a broken arm bone—the skinny bone of the lower arm. The demon tapped with it on the *hedge*, as if it was tapping on a door. Sparks flew from the point of contact.

Eli could feel the heat of the thing, but the demon didn't seem to notice its own temperature or its effect on its surroundings.

The demon leaned in with that one shattered bone, pressing against the *hedge* with the splintered point like a long, filthy fingernail. The point of contact blazed with scarlet light and instantly began to dim slightly, as if energy was being siphoned away.

In her own working, Eli saw Lizzie's necklace go cold as all the stored energy was sapped away.

Liz picked up the battery stone and placed it in her lap, then took the necklace off and coiled it on top. Even he could tell it wasn't going to be enough. She pressed her bleeding finger onto the firepit rock closest.

Liz

Hazy memories slid through her fast and solidified into a surety: heat and wood and stone and icy cold. She had fought it so hard. So very hard. Her amulets had been on the bank of the pool, far away, resting on a rock. She had fallen through the waterfall and into the water, which had washed the mud away, the only thing that had saved her. She should have died. Washing away some of its mud, the demon had reached into the water and pulled her back to the cave. It had been trying to possess her at the same time it was trying to hold a physical form together. Its attention and energies were divided. She fought it. It tried again to enter her, possess her, through her mouth and nose.

She had socked it with a bare fist, hit it with the raw power of the stones, hit it with everything she could draw from the cave itself. That . . . that had worked. It fell apart. But she had landed wrong and banged her head. Fallen into the pool again.

If she hadn't hit her head, if she had stayed and fought, pulling on the ley line, she might have kept it from reknitting its mud body back together.

Using that raw power, she had gotten away. But she hadn't won. The demon had found its shape again and . . . it wanted someone to possess.

It had followed her blood trail down the hill. Her only weapons were her amulets and the freaking firepit rocks. And the blood she had just smeared on them. That brought another memory: the blood she had shed in the water-drenched cave. Even small smears of blood had allowed the demon to track her. But the blood here and there also *might* give her a fighting chance. Her blood here and there might make the difference.

She tightened her grip on his hand.

As she did, another thought occurred. Her amulets had been lying on the rock at the pool to recharge. The flat rock surface that had looked so small and innocuous had been the upper surface of a boulder that had traveled deep underground. That boulder had been touching the ley line far below the pool. As a stone witch, her amulets had instantly attached themselves to the rock-friendly ley line and filled themselves with power to the burning point. The cave was part of the boulder system. There was a connection between the boulder and her amulets and her blood. She might be able to reach the boulder and, through her amulets, draw directly from the raw power of the ley line.

Liz expanded the *seeing* working for him.

Eli

He snarled and cursed, looked longingly at his shotgun. And his backpack. Which was filled with the water. He calculated how long they would have to wait for backup. If they didn't cook first, they'd be thirsty, but they wouldn't die of dehydration. He holstered his weapon and turned off the tactical flashlight. "So what do you suggest?" he asked, voice calm.

"Study it. It was moving fast at first, like a spirit through time and space, but it slowed. It almost feels like, I don't know, as if it's physically present in reality, but also still tethered to its prison. When it entered the campsite, it almost looked as if it was dragging itself across the ground."

"Okay. In my own vision, I see mud and bright brown-orange flames, maybe like Sasquatch if Bigfoot was made out of Play-Doh, set on fire, and bound in twisted reeds and rope. The rope is disintegrating." He couldn't protect Lizzie from a demon. He'd seen what it took to stop and bind a demon. He'd watched the footage over and over again. Onc had nearly killed Jane, and she'd had help from witches and maybe an angel. It had sucked.

"Reed ropes," Lizzie said. "There was a skeleton in the cave, and it had been wrapped in what felt like—looked like—green willow-bark rope, root-rope, and maybe rope made from the tendons of animals. I'm seeing frayed ends in my *seeing* working, as if . . . as if it tore itself away, but . . ." She held up her hand and he took it again. "Tell me what you see."

"I see a line of green energies trailing back along the path where the thing's walking," Eli said. "It keeps jerking one leg as if there's something still pulling it back."

"I think, somehow it's still bound in the cave," Lizzie said, "but not by much. Oh." She stopped. "I think the skeleton was wrapped with copper."

Copper was a precious metal. It had to mean something. Something he could use. By feel, since the moon hadn't risen yet and even the stars were hidden by the tree cover, Eli changed out his ammo, replacing traditional lead ten-millimeter rounds with silver-lead composite rounds. Nothing would stop a demon, but if it had an affinity to precious metals, then maybe the silver would slow it down. He didn't bother to hope. He did what he could. "Tell me what you remember about the skeleton," he said, his voice flat. "Everything. No detail is unimportant, even if it's half guesswork."

She described the position of the body, the biological bindings, the metal chain and how the flat rectangular copper plates were attached to create a chain rope. She described the necklace of stone beads and the single black braid. "I think . . . it was dressed in clothes like tribal people. Definitely not European, so, maybe like the clothes local tribal people might have worn before the European invasion and colonization. Some kind of woven, coarse fabric and tanned hide."

He took her hand again, saying, "Let me see again." When she opened the *seeing* working, he watched the demon and said, "Still Sasquatch. You?"

"Yes. Just lumpy energy."

"What else? What else did you see in the cave?"

She closed her eyes, seeming totally unconcerned with the appearance of a demon in the campsite with them. Crazy witch woman.

"Maybe a bow and a quiver of arrows leaning against the back wall of the cave? Beaded moccasins? The necklace, or maybe two, were all stone, no glass beads. Feathers in its hair."

"Stone beads. Stone witch? Like you?"

"Huh. Okay, that's odd. I was thinking fire witch wrapped in mud. The stone necklace was the only thing not glowing with ley line power." She took a slow breath of what sounded like excitement in the pitch dark. "Maybe they had been infused with null energies. Or even death energies, like a death witch might make."

"Do you see the necklace in with the bones?"

"Hard to tell with all the mud and bones sticking out all over it. It looks like the entire human skeleton could be sticking through the mud." She took a slow breath.

Eli had not a single idea how to stop this thing. Except it was made of real stuff. Physical stuff. Not pure energy trying to manifest as real. That was different. He dialed Alex to update him.

Liz

Liz pulled on all her knowledge of demon lore, which was pitifully small. The demon was either a fire demon, partially trapped and tied to the cave and the ley line, or the skeleton buried in the cave had been a fire practitioner, one that had been tied to the demon either through possession, or through becoming a sacrifice. Not many fire witches survived to adulthood. When they came into their powers, they usually burned themselves up—spontaneous human combustion—or set their family on fire and had to be put down. But the body in the cave had been adult-sized.

In the woods, back along its trail, along the path of the faint green binding, another dead tree went up in flame.

Eli asked, "Can you alter the *hedge* to resist high temps?"

"Maybe. But that means it'll burn through my reserves faster."

"How do we kill it?"

"You don't kill demons. Impossible."

"Jane did." Jane. Not Janie. Maybe Jane when he was talking about the warrior, Janie when he was talking about his adopted sister? It was cute how he divided up the two parts of her.

Liz released Eli's hand. Jane the warrior had killed her sister Evangelina and the demon Evie had called. Or rather, had bound the demon back into hell. Either way, the important part was that Jane had killed Evie. That should have been the coven's job, but they hadn't been willing enough to kill their sister, or powerful enough to stop the demon. And killing Evie had proved beyond any doubt that an Everhart had called the demon to the Earth. That act had destroyed Liz's coven, wreaked havoc on her family, tarnished their rep in the witch community, and shattered her faith in the older sister she had revered. And even though Liz knew—with the rational part of herself—that Jane had done the only thing she could to stop the evil of Evangelina, there was a small, mean, little part of her soul that hated Jane for that. The rest of her feelings were still a mishmash of anger, sorrow, grief, and worthlessness, unable to fix anything her sister had done.

She shoved those feelings away and pulled her thoughts from the past. Demons loved hate. It would use negative emotion to weaken her. To take over more than the blood-taint on her flesh and her soul. If she slipped into hate, the demon could take her over completely.

"No rifle? No steel blade, brought by Europeans? No cross used in the binding?" Eli asked.

He was still talking about stuff in the cave. "No," she said.

"So, by its accessories, we can deduce it was trapped precolonization, in the American copper age. Somewhere between two and four thousand years ago."

"That's what I was thinking, originally, yes. But now I'm leaning to closer to the two K mark."

"Why?"

Liz shrugged. "No one knows why, but according to witch legends, prior to about 50 BCE, there were no demons on Earth, and they all disappeared by 200 CE."

Eli didn't argue with her estimation, which made her relax a little. Most men argued with a witch, asking, "Why?" or "Are you sure?" or saying, "That doesn't make sense." Instead, he made a little humming sound of acceptance and said, "So back two thousand years ago, someone trapped a demon."

"Yes," Liz said.

"About the time of Christ, when all demon lore started," he pushed. "But that religion hadn't reached these shores."

"No. It hadn't. I'm not sure that demons care about geography or religion. Maybe that was the time when all evil was unleashed on this continent. There were a lot of upheavals, even over here, around that time." She looked back at the demon. The flames of its energies were orange and a sick olive color. And the spot where the bone pressed was draining her *hedge* faster than she thought possible. They were well and truly trapped.

"So instead of crosses and arcane religious symbols," Eli said, "this demon was bound in vines and the bones of a human for two millennia."

"Somehow the demon used my bathing in the pool to get free." Had her blood-curse taint helped free it? She applied pressure to the wound on her finger, which started it bleeding again. She touched each stone in the firepit with the finger, strengthening the *hedge*. When she was done, Eli tossed a roll of one-inch gauze and a similar-sized roll of sticky tape into her lap. When she looked up, he was still holding the weapons. Magician. Captain America.

Liz had a bad feeling about this situation. "I was sent here by Golda," she said.

Eli spoke into his cell. "What do you have on Golda?"

Liz remembered the Wi-Fi he'd set up in the trees on the hill, which was great, but they'd need cell chargers. When her finger was wrapped, she went through her essentials and pulled out the cell chargers and cords. Offered one to Eli and plugged in her own.

"Got it." He dropped the cell from his face. "Liz, Golda died three days ago in Suffolk, England."

"Glamours that make you look like someone else are illegal," she said. And instantly knew how stupid that sounded. "Never mind." She called Molly. When the connection went through, she started talking instantly. "I'm in a stone firepit circle with Eli. A demon is pressing against my *hedge*. It was bound in pre-Columbian copper, hidden in a cave behind a water-fall. It looked as if a recent earthquake or maybe just the action of water on the stone caused a cave-in, and when I took a bath in the pool, I saw the cave and went inside. The pool and the cave are directly over a ley line, which makes me think the ley line was used as a power source to bind the demon and the rocks that held it. So it's possible I, a blood-curse-marked stone witch, accidentally released it when I took a look-see."

Molly cussed, witch-style. "Son of a witch on a stick. Does it have a physical form?"

Liz told her what they could see in human sight and in a *seeing* working. She added what little they knew or surmised. "Ideas?"

"I'll research and get back," Molly said.

"Gotta go, bro." Eli ended his call and said to Liz, "Rescue party on the way, dropping in via helicopter. Brute woke up and selected the backup.

Per Alex, the werewolf is in charge. And there's a grindylow attached to his back."

"Brute? Why did Brute . . . ? Oh. Werewolf," Liz whispered. Brute was a werewolf stuck in wolf form by contact with an angel. The wolf had a complicated and bloody history. He lived at the inn with Yellowrock and Eli, one of the only werewolves on the planet not guarded over by a grindylow executioner twenty-four-seven. If the angel-touched werewolf was coming, with a grindy, then they might actually have angel backup.

But.

The presence of a grindylow meant other problems. A grindy meant another werewolf was close to them. A werewolf left over from the last attacks months ago. Eli had said he was armed for werewolf, just in case. "Son of a witch," she whispered. "How long before they get here?"

"Gut feeling? We have two to four hours before they get in the air, find an LZ, land, and then hike in to us."

"LZ?" she asked.

"Landing zone."

Liz searched around and spotted the silver box; she almost touched it before the sensation of heat registered. Using the sleeping bag edge to protect her hands, Liz plucked open the box. The crystal inside was glowing red. "Whatever fake-Golda attached a charm to, it's heading this way too. Fast. What if there never was a dog? What if Golda sent us to chase a werewolf? And I stumbled on the demon."

"Coincidence isn't likely. If there's a were in the area with a demon and a ley line, it was part of the plan."

Eli called Alex. "Ask Brute if a werewolf is in the vicinity."

A tinny voice said, "Brute nodded yes."

"How does he know?" Liz asked.

"He just knows," Eli said.

Liz's stomach tumbled into her gut. Demons were uber powerful, but they were stupid. They wanted a human to inhabit, but they couldn't cross a *hedge of thorns* without a lot of time and a big fight. Werewolves on the other hand . . . With the exception of very few packs, most were like rabid humans. They could think. They could plan. They could hunt.

"How many?" Eli asked. He cursed foully. Eli ended the call and stared out into the dark. That wasn't good.

Grindylows were the enforcers of the were-community. They looked like cute neon green kittens until they went into fighting mode. Liz had never seen it, but they were supposed to have steel claws. Like, five-inch blades, four of them at the ends of each paw when they executed a were-creature who tried to spread the were-taint. If a were-creature got out of line, they showed up and killed it. But so far as Liz knew, they killed it after the fact, after it bit a human and transmitted the disease that caused humans to wake up furry and kill their friends and family.

"The werewolf probably scented the demon energies during the last full moon," Eli said to Liz, toneless, clipped. Even in the dark, she could see that his face had gone totally emotionless, an expression she'd never seen before. It was, maybe, the true Eli, the warrior. "Maybe it got some power or ability from the ley line and when it found human form, it located your not-Golda."

"Or maybe the werewolf *is* Golda," Liz whispered. "A witch bitten by a werewolf."

"The females go into heat and never regain sanity," Eli said. "Jane saw it happen more than once." He hesitated, staring at the silver box. "It was bad."

The silver box blazed red, burning. Using the bedroll, she snapped the top over it and dropped it to the ground. It was energy, even if it was bad energy. If she got desperate, she could try to draw its power into her amulets. "Golda didn't look insane," Liz said, "but then I've never seen a female werewolf, and I wasn't with Golda for long. However, if we're wrong about Golda being a were, then maybe the werewolf, when it was in human form, told Golda about the ley line and the demon energies. And maybe what Golda wanted all along was . . . What? To free the demon?" Liz frowned and then surprise shivered through her. "Golda wanted me to free the demon, let it take me over in vengeance for something, so she could have the ley line free and clear."

"I heard you tell Molly that you may have accidentally freed the demon. How did your magic free it?"

"Cia and I were accidentally contaminated with a blood-curse while fighting a Big Bad Ugly. We still carry the taint in our skin, and any curse is like bait to a demon." She took a slow breath before admitting to the next part. "Worse, we tangled with a demon once. We accidentally trapped it in a circle and managed to bind it back where it came from, but it took everything we had. And it wasn't much more than a green sprite of evil. This one . . ." She shook her head. "This one is bigger. Way more powerful."

Eli cursed succinctly. Liz figured that summed it up perfectly.

The point above her where the *hedge* was under attack by the bone went a pale gray. She unwrapped her cut finger and squeezed. It hurt. A lot. Pain shocked through her from the tiny injury, telling her that squeezing and scraping the wound on the rocks had bruised it badly. The wound broke open and her blood flowed. She leaned in and began to smear it across the rocks. "Check behind me." Her breath gave out. She hadn't admitted even to herself that with the amulets and the battery stone empty, she was expending her own energy on the *hedge*. And they had been at this less than an hour.

"Lizzie?" he asked.

She cleared her throat and strengthened her voice. "Make sure the rocks are all touching each other," she said. "No gaps."

"Got it." He let go of her hand and bent in the small space. He adjusted two rocks for a better connection. The weakness in her hands and her spine eased as the energies flowed more smoothly and the *hedge* strengthened.

But the demon leaned in harder, pressing on that one single point.

The pain returned to her hands and this time ran up from her fingers, wrists, arms, and into her shoulders. Down her spine. Up into her skull. A soft sound of pain escaped her lips. She was panting. Her heart thundered. The ache of power loss pulled her own life-energy out of her and into the *hedge*.

It had been years since she prayed, but now, in desperation, she said a prayer. Nothing happened. "Blade." She held out her hand for the knife Eli had taken back. Without argument, he placed it in her right hand. She cut her left fingers again, two this time. She smeared the blood, too much blood, onto the rocks. She had cut too deep, severing a tiny artery, but when the blood pulsed out onto the rocks, the *hedge* strengthened. Eli knelt beside her when she was done and reapplied gauze, wrapping the fingers tightly, and held it, applying pressure. "Captain America?" she whispered.

He laughed, short and hard, his eyes moving from her fingers to the point of contact with the demon bone. "Not Captain America," he said.

"I had hoped we'd sleep together tonight," Liz said.

"Just to be clear, in case you didn't notice, we're under attack by a mud demon and you're telling me, in the middle of said demon attack, that you were hoping we'd have sex. Sex. Not sleeping while I listened to you snore."

"I do not snore."

"Sure you do. One night you spent at the inn, I was on in-house patrol. I heard you through your bedroom door. Sort of a soft snorting blowing."

She blushed, her face going hot. "Just to be clear, I was talking about sex and you changed it to snoring."

He grinned at her outrage and embarrassment. "I find your snores adorable." He let go of her fingers, stood, and ran a weapons check. He looked longingly at the shotgun outside the firepit, out of reach. "So how do we hold off a demon and a werewolf?" he asked, sounding almost casual. And not even hinting that they might lose this battle. Warrior to the bone.

"Blood," she said, her panting easing. "And—" She stopped, remembering when the *hedge of thorns* opened. The energies had only penetrated the soil by about eight inches. The *hedge* was designed to go several feet underground. "I can try to recharge my amulets via long distance. These in the firepit are already drained." She stopped to breathe, though it didn't really help. "But the rocks at the waterfall were like the tips of icebergs, big buried boulders sitting on the ley line. I don't know if they're close enough to siphon from, but I need to try. And since I left some blood in the cave, I might have a way to tie me, here, to the stones and the ley line." She looked up at him and said, "You hold me upright, make sure I don't fall through the *hedge*, and I'll see if I can transfer some of the ley line energy to my amulets, or to the circle stones here." One part of her mind was already working through the geometry and the methodology of such a transfer. Even if it worked, it was going to suck.

One of Eli's arms went around her. The other was holding that handgun. Which he still couldn't fire unless the *hedge* went down. Bullets wouldn't hurt a demon but might hurt a werewolf if it was loaded with the right ammo. "Silver composite rounds?" she asked.

"One mag. The other is standard, but once the werewolf—or werewolves—are down, the standard rounds will take it out. That?" He inclined his head to the demon. "I need to know what will hurt it."

Liz peeled off the makeshift bandage. "Let's try this." She made a fist and relaxed it; made another. The wound opened again. Liz flung her blood at the *hedge* in front of the demon. Droplets scattered across the defensive *hedge* working.

The demon reacted with a sharp jerk. Pulled away. It growled, a sound like sucking mud.

Liz said, "Okay. Good to know. Blood works. A demon bound since the time of Christ? Beats me. Holy water? Silver? Salt from the Dead Sea? You got a silver cross?"

"Always. The holy water is in my backpack." He nodded to the backpack outside the firepit. He reached inside his T-shirt and pulled out a chain. On the end dangled a crucifix, the kind with the bloody dead Christ on it. The demon stepped back at the sight and roared as if Eli had shot it.

This demon, who had no knowledge of the Holy Land, hated crosses. Interesting. Liz said, "Captain America with a crucifix. I didn't know you're Catholic."

"We'll talk about religion later. After a better date, because this one sucks right now."

Liz laughed and said, "Amen to that." She slung more blood onto the *hedge*. It was her blood, and her *hedge*, and so . . . that was good to know. "Now shut up while I try to pull in more power." She lifted her necklace and ran her unbloodied fingers through the beads and amulets. "Cross worked. Okay, let's try this." She chose a single depleted amulet and wiped her blood over it. The amulet was a silver cross with a bit of ancient glass in the center, glass from the Holy Land, taken from a two-thousand-year-old archaeological site. She looked at Eli in the darkness. "Oh. Prayer. If you believe in that sort of thing."

"I believe. About the size of a grain of a mustard seed, but that's supposed to be enough." When Liz didn't reply, he said, "If prayer will hurt that thing, then I'll pray. I've seen Jane pray and I've seen her when she doesn't pray. And I grew up with a grammaw who prayed like a machine gun. When Grammaw prayed, there was a difference in her and her world."

The demon eased closer and once again placed the sharp bone on the working. The *hedge* shivered at the point of demon contact. That small spot glowed instantly red and then began to dim, much faster this time. The color change went from red to a glowing orange, as the power of the working began to fade.

Eli tightened his hold on her. "Better hurry."

"Yeah. I see that." Liz went limp. She started searching through the upper layer of soil for a stone close to the surface, trying to see what was there and what wasn't. Searching through this ground for rocks to draw power from wasn't easy because there was a lot of rotted organic matter mixed in with sand and microscopic rocks, and there was a layer of clay about eighteen inches under the ground. The layer of clay was smooth and clean and dense, and it resisted her magics. She pried and pressed, and eventually resorted to tapping with her magic, hunting for the vibrations in the rocks buried in the clay. It took too long, but she found an oval one about six inches below the clay surface. Then another. Her connection to the stones was iffy, like an old radio signal skipping in and out, but they gave her a bit of respite and let her draw power into her battery stone and into the ring of stone.

When she could breathe again, she tried to figure out why she was having so much trouble searching through the ground. She had pushed through clay before, so it had to be because all the power in the entire area had been tied up in binding the demon. She searched lower, out, in small, six-inch spirals, draining the power from the energies of the earth stored in each stone. She found a larger rock out, toward the ley line. Another. The clay, with its weird draining energies, thinned and she hit dirt again. Out from here, the clay was just in patches. Her pain decreased and her breath came easier. The *hedge* strengthened.

"You got this, Lizzie," Eli whispered in her ear. "It's working."

Wending her way through the ground, she moved closer and closer to the ley line beneath the pool.

"Put my hand on one of the rocks," she whispered. "Make sure there's blood contact." Her body jostled. She was sitting cradled between Eli's thighs, her back against his abdomen. She realized that he was still holding her upper body upright. His hand felt hot when it took hers and squeezed the puncture site open again before placing it on to a rock. "Keep me bleeding," she said, as she skipped a longer distance to a more remote boulder. The jump this time was closer to eighteen inches and she felt winded just making that leap.

"Would my blood help?" he whispered.

"The prayer of a righteous man," she quoted, thinking it might be from a long-ago Sunday school scripture.

She felt an incredible heat as Eli mixed his blood across her fingers and onto the rocks around them. "There is 'Power in the Blood,'" he said. "That's an old hymn my grammaw used to sing."

"Sing it," Liz breathed.

"My grammaw was as anti-witch as they came. The idea that a witch would cut herself and have me sing about the blood of the Redeemer would either make her throw something at me or hug you. Maybe both." Eli chuckled as if he hadn't a care in the world and said, "Karaoke in the middle of a magical battle. This one's for you, Grammaw." The first notes were as mellow as the starlight teasing through the canopy of burned leaves overhead as Eli began to sing the old hymn. The tones filled the clearing, vibrating in the air, and as Liz breathed in that air, she smiled and relaxed against him.

The *hedge* grew stronger. The cross amulet grew stronger. There was power in Eli's faith and Eli's song. Even if he didn't know it.

Eli

Where to cut yourself when helping a witch keep up a magical protection from a demon hadn't been included in his extensive military training, so he was winging it. Unlike the witch, he chose to make small slices in the thin skin of the thinner part of his wrist, not his fingertips. The skin was thicker on fingers, had thousands more nerve endings, so it hurt more, made it difficult for him to use weapons properly, and healed much slower. Since it worked for him, he tried it on her. Cutting a comrade-in-arms was a new experience for him. He'd taken out his fair share of enemies with blades. He'd picked up a soldier's leg and loaded it into a helo with him once when the guy stepped on an IED, but he'd never actually cut a noncombatant on purpose, except to save a life.

He sang until he ran out of remembered hymns and his voice went hoarse from lack of moisture. He checked his cell every thirty mikes, watching for progress reports texted by Alex. When the *hedge* began to fail again, he cut them both again and mixed their blood onto the rocks. But that didn't seem to be enough. He hunted through all his pockets until he found five plastic-wrapped candies that he kept on hand for patients whose blood sugar dropped. They were old and the plastic was adhered to the candy, but it was better than nothing.

Around the gooey, plastic-y candy, again he sang.

For three hours, Eli cut them both and sang hymns about blood, several songs over and over, until his voice was only a whisper and he had to open another disappearing candy to keep his mouth moisturized. And he cut and cut, not looking at his backpack with the water outside the circle. Not looking at the other bottles tantalizingly out of reach next to their supper. They bled over rocks, and he held Lizzie. He reopened wounds until he needed stitches, wrapping each wound when it got too deep from the repeated cuts and moving on to a different location.

Finally Lizzie stirred and sat up. Her voice was as dry as his when she said, "I've drained all the energy I can from the boulders. The ley line is just beyond the last boulder I can reach, but I can't tap into it from underground. Stupid thing just sits there, glimmering with all that power, tied up in the working that bound the demon." She laughed softly, a hoarse, mocking sound. "If I had a full coven of five or seven, with a properly constructed witch circle, reaching it would have been a piece of cake. Instead, it's like a mirage. Close. And yet not really there."

Around them, the *hedge* began to waver again at the point of contact with the demon's broken bone. Eli didn't tense around her. Didn't give away what he'd seen.

"See this?" she asked. Lizzie pointed down, indicating the bright energies of the silver box. It was glowing in her *seeing* working, a shocking scarlet.

"I see it."

"Wanna know what's funny?" she asked.

"Sure. Tell me a joke."

"Not what I meant, but okay. Why not? Knock knock."

"Who's there?"

"Werewolf. There wolf. And that's why." She pointed out into the woods, beyond the mud demon. With her witch sight, he saw brilliant green-yellow paranormal forms moving toward the campsite. Mixed with the green were dark spots of curse-brown. Not on them, but *in* them. "It's been said that were-creatures were made when an ancient goddess cursed them, so they carry the dark of blood-curse in their skin. Like I do. I'm guessing that means they'll want me."

Eli tightened his arms and legs around her, staring back and forth between the cursed shapes moving toward them and the heated silver box. It was glowing so hot he could feel the fire from only inches away. No question now. Werewolves were tied magically to the amulet in the silver box. They had been sent here.

"When they get here, they'll attack the *hedge* too. And it will go down. That is gonna suck mightily," she said.

He said, "When the wolves get here, you'll have to drop the *hedge* and run away from the demon. Fast. So I can fire at the wolves."

"I'll never be able to run," she said. "I'm so tired my heart hurts when it beats."

That wasn't good. "How long can you hold the *hedge* when they get here?"

"I'm draining myself. If I keep draining my own life energies at this rate, I'll be dead in"—she gave a feeble shrug—"half an hour?"

A very faint, familiar throbbing sound echoed over the hills. Eli went from abject terror at her words to a spark of hope. "Okay. Hang on, Lizzie," Eli said. "The helo's almost here." He shifted her and sent a text to Alex asking for a text number to whoever was on the helo.

"How's your Wi-Fi battery on the hilltop doing?" Liz mumbled. "I just realized you've been texting for hours as I drained rocks and we bled."

"Not so great," he said. "Nearly empty."

The helo grew closer. Dropped low. Eli received another text and the helo moved away. Eli said, "They have our GPS and location and have picked out an LZ. ETA for backup is fifteen minutes, though I got no idea how they'll get here so fast. Can you hang on?"

"I 'on' know," she mumbled. "'f I die, then . . . no."

CHAPTER EIGHT

Liz

Liz could feel a shock roll through Eli like a wave against the shore. He pulled her closer and wrapped them tighter in the bedroll, his body heat against her spine like a furnace, his chin on her head, so that when he spoke it moved against her hair. Casually he said, "Alex just texted me some info about the woman who claimed to be Golda. Her name is Connie Carroll and apparently you killed her daughter in high school."

"Who? I 'n' kill an'body."

"We know. The daughter was a cheerleader and she was out drinking with some friends. Drinking Connie Carroll's liquor and driving Connie Carroll's car. There was an accident."

"I 'member that." Liz sat up straighter and managed to get her eyes open.

Eli fished around in a pocket and handed her a mint. "It'll help to restore the moisture in your mouth."

She looked up at the *hedge* and it was pale yellow all over, with a small brown spot where the demon pressed against it. That was bad. Really bad. She looked around and was surprised it was still dark outside. She was so drained that it felt as if she had been working all night. "How long have we been at this?" she asked.

"Three hours."

"Oh. Well. I'm not tired at all, then."

Eli laughed silently, his belly moving behind her.

"Okay. Where was I?" Liz asked. "Oh yeah. High school. I spotted a car off the road. It had hit a tree. I called the police. Went to the car. Pulled two passengers out. The driver was already dead."

"She accused 'the witch' of killing her daughter."

"Yeah. That sucked. Cia and I had to drop out of school for home schooling."

"She apparently thinks you should have saved her daughter."

"Her kid's brains were smashed all over the steering wheel and her

body was hanging out the shattered windshield. Witches don't do mira-
cles."

"Huh. Connie Carroll fell apart. She's now alcohol and drug dependent.
She lost her job and is about to lose her house. And to her, you're to blame
for all of life's misfortunes."

"Some people are perpetual victims," Liz said. "My gramma says that.
Nothing is ever their fault. It's always someone else's fault. They drink or
hit their spouse or show lack of compassion for their fellow man and get
called out for it, and it's never their fault. So . . ." Liz stopped to breathe.
"After all this time CC decided to act on wanting me dead. Boo fucking
hoo."

Eli barked a laugh at her language. "Alex says she's been working with
a male vampire named Mayhew and a witch woman, also named Mayhew,
who seems to be a descendant of a third person, a vampire witch you
killed?"

"Oh. That's not good. Yeah. Cia and I trapped the Mayhew witch-vamp
after she got free from a long-chained lair and killed some people." She
held up her arms and indicated the skin there. "That's where we got tainted
by the blood-curse magic."

"So all the bad guys you left alive got together and ganged up on you."

"I'm lucky?"

Eli barked a laugh.

"Last time I saw him," Liz said, "Mayhew was in the custody of some
of Lincoln Shaddock's people."

"Shaddock's holding was taken over recently. Maybe he got away then.
I don't remember that from my reports, but that name wasn't on my radar.
Could have missed it."

The demon snarled and pressed in with his splintered bone. The *hedge*
began to fall. "You got any more hymns in you?" she asked, reaching for
the silver box. It had energy. Werewolf energy, but . . . it was better than
nothing. She hoped.

Eli stopped her and wrapped her hand in the bedroll. "Hot," he said.

"Oh. Right." Her brain wasn't working well at all. Even through the
sleeping bag, she could feel the heat. The silver box was so hot it was glowing a weird grayish orange, like a live coal in an old fire, covered with ash.
Eli cleared his voice and crinkled paper as he opened another mint. He

started singing "Amazing Grace." And this time, now that she was listening, it was heartrending. And . . . he knew four verses by heart. As he sang, she removed the wrapping on her fingers and opened the cuts there once more, the pain shivering through her.

Liz looked at the box again. The werewolves were nearly on top of them.

Something roared in the night, directly ahead. Something else answered. A reddish werewolf leaped from the darkness, landing near the firepit. Another werewolf, white with a strange flash of neon green on its back, flew—*flew*—from their left, through the dark and landed on top of the reddish wolf.

Brute. The wolves and the neon green grindylow rolled across the clearing. Fangs and claws, some of them grindylow steel, flashed in the moonlight. Liz glanced up. The moon was overhead, shining through the trees. Too bad she wasn't a moon witch.

The demon made a snorting sucking sound, as if someone wearing boots was squelching through mud. It was laughter. Liz raised her eyes to the point of contact between *hedge* and bone. The demon's bone-claw had pierced the *hedge*. In her *seeing* working, the energies protecting Eli and her separated at the point of penetration. Little frayed threads of her power waved in an unfelt breeze and softly . . . snapped. They began to fall away.

"Hey, demon," a voice roared. "Suck on this!" A bottle blasted through the trees up the hill and smashed into the mud demon so hard that part of the bottle stuck in the mud.

The demon roared in pain and pulled its bone-claw away from the broken *hedge*.

"Jane," Eli said in an understated warning.

It didn't sound like Jane, so that meant she was in an altered form. A frisson of shock shivered through Liz.

"There's more holy water where that came from!" the voice shouted again, closer now.

A rock rolled down the hill into the small clearing. It was lit with brightness, like a single candle in the dark, lighting the campsite. Liz recognized it but her exhausted brain didn't process what it meant.

A half-woman, half-mountain-lion shape raced into the small clearing, a massive pack on her back. Jane was six feet tall with human-shaped arms and legs, but all knobby bone and taut muscle. The light of the stone revealed her to be covered by a golden pelt. She was cat-faced, with the muzzle and nose and ears of a mountain lion. Fangs of a lion. A horrible visage. She screamed and even the demon jerked and turned to her.

Jane was a shape-shifter. She carried silvered bladed weapons in each hand. Vials of holy water and crosses were hanging on her belt and around her neck. And . . .

Jane wasn't carrying a backpack. She had hauled Cia on her back, at speed, through the woods and into the clearing.

Fury erupted through Liz. Her sister was in the presence of werewolves—wild, dangerous werewolves. One scratch or bite, and Cia, a moon witch with a blood-curse taint, would surely go furry at the next full moon. Female werewolves were always insane. And Yellowrock had brought her here.

The demon turned to the other blood-cursed Everhart.

The fighting werewolves bowled into the demon. It didn't even quiver. Five hundred pounds of were-creature and it was as if they had hit a brick wall.

Cia said something into Jane's ear. Jane leaped high and behind and landed on the other side of the firepit. She set Cia on the earth and leaped again, grabbing a branch overhead. Swinging high into a tree, Jane shouted, "Demon. Fight this!" She threw something down from the limb.

The demon howled again. Jane had just dumped a second vial of holy water over the demon. Now was their chance.

"Drop the *hedge!*" Cia shouted.

Liz dropped her broken *hedge*. Eli leaped out, toward his backpack and pile of weapons. "Stupid man," Liz shouted. "It was safe in here."

Cia leaped into the circle of stone. Her fresh strong moon-magic *hedge* spread out and enclosed the firepit. Her magic was the color of moonlight, crystal clear and an amazing red, the color of a blood ring around the moon in certain weather conditions. There were tints of moonbows in it too, flashing here and there.

She was breathing hard, her eyes wide. There were leaves and twigs in her red hair. And she looked fabulous.

Eli trained his shotgun on the wolf fight. "Not stupid. You two and Jane take care of the demon. I'll help with the werewolves. You know, since we now have three attacking." He rushed into the dark.

"Three?" Cia asked, horrified.

The shape shifter dropped from the limb overhead and danced closer to the demon. Jane was holding two silver-plated vamp-killer blades. There were silver crosses around her neck, hanging from her belt, all glowing bright. Her half-form body was wearing a set of black armor that glowed in a *seeing* working, proving that it had been spelled against magical attacks. She dashed across to the demon. With one vamp-killer, she cut ten inches off one of its limbs.

The demon roared, a sound like a mudslide, rock grinding and groaning. It bent over and picked up its severed part. The muddy dollop was instantly reabsorbed. Jane's crosses all glowed brighter. Her yellow eyes were glowing. At the sight of Jane fighting a demon, one freed by her family, again, a hazy memory became crystal clear. She had touched the copper ax. She had freed this demon. Fear and shame slithered through Liz, freezing solid between her ribs. This was her fault. Just like her sister, she had freed a demon into the world.

Then she processed what Eli and Cia had said. "*Three* werewolves are attacking?"

"That's what *our* werewolf said."

Liz tilted her head to her sister. She tried for a snarl and didn't manage it. What came out was more desultory than angry. "Why did you come here? What are you doing here with a demon and werewolves? Cia . . ."

Cia activated a third amulet and the noise in the clearing decreased. "You didn't think I'd notice when a demon touched your blood-curse taint? Ray and I were in the middle of a lovely dinner at Shadows and Lace when my skin flashed sooty. Even Ray could see it."

She repositioned the dirty and burned bedroll to the side and placed a clean blanket on the ground to keep from damaging her designer jeans and her fancy boots. Liz caught a glimpse of her own sooty clothes and figured that the blanket was a good idea. As the oft-photographed main squeeze of Ray Conyers, a famous country singer, Cia dressed the part. "No way was I leaving my twin in danger. I tried your cell and it went to voice mail." While she talked, Cia was laying out her amulets from her hot-pink backpack. "So I called the inn, and when they had a useful GPS, we drove up and joined the rescue party."

In the midst of the calm commentary, the werewolves were howling.

The demon, burned with holy water, was howling too. It flung seven arms around and stomped its three legs. It was changing shape to adapt to its current needs.

Eli was holding his shotgun, aimed at the wolf fight. Silver shot. The moment he had a clear line of fire, he fired at a gray werewolf, a boom that took all the sound in the clearing away, even with the *sound-deadening* working going. The werewolf howled. The reddish wolf whirled from Brute and leaped at Eli. Liz closed her eyes. The shotgun boomed. Boomed. *Boomed.*

Eli

Finally. The Glock and bladed weapons in one hand, he sprang from the firepit. Grabbed his shotgun and the day pack of ammo. Rolled away, into the dark. Shoulder and back absorbing the brunt of the roll, shoving up to his knees. In a single instant, he was on his feet. Checking his weapons and ammo. Trading out the shotgun's extended mag for one with silver shot fléchette rounds. Taking in the battle. Hands moving on muscle memory in the dark.

Jane had the demon busy. Dancing like a dervish. Cutting off bits and pieces. She yanked a cross off her waist, cut off a demon part, and tossed the cross on the mud pie. The demon howled again. Jane stopped to catch her breath and watched to see if that had worked. The demon bent over the muddy bit.

Brute and the grindylow were in trouble. Three wolves in wolf form were slavering and darting at them. The grindy was a juvenile. One on one, the adorable kitten-sized killer could take on a were. Three on one . . . Eli wasn't sure about that. And Brute's white coat showed dark at his haunches. *Blood.* He'd been injured.

Eli downed a bottle of water. Moved slowly through the darkness, shadow to shadow. Shotgun at ready. Waiting for a clear line of fire. A silver-gray wolf leaped. Fangs exposed, growling. Eli fired. Solid hit, midchest. Silver shot. The gray wolf stumbled and met Eli's eyes in the night, the blue like a summer sky. It mewled like a kitten.

The red-coated wolf whirled from Brute at the sound. His reddish eyes locked on Eli. Everything slowed down. The wolf leaped directly at him. Eli adjusted for aim. Calm. Calm. Eyes on the exact spot between the wolf's front legs, midcenter chest, three inches below the neck. Fired. Fired. Stepped to the side. Adjusted aim again. The gray wolf was no longer on the ground. Spotted it in the dark. Fired once more. The gray wolf dodged. Werewolf fast. Missed.

Eli sidestepped left. The red wolf landed where he'd been standing with a vibration he felt through his boots but couldn't hear—deaf from the shots fired.

Four rounds. Six left in the extended mag. Wished he had brought more silver fléchette rounds. Decided he needed to save the last ones. Slung the rig over his shoulder out of the way.

Pulled his Glock. Checked on Jane. Still playing with the demon. Crazy woman.

Checked on Lizzie. Her eyes were on him. He grinned at her. Saw her eyes open wide in surprise and something else. Not sure what. That was for later. He circled away from the firepit.

Liz

Her eyes flashed open to see Eli dodging the flying carcass of a very dead wolf. It landed on the ground with a *whoomph* Liz felt through her butt. Eli aimed at the gray wolf again. Fired. It dodged behind Brute and attacked the big white wolf's flank. Eli slung the shotgun aside and pulled his handgun. His eyes landed on hers. He grinned. Like a maniac. As if he was . . . having fun. Idiot man circled away from the firepit. Liz blinked. Stared. Tried to figure out what had just happened. Her gaze moved from Eli to the fighting werewolves and the killer grindy, to Jane and the demon. Exhaustion weighed her down. She tried to get a deep enough breath. Tried to think what to do next.

"Liz?"

Liz looked away from the warrior to see her sister, concern in her eyes. "Cia? When did we get two more attacking weres?" Liz asked.

Cia thumbed on a glow stone. Reached over and lifted Liz's arms, exposing that they were bandaged and bloody, with crusty red and fresh wet scarlet. Cia shifted her gaze around the rock circle. The stones were bloody too. Liz hadn't realized how much blood she had given. It looked like a battleground. Which it was.

"Well, that's one way to keep a circle going," Cia said. "You want to explain?"

Outside the circle, Yellowrock cut off another demon limb and tossed a cross on it. The demon sucked up the mud, leaving the cross. It took longer than the uncrossed reabsorption. It was like watching animated Play-Doh. In a mad dash, Jane swept up the silver cross on the ground, cut off another demon limb, and tossed the cross on top. Like a game of tag the demon. Yellowrock made a sound like a cat: coughing/hissing/growling. It might have been laughter. She and Eli were having fun.

"Liz?"

"There's a ley line beneath a pool up that way." She lifted a single finger to point in the general direction of the pool and the cave. "The demon was contained in a cave behind a small waterfall. I accidentally set it free." The memory came back to her again, the memory of touching the ax head. Or her foot touching the mud puddle. Maybe both. She had been so stupid. And now she was so tired. "I got back here and opened a *hedge* to protect us, but I didn't have enough power in the battery stone." She stared around the campground, confusion pulling at her. "To power it, I tried to reach through the rocks to the ley line, but . . ."

"But you ran out of *blood*?" Cia sounded mad. She passed Liz a bottle of water. "Drink, you brave, idiot woman."

The demon crashed into the *hedge of thorns*. But with the moon overhead, even with singed tree cover, Cia was megapowerful.

Liz drank half the water. It was wonderful. "I couldn't get through to the line. There was a thick layer of clay and . . . I couldn't get through it. I could only go six inches between rocks."

"Why only six inches? That doesn't make sense. You've gone farther through dirt before. Oh. Wait. Whoever bound the demon tied the bindings into the line. Maybe a form of a *hedge* in the ground and it bound with the clay. Got it. Except—" Cia stopped, her expression thoughtful and faintly puzzled. "How did the demon get free? And in that form?"

Outside the *hedge of thorns*, Jane whirled away, backhanding a cut. It swiped through the demon's mud body, slowing as the blade met bones and whatever else the demon had incorporated to create its shape. The vamp-killer hung there. Jane had put her entire body weight into the strike. The blade was wrenched out of her hand. She was in midair, spinning.

The mud demon reared and struck her in the head. Jane went down. Mud crawled all over her face and covered her nose and mouth. Jane squeaked. Began fighting at the mud, tearing at it with her knobby fingers. Unable to breathe. Fighting to get her airways clear. Watching Jane fight, Liz's mind began to clear too.

The demon turned away from Jane to the *hedge* again.

Jane's hands stopped peeling away the mud, searching on her belt.

Liz's memories were fuzzy, like an out-of-focus camera vision, part memory, part sensation. *Mud*. Unable to breathe. "Drink," Cia demanded.

Liz finished the bottle and wished for more. Her sister slapped a full bottle into her hand. Twin-bond. Mind reader. "There was a mud puddle and a skeleton in the cave," Liz said as she twisted open the bottle. "It used that. And it wants to possess a witch body. I don't know how to send back a demon who already has a makeshift body."

Cia said, "We can rebind it."

Eli rushed out of the dark and tore a vial of holy water off Jane's belt. Upended it over her face. The mud boiled up and slid off. Jane rolled over, coughing. Gagging.

Liz remembered. Like being slammed in the head with the memories, all the memories, all at once. She crawled into the cave behind the narrow falls. The phosphorescent moss was everywhere. Except on the skeleton. The skeleton had been sacrificed for some great cause, or murdered, killed with a copper-age ax, the ax head left embedded in the skull. She had gotten power-drunk from the ley line energies. She had gotten close to the skeleton. She touched the ax. Her foot touched the mud puddle. Power-drunk and not thinking about consequences.

Liz pulled up her knees and put her head on them, letting the final memories flood through her. The ley line energies had opened up pathways through all her magic. The energies in the demon-binding had used the blood-curse taint to get into her. And she had let it. And the demon . . .

The demon had tried to possess her. Twice. Both times by sliming mud into her airways. It had nearly succeeded.

She raised her head and turned her attention to the mud demon. She had touched the ax head that had held it in place for thousands of years. "The demon was bound with copper from up north, around two thousand years ago. When I fought it, I caught a glimpse of all the copper chain and the ax head, and the human skull used in the binding, and then it did that 'mud-to-the-airways' thing to me that it just tried with Jane. I didn't have holy water, but I got away." She remembered her own short fights in the dank, green cave beneath the falls. Remembered falling back and down, through the waterfall, into the pool of water. The pool had washed away the mud. The pool water that ran through stones attuned to the ley line, and at that time, to her amulets. Right. Okay. She had the timeline. And from that she could come up with better geometry than she had on her own.

"Good," Cia said. "We can use the binding material to draw it back. Did it get access to your blood?"

No recriminations, no unnecessary questions. Simple acceptance and pushing forward, as always between them.

Liz rolled up her pants and looked at her knee. She had barked it on the rocks when she was getting out of the cave. She touched her head, which still hurt in a mushy, bruised kind of way. "Yeah. Not much, but enough."

Cia held out one hand. Liz took it. "I'll keep open the *hedge* and the *seeing* working," Cia said. "You try to reach the ley line. See if the magic can be repaired to rebind the demon. If not, we'll figure out an alternative plan." They placed their hands together on the ground of the firepit, and Liz reached into the earth for the ley line. With her twin's power backing her up, she spotted it instantly even through the layer of clay. It was easier to jump from rock to rock, closer to the ley line. The demon had escaped, and the connection binding the demon to the ley line had frayed in the last hours, freeing much of the power. As she edged closer, energy flooded into her exhausted mind and body. The *hedge* around them strengthened.

The demon backed away and grabbed Jane, wrapping its magic around her.

Jane screamed in pain. Her scream was cut off.

Liz shut away the sounds of fighting and concentrated on the demon's magic trail underground, rock to rock, boulder to shattered stone. The trail was a pale light glimmering softly. The cave was just ahead, a beacon she hadn't been able to reach before. But now, her skin heated, following the trajectory of the demon. The skin on her arms ached and burned. She gasped, and heard herself moan, back on the surface. Whatever the demon had done to her in the fight, it was exacting a painful price. On the surface, her sister did something, and the burning eased like a wash of moonlight.

She slid her magic into the cave. It was no longer brightly lit with the energy of the living moss, the phosphorescence glowing in her *seeing* working. Instead it was dark. The gases and the presence of evil had killed all the moss. Where the mud had been was a dark hole about four feet deep, its bottom muddy. In the very center, a deeper hole went down. And down. Noxious gases streamed up from it, filling the cave. At the back of the four-foot depression was the skull, the ax head, and the copper chain coiled around small bones and bone fragments. From the copper ran a single trail of binding up to the surface. Into the clearing where she sat. Geometry. A very messy triangle, from cave overland to the demon, from the firepit to the cave.

"The demon is still connected to the original binding," Liz murmured. "Copper ax head, copper chain. The skull."

"Probably not a sacrifice. Probably the skull of the man or woman it had possessed," Cia said. "We need some of the binding items here, in order to trap it. Then we can force it back there."

"It's got a tether. It can't get much farther away from the pit it was in than it is now. Its maximum distance is the clearing."

"Or is its maximum distance you?" Cia asked.

"Oh jeez." She studied the final binding. She looked back with her witch gifts and inspected her own skin. "You may be right."

"Guilt it up later. What can you tell about the site where it used to be bound?"

With her magic, Liz explored the rocks at the entrance. "The entrance is visible now from the front of the waterfall. I think when I hit my head, I took some rocks with me. We need to get back there and get the original binding material."

"Not us. We're the bait. We keep the demon here while Eli goes."

Liz didn't want Eli in the cave. Didn't want him to touch the metal. Knew this was all her fault because she had gotten magic-drunk and touched the copper ax and the mud. She pulled her magic back to the surface. On the surface, the battle was at a standstill.

Jane was at the far edge of the clearing. She had changed forms, into human, yet she was still coughing. They had thrown everything they had at it, and it was still upright and going strong, the vamp-killer still sticking out of the demon's side. It was ignoring everything in the clearing except the firepit.

Eli was walking guard duty, eyes out to the woods and the dark.

Three dead werewolves were outstretched, all three in partial shift form. They had died full of silver, and so hadn't been able to shift back to human and heal. Brute was on the ground near them, panting, bloodied, and being fed by . . . Lincoln Shaddock.

Shaddock was the Master of the City of Asheville. He was a powerful vamp, and vamps did not feed werewolves, even angel-touched weres. Everyone knew vamps and weres hated each other. Except Shaddock was feeding the wolf anyway, one eye on the *hedge of thorns* and the demon leaning over it.

Then it hit Liz why he was here. The Mayhew vampires were involved in this trap. He had condemned one Mayhew to death and clearly allowed the widower to live. So this was on him, as much as it was on her.

Liz looked up at the demon. It leaned in on the other side of the *hedge*, once again pressing with the shattered bone, draining the energies of their protection. As soon as the moon was below the horizon, Cia was going to lose power. The demon wasn't going anywhere unless one of the twins moved. Then it would follow. And it would likely be able to possess whichever one of them it caught. It would use witch magic to free itself totally. Its first order of business would be to destroy anyone who might try to stop it, so it would kill her family. It would be free in the world. She had to fix what she had messed up.

"Drop the *sound-deadening* working," she said to Cia. A layer of magics slid down into a moonstone in Cia's hand. "Eli?" Liz called.

The Army Ranger turned to her. "There's a cave under the falls at the pool. It's full of dangerous poison gases. Midway to the back of the cave is an oval depression with a muddy bottom. Sitting on the muddy bottom is a chain made of flat rectangular copper pieces, each attached to the next with a floating tab. There's also some bone fragments and a skull with a copper ax head in it. We need a small part of the chain and a fragment of the bone. But you can't disturb the skull or the ax head. In fact, touching anything in the cave might be deadly, even the things we're sending you to get. And when you get back, the demon will likely attack you for the bone fragment."

"Waterfall, poison, hole, bones, ax, and a chain. It may all kill me. Got it." He grinned widely again, the light in his eyes just a little too bright. "Lizzie, I still say this sucks as a date, but you sure do know how to show a former Ranger a good time."

With that, he melted into the dark, grabbing up his backpack as he disappeared.

"Nice," Cia said, staring at his butt.

"Stop that. He's mine."

"No doubt about that at all, sis," Cia agreed. "And the way he looked at you?" She fanned herself as if too warm. "And that nice backside? Oh my . . ."

Liz grinned. "Stop it."

"Mmm-hmm. *Lizzie.*"

"I hate that name."

"Not when he says it."

Ignoring her and the demon leaning on the *hedge* over her, Liz sent her magic back along the trail to the pool and up into the cave. This time, she didn't need Cia's help. She had a trail of her own magic to follow.

Eli

"Waterfall, poison, hole, bones, ax, and a chain. It may all kill me," he repeated. "Got it." He grinned widely again, liking the way Lizzie didn't look away from him. She was seeing him at his best, and maybe his worst. And she seemed to accept that. "Lizzie, I still say this sucks as a date, but you sure do know how to show a former Ranger a good time."

He grabbed up his day pack and melted into the dark. There was no indication of more werewolves, but he wasn't taking chances. He swung the shotgun around on its tactical sling and positioned the weapon at alert, ready for fast firing, but allowing free movement away on the sling as needed.

His night vision had been negatively affected by the glow stones Cia had thrown. Normally it took twenty minutes to get it all back, so he moved with care, following a path he had taken four times before now. He hadn't exactly memorized every rock and root, but he'd been well trained. The landscape was embedded in his short term memory, ready for use. He shifted around a broken tree. Stepped over a downed limb, one with green leaves still on it. That hadn't been here before. The demon might have brought it down or ripped it free. He slowed his pace, in case there were more unexpected surprises. He caught a whiff of the burned trees the demon had ignited, and traces of brimstone. And he caught a hint of something else, something he couldn't identify but that made the hair on the back of his neck stand up. He moved slower. Checking above, around, behind.

Moving uphill, upstream, at night, under a canopy of trees was dicey, but eventually he heard the distinctive sound of the waterfall. Skirted the tree. Checked his internal clock. He had left the clearing twelve minutes ago. Too long. Moonset was coming. Cia, moon witch, would run of out power. Whatever they were going to do with the copper and the bones had to be completed before then.

The pool appeared, just ahead. He drank another bottle of water. Stopped to piss. Took in his surroundings. No sign of another werewolf. So far. But that faint stink. And the warning of his body that said he wasn't alone.

His night vision had improved as he walked, but he'd be in a cave in moments. He'd need a flash. He would need to keep one eye closed to preserve his night sight. No way was he going to risk needing a flash for the walk back. Not with werewolves.

The aftereffects of the gun battle with the furry batshit-crazy weres coursed through him. He stopped and breathed through it. Maybe five seconds. The big battle was ahead. *Waterfall, poison, hole, bones, ax, and a chain. It may all kill me.* He laughed silently. Jane sometimes complained that her life was weird. She had no idea.

He moved the last steps to the pond. The waterfall was noisy enough that his hearing was impacted. There could be a werewolf at the top of the falls and he'd never know. He cursed to himself and repositioned his weapons. Again. Shotgun at the ready. Tactical flash off but ready. Breathed in and out five hard breaths.

Stepped out. Toward the falls. He caught a flash of movement from the corner of his eye. He swung the shotgun toward it. Knowing it was already too late.

Liz

"Grindylow!" Liz shouted, calling the were-killer-creature. "Werewolf at the pool!"

In a flash the kittycat killer disappeared.

"What!" Cia demanded. "What did you see?"

"There's a werewolf on the far side of the falls from Eli."

Cia cursed.

Eli

He swung the weapon. *Too late. Too late. Too late* hammered at his brain.

A second motion ripped across in front of his field of vision. A bright light. A *swish* of sound. A grindylow hit the first *thing* in midair, directly over the center of the pool. Splashed down.

Disappeared into the water.

Son of a bitch.

Waterfall, poison, hole, bones, ax, and a chain. And a fucking werewolf.

Eli felt along the cell wall under the waterfall, the water soaking him. He felt a depression—the cave opening. He pulled a padded bag from his gear, opened it for easy access, and sucked five more deep breaths, blowing out hard each time, filling his body with oxygen and blowing out carbon dioxide and his body's reaction to the werewolf. Just enough hyperventilation to give himself a bit of nonbreathing room. Two minutes. He could hold his breath for two minutes. Under ideal circumstances. That almost made him laugh.

He stepped into the cave. It was black as pitch. Keeping one eye closed, he flicked on the small tactical flashlight and inserted it into his mouth, lips closed around it. Even without taking a breath, it stank like brimstone. His eyes, even the closed one, watered. His skin felt as if flames and dry ice coated his body at the same time. The burned place on his arm where the firepit exploded ached as if it was on fire again. Scorching and frigid.

The walls of the cave were covered with dead vegetation. Slimy water dripped down through the dry, brittle mosses. The stones were sharp, and he had no idea how Lizzie had walked in here barefoot. It had to be a stone witch thing. Carefully, he moved into the cave and shined his light into the bottom of the pit. Eli slung the shotgun back out of the way and pulled his vamp-killer with his left hand and his ten-mil with his right. He lay down on the edge of the pit, checked the cave opening. *Nothing. No were-wolves.*

He turned back to the pit and stretched out the vamp-killer. Adjusted the flashlight with his teeth and tongue. Easing closer over the four-foot-deep hole, more of his body mass over the pit. His legs on the broken stones. The point of the blade barely touched the copper chain lying tangled on the muddy bottom. Gently he slid it toward him, the sound of ancient copper and modern steel and silver clanking dully. When the chain was directly below him, he checked the cave opening: *Clear.* Using the vamp-killer point, he dragged five bone fragments to him. They looked like toe or finger bones. Maybe a batch of both. But they were small and kept sliding past the tip of the blade until they were close enough for him to tilt the vamp-killer and use a wider part of the blade. It took too long. He could hold his breath for two minutes. Under ideal conditions.

His breath was going. He glanced back at the cave opening. A figure crouched, the falling water moving behind it. Shock raced through him. He lifted the Glock. Stopped. *It was small. Not a were. A grindylow.* Twelve pounds of adorable killer, looking like a soaking wet, pissed-off cat. A cat that had just saved his life. And was guarding the entrance.

Feeling a lot safer, but a lot more breathless, Eli went back to the task at hand. Placed the vamp-killer beside the Glock 20. Forced away the need to breathe. Fought the desire to take that desperate breath. He pulled out the contents from the small open bag—six folded handkerchiefs. He hoped the padding would be enough. He levered his body over the edge. Lowered his upper body down.

The position was too much for his lungs. He exhaled. Inhaled. The coughing started, which made him breathe faster. The nausea hit his system. The poison part of the *Waterfall, poison, hole, bones, ax, and a chain*.

With the handkerchiefs, he picked up the bone fragments and placed them on the cave floor. It took too long. The coughing was worsening. Through the folded cloth he could feel the energies of the bones. Sick, burning.

More carefully he picked up one of the rectangular plates and lifted the chain into the air. Sat up. Shined the light over the chain until he found a lose link. With the handkerchiefs protecting his skin from the worst of the magics, he twisted the link free. Coughing harder. Fighting the need to vomit in the midst of the coughing, which could cause him to aspirate.

Eli tossed the chain back into the pit; it landed with a dull clank near where it had been. With the folded cloths, he placed the link and the bones into the padded pouch. Zipped it closed. Caught sight of his fingers in the flashlight. White tipped, like frostbite.

He picked up his weapons. Made his way to the cave opening. The grindylow didn't move and Eli didn't know if that was a good thing or a bad thing. He removed the tactical flashlight and clicked it off, while leaning out through the waterfall, letting it drench his head and back, and he coughed the poison out of his lungs. A couple dozen more coughs. Good clean air. He swore softly. *This sucks.* He breathed deeply again, held it, and pulled back inside the cave. He made sure his treasures were safe, holstered the Glock, and took a firm grip on the cave wall. As he left the cave, he leaned out and let the icy water wash the brimstone stink, the accumulated toxins, and his own sweat off him. Washed the poison out of his eyes. Took in water, swished, and spit. Coughed and breathed.

Dripping, he stepped to the side of the waterfall, changed out his weapons for the shotgun, and made his way to the edge of the cave, near the tree with roots like steps going downstream. On the roots was a human-shaped body, cut and slashed as if a dozen attackers had cut him to pieces. Eli knew he had to report it to Lincoln Shaddock. This was Linc's hunting territory. The vamp would have to handle all the were bodies.

The grindy, looking like a cute kitten, scampered in his wake.

Liz

Eli appeared at the edge of the clearing and dropped a small pack. He was soaked to the skin. He looked ashy with oxygen loss. He was breathing hard and fast, holding his shotgun in one hand and another small bag in the other. He slung back the gun, hefted the bag, and took something in his thumb and forefinger. He asked, "You ready?" His voice was raspy and sounded pained.

The demon turned to Eli. It roared. It lumbered across the clearing.

"Now!" Eli shouted.

The *hedge* dropped. Eli sprinted to his left. The demon pivoted to follow, growing another leg for leverage. With his off hand, Eli tossed something small to the side of the demon. With his other hand, he swung back like a softball pitcher and chucked the bag into the firepit. It landed in Liz's lap.

The *hedge of thorns* blazed back up.

The demon stopped and slid another limb along the ground until it picked up the thing that Eli had tossed. It was a small chip of bone. The chip disappeared, pulled into the mud demon's body. Ignoring the human, the vamp, and the dead werewolf bodies, the demon returned to the *hedge*. It pressed the original bone fragment into the protective energies. At the point of contact, the *hedge* was again brown. The edge of the moon was just below the tip of the hills. It would drop behind them soon. Cia would lose all her power in an instant.

Liz bent her head to the bag. She could feel the power in the copper and bone through the padded waterproof bag. This was dangerous. If she miscalculated, the demon might be able to use this magic to attack Cia. The copper was cold, cold, cold, burning cold. So were the bones. How had Eli touched the fragment he had tossed? His fingers had to be in bad shape.

"How did you know that throwing a piece of bone at it would work?" Cia asked Eli.

"You said it might attack me when I brought back a piece of the bone. So I brought five and gave it one. Basic logic." He started coughing. To combat it he breathed deeper. Hard to do when your lungs are spasming. Liz knew.

"You gonna be okay?" Cia asked. "Because I need to help my twin and you look and sound like you're dying."

"I've been gassed before. I'll recover. Besides, I was only in the cave for three and a half minutes. Your twin was likely in there a lot longer."

Cia eyed her and sighed sadly. "She never has taken good care of herself."

On the ground, one of the werewolves twitched. Eli whirled and fired the shotgun. Which hadn't even been in his hands until that moment. "Captain America," Liz murmured. "Okay. I'm trying to remember what the original binding of the skeleton looked like," she continued. "How much holy water do we have?"

"I have two in my pack," Eli said.

"I have one more on my belt and three in my pack," Jane said from the edge of the trees. Lincoln, standing beside her, looked back and forth between them, faint alarm on his face. Jane tossed the bottles of holy water to Eli, one by one, and he caught them, tucking them into the crook of his arm.

"This isn't enough to wash all the demon's mud away," Liz said, "but maybe there's enough to weaken it. Can you put all the water into one container?" she asked Eli. "Then when I say so, throw it or squirt it on the demon? All of it? At one time?"

"Can do," Eli said. He knelt and opened his pack, removing a silicone baggie. Methodically, he poured all the bottles of holy water into the baggie and zipped it closed.

"Just be so kind as to aim away from me when you throw that shit," Shaddock said. "Begging your pardon, ladies."

Eli gave the vampire his battle smile, a tiny quirk of his lips. "Will do, fanghead."

Liz removed all her bandages and studied her hands and wrists. They were in bad shape. She needed stitches to close some of the cuts. But she needed blood to make this work. She inspected higher and discovered that she was still bleeding from one cut on her lower left arm. That would do. "Okay. I'm going back into the magic of the cave and see if I can begin the rebinding." Liz closed her eyes.

Once more she sent magic zinging through the earth, so much faster this time, an old route through the ground. Into the cave. And right up to the skull. "Hello, you little bastard," she said aloud to the skull. "Did you fight the possession? Or did the power seduce you?" As it would try to seduce her if she failed. And honestly, if she failed, she would want the magical power. That was the nature of all power, to always want more, no matter the cost.

"Dang," she murmured, opening her eyes on the surface, while still holding on to the *seeing* working in the cave, the place of binding. "I need some plant material."

Cia picked up some leaves and twigs and placed them in Liz's lap with the bag. "You can thank Jane's crazy run through the hills for these. I'm lucky to be alive."

Liz smiled. "Do you remember the Irish Gaelic for 'Must remain in place'?"

"Of course."

"Okay. Sit at north."

Cia tilted her head, finding the position of the moon in her witch gifts. She slid around to the side. Liz lifted her now-powerless amulet necklace and opened the clasp. She let all the depleted stones slide off to trickle onto the ground between her knees. She added the battery stone, which was also nearly drained.

"Put all your moonstones into the pile."

"All?" Cia sounded horrified.

"All."

"You screw this up and bust my moonstones, and we are gonna have a long chat, *Lizzie*."

"I screw this up . . ." She hesitated, her damaged fingers on the bag. "I screw this up and you need to get Eli to put a silver bullet in my brain. Because if I screw it up, the demon will drop that mud body and be inside me."

"Well, *hell*," her twin said.

"Pretty much. And you will not let me kill you or leave this place with that thing in me."

"Then you bind that twice-bedamned thing and we'll get it back into the cave."

Twice-bedamned and *thrice-bedamned* were some of their grandmother's favorite cuss words. It spoke to family and witch power and a history of protecting the world with the gifts given to them. Liz nodded. "Right." She looked at the demon. Its shattered bone was pressing into the *hedge of thorns*, widening a dark brown spot of weakness. Her sister's *hedge* was failing. "How long to full moonset?"

"Not long. Make it work."

"Thanks for the leaves." Liz slid her power into the earth and fast back to the cave. With her magic in the cave, and with her magic in the firepit, Liz began weaving the twigs and leaves together with her power, simulating the original biological material. Drawing on the power of the ley line, she picked up the small stones of her amulet necklace and added them to the mix. As the power grew stronger, she added more stones, those still inside the cave. When she had the power all in one place, just below the surface of the cavern floor, she began to weave in the floor and the walls and the ceiling of the stone cave. Granite, marble, a mixed jumble of massive rocks. Unlike Liz, whoever created the first binding hadn't been a stone witch as she understood the concept. Their coven—had there even been one?—had worked magic in ways that felt foreign and like a babble of magic, mixed colors and textures, like a yarn shop hit by a tornado, the skeins all tangled together. The practitioners had used water and green things and woven ropes made of the sinews of animals for the binding. They had put *stasis* workings on the greenery, the sinews, and the stone walls, but the workings had become poorly connected over the centuries. With the cave-in at the entrance, everything had finally begun to rot. Disintegrate. And because of her, it was happening faster and faster. The original binding was nearly torn asunder.

Liz pulled the last remaining power from the firepit, from her own stones and amulets, and from her own flesh. She wove it all together into the *binding* working. She pulled on the moonstones and the moon-power and heard Cia gasp.

With all the power in her grasp, Liz sank deeply into the ley line. The power had a structure, a shape. It was composed of circles and lines, dots and waves, knotted bunches of them all together that looked like weavings. The magic in it moved fast. She had a momentary worry that if she fell in, the energies there would take her through to another time and place. As if space and time were all screwed up here, in the ley line and the dark cave.

She braided and wrapped and twisted strands of the ley line together with her own magic, with Cia's moon magic, and created a strand as dense and heavy as a bridge-spanning steel cable. She braided another. And another.

When she had three cables of power she whispered, "Bone."

Cia put the first piece of bone between her fingers. It burned, like handling a coal from an old, superhot fire.

Liz added the copper rectangle, shoving it under the dressing, pressing them together. She forced them hard against her lower arm, near her elbow, into the bloody mess there. The power of the ley line scorched through her body, fast, filling the stones of the firepit, filling her amulets, filling Cia's moonstone amulets.

Cia made a different sound, a breath of relief that let Liz know how close they had been to losing the protection of the *hedge*. And that it was fully strong again. She added the rest of the bone fragments, pressing them deep into her blood.

Closing her eyes, so her mind could follow only the energies, she pulled in the frayed threads of the ancient *binding* working. Using the copper and the bones still in the pit of the cave, she rewove the old working with the ley line. When it was strong, when it incorporated the entire cave, every rock in it tied into the ley line, she followed the last thread of the original binding back to the demon. She began to tug.

The demon screamed.

Her voice shaking, she said, "Cia, speak the words for 'Must remain in place.'"

"*Ní mór fós i bhfeidhm,*" Cia said.

"Eli," Liz said, a bit stronger. "Now."

She felt it the moment the holy water hit the demon. It lost its cohesiveness. The mud exploded outward, over the *hedge*, over the clearing. It exploded everywhere. Foul stinking filth, the rot of an abattoir. Shaddock cursed. The others said other things.

The demon roared and screamed, and it was the sound of bones breaking, the sound of death and dying and loss and fury. A heated wind blasted through. The scream went higher and higher in pitch until her ears ached with the squeal.

It went silent. Over the deafness of the scream, into the sudden silence, Liz heard a sound like *whooomp*, followed by clattering, popping, sizzling. She opened her eyes to see that a heavy layer of mud coated the *hedge*, dripping down it in globs and runnels. In one narrow open area, she could see out. On the ground beyond the *hedge* were bones and sticks and rotted bindings scattered in small piles near the firepit. Everything steamed as if it had been boiled. A slimy, blackened scattering.

With the power of the ley line, Liz drew all the bones together into a net of energies. They scuttled across the ground to the firepit like spiders and rats, gathering into a single clump. "Drop the *hedge*," she said.

"You're gonna regret that," Cia said. "I know *I* am. I loved these jeans."

The *hedge* fell. The demon's inactivated, rotten mud collapsed onto them. The stench was so intense and foul that Liz nearly lost her hold on the energies. Cia gagged and swore. The filth dripped down their heads and shoulders and backs. Into Liz's shirt, where it slid down her bare skin. She gagged too. But she kept hold of the binding.

"We need a backpack big enough to hold the bones and my necklace and my battery stone."

"You can have mine. I'll never be able to get the stink out," Cia said.

Her twin stepped from the circle, shaking off the filth in spatters of grossness. She emptied out her once-pink backpack and placed it near the bones. "How are you planning to get the bones into the pack without us touching them?"

"Eli, you still got gloves?" Liz asked, knowing the answer.

Eli pulled on a pair of gloves from his kit and knelt beside her. "Ready?" he asked.

"Go for it. Don't let any of them touch your skin."

"Roger that."

Liz watched as he carefully lifted and placed each bone into the backpack, making certain that nothing would shift and touch his skin as he worked. When he had all the longer bones and the fragments from the muddy earth, Liz added the small shards from her bandages and dropped in the copper link. The magic binding clicked into place with an audible sound and an internal vibration she felt in her blood-cursed flesh and deep into her bones. "Now we put it back," she said.

Eli zipped the backpack closed, pulled off the gloves, tucked them into a pocket, and lifted the backpack straps by one hand. After testing whether it would hurt him, he tossed the backpack over his shoulder and slung the shotgun forward. He held out his other hand to her and, careful of her injuries, helped her to her feet.

She was unsteady from blood loss and had to pee so bad it hurt to walk, but she took his hand and let him lead her out of the bloody, muddy firepit back up the hill to the pool. It was a miserable traipse. Her legs ached. Her feet hurt. She stank like a sewer filled with rotting corpses and she was freezing. But Eli's hand was warm and dependable. His touch steadied her. "Shotgun?" she managed to ask through a voice that was rough with misery and overuse.

"Just in case of more werewolves." he said. "Oh, fanghead," he called to Lincoln over his shoulder. "The grindy left a werewolf corpse by the pool. It's all yours."

Lincoln said drily, "Your kindness is boundless."

"Think nothing of it."

They made their slow, precarious way up the hill, upstream. The others—Cia, Shaddock, Brute, and Jane, who looked weak as well water in human form—filed behind them, some of them stumbling in the dark. It took an age, but the pool and waterfall finally came into view. Eli asked, "In the pool or around the side?"

"Much as I would love a good wash right now, I don't want to risk getting the bones wet."

"Copy that. Side it is. It's slippery." He started out and Liz stopped him.

"Maybe I should go first. Just in case."

Eli took a single step back and waited.

Holding on to the tree, avoiding the dead body, Liz climbed up the rocks and roots and eased around the tree. Carefully holding on to stones and trees, her hands aching with each grip, she worked her way across the rock and under the waterfall. Which was icy and glorious for the two seconds it took to get one foot inside and take a sniff.

The gases were still here, but not nearly as dense as before she pulled all the energies into one spot and wrapped them around every bit of stone in here. She could breathe. Holding on to a rock that was now covered with dead moss, she extended a hand back out. Eli placed the backpack straps into her hand and she swiveled her body, bringing it inside, protecting it from the waterfall with her body. Again, washing off some of the mud in her hair was the best thing ever.

Eli followed her, shotgun in his hands.

When they were both inside the cave, Cia came in, muttering about mud and expensive boots and jeans and her hair and how she would never smell good again. If Cia was griping, then things were probably going to be okay. Cia placed a moonstone on a low, broken rock and activated a *light* working. Bright as a candle, it lit the cave. She said, "Oh, looky. A skull, a murder weapon, and everything. Perfect for a Halloween haunted house. I'll have to remember this."

Eli swept the room with his eyes, drew a vamp-killer, and faced back out toward the falls. Guard duty.

The twins discussed whether they had to open the backpack and decided they didn't. Holding on to each other for balance, they dropped the backpack on the copper chain, near the skull. "Take north," Liz said. Her sister moved around the pit and sat. Based on her position, Liz took east. They didn't have to cast a circle, not with the ley line all around them.

"Son of a witch," Cia swore, and shivered. "This feels good."

"Too good. Don't get drunk."

Cia put back her muddy head and breathed in the power.

"Cia," Liz warned.

"I know, I know." She sounded disgusted. "Let's finish this."

"On three, we say the binding, three times," Liz said.

"It's gonna hurt," Cia said.

"Probably. One, two, three."

Together they said, *"Ní mór fós i bhfeidhm."*

The bones in the filthy backpack rattled. The skull shook and rolled over, landing against the backpack. The ley line blazed with power, wrapping itself around the backpack and the bones. The copper chain clinked and rattled and slipped around the backpack. Around the skull.

"*Ní mór fós i bhfeidhm,*" they said.

The chain tightened. The ax head moved and thudded around inside the skull. Liz pulled the piece of copper and bones from her bag and tossed them into the pit. They struck the bones and disappeared.

"*Ní mór fós i bhfeidhm.*"

The ley line sang a note like an angel in heaven, pure and strong and so high it vibrated the stones. And then the ground began to quake.

"Out, out, out!" Liz said, struggling to her feet. Eli yanked them both up by the arms and threw Liz out of the cave, into the hands of Lincoln Shaddock. Vamp-strong, he caught her before she landed in the pool and set her to the side, on the ground. He caught Cia next. And then he grabbed Eli midleap. "Move," Liz said.

The earth quaked and shook. She fell and Eli dragged her along. Shaddock picked up Cia and carried her down the hill. Vamp-fast. Brute growled and disappeared. Which would probably be freaky if she ever examined it too closely. Behind them, the cave shuddered. Rock fell with a landslide, into the cave itself, and into the water. The cave roof came down. They all fell with the impact. Caught themselves on trees or rolled in the dirt.

When the earth stopped moving, the lovely pool was gone. The waterfall above it was a muddy trickle down exposed rock and a layer of mud.

Ní mór fós i bhfeidhm. Must remain in place. Yeah. A rock slab the size of a car would do it.

Liz

"The witch posing as Golda was a member of Romona Mayhew's witch family," Shaddock said, while they waited on the helo at the LZ for an exfil. Military talk from Eli when he called for the helicopter.

Liz and Cia met eyes.

"She targeted you," Lincoln said. "She knew a demon alone or werewolf alone wouldn't hold you. But both?"

"Romona?" Jane said, looking perkier at the name. "I executed her."

Romona Mayhew had been an insane witch-vamp who had drained and killed an entire small village. Liz and Cia had captured her and turned her over to Lincoln and Jane. That meant they had been indirectly responsible for her execution. A shiver of something arcane passed through Liz. Like karma. Or vengeance from the grave.

"Seems that her family decided to punish the Everharts for the death," Lincoln said.

"I guess as soon as we get the stink off us, we have to go after another Mayhew," Liz said, her tone exhausted.

"No need," Lincoln said smoothly. "Bedelia and I took care of her before I arrived here. She's in a null room."

The girls exchanged glances again. Their mama and Lincoln had a history. No one had told them what kind of history, but, from a few hints, they assumed it had been of the romantic variety. Which was just icky gross, especially as Evangelina had mentally, if not physically, seduced Lincoln.

The helicopter thundered directly overhead. They were bloody, muddy, abraded, chafed, and bedraggled. They stank to high heaven. But they had won against the filth of the demon.

Liz

Just before dawn, the twins fell into chairs on the wide porch of the inn to watch the sunrise. They had bathed and showered and washed their hair with the lavender soap that was an Everhart witch family secret, and they were finally clean, smelling a lot better. Liz's wounds had been healed with vampire blood, which was horrible, but Lincoln had insisted, and while she could fight off a demon, saying no to the implacable courtesy of the Master of the City of Asheville had been impossible. Holding hands, Liz and Cia opened a *seeing* working to study their own flesh. "Still have the blood-curse," Cia said.

"Mmmm. Looks a little less dark, don't you think?"

"Yeah. I think so. Maybe . . ."

Liz said, "It was a dirty job rebinding the demon, but somebody had to do it. And since I started this, guess it's a good thing it was me."

"What am I? Chopped liver?" Cia said.

"No." Liz smiled. "You're my other half. Couldn't have done it without you." She looked at Eli. "Or you. Or Jane or Lincoln. Thank you."

"My pleasure, ladies," Lincoln said. "If you'll excuse me, dawn is nigh. I've faced death enough times this night. If you don't mind, My Queen," he said, making it sound like the title it was. "I'd be honored to make use of one of your cottages to dream away the daytime and, therefore, not die with the sun. I do wish to die my true-death in a blaze of glory, but perhaps not this dawn."

Jane waved a hand at him. "Eli? Which one is empty?"

"Cottage number four."

"I'll bid you all a good day," Lincoln said and bowed slightly, like the old Southern gentleman he was. He disappeared. Brute flopped onto the porch and put his big head on his paws. Liz frowned, certain he hadn't been there before.

"I'm ready for bed," Jane said. "Night." She left too. And that left Cia, Eli, and Liz.

Cia gave her a secretive smile, yawned, and pulled her hand free. She walked for the door, saying, "Nite, y'all. Don't do anything I wouldn't."

Her twin went inside. She was alone with Eli.

Liz cursed her fair skin as a blush surged up her neck to her face.

Eli

Lizzie looked worn out and more tired than he'd ever seen her, but she also looked happier. She tugged her hair back over her shoulder, her face a rosy hue in the faint gray light. Eli took the seat Cia had vacated. Silent, he looked out over the inn grounds and vineyard, thinking again about where they might situate an oversized garage. And a permanent helo landing site. Not looking at Liz. Giving her time to think about what she might want to say. He knew what he wanted. He wanted to take her to his room and keep her occupied for a week or two. But it was too soon for most of the things he was thinking about now, considering he had ignored her for a month. He probably owed her an apology for being an ass. A small smile fought its way to his mouth, and he let it. He said, "You said you wanted us to sleep together last night."

"Yeeeah," she said, drawing out the word, seeming to have gotten over Cia's teasing comment. "I'm too tired to even think about that now. But I have to say, fighting a demon and a pack of werewolves was pretty cool as a makeup date for you walking out on me. You almost kept up with me, so I was impressed."

"*Almost?*" he said, his tone disbelieving. Ignoring the "walking out on me" comment.

"Well, maybe better than almost. Your compass and Wi-Fi thingy came in useful. But you didn't have much use for the guns until the werewolves showed up. And by then we had help. All the crystals and stones and amulets were the things that kept us alive. You know. *Magic. Woo-woo* stuff."

He let the full smile free. "'Woo-woo stuff,'" he repeated. "Okay. I'll give you that. Your way kept us alive. Your magic was the better weapon." Eli held out his hand. Waited while she stared at it. He was just about ready to pull it back when she placed hers into his and interlaced her fingers through his. She was still cold. She'd used a lot of life-force in the battle. She'd kept them alive until help came. Eli had a feeling she would have kept fighting until she died from the effort.

He tightened his hand on hers. With every self-protective instinct screaming, he stood, lifted Lizzie onto his lap, and snuggled her in his arms. To help her get warm. *Right.* He was in trouble and he knew it.

He had thought that dating a witch with no fighting skills would be hard. Maybe he'd been wrong. Maybe it was . . . Maybe *Lizzie* was worth the risk. "So, steak soon? In town? Nice place with silver and crystal?"

"Nah. I'm more of a campfire or outdoor grill kinda gal. One without demons and werewolves," Liz said. She rocked her head back to see the sunrise better. He followed her gaze. The sky was every shade of pink and orange possible.

She said, "That was the worst date ever."

"I thought it was terrific. I got to kill werewolves."

She chuckled, her body moving against his. It was the best thing he'd felt all night. The sun peeked over the distant hills and slowly rose until it was a golden ball nestled in hazy pink clouds.

Softly he repeated, "Yeah. You do know how to show a former Ranger a good time."

The Ties That Bind

First published in *Dirty Deeds*, an anthology by Pen and Page Publishing (2024).

Bedelia

The alarm on the outer perimeter dinged. Something had just crossed the basic *warning* working about fifty feet from the house. Bedelia finished pouring her nightly chamomile infusion and waited on the next set of alarms to see if it was the small herd of does that had been moving through the area at dusk. Or an owl. There were owls nesting nearby. One evening, just after the repairs to the house from the recent magical firebombing, the male owl attacked a rabbit exactly atop the middle warning and she nearly expired at the continuous clangor.

As she waited, she added honey to the chamomile infusion. Stirred. Sipped. Patient. Tired of the yard work Mama had demanded all evening. She wanted lilies next summer, and the bulbs had to go just, "There, and there, and . . . no! Not there! Move 'em!"

Bedelia's back hurt, but the yard looked great and—

The central ward *dinged* a distinctive set of soft notes, identifying the uninvited visitor who was approaching through the woods in back. Bedelia's heart leaped. She frowned. Sipped again and calmed her heart rate. Once he was close enough, this particular visitor could hear her heart speed or slow and smell her reactions of any kind. And there was no way she would allow him that satisfaction.

But . . . dear heavens, she had missed him.

She thought about slipping into the half bath and brushing her teeth before applying lipstick as she would have done forty years ago. Or even twenty years ago. But she was too old for that nonsense. Instead, Bedelia walked down the hallway and checked to see that her mother was deeply asleep. Mama was older than dirt—her description, not Bedelia's—but she was still mentally sharp and agile, even at a 102 years of age, and her magic hadn't waned at all. Mama was dangerous when riled, but she went to bed with the sun and rose at dawn, and once asleep, could sleep through hail and lightning storms, perimeter alarms going off, and even this visitor. But Mama had a particular distaste for this one and had no hesitation in telling him so. To keep the peace, and for a moment of privacy, Bedelia was glad Mama was asleep, lying flat on her back and snoring at the ceiling.

Bedelia closed her mama's door softly. She tried to pass it by but stopped in the half bath after all. She brushed her teeth and ran her hands through her short hair. Silver curls sprang up and caught the bright light. Her eyes were shining blue and had lost none of their beauty. But. She glanced down at herself and the comfy housedress and slippers. Too much cleavage showing. Crepey skin. She was so damn old and the extra weight . . .

He *liked* the extra weight. Always had. *Damn it.*

She slid off the old-lady slippers, took in her freshly painted toenails—red, his favorite color—*damn it again*. She sighed, called herself an old fool, and went to the back sliding doors. She stood, silhouetted by the bright kitchen lights, arms loose, body relaxed, and no expression on her face. She didn't turn on the outside lights. Didn't need to. She could see him outlined in the red glow that announced a vampire visitor, behind the middle ward of three, that one a *hedge of thorns*. He was watching her. He always watched her, any time they were near.

He had never been to this house. She had no idea he even knew where she lived now. His last visit was years ago, at her own home, before she had rented it out and moved in with her mama to take care of her. She had put up the exact same wards here as at her own home, and, clearly, he remembered the protocol of each. If he was here, after all this time and after what happened with her now-dead daughter, Evangelina, it wasn't to chitchat. There must be some important reason.

A frisson of danger climbed up her spine on hooked spider feet.

Bedelia reached to the counter beside the glass doors, made a show of picking up her amulet necklace, and slid it over her head. The focal nestled between her breasts, a delicate faceted labradorite with a flash of red and purple. Bedelia was that rare breed of witch who could draw on multiple elements. She could use some stones, some types of wood, and plants. She could collect the power of strong air currents, and when the moon was high, she could recharge any amulet with its power. She was dangerous. He knew it, but she wanted to remind him. She leaned a hip against the counter, picked up her cup of chamomile, and sipped. Waiting. Just in case that danger was behind Linc. Holding him prisoner and waiting for her to let down her guard.

Several minutes passed. She finished her tea. He did nothing, and the sense of danger increased. *Enough*, she thought, and turned to walk away. Lincoln Shaddock knocked politely on the ward. His special specific notes rang out. Those notes hadn't rung through the air in years, not since the last time she ran him off, telling him she was too old and too tired to play vampire games.

Bedelia swiveled back to the slider doors, thinking, watching his body language. With one hand, she lifted her mixed-amulet necklace and pressed the bloodstone amulet between the thumb and forefinger of her left hand. The *hedge* fell in a delicate sprinkling of sparks that looked like a rainbow of fireflies darting hither and thither. Her workings were always pretty, not just utilitarian like anyone could make. A pretty one took skill and power and patience to layer the energies just so. The lights of the falling *hedge* danced across Linc, brushing over him and bursting in a rich red color as they fell. That used to be her special welcome for him. She had never changed it. Linc's eyes landed on her and she knew that not bothering to alter it had been a mistake.

He moved across the lawn to the house, long, lean, lanky, yet with a vampire's grace and easy stride. No one followed him. Whatever the danger she was feeling, it wasn't holding Lincoln Shaddock against his will.

She pressed the bloodstone again and the middle ward rose with another shower of sparks. She opened the slider door, touched the inner ward, and it fell. And Linc was standing there, on the back deck, his eyes on her. He smelled of barbeque, which was unusual for a vamp. They usually smelled of flowers and herbs and, more rarely, of old blood. Linc ran a BBQ restaurant and he often cooked the meat himself. Lincoln Shaddock was not the usual vampire.

Linc

He stood silently in the trees, on the outside of the first ward. He knew to the inch how far back he needed to be to keep from setting it off. He knew because he had courted Bedelia Everhart. Once upon a time, he had crossed over her wards on a regular basis. Bee was a very powerful witch, but like most witches, who seldom altered the style of their magics, she had kept the positioning and manner of her wards the same, though they were much stronger now. It was much more painful than just decades ago to be this close.

With a vampire's eyesight, he watched through the distance and the trees as she made an infusion. At this time of night, it would be chamomile. She was wearing a rose-colored housedress and pretty pink slippers. She had gone gray in the last few years. He liked the color on her, yet his heart wrenched at the sight of it. Once she stopped sipping on his blood, she had begun to age at the rate of most witches. Barring an accident, she would still live to be over a hundred, but she would look it and feel it and she would die far too soon. And take what was left of his heart with her. She sipped her weeds and hot water. He missed the taste of that stuff on her mouth. He missed everything he had given up when she refused to allow him to continue to be a fool. When she had put her foot down. When she had walked away.

Lincoln Shaddock, Master of the City of Asheville, took his life in his hands and passed over the outer ward, striding close to the middle one. The *hedge of thorns*. The Everhart witch family had been working on this ward for decades. This one was a doozie and a half. It might fry him if he wasn't careful. He felt it the moment the ward recognized an intruder. He stopped, watching her, waiting.

Bedelia sipped, put down her cup, and walked down a hallway and out of sight. Once upon a time, that had meant she was checking on her daughters. Now it meant she was checking on her mother. He waited. Eldercare was sacrosanct in blood-servants, so the human need to take care of the old ones, he understood.

When she returned, she was barefooted, and he saw that her toes were painted scarlet. Linc smiled into the dark, and then that smile faded as he wondered if she even remembered.

She picked up her cup and sipped again, staring right where he stood in the dark of a night with an unrisen moon. Witch magic told her where he stood. Her arms were loose, body was relaxed, but there was no expression on her face, no smile of welcome and joy. He watched her. Both of them waiting. Both of them knowing that him being here meant there was a passel of trouble somewhere already.

Bedelia reached to the counter beside her and picked up her amulet necklace. She slid it over her head. Bee always did have a gift for the dramatic gesture. This particular gesture reminded him that she was powerful. She was dangerous. And that she would not be trifled with. The focal nestled between her breasts, and a shot of desire raced through him like the taste of her blood.

She leaned a hip against the counter, picked up her cup, and sipped again. Waiting.

Ah. In case someone had forced me here, he thought. *To this place and time.*

He wasn't certain what to do to assure her he was not hiding a threat in the trees behind him. What had he done that very first time? Something . . . His mind swept back. Had he brought her flowers? *No. He had brought her caviar and smoked salmon and toast points. And a bag of movie theater popcorn.* She had ignored the fancy food and eaten the popcorn.

Bee turned to walk away. Linc raised his hand and knocked politely on the ward.

His special notes rang out. *His notes.* She hadn't changed them. She could have when she moved the wards to this house. But she hadn't. His whole body softened with . . . with whatever Bee had done to him so long ago.

Bedelia returned to the doors. With one hand, she lifted her mixed-amulet necklace and pressed the bloodstone amulet between the thumb and forefinger of her left hand. The *hedge* fell in a sprinkling of red fireworks that proved her strength and her ability as a witch. The scarlet had once been her special welcome for him. She had never changed it. Linc's eyes landed on her, ancient hope held in his cold undead heart.

He strode across the lawn to the house as the middle ward rose again. She opened the glass door, touched the inner ward, and it fell. And Linc was standing there, on the back deck, his eyes on hers. All the love he had ever felt for her was laid bare in his dark eyes. "Hello, darlin'. Thank you for lettin' me in," he said. The paper in his hand crinkled. He had forgotten about the gift.

Bedelia

"Hello, darlin'. Thank you for lettin' me in," he said in his soft, old-fashioned Southern accent. He lifted his left hand, to reveal a brown paper bag spotted with grease.

"Ribs?" Bedelia asked, her mouth salivating. Whatever she had meant to say disappeared at the scent of heaven.

"And a whole chicken. Tater tots. Mac and cheese with bacon from your recipe. It's still the best-selling side in the place. B's-Mac. People order it by the quart to take home."

Bedelia chuckled softly and stepped aside, accepting the bag and saying, "Mama's asleep. Whatever you got to say, we'll have to keep it quiet."

"You eat. I'll talk."

Talk. Oh yes. Trouble and danger somewhere. Trouble followed the old vampire like bees after honey. Bedelia got out a plate, knife, and fork, then poured herself some tea sweetened with stevia. Mama's brush with diabetes had made her change some habits. She arranged two ribs and a chicken drumstick, both coated with Linc's special rub, on a plate with three tater tots and a tiny helping of mac and cheese.

"I remember you being a bigger eater than that, Bee."

"It's late. I don't want to be up with heartburn. And the nice thing about your cooking is that it reheats for leftovers." She lifted a rib in the fingers of both hands and lipped the meat off. It was so tender, she didn't even have to use her teeth. She closed her eyes at the flavors assaulting her. *Heaven in a BBQ rub.* She finished the ribs, ate a drumstick, and tasted the tater tots and a single bite of the mac. It was just like she made, every ingredient unchanged for decades. Full, she wrapped the food, put it in the fridge, and washed her hands. Sat and sipped her tea. He sat across from her at the kitchen table, silent, watching. She put down her cup and studied him back.

Linc was wearing facial hair again, the same look he'd cultivated in the seventies—the 1970s. Even back then, she'd teased him about the jaw whiskers. The look was popular again and Linc was . . . Linc looked good. *Damn it.* "Out with it," she said.

Linc smiled that smile, the one that used to melt her heart. He held her gaze, and everything he was and everything he felt poured into his eyes. "I miss you. I miss you every dawn when I go to bed. I miss you every night when I wake. I miss you when the moon is full and lights the land with a silver glow. I miss watching you dance under the moon, naked as a jaybird, my blood on your lips, your blood on mine. My life is empty and without meaning without you. I love you now and always."

Bedelia looked down at her hands as he spoke, sadness twining through her heart like barbed wire. She didn't speak. Couldn't. She swallowed down her pain and blinked away her tears. Because, *good God in heaven*, it had been too long. She took a breath that shuddered through her chest, and she knew he could smell her sorrow and her love. "I love you too, Linc. But you didn't come here to try and pick up where we left off. We both know that old and worn-out love isn't always the answer. Especially after Evangelina—"

"Your daughter did not seduce me," he interrupted. "She tried. She managed to control me to a point, but she failed at that ultimate revenge and betrayal of you. Old hatred, old love, jealousy, and demon-taint will do that to a human, witch or no."

A sense of relief sailed through her. Bedelia's eldest daughter, by one of the two human men in her past, had always wanted Lincoln. Had always been jealous of Bedelia, of her own mother's power, of her happiness. "I sense . . ." Bedelia stopped and chuckled softly. "I sense a disturbance in the Force."

"That was the most amazing movie," he agreed. "And yes. Evangelina did great harm, but not to my love and devotion to you."

Bedelia intertwined her fingers together, waiting. For a vampire, especially the newly named Master of the City of Asheville, love and devotion meant very different things from what they meant to a woman like her.

Linc said, "One of the girls is in danger. Liz is camping with Eli, on a job to track down a missing dog. The dog was a ruse perpetrated by Romona Mayhew's widower and two females."

Bedelia frowned. "I remember the Mayhew name from somewhere."

"Some time ago, Liz and Cia were hired to find a kidnapped human woman. The wife of one of my people, Romona Mayhew, who was one of the long-chained Mithrans who didn't come out of the devoveo and also a witch, had broken free of her bonds and taken the human female. I didn't know that Romona hadn't been given the mercy strike of true-death, and her husband didn't come to me to rectify the situation because he was still unable to release her. Romona used the life-force of the dead to do blood-curse magic. Your girls took on the blood-curse getting their client's mother free."

Bedelia breathed in with shock, putting it all together.

The devoveo was the ten years of madness that resulted from being turned into a vampire. It was one reason she had never agreed to be turned by Linc. Loss of personal freedom was also the reason she had never agreed to become Linc's blood-servant. There were lots of reasons she had ended the relationship. She shook her head, pushing away the memories and the regrets. "I remember that story." Taking on the blood-curse had been a less-than-brilliant move on her daughters' part, but to this day, they felt that saving a human had been worth it. "Go on."

"The rest is complicated and still comin' clear. A woman named Shania Mayhew was an unaligned witch who was groomed by Romona's widower to believe an evil had been perpetrated by Liz and Cia. Mayhew and she married, an alliance I did not approve. Working together, they discovered a human woman with a perceived grudge against Liz. Her name is Connie Carroll. Together, the three of them conceived a plan to enact vengeance on the twins."

"I remember the Carroll incident. There was an accident involving alcohol and Connie's daughter. She blamed Liz. What did this group do?"

"Shania glamoured herself or Connie to look like Golda Ainsworth Holcomb, of the Ainsworth witch clan, and met Liz in the local hospital."

"Golda died a few days ago. I got the notice this morning."

His face softened with humor. "Your girls are young yet. They don't look at the obits like us old folk."

Bedelia felt a dimple form and then fall away.

"That glamoured female sent Liz on a search for a dog, one supposedly lost after a car accident, off the mountains from Morton Tunnel and Morton Overlook, in the gorge."

"Dangerous country."

"Yes. Liz and Eli took the job together. They have a witch fob that's supposed to be trackin' the lost dog. Pardon me, Bee." He took a call from Alex Younger, a young man aligned with the Dark Queen, Jane Yellowrock. Linc said, "I understand. Thank you," and ended the call. He continued his story to her. "Instead of a lost dog, they found a demon bound into a ley line and it got free. Eli called for backup and extrication via helicopter, and Cia is insisting she be allowed to assist. However, the terrain's rugged and right now there's no moon to facilitate finding a safe landing site, and no moon up means Cia, even if she was already on site, can't assist fighting the demon. Liz and Eli are currently safe beneath a *hedge of thorns*, but they can't last the night and Liz can't fight the demon alone."

As Linc detailed the problem, Bedelia's heart flew from concern to panic. She put a hand to her chest and gripped the labradorite focal stone. The amulet warmed, reacting to her fear. She took a calming breath. Another. But she reached out through the focal to her daughters. *Yes. Liz is in danger.* Linc glanced at her, his eyes intense and kind. "What else?" she asked when she was calm. Because with vampires and witches working together there was always more.

"Brute, the white werewolf aligned with Jane Yellowrock, indicated there's a rabid werewolf pack in the vicinity. Alex Younger has discovered that Connie Carroll was bitten by a werewolf in the last attacks. She was in custody during her first full moon and didn't go furry, but he thinks she's furry now."

Bedelia tightened her grip on her focal. The werewolf-taint would destroy the mind of any bitten female. She shoved away all the things that needed to be said about Evangelina and about the two of them and their past. Saving Liz was the only thing that mattered right now. "Delayed transformation?"

"Or bitten again. Perhaps on purpose. There are such people."

"What are the plans?"

"Eli Younger put a Wi-Fi in a tree. We have their GPS. Half an hour before the moon begins to rise, the helo will take off, carrying Cia, Jane, the white werewolf, and me if we have completed our part, or two of my best Mithran warriors if we're still engaged, to a landing zone yet to be discovered. The twins, working together, can deal with the demon. Jane, Brute, Eli, and the Mithrans can take out the werewolves, including Connie Carroll. You and I, if you choose to accept this mission"—his smile grew at the allusion to an old TV show—"will track down the witch, Shania Mayhew, and take her into custody." Linc watched her carefully. "And then turn her over to the witch council for null room sentencing."

Bedelia frowned at him. "I don't need the help of the witch council to protect my family."

"No. You're a warrior. And I adore you."

Bedelia's eyes flew to his. She opened her mouth to say the things that were cracking open in her heart. Instead she said, "Do we know where this Shania Mayhew is staying?"

"Yes. She rented a house above the French Broad River, just beyond Paint Rock. It rises above the river by a hundred feet or so, right where the river curves—"

"Green shutters? Freshly painted? Across from a small horse pasture?"

Linc looked surprised for a moment. "Yes. How did you—"

Interrupting him again, Bedelia shoved back from the table. "That's the old gathering place of the Coraville coven back in the eighteen seventies. There's a stone circle buried below the ground. It's aligned with the cardinal points, with the motion of the French Broad River, and with a small ley line deep beneath the river. I helped to seal the circle when the Coraville witches died out." And left behind them a prophecy that promised the circle would be sought by evildoers and had to be sealed. But Lincoln Shaddock did not need to know that at all. No nonwitch needed to know that. "I'll need a moment." Bedelia walked away with purpose, moving down the hallway to her room, cell at her ear, calling for her human daughters to come sit with their grandmother.

When the family calls were in place, Bedelia opened her closet and stepped inside. She wrapped her hand around a prybar on the top shelf, shoved clothing aside, and bent at the waist. She raised the prybar overhead and slammed it against the wallboard in the corner. Again. Again. Over and over. It took too long, but the supplies she needed were things she wasn't supposed to have, things she had hidden in the false wall of her closet.

As she worked, she considered the reinforcement witch power she would need to help. Two were old friends she kept up with on Facebook and Twitter. They knew the circle Linc had described because they'd been part of the larger group of witches who had closed and sealed the underground Coraville circle long ago. Moonrise would be perfect for Mable. Clara Anne had buried some stones at north. Bedelia had buried things there too: three focals tied to the circle and to a marble outcropping below the earth not too far away. If she was lucky, the rosemary plant she'd gifted to the previous owners two decades ago would still be growing there. Assuming they hadn't killed it, she would have all her best elements on hand.

The prybar broke through the drywall, exposing the space between her closet and the bedroom on the other side. "Yessss," she hissed. She grabbed up all the magical amulets. Moving fast, she bagged the stuff she'd hidden, pulled leggings on under her housedress, added wool socks and hiking boots, and layered on two shirts. She stuffed the bagged items from the back of her closet into a small shoulder bag and snatched a bulky old-lady sweater off a hanger. The sweater belonged to her mother. Linc would hate it. *Good.*

Quickly she set up a conference call between Mable and Clara Anne to explain the problem. Both witches agreed to meet at the buried Coraville circle. They would help to call the enemy witch. Good friends. They always had each other's backs.

She grabbed up her keys and strode back through the kitchen. She stopped when she saw Linc still sitting at the table. "What," she demanded, wondering why he was still here.

"Bedelia, my darlin'. You left before I could complete my commentary. Shania Mayhew has likely made a pact with the rogue werewolf pack. There may be more of them waiting for you at the rental house, knowing you would track Shania down. *Werewolves*, Bee."

She stopped short. "Well, that's a *thrice-bedamned* situation," she said.

He smiled slightly. "I have three of my best Mithran fighters in an SUV on the road down from your property and another watching the house Shania rented. They're weaponed up with silvershot. Vampires don't go furry. You and your witches will, however, if they get to you. We'll follow you to the house Shania rented and keep watch while you call and fight the witch. We'll kill any wolves that attack."

Bedelia tried to think a way through this. When she was younger there were no were-creatures in the area. She had never been forced to think in terms of battling them. She didn't want to accept Linc's help. But. *Werewolves* . . . and *demons* and—

She shook her head violently. "I accept." Formally, she said the words that would bind her to him. "I accept this help offered to the Everhart Clan witches by the Master of the City of Asheville. What boon will I owe you?"

A slow smile pulled across Linc's face. *That* smile. If the devil had a smile it was that one. "Dinner with me," he said. "At a time and place of my choosing."

"No blood-sharing."

"One sip each," he bargained.

"Wrists. Not throats."

"Done." He turned and left her kitchen. Cursing under her breath, Bedelia placed three small wood discs on the table, discs that could be used to reactivate the wards. Her human daughters would be here soon. They could drop the wards and get inside fine because their blood was attuned to the wards. But they would need to start the wards up again. She looked around at the kitchen and checked in again on Mama. All was well with her, at least. She had slept through the hammering.

Bedelia stopped at the hallway closet door, turned to the side, and prayed. It was a prayer of desperation and fear; tears pricked her eyes. When she was done, she pulled open the hallway closet door, picked up a second bag of tricks, and walked to meet Lincoln Shaddock. Linc, who was the "father of the body" of most of her daughters. The father of Liz and Cia. He had a right to be there to save them. God help her.

"We'll take my car," Linc said when she met him at the door.

Linc

Linc didn't take her hand as he led her to his vehicle. Those days were long gone and all his fault. He'd been a vampire predator first and a lover second. And to use Bedelia's mother's spoken judgment at the time, he'd been a "thrice-bedamned fool."

He opened the door to the car, and she slid in. She smelled of chamomile and his barbeque and that faint aroma of roses in her blood. No other woman in his entire long life had smelled so sweet.

He shut the door and went around to the driver's side, waving away the driver. "Contact Alex Younger. Keep track of what we know about the scene with Elizabeth and Eli. Update me regularly." If anyone could keep his daughter safe, it was the former Ranger. But he was only human. The last communication he'd heard was that they were safe for now under a *hedge of thorns*, the demon was free, and the werewolves were most probably on the way to the campsite. It was a trap, and part of that trap was the result of his error for allowing Mayhew to live after his wife died. When the vampire got away during a breach of his clan home, Linc had known it would come back to haunt him, but it hadn't occurred to him that it would result in danger to his daughter.

Alex Younger had found the Mayhew witch at the home she'd rented and had been tracking her activities via credit card use over the last week. It was not a fast job, even using the programs he'd created to access security cameras, bank records, and the GPS of her vehicle. Mayhew had met several times in restaurants with men who, three months ago, had quit their jobs and changed their lifestyles radically. Alex said their appearances in public matched when the moon was not full, and when full, they disappeared. There was no proof that they were a small rogue werewolf pack, but he assumed so since Brute indicated a rogue rabid pack was in the vicinity.

Law enforcement and all the necessary wildlife and park rangers had been notified, but there was no way any human agency could provide support in the dark in that terrain against a demon and a rogue pack. Worse, they could be infected. His people couldn't. Jane Yellowrock, the Dark Queen of the Mithrans, had a call in to the necessary elected officials, informing them that her people were handling it. But he and Jane both knew it was his job and his failure that led to this. He would owe her a great deal when this was over, and Lincoln hated owing anyone anything.

Linc got in and started the vehicle. Silent, they pulled out of the drive and headed toward Hot Springs, Paint Rock, and the enemy of his beloved.

If Bedelia had any trouble dealing with the Mayhew witch, he would draw on the energies of his people, walk into the witch's home, and rip off her head. No one hurt his family.

Bedelia

She had no idea what to say or how to say it. Not to Linc. But she could plan for the working. She hadn't trapped a misbehaving witch in years. It would be a challenge; just thinking about it made her pulse rate rise and her breathing deepen.

Linc

He watched as she redialed Mable and listened in unabashedly. "Hey, Mabs. I'll be there in forty-five minutes. You and Clara Anne stop at the bottom of the hill and call. If everything's okay, you can come on up. I'll have vampires at the perimeter to fight off the werewolves."

"Ohhh, vampires? The pretty one?" Mable asked.

Bee glanced at him from the corner of her eye and grinned. It was just a little wicked and his heart actually beat once. "Oh yeah. The cutie-pie Master of the City, as you called him once."

"Is he still single?"

"He's a woman-chasing, human-hunting bloodsucker, Mabs," Bedelia said casually, cutting him to the bone. "Why do you care?"

"It's been a while," Mable said with asperity. "I'd like a night of fun and wine and wild sex under the full moon."

"I'll pass that along," Bedelia said, her tone as dry as the Sahara.

"You do that. Tell him I'll bring the wine."

Staring straight ahead, Bedelia ended the call.

Linc said, "'A woman-chasing, human-hunting bloodsucker'?" He touched his chest. "I'm decimated, Bee. I weep at the characterization."

"Uh-huh. You want a date with Mabs?"

"No. As I recall, your friend Mable is a scrawny bottle-blond who smokes clove cigarettes, marijuana doobies as big as cigars, and drinks far too much wine while sitting on her front porch and flashing her charms to passersby when she's drunk."

"Nailed it. She thinks you're cute."

"I am a gentleman of the highest order, well-educated, a fine chef, and utterly charming. I am not *cute*."

Bedelia laughed, the notes cascading through the vehicle like bells in a church.

Walls Linc hadn't even known were built around his heart tumbled to the ground like the broken protections of Jericho.

Bee dialed another number.

Linc drove as the flashes of memories of them together struck through his brain like lightning, burning him.

Bee said, "Clara Anne, don't set the vampires on fire. They're there to keep the werewolves at bay." Clara Anne squeaked a question that Linc missed. "Yes. Werewolves. And vampires. The Master of the City swears to our security. We'll be safe. I promise." That call too ended.

"Don't set the vampires on fire?" Lincoln asked, his tone both gentle and amused.

"Mmmm. She has a new working she's been wanting to try. She calls it a *making vamps crispy* working. But there's a time and a place for everything. Tonight isn't it."

"As always, Bedelia, you terrify me," he said. She laughed again but he meant every word. She had broken him—heart, mind, and spirit—when she walked away. Or, rather, when he drove her away because he was a fool and had wanted her on his terms, not on hers. He thought the decades had healed that brokenness. He'd been wrong.

Bedelia

Linc pulled up to the old Coraville coven home. He stopped, put the SUV in park, and waited, looking out over the grounds and into the rearview. Bedelia followed his gaze behind them, where his people had stopped about a hundred yards back, parked, and got out. They were heavily armed with shotguns and swords. They did that vampire thing where they disappeared into the darkness like wraiths. It was frightening and beautiful and comforting all at once.

"Can you tell if Shania is home?" she asked, turning her eyes back to the house.

"One of my people has been here since I was notified. She's sensed no one in that time. She did, however, tell me that someone had been here just before she arrived."

Vampire noses. When you hunt humans for your dinner, you know when prey is around. Or not. Bedelia frowned, knowing he could smell her dismay.

"Clara Anne and Mable are here," Linc said, not reacting to her scent change.

"Can you get inside and find something the witch has used, only the witch? Something personal? Hairbrush? Toothbrush?"

"Of course." Linc lowered his window and said softly, "Nubit. You heard."

"On it," a voice said out of the dark.

The window went back up. "What else?" he asked.

Bedelia pulled her shoulder bag close and reached inside. There was a lot of witch paraphernalia in it, but the lead-lined box from the closet wall took up the most room. She removed it. Placed it on the dash.

"Bee?" Lincoln asked softly. Clearly he knew what was inside.

"Once we have the personal item, we can call the witch. You will have to tackle her and put them on her. Fast."

"Them?" he asked, the word nearly silky, making her say it.

"Null cuffs," she groused. "No, they aren't legal for me to have. No, the witch council didn't authorize them. Yes, they're dangerous for me to have. Will you put them on the witch when she shows or not?"

Linc took the box. "You know I will. Bee, I understand that Asheville is Everhart territory, but you seemed to know this place the moment I mentioned it. You seemed unsurprised she would come to this exact spot. You seem to know something about this place that I do not. How did you know that your enemy would be here?"

"This is a calling ground. Something like . . . like a myth of power. Like a treasure map. Or King Arthur's round table. When witches move into the area, they always come here, looking for the Coraville witch circle. Looking for power to accomplish some aim."

"So it wasn't a coincidence that she came here, to a place you know about?"

That silky voice. It had once sent shivers up her spine.

"No. Not coincidence. The Coraville circle is buried and locked into a ley line. Most young witches come here on the full moon and try to find the circle, but they can't find it in one night, on one try. It takes patience and weeks, which most witches don't have. Mayhew simply had more resources than most. She *rented* the place."

"I see."

Linc said nothing else and Bedelia pulled her cell and called her cohorts. She told each that the coast was clear. Moments later the witches pulled up behind Linc's SUV. Bedelia got out, slung her bag and the ugly sweater over a shoulder, and met the two witches in the dark of the currently moonless night. The others each carried a blanket and a small bag, and each was wearing her amulet necklace. When they reached one another, they took hands. Together they all said, "Well met and well come. Blessed be, a meeting of three."

"How do we catch this bitch?" Mabs asked.

"You won't like it. We call her. Lincoln Shaddock has a set of null cuffs," Bedelia said, knowing Mable would object, but her old friend surprised her.

"Good. They hurt like a mother, but they stop all magical energies."

"How do you know they hurt?" Clara Anne asked.

Mabs winked at them both and shimmied her skinny shoulders. "I'll try anything once. Come on. Let's get this witch trap set."

"Oh, dear. Age hasn't softened you at all, has it?" Clara Anne asked.

"Nope. Hot-to-trot old cougar here. I like 'em young and don't mind the fangy types."

Bedelia resisted looking back at the SUV. She knew Linc was gone, despite the lack of a door opening and closing. But she didn't look too closely at how she knew he'd melted into the night. Vampires were crafty, silent, and deadly, and Linc had always been much more than he seemed. "Let's clip the plantings we need."

A woman appeared out of the night with a soft popping sound, moving so fast that air was displaced. Bedelia was expecting her, but Clara Anne flinched and Mabs yelped, both dropping her hands. The vampire bowed deeply and, from that vulnerable position, held out a pillowcase. "My lady. These are the personal items found within the abode: a bra and a toothbrush. I placed them in a clean, unused pillowcase. I did not touch them."

It had been a long time since a vampire bowed to her. It was disconcerting. "Thank you," Bedelia said. She took the items, tucking the pillowcase into her shoulder bag. The vampire popped away.

"I hope they don't do everything that fast," Mabs said. "That would be disappointing."

Bedelia laughed softly, thinking, *No. They most certainly do not do everything that fast . . .*

"Let's clip our plant focals and get this show on the road," Clara Anne said. "Moonrise isn't too far off and we need Mable in place." They walked away from one another. Bedelia went toward the house and clipped a few sprigs off the rosemary she'd planted here so long ago. It was massive, taking over much of what once had been a well-tended herb garden. Mabs walked to a rowan tree and, because it had grown so tall, used her scissors to scrape and peel off a bit of bark. She picked up a few leaves from the ground. Clara Anne walked around the house, hunting, and finally came back with a mullein leaf, a stem of wilted-looking sage, and a sprig of silver artemisia. They each tucked their clippings into their small bags.

Holding hands again, the witches crossed the lawn to the flat place just in front of the cliff edge, the precipice where the earth plunged down to a sharp curve of the French Broad River below. The night winds were blowing, inversion layers mixing it up, and the air currents followed the water downstream until they hit the cliff at the elbow of the river and rose fast, up the cliff face, to explode into the clearing. They stood there, silent, peaceful, the wind whipping their hair and clothing. Bedelia pulled all that air magic into her body, the blast of current into her lungs. It was a little like having a glass of wine, heady and freeing. Bedelia felt all the tension she carried in her shoulders evaporate into the air. She dropped her head back, face to the sky. Joyous.

Through their linked hands, she shared the power of the air with her closest friends. Minutes passed. "Ohhhh," Clara Anne said. "Thanks be and glory be."

Mabs, who no longer sounded flirty or silly, but peaceful and wise, used the cadence of ceremony and said, "Well met and well come. Blessed be, a meeting of three."

Clara Anne and then Bedelia repeated the words of gathering. It was old-school language, old cadence, unlike what the younger witches used. Comforting to them all.

They released hands, turned one hundred eighty degrees, and walked back to the spot of the buried circle. Standing outside the buried ring, its power banked, hidden, shielded, and chained, they kicked off their shoes, their feet in contact with the earth.

Bedelia, as the one who called this circle, said, "Let us begin."

"When the Coraville coven died out, we buried items of power, we planted seeds and rootlings of power, and together we bound this land," Mabs said, continuing the words of the ceremony from so many years ago. "Together we three, among a very few others, claimed this place for witches and women of power, but limited it, for the danger its unshackled might could pose to the untrained and the foolish."

Clara Anne took up the narrative. "Together we claimed the land, this place of power, and the buried circle as sacred, sanctified, and sacrosanct, set aside for future use, for such a time when evil would need to be fought, set aside for the women warriors, the witches of this land, to use and call upon."

Bedelia continued, "We expected *men* to try and take it. Instead, those of our own sex have always been drawn here, and once again, one such has sought to use this place for evil vengeance."

Clara Anne said, "The buried circle is a place of power for the women. But its purpose is for the good of humankind . . . and is under . . ."

Together they all said, like a pronouncement, "The Rule of Three."

Together they stepped over the long-buried stones, a single long stride that carried them within.

Mabs said, "For the good of humankind, and beneath the Rule of Three."

"Three women of power," Mabel said.

"And no single power and no single user may *exploit* it or *filch* it or *consume* it unto *evil*," Bedelia said.

"The Rule of Three. So let it be," they said together. The energies began to rise through the earth, a tingling and sense of expectancy, like the feel of lightning before a strike. The air rising up the cliff swept through the circle in a whirl of power, a strong but small tornado.

"Let us claim the circle," Mabs said. "Who shall be north?"

"Bedelia," Clara Anne said, "for the Everhart witch clan has been challenged."

"Accepted," Mabs said. "I shall be east." Mabs went and stood at east.

"I shall be west," Clara said, taking that place.

"And so south shall be vacant," Bedelia said. "I'll place the calling items in the center of the circle." Taking the pillowcase from her bag, she went to the very center of the buried circle and upended it. The two items landed together, the bra wrapped around the hairbrush, and she took her place at north. North meant she was the leader of this *calling* working. She said, "Thrice around the circle we go, sunwise, each time dropping an item of our power at south."

"Sunwise," they repeated, and Clara added, "deosil, sunward, the path of power."

The women dropped a sweater or blanket and anything they didn't want to carry at the moment. Then, as if on the same beat of an unheard drum, they began the trek clockwise around the buried circle, feeling the path with their feet. And each time they passed the cardinal point of south, they dropped something they had planted in the yard and gathered just now.

None of their actions were *necessary* parts of magic. Magic simply *was*. It was everywhere, a part of the universe, a part of all life, a part of every stone and flower. It was energy and life and the beginning of all creation.

Unless one had direct access to ley line energies and had the ability to work raw power without getting drunk and falling over to sleep it off, one had to gather the energy of the universe slowly through meditation, and then channel that power through the math of geometry and a little calculus and physics, while adjusting one's own inner energies to merge with the will and purpose of the group. Tapping into the power of the Earth and stars and sun and moon and water and air and stone, and binding it to one's will, was difficult, but that hard work had been done, sealing the circle here, years ago. Now they had only to claim the energies through the treading of their feet.

The three sunwise trips were done quickly and they retook their places. As one, they sat and got comfy. That part wasn't as easy as it used to be. The ground, even with the ugly sweater beneath her, felt a lot harder than it had been last time, though Bedelia had more backside padding now than back then. They all closed their eyes. Their power rose. The witch energies raced through the buried stones, freed after being bound so long. Released, the circle sent images of other witches who had crossed this land. The last time, the strongest time, was last night. Seven paranormals had gathered here, three of them both witches and *other*. The *other* paranormal energies were unfamiliar, sharp and slivered, cutting and cold, like broken obsidian lying on frozen ground. Bedelia's eyes popped open and found Mabs and Clara Anne staring at her. They had seen the same wrong energies—witch and *other*. The four nonwitch magic users were also *other*.

Bedelia felt through the ground the vibrations of the witches who had tried to find and claim the circle. They smelled the witches on the breeze, tasted their magic in the air.

"Foul," Mabs whispered.

"Abomination," Clara Anne said.

"Can we trap all the witches?" Bedelia asked.

"We only need to call one," Clara Anne said, reminding her. "When she drives up, the vampires can grab her and put the null cuffs on her. From her, your vampires can find the others and claim them. One at a time."

Clara meant that Lincoln and his vampires could bleed and read the captured witch. If she hadn't tasted the abomination in the witches' magic just now, she would have thought the suggestion repugnant. Now, anything that cleansed the Earth of these foul creatures would be the right thing to do.

She linked to the skin cells on the personal items and said, "By the Power of Three, we call the witch." The others echoed her.

Linc

He was watching Bedelia speaking the words of a summoning when the stink came to him on the air. Wet dog. Odd sweet-sick scent overlaying its primary scent. Female dog, in heat. The scent of sweetness and blood and . . . insanity.

Female werewolf. His hunter's mind knew it.

Quickly, he sought his Mithran scions through their fresh blood bond and directed them into different positions. Through that bond, he felt their reaction of shock as the scent reached them all, and he directed calm into them.

A howl shivered through the air, plaintive, desolate, aching. Lost and lonely.

A creature stepped from the darkness of the trees. It stood there, limned in the night in his Mithran vision. A silver wolf in half-form—bipedal, standing upright on clawed paw-feet, naked except where wolf-pelt covered her, she carried a silver athame in each half paw/half hand, and an amulet necklace of wood beads lay around her half-wolf shoulders, marking her an earth witch. She had a full-wolf head, ears pointing high, wet nose, lips drawn back in a snarl.

Had he not seen Jane Yellowrock achieve a half-form of a panther/human hybrid, Linc might have been tempted to spin away and run for his life. But he could handle this werewolf witch just fine.

Out of the woods behind her, another werewolf stepped. Then a third. All female. All in heat. All insane. All three were witches, wearing the amulets of their power around their necks. The Rule of Three as Bedelia had spoken it, but perverted, evil. They were here to claim the Coraville circle and kill anyone who stood in their way. Kill Bedelia if she fought back. And his Bedelia would always fight back.

The wolves raised their wolf heads and howled. His skin shivered. *Holy hell.*

Lincoln glanced back. There was no protective ward around Bedelia and the witches. No *hedge of thorns.* The circle was defenseless. If the witch-wolves attacked the circle, the rising circle of power where Bedelia sat, it was likely they would break it. The rising energies would backlash.

The sitting witches would be injured. They would be unable to protect themselves. They would be killed easily or infected by the attacking were-wolves.

Rage thundered through him. His heart beat. Beat. *Beat.*

He drew on all the power gifted him as Master of the City. Drew on the connections he'd made through drinking the blood of his people, from allowing them to sip of him. All the things Bedelia had hated about his life as a vampire clawing his way to the top of a vampire clan, all these things would now save his love. His family. Raising his head, Lincoln Shaddock screamed the battle cry of his old human self, a ululation of rage. He called his people to war. "To me! To me! Silver. Fire at will!"

Shotguns blasted. But the werewolves were as fast as his kind.

Muzzle open, fangs dripping with the contagion of were-taint, the gray wolf leaped at the circle. Stretched out. Claws sharp as knives and black as the night sky.

Bedelia

"To me! To me! Silver. Fire at will!" Lincoln's battle cry echoed over the grassy land and rolled down the cliff to the water. At the sound, something brittle as glass shattered within her. Icy power rushed through her and back out again, leaving her cold as the undead. His fear and fury pounded through a bond she hadn't known was there. Fear, fury, and . . . *love.*

Shotguns discharged. The concussive force made her instantly deaf.

Her eyes opened. Linc was in midair, leaping higher than was possible. Ten feet off the ground. Something hit him. Bowled them both toward the circle. Bedelia's entire body clenched, ready for the pain that would come when the magics—

Somehow, Linc rolled into a ball and spun to the side. Missing the circle. A creature she had never seen before had clamped its teeth onto his shoulder and neck. Savaging him. *Werewolf.* Half-human, half-wolf, fully a monster.

The shotguns boomed again and again. Two other werewolves fell, full of silver. Writhing in agony on the ground. Bee knew they'd been taken down with silver because they didn't start to shift back to human to heal and live. Two vampires disappeared into the darkness, watching for more, on guard. Another finished off the downed wolves with multiple head shots before reloading. Bedelia was glad the darkness hid the gore from her.

Linc, however, was still fighting the gray wolf. There was blood. Too much blood. He was injured. Fear spiraled through Bedelia.

Clara Anne waved her arms to get their attention. She pointed at the fighting werewolf and mouthed the words *Shania Mayhew*.

"Oh no," Bedelia said. "We called her. We called them."

"She'll want to get in here with us," Clara Anne said, heard over the clamor still sounding in Bee's ears.

"Linc won't let that happen," Bedelia said, knowing that he would protect her to his last breath. Tears pricked beneath her lashes.

Linc rolled across the ground, the wolf snapping, body whipping. Trying to get another bite on his shoulder, flank, or into his gut. Nubit raced close and aimed at the fighting pair but couldn't get a shot that wouldn't injure Linc as well. Were-creatures weren't the only ones for whom silver was lethal. Silver could be fatal to vampires too.

The werewolf dodged to the side, aiming for the circle and the power they had unleashed.

Linc moved faster, cutting the wolf with silver blades. He stabbed straight out, into her left jaw. She squealed. Jerked back on four paws as if to run away. Faster than Bedelia could see, Linc picked the wolf up and threw her against a tree trunk.

She landed hard.

A crunch even Bedelia could hear indicated broken bones.

The wolf was still alive, but she was stunned. Lincoln cut down and hamstrung her before he stepped back. He was breathing hard. Bedelia had never seen him breathing hard. Ever. He was covered in blood.

Nubit, the vampire who had been watching the house and who'd brought them the items of calling, approached the wolf and fired a shot point-blank into the wolf's left hip, the shot so close that it stole most of her hearing. Nubit handed Linc the lead-lined box, and Linc applied three silver cuffs around the wolf's neck like a dog collar. Without human thumbs, the witch would be unable to remove them, and with her body full of silver, she couldn't shift to human and heal.

Bedelia tapped a healing amulet on her necklace and her ears improved enough to hear Linc.

"Watch her. Kill her if she manages to shift. She's a witch and a were-wolf, and might have tricks we don't know about," Linc said. To the others, he said, "Two of you, attend me." They approached and one of them turned the garden hose onto him, washing off the were-blood. Another swiftly cut Linc's clothing away and left it in a pile. Linc was . . . still beautiful. So very beautiful. Naked in the faint light of the moon just beginning to rise. And so very wounded. Gashes and bite marks were all over him, dark in the night.

Linc's eyes met hers and he grinned—insouciant, impossible, infuriating man. Together he and his vampires vanished into the dark.

"What are they doing?" Clara Anne asked.

"He's hurt," Mabs said. "They can heal him with their blood. But it means them bleeding onto his naked self and him drinking their blood and probably a lot of sex."

Bedelia looked down at her hands. And there, right there, was the reason why she and Linc had never worked out. She had been a one-man woman, and Linc had been a vampire, always and forever. She sighed softly. Her hearing was mostly back, so she said, "Rule of Three. Three called, three answered. Evil sought the power and evil was defeated, as the Coraville prophecy claimed. Our time is done, this circle is no longer needed. Let us reseal the energies."

"Let the energies we have used return to the guardianship of the buried stones," Clara Anne said.

"May the moonlight protect it," Mabs said.

"May the earth and the plants, may the air and the rain, may all that is good within the earth and wrought by the Divine protect this ancient place and the circle of three that claims it. Seals it."

Together they raised their hands, mimicking the first time they'd sealed the energies into the ground. They brought down their hands flat upon the ground. Together they said, "It is done. And it is good."

Bedelia pushed upright and felt movement from the cliff. She started to turn to see.

"Down," Nubit screamed.

Bee dropped flat. The shotgun boomed, boomed, boomed. A massive brown wolf landed in the center of the circle, so large the ground shook. The vampire landed beside him. "Close your mouths," Nubit shouted over the ringing in their ears. "Don't breathe!"

She fired. Fired. So many times. Reloaded and fired some more.

Blood went everywhere. All over the witches. All over the vampire. *Were-taint.* It was carried in saliva and blood, which was all over them.

A moment later icy water cascaded over Bedelia. Garden hose. Any in their mouths or up their nasal passages, in their eyes, or a tiny cut . . . Holding her breath, she stood and turned in a circle and let the spray hit her. She pulled off her clothes and stood naked, letting the water douse her. Her friends did the same.

"Inside with the others," the woman said, barely heard. "Into the showers. Strip them and get them clean."

"Apply your blood all over them," Linc said. "Let them sip and spit and then drink. Hurry."

"Yes, my master," a man said.

"Bee," Linc said. "Sip. Wash out your mouth and spit."

Bee opened her mouth. Linc's blood flooded in. She swished and spat and then his wrist was pressed against her lips. She drank. The first sip flooded her mouth and his fear crashed against her, through her. That bond she hadn't known existed opened wide and she burst into tears as his love and horror flooded through her and twined her heart. She drank.

"I'm going to wipe you down with my blood."

"I am uninjured, my master," the female vampire said. "I have washed myself clean of the were-filth. May I take your place?"

"Yes, Nubit. You're right. Hurry," Linc said. Eyes still closed, Bedelia felt the cold, bloody vampire hands patting her down. A blast of air crested the cliff; the night breeze chilly on her wet and now blood-wet skin. But Linc and his vampires were fast and they quickly wrapped her in a blanket that smelled a little of Linc and a lot of horse. "Into my SUV," he instructed.

"My things," Bedelia said.

"Contaminated," Nubit said. "I will burn them all for you. I will care for your personal items, anything that could call you. I will burn them into ash and mix them with the earth."

"You know our ways," Bee said, finally opening her eyes, to see the woman. She hadn't paid attention to Nubit when Linc first called her over. Nubit was short, broad-shouldered, and dark-eyed, with dark skin. She wasn't exactly pretty. She was far more. A warrior. A fighter.

"Yes. I come from a people who had a holy woman. We all knew how to protect her."

"Thank you, Nubit," Bedelia said.

"I'm putting you into the SUV," Linc said." A helicopter'll be landing here soon to pick me up."

"You're going after Liz, aren't you," Bedelia said.

"With the others, yes. I'll bring her back safe."

It was a promise he might not be able to keep, she knew that, but she knew he was her daughter's best bet.

"And Bee. I'll see you just after sunset."

"Mama—"

"Is asleep with the sun." And he was gone.

Bedelia

Bedelia checked on her mama one last time. She was asleep. Snoring softly. She closed the door and padded barefoot away, her favorite housedress swishing around her calves. It was an hour after sunset. She settled on the screened porch, stretched out on a chaise lounge. On the table between the two reclining chairs were two bottles of wine, a white in a terra-cotta chiller for her and an unopened red for Link. She sipped, waiting. Knowing, from the moment he woke, that he was thinking about her. Knowing that he was on his way. By full dark, Linc was here.

The outer perimeter *dinged*, a soft note. The central ward *dinged*, his distinctive notes, as he walked through the woods. Bedelia's heart leaped, and this time she didn't try to still her heart. Where once she had made him knock, mostly to let him know that the power between them was hers, she deliberately pressed the bloodstone amulet between the thumb and forefinger of her left hand.

The *hedge of thorns* fell in that delicate sprinkling of darting fireflies. The lights of the falling *hedge* cascaded across Linc, brushing over him and bursting into that rich red color as they fell, his unique welcome. When he crossed the *hedge*, she closed it and dropped the inner ward. He stepped onto the deck, opened the screened porch door, and entered. He laid a single red rose across her lap, opened the red, and poured a taste.

"Nice," he said, taking the seat beside her, as if he had always done so. Tonight he didn't smell of barbeque. He smelled of a fresh shower and his expression said that his heart was full of hope.

"Thank you," Bedelia said. "Thank you for making certain my witches were safe. If it hadn't been for you and your people, we would have been dead or furry by now."

Linc made a soft *hmmming* sound.

"And thank you for your part in saving Liz and Cia."

"They are brave and powerful, and I am mighty proud of them," he said. "Have you ever told them? About us? About me?"

"No. But I'm rethinking that now. They have a right to know about you."

"I'd be honored for them to know me. And the other girls."

"The problem comes not with the girls. But because of Evangelina, and between us, as it always has been."

"Bedelia, forgive my interruption. But I came here to say something." He put down his glass, swiveled his long legs to the side facing her, and moved the table out of the way. He put her glass aside too and took her hands. "When you ran me off, I was still young for a Mithran. Hotheaded. Difficult. Selfish. I was full of piss and vinegar, and I believed any woman should be tickled pink to be with me. I did not regard you with the respect and honor I should have. And you left." He went silent, staring down at their hands, his thumbs rubbing over her knuckles.

"When you left me, I fell into the vampire ways for all I was worth, thinking that if you thought I was horrible, then I'd just go ahead and be horrible. I hated myself for every single one of those moments. I missed you every single one of those moments. I regretted what I had done and who I had become every single moment. Then one night I woke up and . . . I was done being a man without honor.

"In the last fifteen years, I have neither slept with nor had sexual relations with another person, not a Mithran, not human, not anyone. I came dangerously close with your Evangelina, under her compulsion, but I did not consummate with her. I was able to keep that much of myself from her, because of my love for you. Because you didn't want a man who couldn't be true to you. I have been faithful to my love for you for fifteen years. I do not deserve the love of a woman like you. This I know well. But I profess my love to you, forever, for as long as you shall live. Bedelia Everhart Shaddock, will you allow me to court you once again? To show you, to prove to you that I am yours now and always?"

The bond between them was open, free, and she knew he spoke the truth. Bedelia was smiling softly, her eyes on their joined hands. "Yes."

Linc leaned over and kissed her hands, one and then the other. Moving slowly, in case she might pull away, he leaned in and kissed her gently on the mouth. He was smiling and so was she when he eased away.

"Linc," she said, softly. "We still have a lot of talking to do. But. Something you ought to know. You can't live here because Mama would turn you into a toad if she knew we were taking up again, but I never did sign the divorce papers. We are still, legally, married."

She yelped at the sudden motion, and then she was in his arms, being held like a baby, or like a starlet in an old movie, and he was twirling them. Laughing. That laughter twined through her own heart and set her soul free. She wrapped her arms around his shoulders and held on tight.

ACKNOWLEDGMENTS

No writer is (or should be) an island. In my case, it takes a community to make a book.

A huge thank you to senior editor Jessica Wade, editor Miranda Hill, Alexis Nixon (PR) of Penguin Random House, and production editor Alaina Christensen. Without you there would be no book and no sales at all! Additional thanks to all the editors and copy editors and PRH promotional staff who worked on this project.

My thanks to:

Mindy "Mud" Mymudes, Beta Reader and PR.

Let's Talk Promotions, at ltpromos.com, for managing my blog tours and the Beast Claws fan club.

Beast Claws! Best Street Team Evah!

Mike Pruette at celticleatherworks.com for all the fabo merch!

Teri Lee Akar, timeline and continuity editor. Thank you for keeping track of all the characters and if they are still alive-ish or more deadish. I miss you.

Last but never least, my thanks to Lucienne Diver of the Knight Agency for guiding my career, being a font of wisdom and career guidance.

Faith Hunter is the *New York Times* and *USA Today* bestselling author of several series: Jane Yellowrock, Soulwood, Rogue Mage, and Junkyard Cats. In addition, she has edited multiple anthologies and coauthored the Rogue Mage RPG. She is the coauthor and author of 16 thrillers under pen names Gary Hunter and Gwen Hunter. Altogether, she has written more than forty books and dozens of short stories, and is always juggling multiple projects. Faith sold her first book in 1989 and hasn't stopped writing since. She collects orchids and animal skulls, and loves thunderstorms. She drinks a lot of tea. She likes to kayak Class II and III whitewater rivers. Some days she's a lady. Some days she ain't.

CONNECT ONLINE

FaithHunter.net
 Official.Faith.Hunter
 HunterFaith